The Foiled Knight

By: John C. Stipa

Also by John C. Stipa

Novels:
No Greater Sacrifice, 2009

Short Stories:
Pop Up, 2013
My Grandmother Was A Howitzer, 2012
The Chief of Mischief, 2011
Pegasus, 2009
When Ink Bleeds, 2008
A Lifetime of Vacations, All In One Day, 2008
Passion Takes Center Stage, 2007
Gracie's Web, 2007

Photo Books:
Fire It Up!, 2009

Poetry:
All My Power, 2009

The Foiled Knight
Copyright © 2013 by John C. Stipa

All rights reserved. Any use, storage, reproduction or transmission in any form or by any means of the contents without the written consent of the author is prohibited.

Cover design and illustration: Lorrie Herman

This is a work of fiction, nothing more. Names, characters, places and incidents are the products of the author's imagination or are used fictitiously. Any resemblance to actual events, locales, or persons living or dead, is entirely coincidental.

Sales of this book without a front cover are unauthorized.

John C. Stipa, Herndon, VA
CreateSpace June 16, 2013

ISBN-13: 978-1484820285
ISBN-10: 1484820282

Library of Congress Control Number: 2013908032

This book is dedicated to the most influential person in my life: my late, great mother, Nancy Stipa. She made my life possible.

Map of Abington

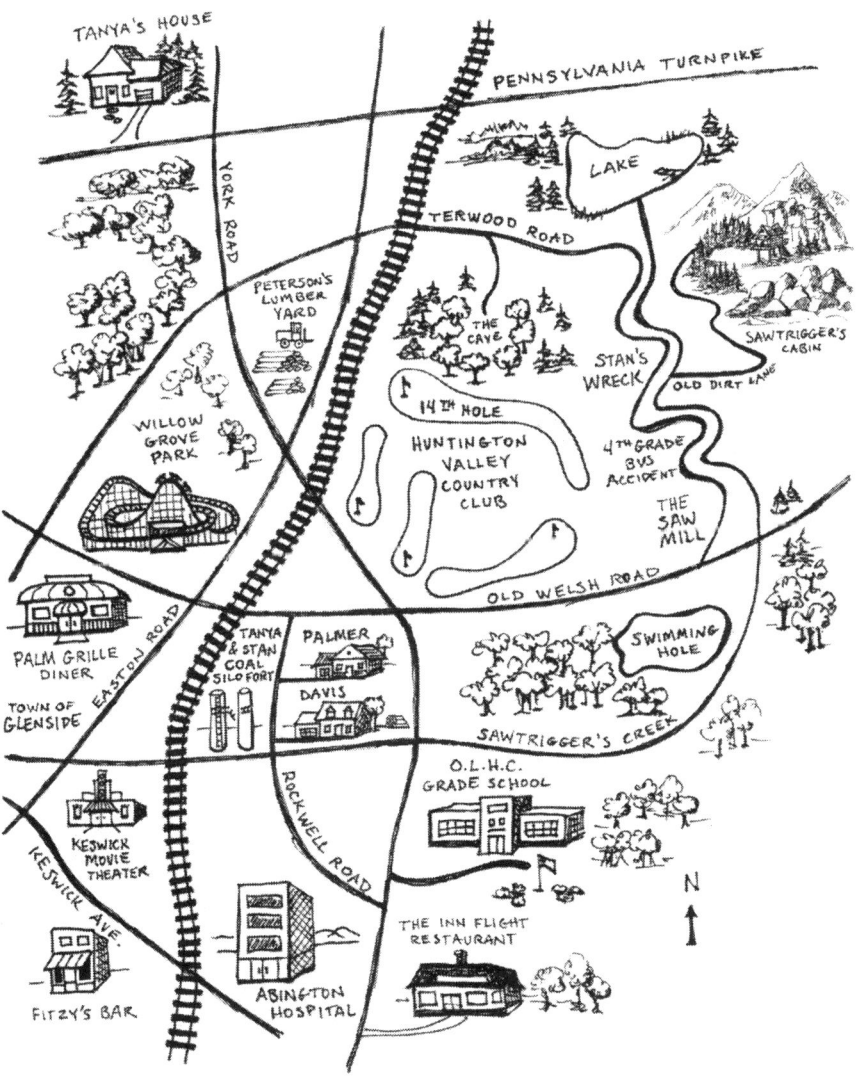

Chapter 1

Stan Palmer elbowed his way through the smoke-filled bar to an empty stool near the taps and clattered his car keys onto the glossy counter. They hardly made a dent against the din of the happy hour crowd and jukebox blasting out *"You've Lost That Loving Feeling"* by The Righteous Brothers. He stamped the snow from his boots and shed his coat.

Tall and lanky with close-cropped black hair, rosy cheeks and unblemished white skin, Stan resembled an overgrown altar boy more than he did the bookkeeper for the local sawmill. He stuffed his Phillies cap into the back pocket of his jeans and motioned to the large red-haired bartender. "Evening, Fitzy, T.G.I.F."

"Hey, Stan the Man!" Doug Fitzgerald called out. The former all-state baseball catcher grabbed a mug from the overhead rack, poured a beer and toyed with it like a shuffleboard puck. "Fastball or curve?"

Stan placed a cupped hand on the bar. "Bring your heat, Koufax."

Fitzy slid the mug down the middle of the wet bar. The glass had barely slapped Stan's palm before it was at his lips.

"Nice scoop," Fitzy said. "Hey, what's up? You're late, it's almost seven."

"Family in a station wagon got stuck in the snow. I helped dig them out."

"Good man," Fitzy said and plopped a bowl of peanuts in front of Stan. "Dinner?"

"Rather have a cheese steak," Stan replied. "How's business?" He spun around in his chair assessing the environment.

Fitzy's was a cozy split-level watering hole with the bar, restaurant and dance floor on the upper tier and a game room on the lower. Everything was made of wood from the bar to the tables to the chairs, stools and floor. Banners from Philadelphia sports teams hung from the rafters. The pool table, dartboards and Foosball games didn't gather much dust.

"Eh," Fitzy said. "Could be better, but I'm not whining."

Stan sucked a gulp and flicked his eyes toward the dance floor. "Eileen been here long?"

"Long enough to get trashed and make a fool of herself."

They took a break to stare at a woman dressed in a skimpy denim skirt, spiked heels and a too-tight-for-her-age leopard top. The leggy brunette wore thick makeup that wasn't enough to camouflage her sagging facial skin. Still, the slow, sultry swing of her hips and daring cleavage was enough to occupy the attention of two young men.

"What do you call it?" Stan asked. "The Come Grind On Me Samba?"

"Hey boy," Fitzy said with a theatrical wave of his hand, "don't you know the mating dance of the old-babe when you see it?"

There was a yelp as the woman tripped over her own feet and fell to the floor. She landed hard on her thigh, legs splaying in awkward angles. For several seconds she lay there in a mess of long hair, broken heels and exposed belly rolls. The young bucks stood back assessing the train wreck, shook their heads in unison and walked away.

Stan leapt down from his stool and knelt by the woman. "Eileen, are you all right?"

She swept the hair from her face and wiped her nose with her sleeve. Her head swiveled searching for the source of the voice. "Do I know you?" She tried to stand, heels flailing about like roller skates on ice.

Stan hauled her up until they were face to face.

The wrinkles of her face seemed to grow deeper as she squinted bloodshot eyes at him. She swayed for a few moments until a scowl formed. "Who the hell are you?"

Stan stared back, staying silent, waiting for any sign of recognition from his former classmate. But despite the close scrutiny, her pupils remained glazed with the stupor of drunkenness. He sighed and bent to retrieve her broken heel, then pressed it into her hand, wrapping her fingers around it. "Nobody," he murmured and turned back to the bar.

Eileen swayed a few seconds until her head jerked as if just having woken up. She pulled at her skirt and attempted to fix her hair. Sufficiently repackaged, she stuck out her chest and clip-clopped away to the sanctuary of her table.

"Eileen Harding," Fitzy said while shaking his head. "What a skank."

"Some things never change," Stan said and took another slug of beer.

"Sometimes that's good."

"And sometimes it sucks canal water."

"Yeah, but sometimes—" Fitzy started, then paused to search the ceiling for his next thought, "—the canal leads a guy to a friendly watering hole."

Stan toyed with his car keys. "And sometimes it takes you to Panama where you get malaria from a mosquito bite."

"Okaaay," Fitzy said, "let's try plan B. Watcha up to tonight?"

Another sip. "Going to my folks for dinner."

Fitzy flipped a white towel over his beefy shoulder. "You shouldn't be drinking and driving."

"I'm just going to have one," Stan said. "Is that okay with you?"

"What are you gonna tell your mom when you give her a kiss hello stinking like this place?"

"You're a helluva salesman for the bar," Stan said.

"It's my place, so I can say anything I want about it. And I'm just showing concern for my customers, is that okay with you?"

Stan shrugged, opened up a pack of cigarettes and stuck one in his mouth.

Fitzy's bushy red eyebrows rose an inch. "Since when do you smoke?"

The cigarette drooped as Stan returned a weary gaze. "What are you, my mother? First you're on my case about having a beer, then you tell me I stink like a pig sty and now you're my health advisor?"

"You calling my place a pig sty?"

"No, you did, remember?" Stan said, then mimicked Fitzy's voice, only deeper: "'It's my place so I can say anything I want about it.'" He rolled his eyes

The Foiled Knight

while shaking his head.

Fitzy spread his meaty palms flat on the bar. "What's eating you tonight?"

There was a pause as Stan lit the cigarette, took a long pull then blew a stream of smoke toward the ceiling. "Nothing."

"Right, who do you think you're talking to? How far do we go back?"

Stan thought a moment. "Fourth grade."

"Yeah, so that's like practically our whole lives. When we were playing ball, I could tell when you wanted to throw smoke and when you wanted to fool 'em with the curveball. I know when a chick's caught your eye—"

Stan clunked his forehead on the bar. "Jesus Christ, not again."

Fitzy preached on, "—and when something's crawled up your butt. I can tell when you've gotten laid and when you're bluffing in poker. And right now, you couldn't bluff nothing from nobody. Don't tell me nothing's wrong."

"I'm just feeling sorry for myself," Stan snapped. "All right?"

"When is the last time you talked to her?" Fitzy fired back.

"Who, Eileen?"

Fitzy stared at his friend with contempt. "You know who I mean."

Stan went silent and slid his mug from hand to hand. Just when it had almost stopped moving, he sent it back in the other direction. For a long minute he didn't answer.

In the middle of the tenth slide, Fitzy clamped a hand on the mug. When Stan looked up with wounded eyes, Fitzy bored back with lasers of his own. The skin on Fitzy's face seemed to turn to thick leather.

Stan sagged on his stool. "Last week."

Fitzy tilted his head.

"It's not that easy," Stan said.

"It is if you would only let it. Brother, you are the most bullheaded—"

"Look Fitzy, I don't feel like talking about it right now. Can't you get outta my face for even two minutes?"

Fitzy studied Stan for a short moment. Shook his head, pretended to wipe his hands of something, then held up his palms. "Yes sir, mister Big Shot, sir." His voice trailed off as he walked to the far end of the bar.

"Crap," Stan mumbled. He stuck his nose in his mug and turned to survey the bar.

It was a typical Saturday night. A good-sized crowd determined to party combined with wings, beer and music led to lots of dancing and laughter. Glenside was a blue-collar suburb of Philadelphia where guys cashed their paychecks on Fridays and were broke by Monday morning.

A crusty old man sitting next to Stan patted the pockets of his work pants. Unintelligible words tumbled from his chapped lips.

"What's the matter, old timer?" Stan said.

"Think I left my wallet at home," he replied. "Shoot, it took me twenty minutes to get here in the snow." He tossed his cap on the bar and smoothed greasy hair across a scalp that was dotted with aging spots. "Dammit, now I gotta skunk back to the witch's castle to get it." All the air seemed to leak out of him.

"Here," Stan said and handed over a ten-dollar bill.

"What's this for?"

"One guy helping another," Stan said and patted the man on the back. "Just don't drive home, okay?"

The man slapped the bill on the bar. "Deal. Thanks, bub."

Stan waved a hand. "Forget it." He turned to face the crowd.

Warren Zevon's *"Werewolves of London"* blared from the jukebox. Stan settled in to try and predict which of two guys would be successful at getting a blonde's phone number when the front door opened and at least a dozen people entered the bar at once. Stan checked his watch: 7PM. *Huh, here comes the Keswick theatre crowd for an after movie drink.*

All of the newcomers had dates. All except one. Dressed in a grungy green army coat, he was large and burly with long arms, a sledgehammer of a chin and a faded yellow trucker cap pulled low over his eyes. The smoky room made it difficult to make out any other facial features, but for a split-second Stan thought he detected a thin line of blood beneath the man's eye. Or was it a scar?

The stranger turned and stalked with hunched shoulders toward the shadows of the far wall near the window. Ignoring everything around him, he turned up his collar, leaned against a post and stared out at the driving snowstorm.

Stan stroked his chin. There was something familiar about the bulky frame. Where had he seen this guy before? An image from Stan's childhood flashed in his brain. *Can't be*, he thought.

A blur of long willowy hair blew by the window, outside the bar. The stranger's thick skull twitched. Suddenly alert, the man reached into his coat pockets, put on woolen gloves and moved quickly to the exit. With a yank on the door handle, he disappeared into the snowy night. A looming mass of darkness floated along the line of windows, in the same direction as the willowy hair

Stan almost completely missed the edge of the bar when returning his mug. He hurriedly threw on his coat and rammed the Phillies cap onto his head. Tossing some bills on the bar, he grabbed his car keys and ran out the door.

Chapter 2

A vibration shivered down the legs of the bedside table, across the carpet, up the headboard and through the mattress. A minuscule quiver. As if someone had closed a door in another part of the house. A sound followed, indiscernible, but annoying still. It went away. Then returned. More of a jangling this time. And again. Tanya Davis woke. The ring persisted. One eye opened. She groped for the receiver.

"Hello."

"Tanya?" A woman's voice, quaking, but familiar. "Can you hear me?"

Tanya raised herself to one elbow. "Yes? Who is this?"

"Oh, sweetie, it's Sandra Palmer. Stan's mother."

Tanya sat up, the brevity in the woman's voice sending stabs of concern through her scalp. "Yes, Mrs. Palmer, I'm sorry. What is it?"

People shouted in the background, their voices short and urgent, sentences in staccato bursts over the siren's din. Then a barked order to "cover him."

"Mrs. Palmer? What's happened?" Tanya asked. Her cat and companion of seven years, Dodger, appeared from beneath the covers. His black and beige coat twitched with anxiety while his ears stood straight up like dual antennas searching for a signal.

"There's been an accident."

A knot formed in Tanya's stomach. "My God. Is Mr. Palmer all right?" The sound of a chainsaw ripped through the line, followed by screeching metal. Tanya shouted: "Mrs. Palmer?"

"Honey, it's not Mr. Palmer who's hurt."

The words 'not Mr.' hit Tanya like a guillotine. She tried to talk, but only a gurgle would come. Her stomach reached the back of her throat. She forced it back down by punching her chest. "Then... then who—"

"It's Stan. He's been in a serious car accident."

Tanya's hand flew to her mouth. A whimper escaped her lips. "Is he…"

"No, he's not, but he's very badly hurt. Look, the ambulance is here now. I've got to go. Meet us at Abington hospital."

Dodger ducked the phone and tumbled off the bed as Tanya dashed for the hall. She snatched her car keys off the mantle and flew out of the house. A painting tilted off-center as the door slammed behind her.

Chapter 3

Tanya whipped through the snow-covered neighborhood streets, the driving snowflakes infiltrating her headlights in a swarm of white hornets. She cranked the heater full blast and turned the wipers on high. "Please God," she whispered, "let Stan be okay." Gripping the wheel fiercely, she fish-tailed around a corner toward the interstate.

As Tanya urged the car up the ramp, the blaring of a horn startled her and she swerved to avoid an 18-wheeler roaring by. The behemoth's wake splattered the windshield with a thick coating of slush and salt. She slammed the brakes and felt the car begin to slide sideways. A pang of terror hit. "Oh shit, oh shit," she hissed. Gritting her teeth, she spun the wheel in the opposite direction. The front tires plowed into the mush, then shuddered followed by a jerk and the vehicle jolted back on course. Tanya heaved a sigh of relief and locked down on the wheel. "Okay, okay; I'm okay!" Her eyes bored through the asteroid shower of white on black.

The defroster struggled to fight off the accumulation on the windshield. She wound down the driver-side window and reached into an icy wind with a bare hand to help the wipers clear the glass, nearly lost control again, then recovered. After ten seconds, she crammed a frozen hand between her thighs. "Screw it. Please just let me get there." A green overhead road sign indicated a half-mile to go. She stepped on the gas, cutting across three lanes, ignored angry horns and barreled toward the exit. Her side view mirror threw sparks into the night as it scraped the concrete barrier. At the bottom of the ramp, she blew through the red light, nearly clipping a mini-van. More horns. *"Shut the hell up!"* she screamed and leaned on her own horn. "Get out of my way!"

Abington hospital appeared over the skyline as she turned onto York Road. Built in the 1920s, the dull beige brick building, lit by bright floodlights, stood poignantly against the storm. Every here and there, darkened windows dotted the magnificent façade in a checkerboard of doom. In contrast, the rooms that were lit seemed alive and healthy.

Tanya screeched to a halt in the parking lot and jumped out, leaving the door open, the heater and wipers firing away, the keys in the ignition, the engine still running. The headlights lit her rainbow socks as she sprinted across the snow toward the entrance.

A blow of warmth slowed her as the sliding glass doors opened to the mustard yellow interior of the emergency room. The chaos that occupied her previous fourteen minutes abruptly stopped. Deep-cushioned chairs sat calmly aligned in perfect rows, their only inhabitants a little boy in Bugs Bunny pajamas being read to by his mother. He looked at Tanya with big brown eyes, smiled, whispered something to his mother, then pointed at Tanya's feet. Tanya looked around. A man and a woman in surgeon scrubs and paisley caps stood in front of a vending machine. The woman laughed flirtatiously. A janitor passed by them, toting a trash can on wheels, plodding along as if magnetically connected to a red line painted on the floor. An elderly man leaned on the handlebars of a wheelchair, pushing a white-haired woman, both chatting happily. Tanya whirled. *Am I at the hospital or the library?*

The ring of a cell phone snapped her head toward a pair of swinging doors. She rushed past the reception desk and burst through to another room saturated with the smell of medicine. Zombie people wandered about in pajamas and trench coats.

"Where is he?" Tanya blurted.

Several heads turned in unison, their faces familiar, but not totally recognizable, as if someone were intentionally shaking a collage of family photographs.

"Tanya!" A woman with haggard gray hair ran toward her, tissues waving in each upturned hand. Sandra Palmer, normally an attractive, smartly dressed woman, looked a wreck. Unbuttoned, untucked and unmatched clothes hung off her. Worry lines riddled her face like a damaged tennis racquet. A beret dangled from flyaway hair and the front of her once white blouse was now stained with blood. Her eyes were bloodshot and her jaw shook uncontrollably. "Oh my goodness," she said, throwing her arms around Tanya. "I'm so glad you're here."

"I came as fast as I could. Where's Stan? What happened? Is he all right? Have the doctors said anything yet? Can we see him? My God, I'm freaking out."

Sandra shook her head. "We don't know much yet, but I overheard something about—" she took a breath "—internal bleeding."

"When did it happen?"

"A few hours ago. He was on his way over to our house for dinner. I was making his favorite dish. He's never late for that..." Sandra's voice cracked and she buried her face into her hands. "This can't be happening. Oh, Stan! Please be okay."

A solidly built man in jeans and a well-worn leather jacket took Sandra into his arms. Fenton Palmer was a tall and silent man of sixty with a ruggedly tan face, square jaw and short black hair just starting to gray at the temples. "It'll be all right, Sandra," he said, his deep voice trying to shake off the worry that trembled his lips. An outdoorsman with serious, but kind blue eyes, Fenton held his wife of forty years in a way that was neither subtle nor suffocating. He turned to Tanya. "He hit a deer and swerved off the road. His car is wrapped around a tree."

"Oh my God. Where'd it happen?"

"On Terwood Road."

"What's happening now?" Tanya asked, glancing anxiously at an orderly pushing a gurney with a bandaged body hooked up to IV bottles.

The weathered lines on Fenton's forehead rippled. "He's in surgery. We won't know anything for hours."

"I'll get everyone some coffee," Tanya said, suddenly shivering.

"Great idea," he said, then noticed her feet. "Good lord, Tanya, where are your shoes?"

Tanya looked down and blinked. "I-I don't know. I must've jumped straight into the car."

"And you've no gloves or coat either?"

"I don't remember even driving here." She tugged at her pajamas as if trying to hide her feet. And then her head suddenly jerked up. "Oh! I left my car running in the parking lot. I've got to turn it off." She moved to go.

Fenton placed a calming hand on her shoulder. "I'll take care of it. Here, take Mrs. Palmer to the waiting area and sit her down and keep her down, okay?" He pressed a blue pill into Tanya's hand and mouthed: *Valium*.

Tanya caught his eyes: *Got it*.

"See that she takes it," Fenton murmured, then scanned the area, his Marine survival training launching him into crisis mode. Quick to evaluate, able to decide judiciously, fearless when acting. Tanya had seen "the look" before when Stan had nearly lost a finger in a lawnmower accident. Fenton had acted quickly then, wrapping the lost digit in ice before rushing to the hospital. "I'll see if I can scrounge up a dry pair of socks for you and maybe some slippers. Have you warm and fuzzy in no time."

"Yes sir," Tanya replied as he walked away, the musky smell of his leather jacket lingering in the air. Her eyes followed the man as he powered through space. With broad shoulders and trim waist, he strode confidently, his hair slicked on both sides as if intentionally groomed to cut down air resistance.

Tanya led Sandra to a cushioned chair in front of a wide screen TV playing a loop of CNN world news coverage. "I'll get us some coffee, Mrs. Palmer. Don't go anywhere." She sped to the cafeteria and fixed two cups, mixing in the sedative before returning. "Here. Sorry it's not very hot, but it's…strong, just what you need right about now."

"Thank you, honey. Couldn't even drink the first cup." Sandra motioned to her stained skirt. "Spilled it all over me." She noticed the blood stains on her blouse, then stared at Tanya. "Dear God."

"Don't think about that now," Tanya said. "I'll go to your house and get you new clothes."

Sandra tried to take a sip, but her hand shook uncontrollably.

Tanya steadied the cup so that she could drink.

"Thank you, Tanya. You always were the sweetest girl I ever knew."

"Don't mention it. I've known you all my life. There's no way I can repay you for all the things you've done for me."

"Well, this is a big one, trust me, and I appreciate it." Sandra took a longer sip, sank into the chair and threw her head back. "I still remember your and Stan's first day of school like it was yesterday."

"Heh, Ernie McFadden."

"Yes." Sandra turned and made eye contact with Tanya, that knowing look of a bond created only by shared experience. "My, how you were a loyal friend even then."

Tanya laughed. "Stan didn't appreciate being saved by a girl."

"That's simply not true." Sandra gulped some coffee, set the cup down firmly and grasped Tanya's hand. "Stan loved it when you were around. Since the day he was born, he was always the shy and quiet one. That's why bullies

The Foiled Knight

like McFadden picked on him." A sneer lurked for a second then went away. "But Stan became energized when you were around. 'Tanya did this and Tanya said that and you're not gonna believe how Tanya told off Ernie in Mrs. Delaney's English class today.' He was a different person when you were around."

Tanya's face pinched and she wiped her eyes. "I was different when he was around."

The two women shared another knowing look.

"You don't have to tell me," Sandra said, smiling, and as she did so, her hand fell into her lap. "My, my. Suddenly I feel very tired. Tanya darling, can I rest my head on your shoulder? I need to close my eyes for a minute."

"Sure Mrs. P., I make a great pillow." Tanya pulled Sandra close, breathing in the smell of honeysuckle that reminded her of piggy-back rides Sandra used to give them at the tot-lot. A memory of Sandra showing Tanya how to remove brownies from Betty Crocker's Easy Bake Oven flashed in her brain and how Sandra's laughter would fill the house at the sight of Stan and Tanya searching the air with closed eyes and innocent noses, trying to hold onto the aroma.

The click of boots on linoleum sounded. Fenton returned and stopped before them, a tight-lipped smile on his chiseled face. "Two peas in a pod," he said. Kneeling, he removed Tanya's frigid socks and replaced them with warm woolen ones and slippers. He then unfurled a flannel blanket and covered the two women. "There. Hope my two favorite girls are comfortable."

"Fenton, you're so thoughtful," Sandra said, her voice slurring. "Tanya, you'll stay a while, won't you dear? Stan will want to see you when he wakes up." She drifted off to sleep.

Tanya mouthed a "thank you" to Fenton while stroking the elder woman's hair. "Don't worry, Mrs. P. I'm not going anywhere."

But it wasn't bravado Tanya felt as Sandra went to sleep in her arms. It was something else. Something unreal. Something unconscionable. A sense of fear and helplessness. Beyond anything she'd ever experienced. Beyond anything that could be known to exist. She glanced down at the smears of Stan's blood on Sandra's blouse and came face to face with bone marrow-sucking despair.

Chapter 4

Tom Morton stared at the elevator panel. The back-lit buttons blinked from bottom to top. Chimes at every new floor fell in step with his heartbeat. The dull hum of hydraulics was like bald tires on a long stretch of highway. In all his years as a nurses' assistant, the pudgy man had never found a way to deal with the lulling effect. His eyelids drooped and for a split second, the paltry light emitted by the fluorescent bulb went completely dark.

Jenny Wilson, a slender woman with frizzy blonde hair reached across the gurney and shook him by the shoulder. "Come on, Morty, wake up! Don't make me do this by myself."

Morty's head snapped, scorching the muscles in his neck. "Ouch." He glanced at the patient just released from surgery: a body wrapped in gauze, bandages and tubes lay on their back on the gurney of chrome. Morty checked his watch, then scraped fingernails through his crew cut, counting on the pain to keep him awake. "I'm on it."

"I don't believe you." Jenny rolled up the sleeves of her pale pink scrubs. "Come on, challenge time. Let's see if that medical training is worth the construction paper you printed your diploma on."

"Game on," Morty scoffed. "Hmm, EKG and EEG to measure heart and brainwaves. IV bag means he's lost a lot of blood." He pulled back the bandages from the patient's chest. "Damn, that's a nasty puncture wound." Morty stroked his beard flecked with gray. "And the ventilator is a dead giveaway that he can't breathe for himself. Did he get mugged and knifed in the chest?"

"Not quite," Jenny said. "Car accident. Hit a deer, a buck. But pretty good otherwise."

The elevator doors opened and they steered the gurney down the hall. Morty pushed while Jenny oversaw the clean passage of the life support equipment.

Room 9, a boring square of baby blue walls, featured a flat panel TV bolted to the wall above two visiting chairs.

"The buck probably came through the windshield," Morty said. "An antler must have pierced his lung. Can you imagine what that felt like? Brain damage likely. Might have to get on dialysis for his kidneys. Did Doctor DeAngelis say if it was okay to let in visitors?"

"Not for a couple of hours," Jenny said, shaking her head. She then added in a low tone: "Doesn't matter though, does it?" Her lips formed a thin line.

They double-checked that the monitoring equipment worked properly and left, their booties swishing a repetitive tic-tic-tic that faded away to silence.

Chapter 5

A steaming cup of coffee appeared in front of Tanya.

"I know it's your third cup," Fenton said, "but you've got the look of someone who's not leaving anytime soon, so I figured you might want something to occupy your hands instead of chewing those beautiful finger nails."

"Thanks," Tanya said and looked over at Sandra, half asleep and stretched out on two chairs that were shoved together. There were no other people in the hospital's waiting room. The TV had been turned off in favor of staring at the floor. Tanya took a sip, set the cup on the table and rubbed her forehead. "What time is it?"

"Five a.m.," Fenton replied.

"He's been in there for hours. When are we going to hear something?"

"When they first brought him in, they told us it would be a while. You really should go home and get some sleep."

"I wouldn't be able to," Tanya said, then realized she was gnawing on her fingernails again and shoved her hands into the pockets of her pajamas.

He shrugged. "Thought you'd say that."

They sat opposite each other, hands folded, listening to the hum of a computer printer drifting from somewhere.

Fenton leaned forward, simultaneously twisting his back and massaging his temples. "I feel so achy," he said, ending up facing Tanya, elbows on knees.

She could see the dark circles forming under his eyes, could smell the coffee on his breath. "The ER waiting room isn't the best thing for your back."

"You got that right." He stifled a yawn. "Excuse me. So what are you doing with yourself these days, Tanya? Still volunteering at St. Christopher's?"

"Couple of days a week. A few hours, in between shifts at work."

"Where are you working? Still at the department store?"

"No, I quit that a while ago."

"Ah," he replied, dragging it to imply "*And?*" without actually saying it.

She opened her palms as if in confession. "I'm waitressing at the Palm Grille diner."

Fenton dropped his arms and leaned back in his chair creating a silence that nearly screamed.

"I know, I know," Tanya said. "But the hours are flexible."

"The place is a dump," he said. "Only two A.M. rejects go there."

"Good tips," she said. "I had a good job at that research firm before I got laid off. Took me forever to find something comparable, but then they went out of business." She looked away. "And without a college degree, well, it's just been...tough."

He tried to study her, but she wouldn't meet his gaze. Finally, he shook his head. "Better than some of the bozos around this town, collecting unemployment, not even trying to find a job. But don't give up. Hey, whatever happened with that dancing thing? Weren't you going to give the theater a try?"

Tanya stiffened, looked down and unconsciously rubbed her leg, started to pick at her fingernails, then frisked her hands. "Um, I was never good enough."

"Not what I heard."

Tanya brightened. "Yeah, says who?"

"Stan. Said you were damned talented. Would've paid money to see you perform."

"Huh, I didn't know he thought that." She took a sip of coffee. "I still take lessons from time to time. It's hard on the bod—" She stopped, then plucked at a pill on her pajamas. "Tough on the feet, you know?"

His stare was hard. The outer edge of his right eye pinched a bit as if having made up his mind about something. "I guess," he said. "Slaved at an assembly line for a while." A faraway look passed across his face. "Hated that time of my life."

There was a bang and an olive-skinned man in blue scrubs and booties emerged from behind swinging doors. Arching his neck, he removed his mask and cap to reveal a drawn face and bloodshot eyes. Sandra Palmer stirred from her slumber.

"Are you the Palmer family?" he said.

Fenton stuck out a hand. "Yes, I'm Stan's father."

"I'm Doctor John DeAngelis, I worked on your son." They shook.

Sandra joined the gathering. "Is our boy all right?"

"No, he's not," DeAngelis said, meeting each of their eyes, one by one. "He's in a coma."

Tanya's hand flew to her mouth.

"Stan's injuries are quite extensive," the surgeon continued. "He has a punctured lung, broken ribs and a ruptured spleen. He will likely have nerve damage as well."

Sandra sobbed and leaned into Fenton.

"There was so much blood when they brought him in," Fenton said.

DeAngelis nodded. "He has a large gash on his forehead. Could have been the steering wheel or maybe it was the deer. We stitched up the external lacerations, but we couldn't get the internal bleeding under control. He went into cardiac arrest and was without oxygen for a long…for a period of time."

No one said anything for three long seconds.

"Will," Fenton started to ask, then cleared his throat. "Will he live?"

"Yes, but we need to run further tests. There's no telling when he'll come out of it. That's not what you want to hear, but I figured you'd want the truth."

"Of course," Fenton said.

Tanya spoke up. "But you said 'when he comes out of it' as if you expect him to wake up."

DeAngelis looked her in the eye. "You're right. I'm sorry about that." He paused. "I should have said *if* he comes out of it."

Sandra whimpered and sank into a chair. Fenton went to her side.

"You can't know that," Tanya's voice cracked. "It's too soon. He's just come out. You still need to do stuff. Give him something, take scans, run tests."

The Foiled Knight

She grabbed the doctor's arm. "You can't know that!"

Fenton jumped up and wedged himself between Tanya and the doctor. "Tanya, honey, you need to go home and get some sleep, you're a wreck."

"I'm fine," she said still glaring at DeAngelis.

"No you're not," Fenton said. "You can barely stand up."

"I don't want to go."

He braced her by the shoulders. "You can't do anything for Stan if you don't take care of yourself. I've got it under control here. Get some rest. Please. Come back later."

Tanya stood in rigid defiance. And then the air seemed to deflate from her body as exhaustion won out. "Sure," she said and made for the exit in a stupor-like stagger.

Fenton turned to DeAngelis. "Doctor, we're all in shock over this. Maybe you could give us an update in a few hours after you've had a chance to look Stan over some more?"

DeAngelis squared his shoulders. "Mr. Palmer, I think you should prepare yourself for the real possibility that your son may never recover."

Fenton's mouth gaped. "That's not possible."

"I'm sorry, sir, I truly am."

"No, I'm sorry for *you*. I'm sorry that you're going to be embarrassed when my son proves your prognosis wrong."

"Test results don't lie, sir."

"And I believe that you believe that," Fenton said, his crystal blue eyes burning with intensity. "But you don't know Stan."

Chapter 6

"Oh Daisy, you money grubbing, two-faced cowardly bitch." Tanya smacked her copy of *The Great Gatsby* onto her coffee table and gulped some wine.

"Can't you see that Jay is helplessly in love with you?" She set the glass of red down, folded her arms across her chest and pinched fabric pills from gamey flannel pajamas. The pinches, at first snippy little tugs, grew in intensity, the fury rising as the visualization of Jay Gatsby lying face down in the pool festered into pinches of her arms. She thought of Stan, imagining what he must look like lying in his hospital bed: tubes, bandages, life support equipment. Her body shuddered as she shook the image from her mind.

She'd spent the entire day sleeping, recovering from the all-nighter at the hospital. Looking down at her five toed rainbow socks, then up the line of her legs, she found a long strand of auburn hair, snagged it with two fingers and unceremoniously dropped it to the ground. Another slug of wine. She reached for the pint of coffee ice cream leaning against a pillow, dug her spoon in deep and plopped a large dollop into her mouth. Then just as quickly, she set the container on the table and snatched the TV remote. "Let's see what a million cable channels have to offer." She surfed through numerous programs, barely pausing on an image before pressing the button. Get rich quick commercials, reality show brawls and guaranteed fat-burning diet scams flashed before her.

"Ugh." She tossed the clicker and watched it bounce off a couch cushion into a bucket of Buffalo wings. The cardboard container tipped over, flinging the bite-sized nuggets about like a game of jacks. "Ah, no way!" She took a napkin and flicked the pieces back into the container, sucking one drumstick clean of its meat in one bite. A glop of hot sauce dripped onto her ratty Elon University sweatshirt. Her chin drooped, eyes following the greasy orange worm as it dribbled down her breast. She flung her head. "Great. Just great." She jammed the bone into the bucket.

Up off the couch, Tanya sock-skated across the hardwood floor towards the kitchen, scattering stuffed animals that were already strewn about. The screech of a cat filled the hallway. "Look out, Dodger!" Dodger scurried away to safety under the couch.

The kitchen was a cramped and eccentric arrangement of white: a small white table, white appliances, a white counter beneath white cabinets. Knives and pots clung to a white metal rack suspended by chain from the ceiling.

Across the white linoleum floor to the sink for a rag of cold water. Tanya blotted the stain until it faded to a smear of orange. "Eh, it'll have to do," she said. She punted a stuffed animal out of the way to get to the refrigerator. On the door, a calendar attached by four Pooh Bear magnets contained phone numbers: her parents, her minister, St. Christopher's, and Stan. She sighed at Saturday's empty square. When she opened the freezer door, a library of Lean Cuisine

The Foiled Knight

microwavable meals stared back at her. "Get. Real," she said under her breath and slammed the door.

The broom found her hands. She twirled to the answering machine on a small white desk tucked into an alcove by the white window. Stooped to double check the zero on the display. A frown. "Damn." Straightened her wooden partner. "Mr. Bailey, whisk me to the dance floor before Violet Bick digs her claws into you. And watch your step, there is a pool hidden beneath the floor that would like nothing better than to drown young lovers like us."

Closing her eyes, Tanya tilted her head back and waltzed. Circles and circles. Around the empty living room warmed by a frilly-fringed Persian throw rug acquired from a deceased neighbor's auction. Past the dust covered mahogany piano and Victrola phonograph. Up and over the couch. To the floor again where she collided with the Victorian coat rack that held a torn rain slicker, a woolen scarf and pea coat. Melted snow pooled beneath a black umbrella leaning against a radiator whose paint peeled in large curls.

She thumbed her nose at a portrait of herself in a dancer's costume, one of three paintings on the wall. The second was of a dancer's feet in ballerina shoes, on point, barely touching the hardwood, ribbons tied around the ankles. The last painting featured a young girl and boy, both dressed in baby blue shorts and white shirts, holding hands as they strolled happily toward a golden sun. While an amateurish oil, it had been framed expensively, a gift from Stan on her 13th birthday. Tanya heard herself sob. Stan had gotten beaten up by Ernie McFadden over that painting. McFadden had been Stan's nemesis for as long as she could remember.

Into the dark hallway she stormed. Tripped over a telephone book left open on the floor and finally into the bedroom where she flung herself onto the bed, tears streaming from her eyes. She reached for a tissue on the nightstand and honked her nose. A minute later, Dodger appeared and flounced into the nook of her belly.

Tanya cuddled around him into a ball. "Ernie McFadden," she whispered. "Good God, Dodger, be happy you don't have enemies like that."

Even Sandra had remembered Stan and Tanya's first day of first grade. First time on a bus. First time they had been away from home for more than a few hours.

Lunchboxes clunked and backpacks swished as the children had exited the bus and tromped down the paved driveway to Our Lady Help of Christians Elementary. Understated, yet practical, the one-story beige brick building consisted of only eight classrooms, a resilient facility that used its gymnasium as its cafeteria, theater, science hall and storage facility. Nuns ran the place and anyone caught fooling around made the walk of shame to the principal's office where the acoustics were intentionally designed to let the entire school know just who was in trouble and by how much.

The bell rang at 7:20 signaling everyone to gather by grade and form straight lines, by height, girls on the right, boys on the left. The younger kids stumbled their way through the Pledge of Allegiance while the seventh graders made farting noises at key syllables.

Stan, being among the shortest, stood awkwardly near the front of his line.

The first grade girls all chatted happily, examining their dresses and commenting on their lunchboxes or backpacks. Tanya talked to no one, the pair of girls in front and behind her oblivious to what she thought was a pretty blue dress. She looked up and noticed Stan staring at her. He smiled, sending a waffle of joy through her. She smiled back and waved.

A stocky, long-haired boy kneed Stan in the calves causing Stan's legs to buckle. His metal lunchbox fell to the pavement, springing open the lid. Stan's lunch and Thor thermos spilled onto the ground.

"Hey, look at the sissy with the blonde-haired girl on his thermos!" Stocky boy shouted. Hysterical laughter exploded from the other boys.

Stan flushed a deep red and scooped everything back into the lunchbox. "That's not a girl, you jerk. That's the mighty Thor, and he can destroy anything with his powerful hammer."

Stocky boy laughed and snared Stan's lunchbox, holding it high above his head. "Yeah? Can he jump high enough to get your lunchbox before I dump everything onto the ground again?"

Stan leapt with all his might, but couldn't reach. "Give it back."

A third boy crouched behind Stan. Stocky boy pushed Stan backwards. Heels flying into the sun, Stan toppled through space onto his back.

"Good one, Vinnie," the stocky boy said to his still-crouched accomplice.

All air expelled from his lungs, Stan lay there frozen, his eyes in shock, not understanding why he could not breathe.

"Leave him alone, Ernie McFadden!" a girl's strong voice commanded.

Ernie wheeled to face his new opponent. "Who are you?"

"Tanya Davis."

"Shut up Nya-Nya Davis and get back in line."

"You're not the boss of me."

Ernie's sneer reached from one side of his face to the other. "Don't you know that dress is see through and everybody can see your underwear?"

Tanya's jaw dropped and she jumped back in line as the playground roared in delight at the first day's entertainment.

Ernie spun suddenly. There was a crack and the snap of his head as Stan punched him in the nose. Blood spurted like a wild spigot. Ernie grabbed the lapel of Stan's blazer and drove a punch into his face that sounded like thunder and lightning striking at the same time. Stan went down hard.

"Hey!" Tanya shouted. Ernie turned to take the full brunt of a kick to the groin. He doubled over, grabbing his private parts. Tanya swung her lunchbox and clocked the bully, ripping a gash under his eye. More blood hit the playground. The other kids formed a circle, chanting "Fight! Fight!"

Stan jumped up and slugged Ernie who staggered backwards. Ernie recovered and came at Stan, unleashing a furious barrage of punches that knocked Stan down again. But not for long as Tanya bashed him again with her lunchbox.

Rushing footsteps approached. "Break it up!" a man's voice said. In seconds, teachers were pulling them apart and the fracas was over.

"Follow me," the leader of the adults said. "You three are going to the principal's office."

The Foiled Knight

Tanya, Stan and Ernie skulked away as the rest of the school moaned, "Ooo, you're in trouble."

They were led to a small wooden bench set just outside the principal's office. A bulletin board, covered with pushpins and notes, hung on the wall.

"There's not enough room for all of us," Tanya said.

"Try to squeeze in," the man said before disappearing into the adjacent nurse's office, returning with a butterfly bandage, a tissue and an ice pack. He pinched together the skin under Ernie's eye and affixed the butterfly, then handed the bruised youth the tissue and ice pack. "For your nose."

Ernie snatched the items and applied pressure to his still bleeding nose while pressing the ice pack to his forehead. He said nothing, his glare hurling silent knives at Stan.

The man rolled his eyes and walked away. "You're welcome."

The door to the principal's office was a solid mass of brown. No peep hole, no name plate, no notes of any kind tacked to its face. It loomed before them, seemingly from floor to ceiling. Tanya chilled, waiting for the Bogey Man to burst through and suck them into a cave of worms.

After a few minutes, Ernie's nose stopped bleeding. He dropped the icepack and removed a push-pin from the bulletin board and set about punching holes in an index card containing key contact phone numbers until they were obliterated.

Tanya removed a doll from her backpack. "Don't you love Gracie's hair?" she said. "It's so soft."

Stan reached over and ran his fingers along the blond strands. "Huh."

"I'm going to name my baby Gracie someday," Tanya remembered saying.

And how Stan had smiled.

And unfortunately, how Ernie had sat down defiantly, a look of grotesqueness on his face. "I can't believe you play with dolls, Stanley."

"I wasn't playing with it," Stan said. "And don't call me that."

They had tried to butt-shove each other off the bench only to knock Tanya to the floor. Ernie had laughed raucously while Stan leapt to her side.

Never were two boys more different Tanya thought. One a mischievous punk, the other a fine man in the making. She'd hardly seen one over the past twenty years and couldn't care less. The other, the one that mattered, lay near death in a hospital bed.

She squeezed Dodger tightly.

Chapter 7

Sandra and Fenton Palmer shuffled arm in arm along the hospital hallways, avoiding rushing doctors and nurses while nervously peeking into rooms of other patients. Distraught faces of other families stared back, their eyes glassy and passive, not even cognizant of the fleeting moment of shared stress.

The early morning sun streamed in through the windows in stripes of orange. Fenton stopped to buy a cup of coffee from a vending machine and then at the nurses' desk to ask Morty for directions while Sandra filled a vase for daisies. They took only one wrong turn, but used the colored lines on the floor to get back on course. Tissues in hand, they stopped at the door to Stan's room.

Fenton put a strong arm around his wife. "Are you ready for this?"

"I've got to be," she replied, then sniffing mightily, marched into the room.

Sandra's gasp a second later startled Fenton. He rushed in to find her at the foot of the bed, hand covering her mouth, every part of her trembling. "Oh, Fenton, look at our boy."

Stan lay on his back, a virtual mummy in white bandages, only one purplish-black eye visible and swollen shut at that. A dark red gash with stitches cut across his forehead like a crooked zipper. Tubes ran out his nose and mouth to a machine that made a mechanical air sucking noise while other boxes displayed screens that beeped and blipped.

Sandra pulled a chair close to the bed and squatted on the edge. She stroked Stan's left hand, worry lines etching themselves deeper into her face with every beep. Fenton came up behind her and placed a hand on her shoulder. She lay her head onto Stan's hand, tears streaming down her cheeks.

* * *

An hour later, Jenny padded softly into Room 9, hesitated a moment at the two zombies in visitor chairs, then extracted the clipboard from the basket at the foot of Stan's bed. Fenton and Sandra, looking drained and rumpled, stirred at her presence.

"Don't get up," Jenny said quickly. "I just need to check some vitals." She stopped, noticing the daisies on the window ledge. "I'm sorry, but flowers are not permitted."

"Oh, we, um, didn't," Sandra said. "Really? Flowers?"

"It's the bacteria. Too much risk of infection." Jenny's eyes shifted nervously from Sandra to Fenton. "They should have told you."

Fenton stood. "It's all right, we understand." He took the vase and exited for a second, placing it on the floor just outside the room.

Jenny made some notations and left, returning almost immediately. "I'm sorry to keep barging in. There's someone here to visit. I can send them away if you're not up for it."

"No, it's all right," Sandra said, then turned to Fenton while fixing her hair.

The Foiled Knight

"Who do you suppose it is?"

Fenton shrugged and tucked in his shirt.

A husky man with a weathered face wandered tentatively into the room. He wore a chestnut-colored field coat from LLBean and a Phillies baseball cap pulled tight over short, fuzzy red hair. He waved a meaty hand. "Mrs. Palmer? Mr. Palmer? Hi, it's me."

"Oh, Fitzy, hello," Sandra said. "Come in."

Fitzy's muscular arms swallowed her in a huge hug. "I couldn't believe it when I heard." He shook hands with Fenton. "How is he?"

"He's had a bad break."

Fitzy moved closer to Stan, gulping at the sight of his stricken friend. "Oh my God."

"Lots of broken bones and some other injuries," Fenton said. "And now he's…" He didn't finish the sentence, managing to motion with his hand.

"What happened?" Fitzy asked.

"Hit a deer on Terwood road. You know where it gets real narrow and twists and turns by Sawtrigger's Creek?"

"That area is overcrowded with them." Fitzy yanked the hat from his head. "I *told* the game commission they should do something."

"Well, now they have a real reason to."

"Can he hear us?"

"No."

"It's not fair," Fitzy said and rammed the cap back onto his head. "I just talked to him last night. He stopped in for a beer before heading to your place. He was fine."

Jenny returned with Morty to change Stan's bandages.

"I'm gonna go," Fitzy said. "It's a bad time and you probably want to be alone with Stan. I just wanted to see if there was anything I could do."

Sandra turned toward Fenton. "Dear?"

"Nothing comes to mind, Fitzy," Fenton said, then straightened, "Oh wait, I know. If you don't mind, find out where the police towed Stan's car and get any of his valuables out of it? Could you do that?"

"Sure thing."

"Thanks, you're aces. And there's a vase of flowers just outside, if you could take those away."

"Got it. What should I tell people?" Fitzy tugged at the brim of his cap. "Everyone is afraid to call the hospital."

"I didn't even think about that," Fenton said.

"No one wants to be a nuisance," Fitzy said.

"I know. Just tell them Stan's been in a bad car accident, but doctors worked on him all night and he's alive."

Fitzy glanced tentatively over Fenton's shoulder at Stan "Is he—?"

Fenton stared into Fitzy's concerned blue eyes. "He's going to make it."

A scrunched face asked the next question without uttering a word.

Fenton braced the younger man's shoulder. "I don't know, Doug. I just don't know. One day at a time, right?"

"Right."

"Good," Fenton said. "Thanks for coming. Says a lot about you."

Fitzy's boots squeaked on the tile floor as he walked away.

Fenton stopped at the nurse's station and asked Jenny if another chair could be brought to Stan's room.

"I think we can handle that, Mr. Palmer."

"Thank you."

A few minutes later, hollow footsteps sounded on the linoleum floor. They stopped just outside the room. Then a pair of heads peered around the corner of the doorjamb, their timid eyes searching for signs of recognition.

"Sandra?"

Sandra perked at the sound of the familiar voice. "Laura?"

A woman dressed in a navy blue pea coat over jeans appeared in the entrance followed by a large, athletic looking man.

"Oh Sandra, Fenton, we are so sorry, we came as soon as we could." Laura Davis, a tall and curvaceous woman with caring green eyes reached for Sandra. The two women hugged for several moments.

"I'm so glad you're here," Sandra blubbered.

Kurt Davis placed a hand on Fenton's shoulder. "How are you holding up, partner?" At six-foot three and two hundred and twenty pounds, Kurt still struck an imposing sight at sixty years of age. He stuck out his right hand, which Fenton promptly shook.

"We're still in shock," Fenton replied.

"How is he?" Kurt asked. His eyes narrowed at the IVs and tubes.

"Not good," Fenton said. "All banged up, inside and out; on the operating table for hours." He relayed what else they knew about the accident.

Laura peeled off her coat. "Goodness gracious, it's a miracle he's alive."

Sandra nodded. "The doctors said he was really lucky."

"Will he be all right?" Kurt asked.

"Too soon to tell," Fenton said.

"He's a tough nut. Just like his old man."

"Thanks, Kurt."

"What did the doctor say?"

Fenton answered with an uncomfortable shake of his head and a grunt. Something unintelligible mumbled from his lips.

Kurt paused trying to decipher the words, then watched as Fenton wandered aimlessly around the room, finally pressing his forehead against the window. Kurt made eye contact with Laura who mouthed a silent: *Let it go.*

"Oh," Kurt murmured and removed his coat. "Have you been here all night?"

"Yes." Fenton's breathing steamed the glass. "Tanya was here too."

"Tanya?" Kurt said.

Sandra took Kurt's coat and hung it in the closet. "For several hours," she said then suddenly went still and her shoulders bowed as if her arms were carrying heavy sacks. Her chin dropped into her chest and she stood motionless for several moments with her back to the others. A loose thread dangling from her blouse captured her attention. Then as if deciding something, she yanked the thread free, turned and made eye contact with Laura. "I called her."

The Foiled Knight

Laura paused for a few seconds to read Sandra's face. With hair unkempt, mascara smeared and lips that would not stop trembling, she presented a picture of stress and exhaustion. But it was Sandra's eyes that Laura focused on. Dark and direct, they pleaded out a silent distress call.

"I understand," Laura said and squeezed Sandra's hands.

"But we sent her home to get some sleep," Sandra added.

"Of course," Laura said, then cleared her throat. "What can we do?"

Sandra wiped her nose with a tissue. "At this point, I don't really know. He doesn't have any pets or plants that need looking after."

"What about his work?"

"I've already spoken to his boss at the mill," Fenton said.

"Do you need anything taken care of at the house?" Kurt asked.

"Maybe grab the mail?"

"You got it."

"And toss the newspaper in the foyer. You know where the key is, right?"

"I'll take care of it."

Laura edged close to Sandra. "I'll go to the store and make up some meals and freeze them so all you have to do is heat them up."

Sandra hugged her friend again. "Thank you."

"Whatever you need, you just ask," Laura whispered into Sandra's ear.

"Okay."

"Here," Laura choked out. "I brought you something." From her pocket, she pulled an ornate rosary made of golden oak. "It's the one I brought back from The Vatican." She pressed it gently into Sandra's hand.

Sandra looked into Laura's eyes with watery ones of her own.

"You need this now," Laura said and kissed Sandra on the forehead. She tightened her arms for emphasis. "I love you."

Sandra squeezed back. "I love you too."

"Come on Kurt," Laura said. "We should go." They grabbed their coats and left.

* * *

Sandra and Fenton were halfway through their second rosary when they heard a meek knock at the door.

"Hello? Mr. and Mrs. Palmer?" Tanya's face leaned inside the door frame. "Can I come in?"

"Yes, of course, honey," Sandra said. "You just missed your parents."

"I know, I ran into them in the parking lot."

Fenton stood. "Here, you can have my chair."

"No," Tanya said, holding up her hand. "I didn't mean for you to get up."

"It's all right," Fenton said. "I can't sit still that long anymore; my back will stiffen up."

But Tanya heard nothing as her gaze focused on Stan. Her lips immediately began to tremble at the same time as her hands which she used to cover her mouth to steady both. Water built up in her eyes and the whimper of a wounded deer sounded from deep within her. "Oh, Stanny." She rushed to his side, her hands reaching out in spastic gestures to touch him, never actually doing so in fear of disrupting his life support equipment. Arms not knowing where to go, they crossed themselves three times before returning to their original position.

Sandra sidled up behind Tanya and braced her shoulders.

Tanya's entire body shook. "Oh, look at him." She rested her hand on his. "How is...will he...oh, Christ. Is he going to be all right?"

"Not sure yet," Sandra said.

"Can he hear me?"

"I don't know."

Tanya kissed the tips of her fingers then gently touched his face.

"He just lays there," Sandra said sniffing. "And those annoying machines just keep wheezing and beeping away." She blew her nose. "I guess I shouldn't call them annoying considering they're the only things keeping him alive."

"He's gonna be okay, Mrs. P."

"Of course he is. Any minute now, he's going to open his eyes and ask for a greasy, grimy cheese steak."

Tanya choked. "With onions and cheese wiz."

"And a side of French Fries," Sandra added.

"Lordy, don't forget the gravy on the Frenchies."

"Right, then wash it down with root beer in an iced mug."

"And cap it off with a monster belch," Tanya said. The two women tried to break into laughter, but the best they could generate were faint smiles.

Sandra took another tissue and wiped her eyes and nose. "Oh, you've got him pegged all right."

"All those double dates through high school."

"Seems like such a long time ago," Sandra said, her voice trailing away.

Tanya felt a knot form in her stomach at the sight of Sandra's mouth twitching, her sagging shoulders, and the trembling hand that held the now wrinkled tissue. She rubbed Sandra's neck. "How long have you been here?"

"I don't know," Sandra sighed. "I called in to work; they said take all the time I need." She shook her body as if shedding a chill, then turned to appraise Tanya. "What about you? Are you all right?"

"I'm fine."

Sandra squared her body to Tanya, eyes now on a motherly hunt for problems. "When is the last time you ate a decent meal?"

"I ate tons last night."

"I mean a home-cooked meal, not Buffalo wings and ice cream."

Tanya gawked at her.

"Oh please, Tanya. With Stan, nothing is a secret where you're concerned. He's told me on numerous occasions how you abuse your body when things are troubling you." She smoothed Tanya's hair. "Looks like he was right, too. Your eyes are sunken into your skull and you're white as a sheet. Those clothes are falling off you and your hair looks like a rat's nest on fire..." She stopped the barrage when Tanya's head sagged. "Oh my goodness," Sandra continued, "listen to what a nag I am. I'm sorry, you didn't deserve that tirade."

Tanya shook her head. "Don't worry about it."

"No, it was uncalled for," Sandra said. "We're all just so stressed out. Can you forgive me?"

"Of course," Tanya said sullenly before leaning forward and burying her face in her hands.

Sandra started to say something then stopped. A memory of the night she and Fenton had been playing cards at the Davis house flashed in her mind. The night a teenage Tanya had come storming in after breaking up with her then boyfriend. Bursting with tears, Tanya had rampaged through the house, hands covering her face in the same way before slamming the door to her bedroom.

Sandra made eye contact with Fenton and flicked her eyes toward the door.

Fenton nodded, then cleared his throat while mumbling something about needing another cup of coffee. He kissed Sandra and made for the door, disappearing into the hallway. The click of his boots faded quickly.

Sandra rubbed Tanya's back. "What's wrong, sweetheart?"

"Stan and I met for lunch last week. We sort of got into a disagreement."

"About what?"

"About what I'm doing with my life."

"Oh, he can be hardheaded," Sandra said.

"No, he was right. I'm barely making ends meet. I may have to move back in with my parents."

"Oh, well, there's worse things. You could be on the streets."

Tanya nodded. "This is true."

"Or in a shelter."

"Also true."

Sandra rubbed her back a bit harder.

"Or work at a job that's beneath you," Tanya droned. "Mr. Palmer about said the exact same thing to me."

"I'm sure Stan did too."

"Just a few times," Tanya said. "I should have listened."

The room got very quiet and they both looked at Stan, still wheezing and beeping away.

Chapter 8

Heavy boots clopped across the slush-covered parking lot toward the hospital's emergency room. Clumps of black slop flew from the well-worn tread. Through the sliding glass doors they carried the lumbering man wrapped in an army-green coat. He stopped at the center of the room, removed ratty gloves, and scratched a whiskered throat. Alert eyes scanned left and right until locating the sign indicating: Reception.

* * *

Jenny slung her stethoscope around her neck and massaged her eyes with the heels of her hands. Washed her face then leaned on the bathroom sink, studying her thirty-nine-year-old face in the mirror. A sharp featured woman with clear hazel eyes and pale skin stared back. *Still attractive,* she smiled, despite the lines that etched the corners of her mouth and across her forehead.

Pushing through the door, she slunk on lead feet back to the nurse's station and tossed the last of the clipboards into the wire basket. With a sigh, she bent forward at the waist, placed her palms flat on the linoleum floor and stretched her lanky runner's frame. Counted to twenty, enjoying the burn in her hamstrings before standing again. She gathered her frizzy blonde hair into a manageable pile and secured it with a scrunchie. A check of her pager revealed only two callbacks. She studied the patient status board behind the desk. *Busy day, but not too bad.* Seventeen new cases, all admitted and in various stages of treatment. *Huh, I might even be home in time to actually cook myself a decent dinner for a change.*

Oblivious to the ding of the elevator, she raised the coffee mug to her lips. A frown creased her forehead. "Good god," she whispered and scowled at the murky puddle of crude oil that had coagulated in the cup. "Morty!"

Morty popped his head out of a doorway. "Yo?"

"Hey, my coffee's turned to gunk. Can you make a new pot, please?"

"Sure thing."

Turning, Jenny nearly cried out at the imposing figure that loomed at the desk. A burly man with an enormous head, weathered skin and deep-set brown eyes stood before her. His unruly hair sprouted from under a black knit cap. Thick through the neck and back, the man stooped under muscular shoulders, in the way a sea captain hunches against an angry ocean. Beneath his right eye, a scar pulled the skin downward slightly, revealing the white of his eyeball.

"Good afternoon," the man said, his arms stretching nearly the entire length of the counter. Long, grimy fingers drummed on the hard surface, the sound of the nails clicking like hooves on cobblestones.

Jenny looked down, trying to suppress the trickle of fear that pinched at her bladder. She cleared her throat, but did not look up. "Good afternoon."

The stranger scratched his nose. "A friend of mine was in an accident."

The Foiled Knight

Jenny glanced up. A short gasp escaped her lips as the man smiled, a lopsided grin as if he could only speak out of one side of his mouth. His two front teeth showed the faintest of blue outline where they met the gums. A dental bridge.

"Anything wrong?" he asked.

"No, er, nothing wrong," she said, fumbling with the charts in the wire basket. "Long shift, you know?"

"I can imagine," he replied. "I'll bet the overnight freeze didn't help. Lot of old people bust their hips when the sidewalks ice over."

Jenny started. They *had* had an unusual number of elderly people come in with broken limbs.

Noticing her look of surprise, he added: "I worked as a janitor at an old folks home a while back."

"I see," she said, then gathered herself. "What's your friend's name?"

"Palmer. Stan Palmer."

She looked up with quizzical eyes. "You're a friend of Mr. Palmer?"

"Yup. Been friends for years," he said, then jutted a wide chin and scraped at his unshaven throat with the backs of his fingernails. "Played football together."

"Oh."

"Yeah, Stan was an animal on the field. Man, could he hit."

Jenny rolled her eyes. "I'm not much for violence."

The stranger paused. "Don't blame you. But me and Stan lost touch over the years. You know how it is."

Her mind drifted away for a moment. "Yes, actually I do," she said.

"Really? I would think any guy would want to stay in touch with a looker like you." His eyes dropped below the counter at her trim figure.

The hair on Jenny's neck bristled and she tugged at an earlobe. Compliments weren't something she normally received. Not ones that weren't induced by alcohol anyway. She leveled her eyes at him. "Sorry, but only people on my list of family and friends are allowed in."

The man smiled. "I don't need to see him."

Jenny's face blanked. "But I thought—"

"I'm not too good with hospitals. Reminds me of when my old man was laid up for a few months in traction."

"Oh, okay, um, I mean, sorry to hear that."

"Don't sweat it. I was just hoping you could tell me if he's gonna make it."

"I can't release that kind of information," Jenny said.

The man continued on, as if he hadn't heard her response. "Friend of mine is a cop and said he hit a deer and is in a coma."

Jenny shook her head.

"What?" the stranger said, "No, he didn't hit a deer or no, he isn't in a coma?"

"I'm shaking my head because I can't tell you."

"Why not? I'm his friend and all."

"Hospital privacy rules."

"Oh, right, I mean sure, I totally understand. Creeps and all." A pause. "But he's lucky to be alive, huh?"

Impassive eyes focused on the man without blinking, their color intensifying ever so slightly.

The man leaned close. "Can you tell me if he's said anything yet?"

"No."

"Of course, stupid question. Cause if he *wasn't* in a coma, he'd be telling me himself what happened, right?"

"Right," Jenny said, then quickly, "Wait. What? No. I mean, er, when I answered, I was speaking hypothetically. I did not confirm whether or not he is in a coma." Her face contorted in confusion.

An oily grin rippled across his wide jaw. "Of course you didn't. And there's no way you're gonna tell me if he'll ever come out of it, is there?"

Jenny frowned. There was something about the way the man tapped the countertop. After a few seconds of silence, she shook her head, picked up her coffee mug and set it down with a decisive *click*. "Look mister, why don't you go to the library and check out a book on the subject because I told you, I can't release information about a patient."

The man said nothing for several seconds, the silence replaced by the clacking of his fingernails that had picked up in tempo. "Damn, that's too bad."

"Have you been in touch with his family? They're here every day."

The man checked his wristwatch. "No, and darn, too bad I'll miss them. Gotta go to work. They wouldn't remember me anyway." He turned to leave.

"Hey," Jenny called to him. "Who should I say was asking for him?"

The only reply was the sound of a dirty fingernail stabbing the elevator down button.

Chapter 9

Darkness hung low over the deserted downtown of Abington. 5:45 AM. That time of day when night clings to its last remaining moments, just before giving way to dawn's pale blue curtain. When steam escaping from sewer grates appears the dullest of gray.

Cold and desolate streets lay still, their slumber broken only by the soft pat-pat-pat of a determined jogger bundled in earmuffs and leggings. A newspaper truck dropped off stacks of the morning edition tied up with jute. They hit the sidewalk like blocks of frozen granite. Traffic began to appear as the jogger and truck headed east, their profiles looming dark against the growing ball of a yellow sun inching its way above the horizon.

One lonely ray of sunlight found its way through the window of the ninth floor of the hospital, illuminating the fast moving legs of Sandra Palmer. Her heels pounded an echo off the walls. In her leather-gloved hands, she held a folded newspaper snagged from the sidewalk bundle.

Just past the nurse's station, she leaned into Stan's room and spotted Tanya: head lying on the edge of the bed, eyes closed, snoring ever so slightly. Padding softly, Sandra slid past her and kissed Stan on the forehead. The bandage around his head felt rough on her chapped lips. She turned her cheek to it and closed her eyes. So smooth now, so soft, so tender, she fell into a soothing rhythm, across and back, savoring the sense of tranquility.

After several moments, she stood back and stroked Tanya's hair. Tanya woke with a start. "Shhh, it's just me," Sandra said. "Same?"

With a yawn, Tanya arched her back and stretched her arms. "Same."

"I was afraid of that," Sandra said.

"Doctor DeAngelis stopped by last night," Tanya said. "He's going to run more tests."

"That has to be a good sign," Sandra said, eyebrows raised hopefully. "They wouldn't keep running tests on him if it was hopeless. Right?"

"I guess," Tanya said. "I told him that you would be in this morning."

"Okay, thanks." Sandra stroked Stan's hair. "He's so peaceful."

"I know," Tanya said. "I keep praying he would just sit up and say: 'Let's get out of here.'"

"If only," Sandra said, her voice fading away. "Will you be able to stay with him today?"

"No," Tanya murmured. "I have to work."

Sandra's knees buckled slightly. "Oh."

Tanya leapt up and bolstered her with a strong arm. "But I'll be back tonight."

"Good," Sandra said, somewhat improving in spirit. "Stan will like that."

There was a moment of silence as she looked longingly at her son, then a sigh. "I hate it that I can't stay here all day, but somehow, it helps if I keep moving." She went silent. A shaking hand rose to cover trembling lips. "Even if he can't."

Tanya moved in close. "Hey, Mrs. P. It's going to be okay. He's a fighter."

"And he's in good company," Sandra said, leaning into her.

Tanya squeezed her tight. "Did you see what I brought?" She pointed to the painting Stan had given her that was now leaning against the window.

Frozen in time, the boy and girl smiled at each other, he admiring her pigtails in ribbons, she the smell of a flower that he had picked. The dirt path upon which they walked in bare feet was bordered on both sides by a black thicket of densely leaved trees, their thorny branches holding a mangled kite and an empty bird's nest. Blue specks peeked between the tree trunks, the creek where they used to explore.

"It's beautiful," Sandra said.

"Stan gave it to me as a present on my 13th birthday."

"I remember him working on it."

"I know you were disappointed the hospital wouldn't let you bring in real flowers," Tanya said, "so I figured this would be the next best thing."

Sandra gently touched the flower held by the girl. "A daisy."

"I remember him picking it," Tanya said, running her fingertips down the canvas. It had been early June, seventh grade. A typical day of exploring for her and Stan.

"Hey Teedy!" Stan had shouted. "Commere. Look what I found under this rock." With a bony arm, he held up a mud-green colored crayfish.

"Ewe!" Tanya had replied, holding her sneakers above the water line as she stepped gingerly on the slippery stones along the base of the creek. "Put it back. Sawtrigger's Creek is the only place around here where he can survive."

"No way. This is the same bugger who bit my toe last time we were here."

"That was two whole days ago and there's a bazillion of his brothers and sisters in here. How can you possibly know he's the same one who bit you?"

"Because he's got a smile on his face that's saying: 'Mmmm, you were tasty.' He must like toe jam."

Tanya winced. "Stan Palmer, that is just too gross for words."

Sawtrigger's Creek ran perpendicular to Rockwell Road, the street on which Stan and Tanya lived. Lined on both sides with sycamore trees, their branches so large they reached from one side to the other, forming a tunnel. Thick as they were old, the trees' roots broke up the sidewalk into a rollercoaster of concrete that the kids rode with their skateboards. Two-story colonial houses, each with a wrap-around front porch and dormer windows, nestled into their expansive shade. In every yard lay a bicycle, or a slingshot, or a baseball bat, or wooden fence with a loose board.

Rockwell acted as a convenient cut-thru from Welsh Road to York Road, the main drag through the small town of Abington. Built into the north side of Huntington Valley, the road followed the landscape's "V" that naturally guided rain water run-off to Sawtrigger's Creek. Old Man Sawtrigger, a train conductor and Abington's most generous citizen, had fought local builders from developing the area, holding firm to the town's desire to be a place where kids could "experience the life of Tom Sawyer" — which meant room for nature.

The Foiled Knight

Stan tossed the crayfish back into the water and climbed up the muddy embankment, latching onto low-hanging tree branches for stability. The sun had found a hole in the canopy cover, lighting up a large flat rock that stuck out over the water like a diving platform. Stan pulled himself up. "Did you finish your history project?"

Tanya waded to shore. "Not yet. Probably do it on Sunday. Why do we have to study so much Civil War? I hate 7th grade."

"It'll be over soon." He picked up a rock and hurled it at a squirrel skittering along a tree branch. "Before you know it, we'll be in high school." He peered at a circular pool of clear water ten feet below. "Think I can do a back-flip off this ledge?"

"I wouldn't," Tanya said. "It's not deep enough."

"Is too," Stan said and pulled off his shirt leaving him in ragged cut-off jeans. His scrawny body glistened with sweat in the bright sunlight. "Ernie McFadden dove in head first last summer."

"Yeah, and you know what happened to him."

"Ernie is an idiot," Stan said. "Everybody knows you're supposed to put your hands out in front of you so you don't scrape bottom with your face."

"He lost all his front teeth."

Stan chuckled. "Yeah, now he's one helluva whistler."

"Is it true he got caught peeping from one of the stalls of the girl's bathroom?"

"Yup. And... he had a mirror."

Tanya gawked, then shook herself. "Disgusting!"

"Got a whole summer of detention for that one," Stan continued. "And then his dad caught him with a bunch of nudey magazines."

"What is he, some kind of pervert?"

"Pretty much," Stan said and took up a diver's position, balancing with just his toes on the edge of the rock and his back to the water.

"That rock doesn't spring like a diving board, silly," Tanya said.

"Waa-Waa."

"You need a good spring to get past the rocks."

He looked down, judging the distance. "I'll just push harder with my legs."

She took an urgent step forward. "Stan, don't."

"I can do this, Teedy."

"It's too far!"

"No it's not. I always whupped Ernie's butt in the long jump."

"But you're not running!" she exclaimed and covered her face.

With a pinwheel of his arms, Stan leapt up and around into a perfect back-flip, hitting the water cleanly with pointed toes. The ripple of water from his splash had just spread to the banks when Stan's head broke the surface. He shook the hair out of his face. "Told ya."

Tanya peeked out between her fingers and relaxed when she saw Stan's wide grin. "You are such a daredevil," she said. "I think I hate you."

"Don't ever let anyone tell you you can't do something, Teedy."

She scrambled up the embankment, slipping and sliding until she reached the rock platform. Throwing her sneakers ahead of her, she climbed up. The sun-heated rock warmed her chilled feet. "Think I could do it?"

Stan laughed. "Yeah, right."

"Don't you dare laugh at me."

"Teedy, listen to me, don't do it."

"Like you listened to me?" She stepped to the ledge and pulled off her shirt revealing a training bra. "Any comment out of you Stanley Palmer and I'm beating the shit out of you."

"Holy mackerel," Stan said, "you're serious."

She held her arms out straight. "Tell me what to do."

"Just count to three and jump up and out. That's important, you gotta go up *and* out."

"Up and out," Tanya said, taking several quick breaths. She dropped her arms. "I'm scared."

"So don't do it."

"But I want to."

He rolled his eyes. "So do it."

"You're no help."

"Want me to do it with you?"

She shot daggers at him. "No."

"Quit stalling and go."

"What if I miss?"

Stan made for shore. "I'm coming up there." He hoisted himself onto a log at the edge of the water.

A look of determination pounced on Tanya. With rigid force, she locked her arms in front of her, took a deep breath and sprung from the rock platform going up and out. But not all the way over. She clapped the water in an awkward belly flop and disappeared below the surface. A moment later she reappeared, strands of hair snarled across her face. "OUCH!!!"

Stan fell back onto the grass, guffawing, his feet pounding the ground.

"God my stomach hurts," Tanya said, falling into laughter with him. She pushed the hair away and swam toward him.

"Totally awesome," Stan said.

She climbed out to stand before him, her belly sticking out from beneath the training bra that was now see-through. Rivulets of water ran from her hair and down her plump torso. She plopped down next to him and kissed him on the cheek.

He cocked his head. "What was that for?"

"For not staring at my chest."

He smiled, but said nothing.

She smiled back. "What's so funny?"

"I don't know. Wasn't expecting you to say *that*." He got to his feet. "Wanna head over to Sawtrigger's cabin?"

The quizzical look faded from Tanya's face. "Nah, too far. Let's explore the train yard instead. But you'll have to help me up."

He shrugged. "Okay." He held out his hand. She took it and stood, rising until she was face to face with him, their bodies only inches apart, water droplets hitting each other's feet. The beauty of her face caught his breath: her dimpled chin and petite nose with the barely perceptible triangle of freckles on one nostril. And that flashing smile, the whiteness of which blinded him from acknowledging the crookedness of her teeth. Pomegranate lips, still stained from the blueberries they had eaten earlier, came together in a clumsy pucker. Waiting. Inviting him. Their poutiness mesmerizing him. He studied the small white line of a scar that ran along her upper lip, the result of a bus accident in fourth grade. And her skin. So tan except for the hints of purple and red where the acne would soon ravage her cheeks.

He shifted to her eyes that were greener than maple leaves. A hypnotic pair that didn't try to hide her willingness, ones that caused a prickly heat to scald the back of his neck. Flushing, he turned away. "We'd better go if we're to be home in time for supper." He reached for his backpack and slung it over his shoulder.

"Okay," she murmured and pulled her shirt over her head.

They strolled along the dirt path that ran by the creek's edge, holding their sneakers by the tips of two fingers. She reached for him. Hand in hand they walked, saying nothing, content to enjoy the slight breeze and perfect temperature. Trees were in full bloom, and nature busy in the never-ending cycle of survival. Birds nested. Bees pollinated. Fish hunted food and laid eggs. The path felt smooth on their feet and dirt just beginning to collect between their toes when Stan had darted to a clump of wild daisies growing from the side of the creek. Plucking one, he had returned to Tanya's side and handed it to her.

She remembered inhaling the sweet fragrance and she breathed in trying to experience the joy again. Her eyes snapped open at the repulsive smell of Stan's hospital room. There was nothing pleasant about it. Tanya shivered at finding the right way to describe it: it was if everything just...died.

Chapter 10

Detective Mike Ciquero peeled off his leather jacket, fixed a cup of coffee and deposited his girth into the swivel chair behind his oak desk. His office in the Glenside Police Station was as plain as it was small. Oblivious to the ringing of phones and other activity going on around him, he opened the folder on his most recent case, spread the contents across the surface, and set about studying the facts. Female, fourteen, reported missing the night of the snowstorm.

Holly Mathews, local girl, good student, no history of any trouble. According to her parents, a fairly typical teenager, just getting into boys, played tennis and spent a lot of time doodling in a art pad. By all accounts a good kid. Nothing to suggest she might be a runaway.

Last assumed whereabouts: the Keswick movie theater, supposedly to see a five o'clock show. No one at the theater, however, could remember her. The parents claimed she didn't have a boyfriend so nothing to suggested she lied. Interviews with friends confirmed that. When Ciquero had interrogated shop owners in the immediate vicinity, he got nothing. A check of the girl's cell phone records revealed she'd made only one call since earlier that afternoon – to the pet store where she volunteered – to verify her hours the coming week. Ciquero and another policeman had scoured the streets and alleys in the area, coming up with nothing but soggy boots. He'd checked into everything he could think of and had nothing to show for it.

He stroked his mustache and thought some more until his brain began to hurt, then gathered the meager notes into the folder and shoved it away. "Where are you, Holly?" he whispered.

Tall with dark hair, dangerous green eyes and a rugged, swarthy complexion, Ciquero presented an imposing presence when interrogating suspects. And yet while he looked the part of Italian swashbuckler, his demeanor didn't deliver it.

So far, it had been an unremarkable twenty-year career. He didn't graduate top of his class, hadn't earned any awards or progressed through the ranks like everyone else. His shining moment arrived just a few years ago when he made detective, something the high fliers did after five years. Most of the guys he came up with had since moved away to become police captains in other cities. Not that that bothered him. Small towns like Glenside didn't generate violent crimes like in the city. The lower the risk, the longer the life. Unlike his father who craved confrontation. Craved it so much that he couldn't back down from any altercation, a mindset that earned him a trip to an early grave.

Tony Falbo, the station tech, leaned into Ciquero's office. "Hey Mike. I think I got us a break."

Ciquero took a sip of coffee and peered over the tops of his wire-rimmed glasses. "Yeah? Tell me you've got video of the girl on a security camera."

The Foiled Knight

"I wish," Falbo said. He held up a computer printout. "It's a list of 911 calls the night of the storm."

Ciquero's eyebrows rose.

"There were nineteen made that night," Falbo said.

"Nineteen?" The eyebrows dove.

"Yeah, everybody has problems during a storm."

"Is one from her cell phone?" Ciquero asked. "How come it wasn't on the phone company's read out?"

"I don't know who they belong to," Falbo said. "You're the detective." He dropped the printout on Ciquero's desk and walked away.

Ciquero dialed the first number.

A female voice answered after three rings. "Hello?"

"Hello, this is detective Mike Ciquero, Glenside police. I'm following up on a 911 call made from this number last Saturday night."

"Yes, what about it? My father's fine."

"Your father?"

"Yes, he started having chest pains after shoveling the driveway so we called 911. But he's fine, he just overexerted himself."

"Oh, um, I'm glad to hear he's feeling better." Ciquero hung up and massaged his forehead. *Good grief,* he thought to himself, *I'm going to get every lost dog or domestic dispute case in the county.*

Sighing, he took a pen, drew a line through the first number and dialed the next one on the list.

Chapter 11

"Tanya, wake up, honey," Sandra said.

Tanya's eyelids pried open a crack. "Hmmm?" Rainbow socks came into focus, then an easy chair. A magazine on the floor, its pages slightly wet from the melted snow from her boots; the window, black, save for the distant blinking light of an airplane inching across the night sky. Her eyelashes fluttered open at the sight of Sandra Palmer standing before her.

"Oh, hi Mrs. P., I must have fallen asleep." A sudden nervous glance at Stan's face in the shadows. She jerked up. "Is everything all right?"

"Yes, it's the same," Sandra said, her meek voice afraid to challenge the silence in the hallway. "If that's what you mean by all right." She turned on the fluorescent light above Stan's bed.

"What time is it?" Tanya asked.

"Almost seven."

"Really? Wow, I've been here all day."

"I thought you had to work?"

"I asked to have the night off."

Sandra tilted her head. "Why?"

"I feel bad that you haven't been able to be here as much as you'd like. Figured I'd stay."

"You're precious," Sandra said, "but you've been here a long time and you need to eat. I just spoke with Dr. DeAngelis and nothing is likely happening tonight. Let's get some dinner. We could go to the Inn Flight across the street."

"Sure," Tanya said. She slipped on her boots and retrieved her coat. "It'll be good to stretch our legs."

"I could never work in a hospital," Sandra said as they walked to the elevators. "So...medicinal. Like someone used iodine to scrub the floors." She pulled on leather gloves, hit the down button and buried her nose in the collar of her coat.

"Well, their coffee won't win any awards," Tanya said. "I always wondered what mechanics did with the used oil they drained from cars."

"Good God, that's horrible. What made you think of that?"

"Sorry, didn't mean to gross you out. It's something Del used to say."

"Oh, I forgot," Sandra said. "He works on cars, doesn't he?"

"Yeah. Well, he did. Got fired. Again. Now he's working for Macino Construction. It's owned by Vinnie Macino, a guy we went to school with." The elevator doors opened and they stepped inside making room for a janitor pushing a mop bucket on wheels. They rode in silence until they reached the ground floor and were out the front doors.

Cold air buffeted them forcing them to hold the handrail as they descended the steps. The snow had been blown away onto both sides of the sidewalk. They

The Foiled Knight

hooked elbows and strode through the chute with white shoulders.

Arriving at the street corner, they looked both ways before dashing across the four-lane road. Their scarves fluttered behind them like dual tails of a kite.

The Inn Flight restaurant, a small stone structure with a central chimney, was a quaint little getaway specializing in steak and seafood. Flood lights lit the snow-shoveled walkway to the entrance.

Inside the front door, a soft glow of lighting and saxophone music greeted them. Cozy booths lined the walls around a hearth burning a roaring fire. They removed their coats and strolled past the bar made of golden oak. Pilot caps, goggles, leather jackets, insignias and other flying paraphernalia adorned the walls. Toy airplanes, WWII miniatures, hung from the ceiling.

Sandra waved at the bartender. "We're here for a late dinner. Can we seat ourselves?"

"Yeah, sure, take the round booth."

They found an empty cove in the corner.

Sandra's cell phone rang from within her purse. She dug it out. "Hello Fenton. No, we're at the Inn Flight getting dinner. Come join us." She listened. "Okay, I'll order something for you." She slid the phone away. "Fenton is on his way over."

"Good," Tanya said. "Will he let me contribute to the check this time?"

"No," Sandra said, smiling slyly. "So don't even ask."

"Not fair, I do work for a living."

Sandra put her hands up in surrender. "You know how he is. You're like the daughter he never had."

"Maybe he'll let me leave the tip."

"Maybe," Sandra said, her eyes dancing.

A young and well-built blond man dressed in a leather jacket, aviator pants and boots approached. "Good evening ladies. My name is Steven and I'll be taking care of you this evening. Can I start you off with a drink?"

"I'd like a beer," Tanya said. "Mug of whatever is on tap is fine."

"And for your sister?" Steven said, flashing a confident grin.

"Easy, stud," Sandra said laughing. "White wine and a Sam Adams."

"Coming right up." He scribbled on his pad and dashed away.

Tanya's face screwed up into a puzzle. "So what were we talking about?"

"You and Del."

"Oh."

"Yes, oh," Sandra said. "So what do you mean he got fired again?"

Tanya shifted uncomfortably in the booth, the friction of her legs on the leather seat sending out a groan. "For getting into a fight with a customer."

"For God's sake, over what?"

"Who knows?" Then a sigh. "Any little criticism sets him off."

"He's got such a temper."

"Tell me about it," Tanya said, absentmindedly rubbing her cheekbone with the back of her hand.

"He turned into a real louse," Sandra said. "He wasn't always that way."

"No, he wasn't. Never the same since he lost that job at the mill."

"Fired, remember? For stealing from people's retirement accounts. Don't feel sorry for him, Tanya."

"Blamed me for everything," Tanya said, tugging her hair. She gazed longingly at a young couple sitting thigh to thigh at another table.

Sandra reached across the table and covered Tanya's hands with her own. "You did the right thing by divorcing him early. You were too young."

"Never should have gotten married, period," Tanya said.

"Woulda, shoulda, coulda."

"Stan tried to warn me."

Sandra patted Tanya's hand. "He was good at that."

"Said I should have continued with my dance, even if only as a teacher."

"He always knew you best."

"Yes he did."

"When's the last time you went to a show?" Sandra asked.

"Couldn't tell you."

"I got some tickets from my boss, he can't use them. You want them?"

Tanya's eyes perked. "Really?"

"Really. They're good seats too. Take a friend, you deserve it."

"Thanks Mrs. P."

"Don't mention it."

Tanya thought for a moment, then smiled. "Think I'll ask my mother."

"Great idea," Sandra said and squeezed her hand.

They paused as Steven delivered drinks. "Are you ladies ready to order?"

"I know what I want," Sandra said and looked at Tanya to confirm she was ready also. "I'll have the Shrimp Scampi over linguine."

"And for you?" Steven said to Tanya, avoiding Sandra's amused stare.

"My *sister*," Sandra interrupted, snapping Steven's head in her direction, "will have the grilled chicken Caesar salad." Sandra flicked a glance at Tanya, widening her eyelids at the same time.

Tanya nearly spit out her beer, a look of eager anticipation filling her eyes. "Don't forget brother Fenton's order, sister. It wouldn't do to have him turn, here, in public."

"Um, *turn?*" Steven said.

"Yes," Sandra said. "Our brother becomes quite violent if not fed timely."

Steven's eyes shifted from one woman to the other. "Violent?"

"Mmmm," Sandra hummed with a dramatic nod of her head.

Steven looked about. "Er—what would your brother like to eat?"

"Brother Fenton's food!" Sandra exclaimed. "How our minds do wander, sister. But I suppose it is the drink that does us in."

"You were always the lush," Tanya said. "That's why Mother loved me best."

A worried look collapsed Steven's face. "Maybe I should come back?"

Sandra snared him by the pocket. "Nonsense."

He shied away. "I don't know what game you're playing, but I would appreciate it if you would just let me take your order." His face burned as red as the fire behind him.

Sandra and Tanya went silent for several seconds. Steven stared back, beads of sweat dappling his forehead.

The Foiled Knight

"I do believe he means it, sister," Tanya said.

"Damn straight," Steven said, wriggling his shoulders.

"Very well," Sandra said. "Our brother will have the New York Strip."

"And how—"

"Raw," Sandra interrupted, her face lifeless.

Steve looked at Sandra, his pen and pad frozen in mid-air. "Raw?"

"He's just gotten off work, so he'll be famished."

"What is he, a lumberjack? Next thing you'll tell me he chases bears."

"No, he hunts shark."

Steven's eyes rounded on them. "Uh-huh,"

"Hey, where's my food?" Fenton Palmer said as he came up behind Steven. "I'm so hungry I could eat a bear."

Sandra and Tanya burst out laughing as Steven ran from the table. Fenton stood looking quizzically at the retreating server, then at the two women. He shook his head and chuckled. "Poor guy never had a chance."

Fenton climbed into the booth next to Sandra and kissed his wife. "Don't beat the guy up until *after* he brings our food."

"He hit on me," Sandra said.

"Can you blame him?" Fenton said and winked at Tanya while taking a gulp of beer. "No really, what'd he do to set you magpies off?"

Sandra leaned back in her seat. "Careful, brother, or sister Tanya and I will bring Mother's wrath down upon you as well."

Feigning horror, Fenton shed his coat. "You're in a good mood."

"Oh what a joy to laugh for once," Sandra sighed. "I needed it. These past few days have been such a strain, it feels good to release it."

"Laughter is a good thing," Fenton said.

"How'd work go?"

"Augh, another long day at the lumber yard." The words came out in a tired exhale of breath.

Sandra studied her husband. His face, always rugged, seemed troubled, as if caught in a permanent state of frowning. Deep creases cut into the corners of each eye. His powerful arms leaned on the table surface, deftly sliding his mug back and forth, never quite letting the glass leave his touch. "You're a good man, Fenton Palmer," she said and stroked his hair that was still damp from a hasty shower. "You're with friends now, so enjoy a frosty Sam, eat a good steak and let it go."

"You're not working tonight, Tanya?" Fenton asked.

"Took the night off," she answered.

He looked at Sandra and caught the subtle shake of her head. "Any news on Stan?"

"No change."

Fenton's head dipped slightly, the muscles in his jaw clenching. "Damn."

Sandra put her arm around his shoulders. "But Doctor DeAngelis is going to run further tests. We should hear something in a day or so."

"What kind of tests?" he asked.

"CT scan. MRI's. Electro-something-o-gram. Can't even pronounce them, but they should give the doctor a better idea of Stan's long-term prognosis."

Fenton took another drink of his beer and set the mug down without a sound. His sideburns seemed whiter since the last time Tanya saw him only a few days ago. The tip of his index finger ran along the rim of the mug, then down the side, wiping the condensation into the napkin. He stared into the suds, his forehead rippling. "What if he's brain dead?"

The table went quiet. Sounds from the restaurant filled the awkward silence. Glasses clinked while conversation from other tables buzzed in a fuzzy drone. Tanya stared into the fire. Sandra removed her arm from around her husband's shoulders. There was the sound of waiters gathering around another table and singing "Happy Birthday." Finally, Fenton rapped the table with his knuckles and looked up. "Jesus, I didn't mean to bring everyone down like that. I'm sorry." He rubbed his forehead briskly.

Tanya bit her lip.

"It's all right, dear," Sandra said, scooting close to him. "You are just saying out loud what we're all wondering ourselves."

"I don't think I could handle seeing Stan like that for the rest of his life."

Sandra touched his forearm. "You don't know that."

"Can't talk or think or move," Fenton continued.

"Stop it."

"There's so many tubes coming out of him."

"You're getting yourself all—"

"Can't even take a crap like a man."

"Fenton—"

"What kind of a life is that?" He banged the table. "He's like…"

"Don't—"

"A vegetable."

"Don't say that word!"

"Stan wouldn't want to live this way," Fenton fumed. Heads from other tables turned.

Sandra gripped his arm. "Calm down. We'll figure it out."

He raked his scalp with tense fingernails. "How will we pay for his long term medical care?"

"Won't his employer cover it?"

"Not all of it, and it certainly won't be forever."

"Whatever it is, it's better than nothing. We'll just have to manage."

Just then a different server than Steven delivered their food. The table went quiet as the plates were distributed.

Fenton snatched his knife and drove it into the center of his steak. "Do we even know if Stan made a will or who has power of attorney to make decisions on his behalf?" He ripped off a jagged chunk of meat. "I don't even know the name of Stan's lawyer."

"It's Alan Malone," Sandra said. "But it's too soon to talk like that."

Fenton set his knife and fork down. His eyes were tired. "Then when?"

"Tomorrow," Sandra said. "Next week, what difference does it make?"

He went quiet, took a sip of beer, ran his hand through his hair again, then focused on Tanya. "I'm sorry about this. Sandra and I shouldn't be having this conversation in front of you."

"Maybe I should leave," Tanya said, grabbing her coat, "so you and Mrs. Palmer can be alone."

"No," Sandra said. "Stay. He needs to know."

Fenton stopped rubbing his eyes. "Know what?"

Sandra looked at Tanya. "Tell him."

"Stan does have a will," Tanya said, poking at her salad. "I've got a copy of it in my safe deposit box." She hesitated.

Fenton's palms opened. "And?"

"He prepared an advance directive," Tanya said. "It's like a living will."

"What's it say?"

"I'm not a lawyer, okay? But if Stan is pronounced incompetent, then I've been granted power of attorney for medical decisions for his care."

"Incompetent," Fenton said. "Kind of an abrupt word."

Tanya shrugged.

"Who decides if he is incompetent?" Fenton said.

"The doctor," Sandra interjected.

"Lot of good that does us," Fenton blurted. "We've already seen where he's at on this whole thing." He ripped a bread roll in half, started buttering it, then stopped. "Wait, why would Stan give it to you? I mean, no offense Tanya, but why wouldn't he want his parents to have that responsibility?"

"He thought, um, that you and Mrs. Palmer would be, er… gone… before anything like this would be necessary."

"How long ago did you two talk about this?"

"Thanksgiving."

Fenton thought a moment. "Right after I had that cancerous mole removed."

Tanya nodded. "That's what triggered it." She toyed with her glass. "God, that sounds so insensitive."

Fenton leaned back, his face disappearing into the shadows, knife and bread still in hand. He sat unmoving for several moments. Then his eyebrows rose and they heard him blow out a gust of air, the long slow hiss of a man staring at himself in the mirror. "No it doesn't, actually." He came back into the light. "Parents don't expect to outlive their children. What, specifically, does the advance directive say as to his care?"

Tanya looked at Sandra who nodded and said: "Go ahead."

"Specifically," Tanya said, "that he refuses kidney dialysis and designates me as his surrogate to make medical treatment decisions."

"Kidney? What?" He paused. "Then why did the hospital resuscitate him, perform surgery, and hook him up to all those machines? Don't get me wrong, they absolutely did the right thing, but based on what you just said, seems like they weren't supposed to do anything."

"No, you're not hearing me. The directive doesn't say anything about do not resuscitate. All the document addresses is the dialysis and a surrogate."

"What kind of document is that?" Fenton said. "Seems incomplete."

Tanya looked at Sandra who raised her eyebrows, but said nothing.

"What did this Malone guy say?" Fenton continued.

Tanya set down her fork. "If the document does not specifically address the medical condition, then I have authority to decide what care he is given."

She paused, studying Fenton and Sandra, wishing they would say something. But they sat quietly, their expressions void of life. Tanya's eyes flitted from one to the other. "But please, you and Mrs. Palmer have to *know* that I would never make a decision without talking to the both of you first."

Fenton and Sandra made eye contact. A flash of mutual thought passed between them. Fenton's mouth hung open for a split second, then closed slowly as he sat back. He shook his head, eyes glazed, looking past Tanya in a blind person's stare.

Tanya felt as if some unspeakable dark secret had just been kept from her.

They ate the rest of the meal in silence.

Chapter 12

"Thanks for dinner, Mom," Tanya said. "It's nice being back home."

"You're welcome," Laura said. "It's nice to cook for you again."

"Kinda makes you wish I were still living here, huh?" Tanya asked as she placed a dirty plate into the dishwasher.

"Eh," Laura grunted. "Wouldn't go that far." She held a stoic face for a moment, then smiled. "Just kidding. Come on let's get changed." They made their way up the stairs to the master bedroom. "Actually," Laura continued, "it would be good to have someone around. Your father and I aren't getting any younger."

"Bah, you two are in great shape, physically and mentally," Tanya said, caressing the ornate wooden frame of a full-length mirror made of dark cherry. "I don't remember this, when did you get it?"

"Bought it at a sheriff sale auction. I think it goes well with our bedroom furniture, don't you?"

Tanya glanced around at her parent's bedroom. "Eh." She tried not to look at her mother, but the instant their eyes met, they both burst out laughing.

"You're a stinker," Laura said.

Tanya slipped on tight black pants and a stylish top, stepped into high heels and modeled in the mirror.

"Oooh, I love it," Laura said. "Turn around."

Tanya performed a perfect pirouette.

Laura sighed. "Oh, I remember when I had that kind of figure."

"Why thank you, mother," Tanya said, smiling. "But don't talk like that. You still turn heads, I've noticed."

"Heh, you're a sweetheart," Laura said. She brushed her hair out of the way and put on earrings. "Tell me again where we're going?"

"Walnut Street theatre," Tanya said. "Mrs. Palmer got tickets through her work."

"So nice of Sandra to think of us. Remind me to thank her."

"I will," Tanya said. "It feels weird though."

"Weird? How?"

"I feel guilty going to a show when Stan is in the hospital."

"You can't stop living your life, Tanya."

"Mmmm."

"And it's wonderful that you are doing so much to help them out," Laura continued, "but if you don't take a break now and then to recharge your batteries, you won't be able to help at all."

"Yeah, I guess you're right."

"You know I'm right."

"Okay, okay. You ready? I'll drive."

An hour later, they were in their seats, drinks and playbills in hand.

"What's it about?" Laura asked.

"The trials and tribulations dancers go through to audition for a part. You'll love it, lots of singing and dance numbers."

The theatre lights dimmed and the curtain disappeared into the ceiling. A narrow spotlight brought the female lead to life as the soft tones of a violin floated up from the orchestra. The entire first act consisted of a ballet solo.

At the end of the number, Laura clapped loudly. "You used to be able to do that."

"A hundred years ago," Tanya mumbled. "The program says the next scene has everybody."

The pulsating beat of a bass drum brought the crowd to life as men and women dancing in pairs flooded the stage. A tall redhead in a short black skirt and royal-blue top entered from the wings.

"Wow, look at that outfit," Tanya said. "She's hot!"

From the other side, a man of similar height, dark skin and powerful thighs emerged wearing all black and matching hat. The woman sprinted toward him and jumped onto his chest, wrapping her legs around his torso. The cast parted and the pair launched into a lively salsa routine.

Tanya followed the red-head and her partner, marveling at their perfect unison. With hands clasped and frames erect, they whirled across the stage, joined at the waist, their movement's mirror images of each other. Turning her back to him, the woman's curvy physique rolled and her hair tumbled across her chest as her upper body writhed in a carefree release at his tender touch. Facing him, she snaked her leg around his, her calf massaging his thigh, losing herself in the throes of smoldering rapture. She bounded away, he in close pursuit. Into the unknown she leapt, landing safely in the sanctuary of his arms, a look of pure contentment on her face. They embraced; his arms encircling her, engulfing her, adoring her.

He released her to twirl on pointed toes, the centrifugal force fluttering her skirt like a magic carpet. She snapped to a halt, a hooded glare of lust emanating from under her Medusa-like mane. Not backing down, he opposed her. The bass drum thumped: the duel was on. Like primal creatures preparing to attack, they stalked each other as the remaining dancers surrounded them. The woman drove her fingers up into her hair, rocking her pelvis. Spinning, she whipped him with red lashes of hair. He fell to the ground feigning death. The victorious female rushed over, her hands on her cheeks, upset at having vanquished her would-be mate. Prodding him with a toe, she recoiled as he suddenly sprang to his feet. Simultaneously, they lunged for each other, the full body contact audible to the audience.

Number after number the duo performed their enchantment. Tanya shifted in her seat, wiping sweat from her forehead. The couple's attraction for each other kindled a longing within her. Their artistry, the way their bodies merged, and their smiles of unbridled joy caused moisture to well in her eyes. Drawn to the edge of her seat, Tanya's hand clutched at her heart, wishing she could once again experience the thrill of perfect harmony with a shadowy partner of her own. Who was this man with the ability to surface such raw emotion within her?

The Foiled Knight

She tried to glimpse his face, but the hat shielded his features, an invisible silhouette.

The man grasped the red-head firmly at the waist, fingers sinking deep into her hips, and lifted her, high over his head. She extended her arms like wings, her sleek body rising with the graceful uptake. Tanya's soul soared. Imagining herself on the palms of his hands, she took flight alongside the dancer. Floating through the clouds, Tanya beamed, the elation on her face reflecting in the man's electric blue eyes illuminated now by the bright lights. A smile unleashed itself above the square jaw of Stan Palmer.

Tanya's program fell to the ground. "Oh!"

"What?" Laura asked, wild eyed.

Tanya felt a prickly heat swarm her body. She rubbed her eyes, hyper-focusing on the male dancer. The euphoria dissipated at the realization the only resemblance was the dark hair. She flushed at how silly it would be to tell her mother what she had just imagined and turned back to the performance. "Nothing."

In the final scene, the man spun the woman like a top causing her long hair to fly. His other hand never left the small of her back and when she finished rotating, he pulled her into him. Slowly, savoring the contact, as if he wanted it to last for eternity. Chests heaving, their bodies meshed, trying to become one. Their eyes, wide and bursting with passion, bore into each other with wolfish desire; their mouths smiling in that knowing way. When she leaned her head back exposing her graceful neck, he dove in, nuzzling her soft white skin. The number ended to thunderous applause. "They're beautiful," Tanya gushed, unable to hold back the tears. "That was…that was…"

"Hot?" Laura said.

"That wasn't just hot," Tanya said. "That was molten." She bolted up, clapping hysterically. "Bravo!"

Eventually the applause died down and the crowd began the arduous task of filing out and reclaiming coats.

"I remember going to your dance recitals," Laura said on the ride home. "You were so cute in your little pink outfit."

"I remember Mrs. Lehman's studio."

"What a drafty old barn of a place. I think she taught when I was a girl."

"Huge dance floor."

Laura nodded, "But the changing area was like a closet."

"And cold too."

"Haha, remember that time I asked Sandra to pick you up and she brought Stan with her—"

"—and he broke the sink in the bathroom," Tanya finished.

"Sandra told me she chased him into the backyard with all the girls staring out the window." Laura burst into laughter, but then realized Tanya did not join her. She quieted down.

A few moments of silence passed between them.

"Good times," Laura murmured.

"Mmmm," Tanya said in an equally low voice.

Laura cleared her throat. "Hey, you okay?"

"Who me? Yeah."

"Thought I lost you for a—"

"Did you know," Tanya cut across her, "that Stan was the first person I remember telling that I wanted to be a dancer when I grew up."

"Oh? What did he say?"

"That I'd be good at it."

"You *were* good at it, Tanya."

"He said I had nice legs."

"Still do." Laura eyed her sideways. "What? You think you don't?" She watched as Tanya turned on the radio, then checked the rear view mirror. Followed Tanya's hand as it played with her hair, then nervously fidgeting with a button on her blouse, then back to the steering wheel, ultimately dropping to her knee where she slowly massaged.

"I guess," Tanya finally said.

"What's that mean?"

There was another stretch of quiet as Tanya stared straight ahead.

Laura clicked off the radio. "Pull over."

"What, here?" Tanya said.

"I want to talk," Laura replied.

Tanya found a spot off the road and set the brake.

"What's wrong," Laura said bracing Tanya's shoulder. "All of a sudden you're a million miles away."

"It's nothing."

"Can't be nothing."

Tanya sighed. "I've always been touchy about my looks. You know that."

"I didn't mean to bring up bad memories."

"I know you didn't. I don't know why I'm acting this way."

"I've never confessed this before," Laura started, "but it always crushed me the teasing you took growing up."

"Mom—"

"I know how difficult it was for you."

They stared at each other, woman to woman. A contest that quickly turned into mother to daughter. A contest Tanya had never won in her life.

"Middle school was the worst," Tanya said.

"I always felt like," Laura started, then stopped. She looked down, took a deep breath, then focused back on Tanya with troubled eyes. "I felt like a failure as a mother for not recognizing it sooner."

"What? No—"

"Yes, it's true."

"You weren't a bad mother," Tanya said. "Besides, I'm over it."

"I guess it just didn't register with me," Laura said as she stroked Tanya's hair, "that kids could be so cruel. Or maybe I just didn't want to believe it."

"I don't blame you."

"I should have done more to boost your self esteem."

"Mom! I told you, I'm over it. It's not your fault."

"Then what is it?"

The car shook from gusts of wind from passing vehicles. Several moments passed.

Laura studied Tanya rubbing her knee. "Are you depressed about your dancing?"

Tanya's hand recoiled into her lap where she fumbled her thumbs.

"You can tell me," Laura said and took Tanya's hands into hers.

"I'm just feeling sorry, no, disappointed, in myself."

"It was a difficult time for you."

"But I shouldn't have given up."

"You're being too hard on yourself."

"Am I?"

"Yes, that was a terrible thing to experience. I wish I could have done more to help you through it."

"How?"

"I don't know. Help you with the depression. Get you started on the right path again. Something."

"Now who's being too hard on themselves? I was unfixable."

Laura lifted Tanya's chin. "Look at me. You're a smart and kind and giving person. What happened, happened. It's in the past. And you are beautiful, both on the outside and the inside, where it matters, right?"

"Right."

"It's time to move on."

"I know."

A siren wailed toward them then faded away.

"You okay?" Laura asked.

"I'm okay."

Laura reached across the seat and caressed Tanya's cheek. "You sure?"

"Mom, I'm not twelve."

"No you're not," Laura said and leaned over, arms open.

Tanya melted into the embrace, the warmth spreading through her entire body. "Mom, what do you think about me going back to school?"

"I think it's a great idea," Laura said and rubbed Tanya's back. "Your father and I have always wanted you to finish."

"I might need a loan."

"Don't worry about that."

"And I was sort of serious when I said I might need to move back in with you and Dad."

"Anything you need."

Tanya pulled away and wiped her eyes.

"You okay to drive?" Laura asked.

"Yeah, I think so."

Tanya accelerated back onto the road and in ten minutes pulled into her parent's driveway. "Thanks for being my date, Mom. No fun going to a show alone."

"You're welcome," Laura said. "Thanks for driving."

"We should do this more often."

"I'd like that," Laura said. She hugged Tanya and moved to get out, then stopped. A look of contemplation took over her face. "No, I can't leave yet."

"What?" Tanya asked.

"You want to tell me what happened during the show tonight? When you dropped your program."

Tanya's eyes flinched.

"I knew there was more to this," Laura said.

Tanya frisked her hands together. "It's been a while since I've been to a show. I'd almost forgotten how moving they can be. So powerful yet with such grace. It was like I was there, in the lead male's arms." Her voice had become almost a whisper.

Laura touched Tanya's hands. "Go on."

"So on that one lift, the lights were right on the man's face. It felt as if he were looking right at me. And with his blue eyes and dark hair, well, for a second I swear it was Stan."

"I know why," Laura said. "It's because you've been spending so much time at the hospital staring at his face."

"I've never felt anything like that, Mom. It hit me, hard."

"I can tell. Dance has always reached you at the deepest level."

"Am I cracking up?" Tanya asked.

"Of course not. You're going through an incredibly stressful situation."

"Oi! Talk about stress. I had dinner with the Palmer's the other night."

"What did you talk about?"

"Mostly Stan's care. He gave me legal power to make medical decisions for him if this ever happened."

"Is that a surprise?"

"Yeah, no, maybe, I don't know."

"What did Fenton say?"

"At first it seemed to bother him, then he thought about it. He said he understood it, but I'm not sure I do."

"Why?"

Tanya hesitated. "I feel like there's more. Like Stan's trying to tell me something."

"Like what?"

Tanya shook her head.

They sat in a quiet, but this time comfortable silence for a few moments.

"On this, I might be able to help," Laura said, grinning.

"I'm all ears," Tanya said.

"It may sound simple, but you just need to look for the signs."

"What signs?"

"You said he was trying to tell you something. So start listening."

"Listening," Tanya said.

"No one knows him like you do."

Tanya's forehead rippled as she considered the statement.

"Trust me," Laura said, patting Tanya's hand. "Sleep on it. When you wake up, you'll be fresh. Eventually it'll come to you. Are you scheduled at St. Christopher's tomorrow?"

"For the morning, probably go visit Stan after that."

"Sounds like a plan." They hugged and Laura hopped out. "I love you."

The Foiled Knight

"Love you too, Mom."

Tanya stared as Laura waltzed across the lawn before stopping at the landing just outside the door. She faced Tanya and performed a clumsy pirouette, then tried a high kick, nearly losing her balance. Tanya laughed and leaned out the window. "Don't hurt yourself!"

Laura beamed, waved and disappeared inside.

Tanya leaned on the steering wheel. Talking with her mother felt good. Felt familiar, something that had been lacking in her life lately. In her teens, they had shared intimate thoughts all the time. But ever since she'd gotten older, moved out, starting working two jobs, it became more of a rarity that they got to spend any time together, let alone soul-baring heart to hearts.

Talking about her relationship with Stan felt familiar too. More natural than anything else. Comfortable. He wasn't quite a brother, but not a boyfriend either. Somewhere in between. How many times had Tanya relayed stories about their hijinks? And not always the good ones. Her mom was good that way, never making judgments about the bad behavior. Well, willing to listen to it anyway and not rat them out.

Laura had been very understanding about Stan and Tanya's penchant for exploring and experiencing life. Like that day in seventh grade when they had gone swimming in the creek and he had taught her how to do a back flip. It was the same day she had confessed to Stan her dream to be a dancer.

They had been walking along the dirt path from the swimming hole to the point where the path rounded a bend and the creek disappeared into a tunnel under Rockwell Road.

Across the street, silos from Abington's long since defunct coal business stood against the clear sky in huge pillars of silent concrete. Mangled wrought iron ladders had hung haphazardly from the sides, their twisted rails the victim of the elements and neglect. Behind them, railroad tracks stretched into the distance, their usage now restricted to commuter trains.

Stan and Tanya looked both ways before sprinting across Rockwell to a field of grey crushed stone. They stopped to don their sneakers and picked their way between ancient rail cars, spare track stacked atop oily timbers, tools and other scrap metal. Rabbits skittered about. Knee-high weeds sprang up everywhere.

A sign suspended from a metal chain reading: *No Trespassing!* blocked their path. Stan held it up so Tanya could duck under. Just beyond lay a rusting car that had once roared up and down Rockwell before its owner ditched the classic for some foreign made model.

"'68 Chevy Camaro convertible," Stan said. "Coolest car ever. 454 under the hood, nothing could take it. I'd like to own a car like that someday."

"You just like it because it's royal blue," Tanya said.

"Nuh-uh. Look at the white pinstripe and the flecks of metallic in the paint job, the curves, the Cragar rims and those slick tires. They couldn't have been street legal. And man! Get a load of that Hurst stick shift. It practically scratches the ceiling."

"How do you work it if it hits the roof?"

Stan wrinkled his brow. "I dunno, but it sure is boss. When I hear *Radar Love* or *Long Cool Woman* on the radio, I fantasize that I'm driving this car."

"Love those songs," Tanya said. "Especially the beginnings. Make me wanna take off for the shore."

"Yeah," Stan said, resting both palms on the door. "You're gonna see me in a car like this someday."

"You'll buy anything if it's that color."

Stan laughed. "Remember that cheep-o aluminum baseball bat I had to have for Little League?"

"The one that turned into a noodle?"

"Don't remind me," he said, picking up a rock. "I begged my dad to buy it for me." He aimed for a telephone pole and threw, but just missed wide, hitting an old metal water tank instead. The clash of the rock's impact echoed in their ears. "Promised to cut the lawn for free all summer."

"Lasted one game," Tanya said.

"What a piece of crap. I was such an idiot to buy it for its color."

The sound of a rattling chain turned their heads. Then the patter of feet on gravel and a guttural sound that couldn't be human. They froze as a Doberman Pinscher, eyes wild, teeth bared, hurtled around the corner of the water tank. A short section of tether chain still attached to its collar flailed about.

"*RUN!*" Stan shouted and shot off in a sprint.

Tanya, her eyes wide, did not move, her body locked in panic.

"To the silos!" Stan yelled over his shoulder.

With a lurch, Tanya's feet shuffled. First a step. Then two. A fleeting glance. Fifty feet away.

"Teedy! Come on!"

She looked at Stan, terror ripping across her face. "I can't make it!" Her lower body went numb. She stumbled. The Doberman growled an ugly menacing snarl. Thirty feet.

"Yes you can! Sprint!"

Tanya got up, but she couldn't take her eyes off the frenzied animal. Twenty feet, closing fast.

"Teedy!" As the words scorched Stan's throat, a feeling of dread weakened his spine. *It's too late.* He watched in confusion as Tanya stopped running, rendered limp by the Doberman's eyes that were blazing coals of fury. Gawked in helpless horror as she dropped to a crouch in surrender, a whimper escaping her throat, daisy petals scattering along the ground. "*TEEDY!*"

Stan tried to step forward, but his legs, numb in disbelief, buckled under him. No time. He bent over, reached mindlessly for a rock, fumbled it, cursed, then latched on tight. Standing now, he felt a rush of blood drain from his brain and a jolt in his shoulder as he threw. The missile struck the animal in the ribs with a crack. The dog yelped, skidded sideways, then toppled over, crashing head first into an iron train wheel. With teeth gritted, Stan snatched another stone and fired again, striking the now dazed Doberman in the rump. Another howl of pain and the dog rose to its feet and scurried away into the maze of junk. Tanya lay still on the ground, crying.

Stan stepped toward her. "Teedy? Are you okay?"

Tanya jumped up and ran to him, tears of fright watering her eyes. She slammed her body into his. "*Oh, my God!*"

The Foiled Knight

He wrapped his arms around her, surprised by how she filled his embrace. "It's okay."

Her body shook against him in huge sighs of relief. "Is it gone?"

"Yeah," he said, suddenly aware of their thighs touching and her heaving chest. He pressed his hands into the softness of her back. A gritty combination of sweat, adrenaline and body odor rankled his nostrils, but he didn't let go.

She gulped another giant suck of air, and buried her head into his chest. "Are you sure?"

He smoothed her hair with a gentle hand. "I'm sure."

"Did you do something to make it go away?"

"Yeah, I threw a rock at him."

"Sounded like you hurt him."

"Nailed him twice. He's not coming back."

"I was so scared."

He pulled her tight, daring to rub her back, his hands slowly following the contour of her upper body, fascinated by the softness of her flesh. Felt her wet training bra through her shirt, his fingers delicate now. Stopping at her waist, then traveling below, so soft and curvy, then back up, slower this time, more confident that she wasn't shying away. "You're safe now, Tanya."

A few more heavy sighs and the trembling stopped. She leaned back, her face racked from the fear, and wiped her eyes with her sleeve. "Where'd that dog come from?"

"I don't know. Maybe the owners finally decided to do something to keep people out."

"They should put up a sign."

"They did."

Tanya huffed. "Well 'no trespassing' ain't makin' it."

"Yeah, you're right." Stan smirked. "It really should say: 'Warning, freaky psycho dog from hell will bite your face off.'"

She half-cried, half-giggled.

Stan smiled. "Gonna be okay?"

"I think so." She pulled away from him and attempted to organize her hair.

"You look fine."

"Yeah, right," she replied and looked into his eyes. "I almost peed myself."

"You're better than me. I would've crapped my pants."

She managed a laugh.

"Let's go home," he said.

"I don't want to. Not yet anyway. Can't we stay out just a bit more?"

"Thought you'd wanna go after that."

"No, I'm all right, really."

"Let's get to higher ground in case I'm wrong about that dog coming back." He took her hand and led her to the base of one of the twisted iron ladders that scaled the outer face of the silo. "Want me to go first?" Stan asked.

"No." She took hold of a crusty-brown rung and began to climb. "Out run a rabid dog? No can do. Climb a dumb ladder? That, I can handle." Stan followed with eyes closed as crumbs of rust rained down on him.

Ten feet up, Tanya opened a two by two foot cast iron door set into the base of the silo and they both wiggled through the square opening into darkness. Inside, Stan crawled to a crude table they had constructed from pieces of a wooden spool traditionally used for transporting commercial wiring. In the barrel core of the spool, they had removed a board to create a cubbyhole for Stan's Thor lunchbox that protected matches and candles. Lighting one, he dripped hot wax onto the flat side of the spool and set the candle into the improvised glue.

The interior of the silo, at fifteen feet in diameter, was a cylinder of crumbling gray concrete. Another rusty ladder, bolted to the wall, stretched skyward into blackness. There was a tiny opening near the top where coal had been transferred by conveyor belt from train to silo. Stan and Tanya had swept out any remains of coal and debris and replaced it with sand that now covered the floor. Keeping the iron door closed kept the pigeons out, but not the smell of coal. As far as they knew, no one else ever used the makeshift fort.

Stan took off his backpack, removed a blanket and spread it across the sand. "Presto change-o," he said. "One comfortable hideaway." From a Velcro pocket, he extracted two cans of chicken spread and some crackers. He peeled off the lid, then went back to the backpack and thrashed about. "Crap. I forgot a knife."

Tanya kicked off her sneakers and stepped onto the blanket, her feet sinking into the softness. She sat next to Stan and scooted close. "It's all right. People who survive rabid dog attacks are allowed to eat with their hands." Dipping her index finger into the can, she spread a dollop onto a cracker and motioned that she wanted to feed him. He opened his mouth wide and she pressed the treat in, letting her finger linger on his lip for a split second. "How is it?" she asked.

"Mmmm. That hits the spot. Here, let me fix you one." He smeared a glob onto a cracker and held it out for her.

Tanya nudged closer, took hold of his wrist, and guided the cracker into her mouth. "Oooh, that is good."

"Being chased by wild animals makes you hungry." He fixed another.

The morsel melted in her mouth. "Got anything to drink?" She pulled her knees to her chest and folded her arms across her shins, tucking her chin between her legs.

"Just some Kool-Aid. *Oh, yeaaaaah!*" he sang the ad jingle while unscrewing the cap from a thermos. He turned the cap upside down and poured her a cup.

Taking it into her hands, she moved to sip the cherry-flavored juice, but stopped at her lips. "You saved my life today."

His only response was a blurt of embarrassment. Then a blank stare at his feet as heat scalded his face.

"You were very brave," she added.

A hand through his hair and a pick at his sneaker. "Shoot, Teedy. That dog would have ripped you to pieces. I had to do something."

"I know." She set the plastic cup on the table and shifted position so that she faced him, her legs curled underneath her. "I'd like to thank you."

He stared at her nervously. "You're welcome."

She smiled and pushed a strand of hair from his forehead. "I didn't mean with words."

Stan's face scrunched into a puzzle. "Huh?"

The Foiled Knight

Tanya leaned forward and kissed him on the lips, a soft and tender coupling that lasted several seconds. She pulled away and stifled a laugh at the look on Stan's face. Eyes closed, lips still puckered, he looked to have been transported to another planet.

His eyes opened. "Wow. Teedy, that was awesome."

She giggled. "You're welcome."

"Can we do it again?" he said. "I mean, that is, um, if you want to."

"For Stan, my man? Of course." They kissed again, this time longer.

Stan planted his hands on Tanya's back and didn't move them an inch, afraid of where they might go. He didn't care, the excitement of this newly found pleasure more than enough to fill the fantastical joy of the moment. Tanya's lips were soft, wet and squishy. Every hair on his body felt electrified as he felt her tongue meshing with his. She pulled away.

"They call that a French kiss," she said. "When you use your tongue."

"How come the French get credit for inventing it?"

"I don't know. Why do you care?"

A look of awakening flashed on his face. "I don't," he smiled and rolled her onto her back, kissing her again.

After several minutes of necking, Tanya pushed him away gently. "Hey, you're a pretty good kisser."

"So are you."

"Liar."

"Am not."

"Are too."

He lay on his back, his head next to hers. "Here we go again. Might as well have lunchboxes in our hands. Remember that? First grade?"

"Lunchboxes at twenty paces," she said before exhaling a big belly laugh that terminated in a snort. Covering her mouth in embarrassment, she broke into hysterical laughter. Stan joined her.

After several minutes of jovial convulsions, they quieted down and lay in silence on the soft blanket, staring at the ceiling.

Tanya pointed to the dilapidated ladder along the interior wall of the silo. "Hey, Stan, how far does the ladder go?"

"All the way to the top. Me and Vinnie tried to climb it once, but we only got about three-quarters of the way."

"How come?"

"There's a stretch of the ladder that must have gotten damaged or rusted out. We didn't trust the rungs to hold our weight. So don't even think about it."

"What? No. I was just curious."

"Good, because you'd fall and break your neck."

"When did this place shut down?" Tanya asked.

"Not sure. Maybe five years ago? All the workers lost their jobs. That's why I want to go to college someday so I don't have to work some grunt job."

Tanya rolled onto her stomach. "Stan, I want to ask you something, but you must promise not to laugh."

"So ask."

"No, you have to promise."

"What? That's geeky."

"Say you'll promise."

"No."

"Why won't you promise?"

He sat up. "Cause I haven't heard it yet."

She folded her arms across her chest. He let her pout. They stared at each other for a long moment.

"Okay, I promise," he said.

"Good, now lay back down," she said. When he obeyed, she took his hand. "Do you ever dream about what you want to be when you grow up?"

"Um, I don't, er, yeah, I guess so, sometimes."

"What do you dream of?"

"Well, mostly I dream about becoming a writer. Make up stories and stuff."

"What kind of stories?"

"Sci-fi, maybe horror."

Tanya pulled her hand away. "Ugh."

He re-took her hand. "Maybe The Foiled Knight would zoom down—"

"The who?"

"The Foiled Knight. He's the hero in my stories."

"But why foil?" Tanya asked. "Why not shining armor?"

"Because shining armor's already been done. What was it that Mrs. Delaney called that?"

"Cliché."

Stan nodded. "Yeah, that. So I'm making him different. And it's not just any old foil. This stuff is specially treated to repel anything. Lasers, arrows, even bullets."

"Specially treated? With what?"

"A special power that is beamed down to him from his space Goddess." He squeezed her hand.

A wistful look captured Tanya's face and she smiled back.

"So, yeah," Stan continued. "The Foiled Knight would swoop down on Pegasus to save the damsel in distress."

"It's perfect," she said, then added, "What else?"

Stan thought for a few moments. "I think I'd like to write little short stories, create interesting characters and places no one's ever been to before. And the guy will always get the girl in the end."

"Sounds neat."

He twisted his head. "How 'bout you? What do you dream about?"

"I want to be a dancer."

"Really?"

"Uh-huh. I love hip-hop and jazz and choreographing my own routines. Last year, my mom took me to New York to see a show. It was wonderful. A dancer on Broadway, now *that* would be the life."

"That's cool. You'd make a good one, Teedy. You've got the legs for it."

"Ugh. My legs are fat."

"Are not. And they'll get even nicer if you keep going to dance classes."

"You're just saying that."

The Foiled Knight

"Nuh-uh. I've always thought that. Besides, if you give up your dream, you die. It'd practically be the same thing as committing suicide." He cocked his head and grinned. "And if you do that, I'm beating the shit out of you."

She beamed. "When we get to high school and college, I'm gonna try out for school plays and everything."

"That's more like it. Wish I could try out for something."

"What about the baseball team?"

Stan had laughed at that. "Are you kidding?" He waved a hand across his gawky frame. "I'm not exactly the athletic type. Guys in high school are huge."

She remembered him posing like a body-builder.

"Aren't guys supposed to have biceps?" he said. "And look at my ribs. They stick out like those pictures from National Geographic."

"Yeah, maybe you're right," she had said. "But the way you threw those rocks…"

Stan had been skinny. And he did end up going out for the baseball team. But that was a long time ago and Stan couldn't pick up a rock to save anyone. Tanya gripped the steering wheel tightly. Now it was he who needed saving.

Chapter 13

Ciquero drove north on Easton Road, away from Glenside, on his way to Abington. The visit to the Palmers seemed a long-shot, but his department had exhausted all of their leads on the Mathews girl disappearance. Not that they'd ever had anything solid, even in the beginning when everyone's memory should have been fresh. "And it's been two weeks," he whispered.

Reaching the traffic light at Old Welsh Road, Ciquero waited the entire length of the red light even though he was turning right. He waited because caddy corner to him stood the crumbling remains of Willow Grove Park, the scene of his father's death. Once a thriving theme park in the 1900's, the place had fallen into disrepair. Paint peeled from rotting timbers of the famous Thunderbolt roller coaster, weeds climbed the rusting chain link fence, and the marquee sign hung haphazardly from a stubborn screw.

It had started as a mild dispute between Ciquero's father and a bald red-neck over butting in line that escalated into a heated argument. A then 9yr-old Mike watched as the monster body-slammed his father to the asphalt, cracking his skull, killing him instantly. Ciquero found out later that the thug had been wanted in Oregon for armed robbery and should have been in jail. From that day forward, Ciquero committed himself to catching bad guys.

The honk of a horn brought Ciquero back to the present and he gunned the unmarked cruiser around the corner. Crossed the bridge over the railroad tracks and turned right onto the calmness that was Rockwell Road. Glanced from the piece of paper in his gloved hand to the numbers on the mailboxes and found 1777 on the left. His tires scraped the curb as he eased to a halt, set the brake and studied the house.

The residence, a tiny box of a two-story house with a white stucco exterior and a green-shingled roof, sat peacefully away from the sidewalk. A matching white stucco retaining wall buttressed the front yard that stretched the length of the property and formed a stage-like front yard that was nothing more than a square patch of grass surrounded by wrought-iron fencing with hydrangea bushes around the perimeter. An asphalt driveway scooted up the left to a detached two-car garage in the back.

Ciquero adjusted the collar of his winter coat before climbing out into the icy wind. He followed the retaining wall and strode up the driveway to a break in the railing. On long legs, he vaulted the flagstone steps to the front porch and rang the doorbell.

A tall, well-built man with graying temples opened the door. "Yes?"

"Mr. Fenton Palmer?"

"That's right. And you are?"

"I'm detective Ciquero, Glenside Police." He presented his badge. "I'm investigating a missing person case."

The Foiled Knight

"Missing person?"

"Yes, a fourteen year-old girl, Holly Mathews from Glenside."

"I read about that in the paper."

"I'd like to ask you a few questions. I don't know if you can help or not, but our investigation has reached a dead end. It will just take a minute."

"I don't know how I can help," Fenton said and pulled open the door, "but please come in." He took Ciquero's coat, hung it on a hook and guided the detective into the living room. "Can I get you some coffee?"

"That would be terrific, thank you. Black is fine."

Fenton disappeared into the kitchen giving Ciquero a chance to study the room. Modest furniture, nice carpeting, a floor to ceiling bookshelf filled with classics and family photos, an oil painting of hunters on the wall, a crucifix above the mantel, and immaculately kept. *Seems ordinary enough,* he thought.

Fenton returned with two steaming mugs. "Careful, it's hot."

Ciquero took the mug and cradled it in his hands, allowing the heat to warm his fingers. He took a sip. "Boy, that's good, thank you."

"Don't mention it," Fenton said. "Here, please sit down." He motioned for Ciquero to take the couch while he claimed an armchair. "How can I help?"

"Ms. Mathews was last seen two weeks ago," Ciquero said, "walking home from the Keswick movie theater, the night of the storm."

"Anyone with her?"

"No, by all accounts, she had gone by herself."

"Teenage girl," Fenton said, "walking home from a movie, by herself."

"I know, but her parents were okay with it; she'd done it on numerous occasions and had her cell phone. And she only lives a few blocks away."

Hmmm, Ciquero thought, *but maybe the pattern exposed her to some creep.*

"What's the theater say?" Fenton asked.

"No one remembers anything. Not what kind of coat she wore, if she got popcorn or if she even bought a ticket."

"What's she look like?"

Ciquero dug out a photo from his front pocket.

Fenton studied the picture. "Cute girl. You'd think the teenage boys working there would have noticed her."

"I had the same thought. But they don't remember her." Ciquero ran a hand through his bushy hair and adjusted his glasses. *No one ever does.* In all his years on the force, he never understood that phenomenon.

"What about outside?" Fenton asked. "I've been to that movie theater, there are shops up and down the street. Are you sure she didn't stop in somewhere, maybe to look at some magazines?"

"We talked to all the shop owners and got zip."

"And she didn't call anyone? Seems like a young girl would have been going 100 miles an hour texting or talking to friends about the movie."

Ciquero shook his head. "We interviewed several of her close friends and even checked phone company records. Nothing."

"Well then, I'm confused," Fenton said. "The Keswick is in Glenside. That's miles from here. Why did you think I could help?"

"When something like this happens," Ciquero said, "and we run out of leads, we look for other possibilities. Anything unusual. One of the unusual things from that night was a call to 911 from a cell phone belonging to Stan."

Fenton stopped sipping his coffee. His alert eyes focused on Ciquero. "Stan? Our Stan?"

"Yes, I tried calling him, but no one answers. I went to his home, but the place looks deserted, so I came here."

"You think maybe he saw something?"

"We're hoping."

Fenton rubbed his chin. "What time was the movie the girl went to see?"

"5 PM," Ciquero said, sliding forward in his seat.

"And how long was the show?"

"A little over two hours."

"Which puts her walking home between 7-7:30 PM," Fenton mused.

"Right. And not long after that, dispatch got the emergency call from your son." Ciquero edged forward, his detective's instinct beginning to tingle. "Do you know where Stan is? Can we speak with him?"

Fenton rubbed his forehead. "I'm sorry to do this to you, but I can explain away the coincidence. Stan got into a near-fatal car accident that night."

Ciquero's face halted as if put on pause.

"Hit a deer," Fenton continued. "Wrapped his car around a tree."

"My God," Ciquero said. "Is he all right?"

"It's touch and go. He's in a coma. Doctors are running tests on him every day it seems. They don't know if he'll come out of it." Fenton picked up his mug, then slowly set it down. "He was calling from the accident."

Silence again.

Fenton studied the man. "How did you get a hold of the 911 call and not know it was related to Stan's accident?"

"Paramedics respond to calls like that, not us," Ciquero said. "And there were a ton of accidents that night. No way for us to put the two together." He leaned back, thinking it through. "The call only lasted a few…there was no way to… we couldn't—" He pounded a fist into his thigh. "Dammit. Where did it happen?"

"Terwood Road."

Ciquero paused to look at the ceiling, then blew out a gust of air. "Ah, now it makes sense why he said 'in the woods' on the call. It's the only thing we could make out. The deer are bad in that area. Almost hit one myself one time. Jesus, this is awful."

Fenton leaned forward, elbows on knees, hands folded, thumbs pinching the bridge of his nose.

Ciquero caught the subtle hint. He set his cup on the coffee table and stood. "I'm terribly sorry, Mr. Palmer. There's no way your son could have seen anything."

"I'm afraid not."

"Sorry to have bothered you. I'll let myself out."

Fenton followed him to the door. "Wish there was more I could do."

Ciquero pulled on his coat. "I hope everything turns out all right." He opened the door, took a step outside, stopped, then turned around.

The Foiled Knight

"Detective?" Fenton asked.

"Mr. Palmer, I don't know why I didn't think of this before, but can you tell me where your son was going the night of the storm?"

"Yes, he was coming here for dinner."

"Huh. And you said the accident was on Terwood Road."

"Yes, that's right."

Ciquero stopped buttoning his coat. "But Stan lives in Glenside, which is southwest of Abington."

"I'm not following you," Fenton said.

"Terwood Road is on the east side of town, on the other side of Huntington Valley Country Club. Why would he go way over there—in a snowstorm no less—when it's a straight shot to your house up Easton Road? A main road that would have been plowed."

Fenton thought for a few moments, then shook his head. "He works at the saw mill as a bookkeeper. He could have been dropping something off, but I have no way of knowing."

Ciquero's face fell. "Damn, we just can't catch a break. But I had to ask."

"Although," Fenton said. "Fitzy might know."

"Who's that?"

"Doug Fitzgerald, the owner of Fitzy's bar in Glenside. He and Stan are like best buds. Don't know why I didn't think of it before, but he said Stan stopped in for a beer before heading here."

"Okay, we can check that out," Ciquero said re-buttoning his coat. "Thank you for your time, Mr. Palmer. I hope your son pulls through." Pulling on gloves, the detective scrambled down the steps.

"Thank you," Fenton mumbled and closed the door. He took a few steps across the living room and stopped by a black and white aerial photograph of the county taken at the turn of the century. Even though mostly farmland at the time, Fenton easily found Abington to the north by spotting the white framework of the Thunderbolt roller coaster at Willow Grove Park. He traced the white line of Easton Road as it traversed southwest from Abington, straight to the small town of Glenside. And there, snaking its way east out of Glenside and through Abington, was Sawtrigger's Creek. With his index finger, he followed the water's path eastward, all the way to the far side of the photograph, all the way to the twisting line of Terwood Road.

Fenton stroked his chin, whispering to himself. "Yeah, Stan, why *didn't* you just come up Easton Road?"

Chapter 14

Holly Mathews lay shivering on her side in the dark and drafty room. Her skin was raw from the chafing rope that bound her wrists and ankles. The handkerchief that gagged her tasted worse than cooked liver. Barefoot and gloveless, she wore only jeans and a thin cotton blouse. The kidnapper had taken her coat, hat, boots and scarf. Cell phone too. In return, he had covered her with a ratty burlap blanket that smelled of mold and urine. A blast of icy wind from beneath the floor ripped through her bones.

The room itself was an old tool shed made of rotting wood with a simple A-frame roof and no windows. A lumberjack saw, rusty pick axes and a camping lantern hung from hooks on walls that were stained with splatters of animal blood. The splinter-infested floorboards were dappled with knots and exposed nail heads that dug into her hip, ribs and skull. Every now and then, a shiny long bug with a million legs would appear through a crack in the floor and slither across her cheek or up her pant leg. When that happened, she bit into the handkerchief and held her breath, waiting for it to scurry away.

Her hair, once brown and straight, was now black, mangled and crusty from having sopped up the blood from her broken nose and split lip. How long she'd been there, she couldn't remember. More than a week, maybe a month. It was all beginning to blur from her memory as the hunger pangs and thirst cramped her stomach. At least a day had passed, possibly two, since he had last checked on her. An event that filled her with a mixture of relief and horror. Relief because it meant she would be fed. But not until after enduring his violent lust. His boots heavy on the ground. The scratch of the wooden latch sliding. A creak of the door. The stench of his body odor and whiskey breath. And then, inevitably, his hands rough on her pelvis. She squeezed her eyes shut.

When it was over, he left behind a plate of chicken scraps by her nose. The pain between her legs made it impossible to be grateful for the meager offering. But she knew she had to eat. Like a blind dog, she shoved her face into the plate, searching ravenously with her tongue for anything resembling food. Tears filled her eyes as she lolled her head against the ground. The gag muffled her shout of anguish, but she screamed anyway. *"Somebody please help me!"*

Chapter 15

The 7 o'clock show had already started by the time Ciquero walked into the Keswick Movie Theater. He bypassed the ticket booth and concession counter with a flash of his badge and strode quickly across the thickly padded red carpeting on way to the manager's office.

Ciquero peered in at an elderly man with ruffled white hair pouring over employee scheduling reports. He knocked. "Evening."

William Croce removed his glasses and set them on the desk along with the reports. "Hello, Detective. How are you? Any luck finding that girl?"

"Not yet. Anyone remember anything since last time I came by?"

Croce scratched his neck. "No, I spoke with all my employees and told them if anybody knew anything to call you directly." He plucked a business card from the bulletin board on the wall. "Still have your card."

"Hmm, okay, well, I was in the neighborhood, thought I'd check."

"Want me to get them together?" Croce said. He stood and moved to put on a thick gray sweater from the coat rack.

"No, don't want to disrupt business. As long as everyone knows to contact me, that's all I can ask."

"Lemme know," Croce said, sitting back down. "Anything to help."

"I appreciate that," Ciquero said. "There is something you might be able to help me with." He pulled out a photograph of Stan from his coat pocket. "Do you happen to recognize this man?"

Croce re-donned his glasses and studied the photo. "Sure, that's Stan Palmer. It's an old photo, but that's him."

"How do you know him?"

"We sometimes work together on Rotary Club projects. Good guy."

"How long you known him?"

"Years. Shoot, I remember going to watch Stan pitch for the high school." Croce narrowed his eyes. "What? You don't think he's involved somehow with that girl's disappearance do you?"

"Just routine," Ciquero said with a wave. "You heard about his accident?"

"Yeah, I've been praying for him. Rotary will be hurting until he gets back on his feet."

"How's that?"

"Stan is a handy guy, level headed, knows everybody, everybody likes him." Croce winked. "When the town council tries to throw up a road block on something, we send Stan in to be our spokesperson." He leaned back and folded his hands over his belly. "Stan always was a good closer."

"Sounds like a decent guy."

"He is," Croce said, then added, "and he's a regular at church." He stared at Ciquero with a sudden seriousness. "If you know what I mean."

"Right," Ciquero said and cleared his throat. "Well, gonna take off."

"Okay, hey, why not come back with your lady friend and catch a movie?"

"Just may take you up on that," Ciquero said. "Be safe."

"Will do," Croce said and went back to his reports.

Ciquero pushed his way through the door of the theater and onto the sidewalk. Looked left, all quiet, then right, more quiet, then straight ahead as a group of twenty somethings made a singing exit from Fitzy's bar. For the split second the door remained open, sounds of laughter and music cheered the air. He stepped off the curb and crossed the street, not bothering to button his coat.

The bar had that mid-week not quite as busy as a Saturday night as one might predict feel to it and Ciquero had no trouble finding an empty bar stool. He caught the eye of the bartender and motioned for service.

"Hello," the large red-haired man said. "Welcome to Fitzy's." He pointed to an array of taps. "What can I get you?"

"How you stocked for dark beer?"

"Ah, a man who knows quality. Have just the ticket." The giant flicked a mug from a hook in the rafter and poured. "Start a tab?"

"Sure," Ciquero said. "And can you tell me how I might find the owner?"

Fitzy set the mug on the bar. "That would be me." He stuck out a paw. "Doug Fitzgerald, your host and deliverer of legendary service."

They shook. Ciquero thought he might lose his hand if he didn't hold on tight. "Legendary service. That's something you don't hear every day."

"What can I say," Fitzy said with a smile. "And you are?"

Ciquero slurped some suds. "Oooh, that's good. Detective Mike Ciquero, Glenside P.D."

"Pleased to meet you, detective. Not many of Glenside's finest I don't know. How is it I don't recognize you?"

"I'm a Glenside Pub man myself, no offense."

"None taken," Fitzy said, eying the beer. "You off duty?"

"I'm good for one."

"How can I help you?"

"Do you know a Stan Palmer?"

"Yeah, Stan's a good friend of mine."

Ciquero held his mug at his lips pondering the statement. "He a regular?"

"If you call two or three times a week regular, then yeah. Why?"

"Just checking on something. When is the last time you talked to him?"

"Couple of weeks ago. Saturday."

"Remember what time?"

"He usually stops in after work, five-thirty, six. What's this about?"

"I told you," Ciquero said, shaking his head, "just checking on something. Does he get off work at that time?"

"Yes, he works at the mill. He's a bookkeeper, nine to five."

"He works Saturdays?"

"During tax season? Oh yeah."

"And you talked to him…" Ciquero paused as a patron opened the door to leave, offering a clear line of sight to the Keswick Movie Theater. "…here, between five-thirty and six?"

The Foiled Knight

Fitzy scanned the ceiling. "No, not that night."

"Oh?" Ciquero said, peering over the top of his glasses.

"No, he got here late that night, about seven. It was the night of the storm. Everybody got bogged down that night."

Ciquero pursed his lips, then nodded. "True. Did you talk to him?"

"Yeah, not much, he was having dinner at his parents so he stopped in for a quick beer, then left."

"What did you guys talk about?"

"I dunno," Fitzy said with a shrug. "Stuff."

"Stuff?" Ciquero asked. "You said you were good friends. Had to have talked about something."

Fitzy placed his meaty palms on the bar. "Detective, when you're out with your buddies and you come home and your wife asks you what you guys talked about, what do you say?"

Ciquero paused to consider the scene, then laughed. "Stuff." He took another gulp. "That pretty typical of him? To have one and leave?"

"Pretty much," Fitzy said. "One can Stan. Hey, don't get me wrong, he's a good guy, just not a big drinker."

"You said he was going to his folks for dinner. Did he talk to a girl, maybe got sidetracked trying to pick her up?"

"No," Fitzy said, paused, then chuckled to himself.

Ciquero observed the body language and how the bartender had swiftly gone somewhere else in his mind.

And as if on cue, Fitzy flipped the bar towel over his shoulder. "Stan's not a skirt chaser, detective."

"How do you know that?"

"I've known him since we were kids. He's just not. He's a good guy."

Ciquero studied the face of the man and looked for a sign that said *cover up*, but only deep sincerity shone in the man's eyes. "He got a girlfriend?"

"Not at the moment."

"Anything unusual happen that night?"

"You do know that Stan got into a car wreck that night?" Fitzy said, more accusation than question.

"Oh?"

"Yeah, he's in a coma in Abington Hospital."

"I'm sorry," Ciquero said and stood, removed some bills from his pocket, tossed them on the bar, took another swig of beer and left.

Chapter 16

Tanya dragged herself out of bed, took a disinterested shower where she forgot to shampoo her hair, changed clothes and clopped wearily to the car.

Sloppy road conditions made traffic impossible on her way to her second job at St. Christopher's Hospital For Children in Philadelphia. Tanya had volunteered there for fifteen years. It didn't take away from her time at the diner; St. Chris's only needed her a few hours a week to help with morning meals, read to the really young ones or help with crafts.

An attractive brunette in pink scrubs glanced up from the coffee machine as Tanya hung up her coat. "Morning sleepyhead," Marian Gimpel said. "How are you today?" She poured a second mug and set it on the counter.

Tanya scooped up the mug. "I'll be fine after I inject this right into my bloodstream."

Marian's hopeful eyes rounded. "Late night?"

"Yeah."

"What's his name?" Marian asked, her diabolical laugh travelling across the ward.

"Funny," Tanya said and slugged a big gulp. "No, I've been spending the last few nights at Abington hospital. Friend of mine was in a bad accident."

Marian covered her mouth. "Oh my God. Are they all right?"

"I don't know."

"Should you be here? You're gonna be zonked."

Tanya shrugged. "I'll just pound some coffee."

"Well, all right, but lemme know when you run out of gas. Okay?"

"Deal. Where am I today?"

Marian checked her clipboard. "Breakfast, then physical therapy. And if you're up for it, the kids want you to read more Harry Potter."

"Oooh, that's right, the troll is about to invade the castle."

"I just might sit in on that performance," Marian said. "You do have a way of making it entertaining. The kids love you, especially that little Cassandra." Her kind face tilted a bit as she fought back the emotion. "What a cutie."

Tanya set her coffee down and hugged Marian tight, whispering in her ear, "You're the best." Letting go, Tanya snared rubber gloves from the cabinet and strode away. Before rounding the corner, she flashed glistening eyes of her own over her shoulder.

Marian's mega-watt smile flashed bright. "You're welcome!"

* * *

"Okay, who wants to try a spoonful of the yucky-mucky icky-sticky stuff?" Tanya asked and held up a spoonful of pureed carrots.

The room buzzed with coaxing and conversation from several volunteers over breakfast. Cheerful music played from a small iPod box. Balloons and other rainbow-colored art brightened the walls painted sky-blue. Every now and then a spoon would clatter to the floor eliciting laughter from the group.

A wide pair of green eyes stared back at Tanya. They belonged to the most adorable three-year-old girl she had ever seen.

Cassandra Broadhag had been a patient at St. Christopher's for about six months ever since her parents started noticing unusual behavior that included reduced ability to make sounds, difficulty making eye contact, and irregularities when playing with toys. Doctors suspected autism. No one had made any progress with the toddler until Tanya volunteered to try a month before. She hadn't even met the girl's parents yet.

With a bowl-shaped haircut, delicate bangs and dimples to melt one's heart, little Cassandra sat fixated on Tanya, all the while sucking her thumb. Tanya studied the youngster. *She's definitely locked on to me*, Tanya thought. *I don't know what the doctor's are talking about.* Three long seconds passed. Then without further prompting or saying anything, Cassandra removed her thumb and opened her mouth.

Tanya tipped the spoonful in and had just barely removed it before Cassandra's thumb returned to close the window.

A look of contentment passed across the child's face and she removed her thumb again. Tanya quickly reloaded and got in another, bigger, scoop.

Cassandra sucked for a few seconds before a big smile took over her face.

"Oh," Tanya whispered quietly, her pulse surging. "So you like carrots, is that it?" She got another spoonful ready.

The window opened again and Tanya delivered with perfect timing. Cassandra gulped the mouthful down. "I believe you like carrots," Tanya cooed and rubbed her nose against Cassandra's. "Yes, you do. You gorgeous little girl. I knew I would find something you liked." She dipped the spoon into the jar and smeared a tiny bit on the end of her own nose. "Uh, oh! Look at what Aunt Teedy did now."

Cassandra howled with laughter, banging the palm of her other hand on the serving table before resuming sucking her thumb. Then, as if rehearsed, she removed the thumb again. Tanya was ready. The routine went on until all the carrots were gone.

Marian entered the room with an armload of books.

"Well!" Tanya exclaimed. "You certainly ate well today, didn't you little Cassie?" She set the empty jar down and held up two arms as if signaling a touchdown.

"What's this?" Marian said. "Is the rumor true? Word on the floor is Cassandra actually ate carrots."

"Not just ate them," Tanya said, "She devoured an entire jar."

"What? Get out of here."

"Not kidding," Tanya said, holding up the jar and looking at Cassandra for confirmation. "Cassie, did you make carrots all gone?"

Cassandra mimicked Tanya and raised her arms in triumph. "All gone!" And as quickly as she had raised them, Cassandra dropped her arms down to take up her usual position of contentment, sucking her thumb.

Tanya and Marian gawked at the youngster.

Marian pointed and her mouth opened, but no words came out. Her head swiveled toward Tanya who stared back with equal shock.

They whispered in unison, "She spoke."

A few seconds passed.

"She spoke! Cassie spoke!"

The room of volunteers cheered as Marian and Tanya gleefully hopped around the room, hugging each other, celebrating the first words uttered by the toddler. Other nurses entered the room to join the party. A janitor popped his head in to see what all the commotion was about. Marian sprinted to the telephone at the nurse's desk to deliver the good news to Cassandra's parents.

A gala-fest sprouted all around Cassandra out of seemingly nothing. The child paid no attention to any of it, her eyes riveted on her "Aunt" Teedy, the most adorable person Cassandra had ever seen.

* * *

"Oh my," Marian blurted, "I am so proud of you." She hugged Tanya again. "Come on, let's talk while we walk." She led Tanya to the nurse's lounge.

"I knew something was happening when she went gonzo for the carrots," Tanya said. "But when she spoke, it was like, whoa."

Marian sauntered to the vending machine, deposited some coins and selected a soda. Popping the top, she took a long sip. "Wait till you meet her parents, they will be so happy."

"When are they supposed to be here?" Tanya asked.

"Pretty soon I imagine, I called them half an hour ago."

"I hope it's not too much longer, I'd like to get home and crash for a few hours before going back to visit my friend."

"Nice going," a nurse entering the room said. She patted Tanya's shoulder.

Tanya blushed. "Thanks."

"Don't be embarrassed," Marian said. She set her soda down at an empty table and sat in a plastic chair. "You're a celebrity. Enjoy it."

"I'm just not used to getting compliments."

Glancing confusedly at Tanya, Marian started to say something when a disembodied voice spoke. "Marian Gimpel, please come to Reception. Marian Gimpel, Reception."

"Must be the Broadhags," Marian said. "Come on, I'll introduce you." Scooting her chair back, Marian grabbed her soda and head for the door with Tanya close behind.

They wove their way through the corridors of St. Christopher's until they reached the expansive reception area. Marian hurried to the desk. "Hi, I'm Marian, you just paged me?"

The receptionist was on the phone handling another call, but covered the mouthpiece for a moment and pointed with her eyes. "By the window."

Marian looked around and spotted a couple, both wearing matching ankle-length cashmere coats. She slapped the counter. "Got 'em, thanks." She covered the distance to the man and woman in a half-walk, half-skip. "Mr. and Mrs. Broadhag."

The man turned at the sound of Marian's voice. Richard Broadhag, tall and immaculately groomed, with the serious face of someone who pondered world

The Foiled Knight

financial issues, stood with a presence of an ambassador. He extended a gloved hand. "Nurse Gimpel, so good of you to call." His Breitling wristwatch reflected a sharp stab of sunlight at Tanya's eyes.

The woman at his side turned as well. Tanya gasped. Mrs. Broadhag, a buxom blonde in high heels was taller than her husband with a sharp nose, a perfect smile and heavy red lipstick. She moved to offer a hand, but it dropped to her side as she looked past Marian. Her faced became confused. "Tanya?"

The heat on Tanya's neck spread from her scalp to the middle of her back, but she approached the woman. "Hello, Ronnie. Long time no see."

"I don't believe it, what's it been? Twenty years?"

"Something like that."

"How do you two know each other?" Marian asked.

"We went to high school together," Tanya said.

"And grade school," Ronnie added.

"That's true," Tanya said. "We go way back, don't we?"

"Must have some stories to tell," Marian said.

There was an awkward split-second pause, then both Tanya and Ronnie spoke at once. "Oh, yeah."

Marian looked back and forth between the two women. "Uh-huh."

"I guess you heard about Stan?" Tanya said quickly.

"Stan," Ronnie pondered. "Stan Palmer? No, what happened?"

"He was in a bad car accident. He's in a coma."

"Oh no, I hadn't heard. Where did it happen?"

"Terwood Road. Hit a deer."

"Will he be all right?"

"Don't know," Tanya said.

"My God, that's terrible."

No one said anything for a few moments until Ronnie spoke up, "I feel bad. Ever since I moved away, there are so many people I've lost touch with."

"Don't beat yourself up, it happens to all of us."

"What are you doing with yourself, Tanya?"

"Nothing much."

"Are you married?"

"No," Tanya replied. "But you seem pretty happy."

"I met Richard in college," Ronnie said, hooking her husband's arm and mooning him a warm smile. "Where did you end up going?"

"Elon," Tanya said.

"That's right. You studied dance, didn't you?"

"Yes, I did."

"Jazz?"

"Little bit of everything actually."

"Do you still dance?" Ronnie asked. "You must, because let me tell you, you've held up pretty well."

"Thanks Ronnie, you look great yourself. No, I don't dance anymore. But I'm thinking of opening up my own studio, do some teaching."

"That's great. Do you live in the city?"

Tanya shook her head. "No, just outside of Glenside, off the turnpike."

"Really?" Ronnie said. "Richard and I are moving back to the area. We bought a home in Huntington Valley. We should have lunch and catch up."

"I'd like that," Tanya said. "I still can't believe you're Cassie's mother."

"Cassie has been the greatest thing for us," Ronnie gushed. "Helped me find myself. That and Richard." She suddenly paused as if summoning strength, then looked at the floor, took a pensive moment, then looked up again. "I was so mean in high school." She looked hard into Tanya's eyes. "It took me a long time and about ten grand in shrink fees to admit that." She reached for Tanya's hand. "Hope you can forgive me."

Tanya gawked. "I didn't, um, it wasn't, er, I don't know what to—"

"You don't have to say anything," Ronnie said and squeezed. "I know I was the bitch." She cleared her throat and wiped her eyes with a tissue. "Isn't it great news, about Cassie?"

"I'll say," Marian said. "Tanya got her to eat vegetables. She's spatially cognizant, her brain recognizes stimulus and she can respond in like manner."

Richard looked puzzled. "Come again?"

"It means you can have a conversation with her," Tanya stated.

"I didn't know you were trained as a psychologist, Tanya," Ronnie said.

"I'm not," Tanya said. "I just, um, volunteer here."

"Oh, well, good for us that you do," Ronnie said and hugged Tanya tightly. "We are so excited. Can we talk to a doctor?"

"Yes, of course," Marian said and led the Broadhags down the corridor.

Ronnie threw a smile over her shoulder at Tanya. "I'll call you. Say hello to Mr. and Mrs. Palmer for me. I'll say a prayer for Stan."

Tanya waved and returned to the break room. Collapsing into a chair, she drooped her head until it clunked against the lockers. She sat thumping her head for several moments before leaning back.

Ronnie had been one of the gang, ever since first grade. Girls scouts, sleepovers, even took dance together for a year. They had been friends. But Ronnie was right, high school brought out the worst in her. Like at their prom when she stole Tanya's date.

"Mom! No more pictures," Tanya had said. "We're gonna be late."

The Davis residence, a stylishly decorated home with new carpets and a fresh coat of scarlet paint, had buzzed with activity as four high school seniors moved from spot to spot as Laura directed prom-night photography.

"Just one more," Laura said from behind a camera. "Let's have the girls make like Charlie's Angels and the guys do the Heisman Trophy pose."

"Guns and poses," an athletic boy with a spiked haircut said. "Would make a good name for a rock band."

"Del Guidry, you sure know how to make me laugh," Laura chuckled. "Do you know how to get there?"

A burly boy with mutton chop sideburns and scary eyes leaned in between them and spoke before Del could answer. "Yes, Laura, he does."

"That's Mrs. Davis to you, Ernie."

Ernie McFadden's eyes slid down her petite figure. "Lookin' mighty fine, Mrs. Davis."

Laura glanced up from the camera lens. Ernie's toothy smile leered on a

The Foiled Knight

skull too big for his frame. With a bulky forehead, overgrown back, and thick, long arms, he resembled an ape-man in a tux. She rolled her eyes to mask the stab of fear tingling her neck. "Del, will everyone fit in the Jeep?"

"I cleared out the back seat so Ernie and Wheels should fit no problem."

Ernie cackled. "Can't believe you keep your dad's porn mags in your car."

"That not true, Mrs. Davis," Del said. "Don't listen to him." With a punch to Ernie's shoulder, he added in what he thought was a whisper: "Shut up, dickhead. Stop trying to get me in trouble."

"Both of you shut up," a deep voice commanded from the adjoining room. All heads turned as Kurt Davis filled the doorway. Dressed in faded jeans and Rockport loafers, his muscular arms stretched the fabric of his Oxford shirt. He scratched his flat-top haircut, a move that accentuated a bulging bicep, "And watch your language in our home."

He entered the room, moving with the quiet grace of a puma. Alert blue eyes flicked back and forth from Del to Ernie, waiting for either to make a move, an instinct highly developed from his years of playing free safety for the Philadelphia Eagles. "Either clean up your act—" he eased to within inches of Ernie's face, let Ernie get a good whiff of his stogie drenched breath "—or you're gonna be hating life."

Ernie's glaring eyes focused on Kurt who glared back. The duel lasted for several moments until Ernie melted under the unrelenting burn. "Sorry."

Laura cleared her throat. "Ernie, why don't you pay attention to your date and see if Margie wants anything to drink."

"Wheels?" Ernie said loudly, "you thirsty?"

A short girl with round eyes and a Madonna hairdo appeared with a soda in her hand. Margie Wheeler's white dress clung tight to her curves. "Already got myself something."

Laura turned to Tanya. "Is Fitzy coming here?"

"No, he and Theresa are going with Kevin and Patti. They rented a limo."

"What about Stan?"

"Linda cancelled on him at the last minute," Tanya said."She's going with someone else now. So he's going with guys from baseball."

"Oh. Well. That stinks for Stan."

"So does having to drive a beat-up station wagon to the prom," Ernie said, trying to hide a smirk behind a fake cough.

Laura ignored the comment and turned to Del. "Prom's over at midnight. Tanya's curfew is 2 o'clock." She then faced Ernie. "And there will be no drinking tonight, right?"

Silence.

Laura's voice rose a decibel. "I said there will be no—"

"All right!" Ernie snorted. "No drinking. Now can we get out of here before someone suggests a cavity search?"

Kurt glided to Ernie's side. An iron right hand clamped down on the tendons just above his elbow, the entrapment so calm, no one noticed anything out of the ordinary until Ernie grimaced in pain. "Careful how you speak to Mrs. Davis, boy," Kurt murmured. He let go his grasp.

Tanya snared Del's hand and whisked him toward the door. "Come on."

Ernie winked at Del, whispering so that Laura could not hear. "You got the case of condoms and kegs of Moonshine whiskey?"

"Huh?" Del replied.

The corners of Ernie's mouth turned up slightly at the joke, enjoying Laura's suspicious stare, then followed with a pretend friendly wave. "Never mind." His smile evaporated as Kurt stepped in behind her. "Let's go."

* * *

Del roared his Jeep down York Road, weaving in and out of traffic.

"Be careful," Tanya said. "We've got plenty of time."

Ernie let out a loud belch. "Not going fast enough if you asked me."

Red lights flared in front of them. Tanya screamed. Everyone jerked forward as Del locked up the brakes. The Jeep narrowly missed slamming into the back of a mini-van.

"You're driving like a maniac!" Tanya yelled.

"Nag, nag, nag," Del said, turning to Ernie in the backseat. When Ernie nodded his approval, Del smiled.

Tanya's mouth fell open.

"What?" Del said.

"Just slow down," Tanya said.

"Or what?"

"Or let us out."

Del said nothing, pleading into Ernie's eyes in the rear view mirror.

"You really think we want to go to this stupid thing?" Ernie asked.

Tanya whirled in her seat. "Then what the hell are you going for?"

"Yo, bitch," Ernie said. "Calm yourself." He scratched his throat. "You know Del, maybe we should dump them out like they asked." Catching Del's eye in the mirror, he winked.

Del acknowledged the signal with a nod and swerved to the valet entrance of the hotel, cutting in front of a stretch limo. The blare of the limo's horn drew smiles from Ernie and Del as they leapt out of the vehicle. Together they sprinted in the direction of loud music.

"Do you think they know we haven't even gotten out of the vehicle?" Margie said, pulling a wrap over her shoulders.

Tanya fixed her hair in the rear view mirror. "Boys."

They hopped out and clacked their heels inside and found their banquet room. As they stepped through the door, pulsating music pounded their ears while flashing strobe lights and multi-colored spotlights swept the giant room. Circular tables, covered in white tablecloths and paper mache centerpieces, surrounded a dance floor alive with gyrating youth. The band, a group of teens in glittering gold jackets, jumped about on stage, flailing at their instruments. An assembly of teachers gathered in a corner, pointing at dancing couples, trying to decide when to step in and on whom.

"There's Eileen and Ronnie," Margie shouted.

They joined a circle of other teens, each wearing a different color, the boys looking at anything but their dates, the girls staring into their drinks.

"Hello ladies," Margie said. "Hey Ronnie, looking hot, girl. How'd you get out of the house with that plunging neckline?"

The Foiled Knight

Rhonda "Ronnie" Heatherton, a tall blonde with striking features and piercing blue eyes, was dressed in a fire-engine red dress with puffy sleeves. "Clueless parents, that's how," Ronnie replied while retouching her lip gloss. "Damn, Eileen! Those are some serious heels."

Eileen Harding, a vivacious brunette in a backless blue sequined dress flashed a brilliant smile. "Don't you just love them? My legs are already smoking, but in these things, mmm, lookout Vinnie!"

"That dress hardly covers your rear end," Tanya said. "One puff of wind and everyone's going to see your underwear."

"Who says I'm wearing any?" Eileen replied with a crooked smile. "Nice frock, Tanya. Don't you know it's okay to show a little skin on prom night?"

Tanya's face turned red. "You're supposed to wear floor length to a formal." She waved a presenting hand down her emerald green dress.

"Where did you get it, your Grandmother's closet?"

The other girls giggled along with the insult. Tanya walked away toward the beverage table, her head hung.

"Holy shit, Eileen," Margie said. "That was cold."

"I can't stand that klutz," Eileen sneered. "She'll never be in our league."

"What does Del see in her?" Ronnie said.

"She wasn't much in middle school," Margie said, "but you gotta admit, she's got a rockin' body. And nice legs. She doesn't like to show them off, but I'd rate her ahead of you, Eileen. Is that why you hate her? You jealous?"

"I'm not jealous of anybody," Eileen snapped. She tried to control her eyes, but found herself staring at Tanya's sleek figure. "She has nice hair, I'll give her that."

"She doesn't have much up top," Ronnie said.

"Maybe not like you," Margie said. "But trust me, she can hold her own in that department. Enough to turn Del on anyway."

"He's cute," Ronnie said. She crossed her arms which pushed up her breasts. "He could do so much better."

"You give him way too much credit," Eileen said. "Yeah, he's a nice guy and kinda hot, but ever actually talk to him? He's as dumb as a stump who can't think for himself or put two sentences together. He's only got two interests: sports and you know what. He's going nowhere."

"His parents are divorced," Margie said. "Ugly too, my Mom says. All they care about is their money."

"Tanya helps him with everything," Eileen said. "Tutors him, fills out his college applications. Without her, he wouldn't be graduating or eligible to play football next year."

"She's like his brain crutch," Margie said.

Eileen nodded. "Exactly."

"Well, I think he's delicious," Ronnie said.

"Then now's your chance," Margie said. "He and Tanya got into a fight on the drive here."

"Really," Ronnie said. "Coming without a date wasn't a bad idea." She reapplied a layer of lipstick and pushed her breasts to the edge of her dress. "See you ladies later."

* * *

Tanya weaved along the outskirts of the dance floor, a spectral figure that floated among the crowd. Invisible. Ethereal and spooky at the same time, oblivious to everything. And everyone. Neither being talked to, nor initiating contact. An expression of utter loneliness flagged her face. As the band changed songs, she refilled her drink and leaned against a marble pillar. She felt a tap on her back.

"Hey Teedy."

Tanya turned and smiled. "Stan! What are you doing here?"

"Same thing you are, dummy."

"That was so shitty of Linda to bag you. I didn't think you would come."

"Ah, better than hanging out at home like a dorky spider. You look spectacular."

She blushed. "Thanks."

"Your hair is so pretty and that dress. It's—" He hesitated.

The breath caught in her chest. "It's what?"

"It's, like, wow. So green. Really brings out your eyes."

She exhaled and felt the dimples form in her cheeks. "Aw, how sweet. You look pretty good yourself. Where'd you get your tux?" She smiled as he fussed with his hair and tie that would not stay straight. Almost laughed out loud as he tugged at his crotch, trying to adjust the tuxedo pants.

"Glendasheries," he answered. "They had a deal going on."

"Sure they gave you the right pants? Those things are like, *way* too short."

"And tight," he added. "It's like wearing a Chinese torture garment."

"Who cares," she said, chuckling. "At least you're talking to me."

"Yeah, what's the deal with that?" He looked around. "Why all alone?"

She pointed to a pack of boys huddled in the shadows. "Del's over there doing shots with Ernie. Guess I need to find another ride home."

"Man, that sucks."

They looked at each other. First a sly grin, then the cock of each other's head, followed by nervous giggles.

"Wanna dance?" he said.

"You bet!" she replied and grabbed his hand.

They dove into the middle of a writhing mass of humanity.

* * *

"So what's the plan?" Ernie said. "Stay here all night or do we blow this joint and head down the shore? What do you think Vinnie?"

Vinnie Macino, a strapping boy with dark skin and a dazzling smile, scanned the dance floor. "I say stay here, see what shakes. Got my eye on Eileen Harding. Did you see what she's wearing?"

"Hey, *Delward*," Ernie said. "Don't look now, but someone is moving in on your prom date." He nodded at the dance floor.

Del had been talking to Ronnie who had joined their group. It took Ernie three tugs on an elbow to draw Del's focus away from Ronnie's V-neck. Del's eyes got wide. "What's Palmer think he's doing?"

"He's doing better than you," Vinnie smirked.

Del yanked off his tie. "I'm gonna kick his ass."

The Foiled Knight

Ernie grabbed Del's arm. "And then what—get kicked out for fighting? They'll smell alcohol on your breath, which will get you in deeper shit. Maybe even lose your license. Probably nail us too. Then none of us will graduate."

"I can't just let him steal my prom date," Del fumed, trying to break loose.

Grasping Del's tux lapels, Ernie pressed the smaller boy to the wall. "Knock it off, you ditched her." Releasing Del, Ernie scratched his throat. "But you're right, that little shit Palmer shouldn't be allowed to walk so tall."

Vinnie smiled. "Ernie's got a plan, don't you, brother?"

Ernie smiled and turned to Ronnie. "Wanna go to a hoppin' pool party?"

Ronnie's eyes widened with excitement. "Sure!"

"Good, tell your girlfriends to meet us on Terwood Road, behind Huntington Valley Country Club, the service road. Got it?"

Ronnie clapped her hands. "Ooooo, this is so exciting." Arms waving, chest flapping, she pranced across the room to alert her friends.

An evil grin cast upon Ernie's jowls. He turned to Vinnie. "Ronnie is tight with Wheels. They'll talk Eileen into coming."

"Dude!" Vinnie exclaimed. "If you get me in with Eileen, you're a god."

"What about me?" Del said.

Ernie shook his head. "You got Ronnie, small boy, what else you want?"

* * *

By the time they had danced to their fifth song, a sweaty Stan and Tanya were laughing hysterically at each other's spastic moves. Tanya's heels were in the corner as was Stan's jacket. When *"Shout"* came on, they pogo-jumped like maniacs across the parquet floor. On one hop, Stan slipped and fell onto his back and began wiggling like a worm. Tanya joined him. They ended the number doing a series of double high fives until the music went silent.

"This is so much fun," Tanya said, gasping for breath.

"Look at your dress," Stan said. "It's a mess."

She looked down and shrugged. "Oh well, got my money's worth."

"Unchained Melody" by The Righteous Brothers floated from the speakers as the lead singer announced it was their last number before taking a break. Tanya and Stan stood still, not looking at each other, silent, both thinking the same thing. Finally, Tanya mumbled, "Whaddya think?"

"I'll give it a shot." He held out his arms.

They rocked back and forth in a comfortable, but cordial closeness, eyes fixated on each other, neither caring about the perspiration each felt, both enjoying the honeyed emotion from the violin and contact of each other's body. The beat, slow and smooth, guided their feet, relaxing them. A slight adjustment and their hips were touching. Stan's arms slid farther behind Tanya's hips to her back. She nudged closer and melted into his embrace.

Stan probed into Tanya's silky hair. She could feel his chest expand, breathing in her perfume. His cheek found her ear and he sang a verse. *"Lonely rivers sigh, wait for me, wait for me. I'll be coming home, wait for me."* Closing his eyes, he dipped his head, using his nose to explore. Discovered her neck, sweet and tender against his lips. Rubbed his forehead back and forth along her skin, so slick, so intimate. She titled her head to the side and fluttered as he kissed her nape. She felt a tremor through his body when she did the same to him, adding a nibble on his earlobe. He pulled her close.

"This is really nice, Stan," she whispered.

"It's like, the best dance ever," he said. "You're so soft, Teedy."

He felt a stab in his shoulder and pulled away to see Del, a smirk on his face.

"Trying to steal my prom date—" Del moved an inch closer. "Stanley?"

"She's not your date," Stan said. "You dumped her."

"Yeah, but I'm supposed to be her ride home."

"Not anymore."

Del's jaw clenched. "Whatever. Look, we're going pool-hopping at the country club, wanna come?"

Tanya leaned away. "I don't know…"

"What's the big deal?" Del asked. "We do it all the time."

"Who's all going?"

"Everybody. Me, Ronnie, Eileen, Margie, Vin, Ernie."

She looked at Stan. "What do you think?"

"What else you gonna be doing?" Stan asked.

"We're just going swimming, okay?" Del said. "You in or out?"

Stan stood silent.

"What else you got planned?" Del said. "A greasy breakfast at the Palm Grille diner? That's for geeks and losers."

A sense of awakening emerged on Tanya's face. "He's right. I always miss out." She patted Stan's arm. "Will you go with me?"

Stan squirmed in his tux. "Ah, man, I don't think so…"

"Come on," Del said. "Can you imagine the stories that will come out of a night of pool-hopping?"

Stan hesitated, then turned to Tanya. "When do you have to be home?"

"Two."

"You got time," Del said.

"Please?" Tanya said. "I want to do this." Her fingers grasped Stan's sleeve and tugged gently.

Stan looked from Del to Tanya then back to Del. "Oh, all right."

"Yay," Tanya said, hopping several times.

"Cool," Del said. "Meet us at Terwood Road behind the country club. You know where the service road dead ends?"

"The Cave?" Stan asked.

"Yeah, the Cave."

* * *

Stan pulled off Old Welsh Road and onto Terwood Road, a dark and twisty, two-lane gravel road lined by oak trees. Stan clicked on his high-beams. The immediate quarter-mile lit up in a burst of ghostly white while deformed shadows streaked into the wilderness. Stan gripped the wheel tightly to avoid the deep gullies that surrounded them.

"Remember what happened here don't you?" Tanya asked.

"Stupid bus driver," Stan said. "Not hardly room for one car let alone an obnoxious oil truck. Our bus never had a chance."

Tanya opened the sun visor's mirror and studied a faint scar extending from her upper lip. "This will never let me forget it." She pointed at a hole in the tree

The Foiled Knight

line. "There's the old dirt lane to Sawtrigger's cabin. Anybody ever go back there anymore?"

"Not for years," Stan said. "Ernie and Del used to sneak out there and smoke pot once in a while, but it's a pile of shit these days."

They rounded a bend where the road forked. Stan yanked the wheel to the left onto the service road used to make deliveries to the country club. The road was bracketed by more trees and a chain link fence overgrown with weeds and vines. Moths fluttered in the dull yellow glare of a lonely street light. Stan's headlights revealed the neon-red brake lights of two other cars coasting behind trees and out of sight. The service road to the country club ended at the fence line where it appeared to continue into darkness. The tree branches had grown so thick overhead, they completely blocked out the light, creating a massive black hole. "The Cave" was a favorite make-out spot for teens with cars. Stan pulled in behind the others and killed the motor.

The youth gathered around Ernie. "Listen up," he said in a hushed voice. "Leave your keys in the ignition in case we have to bolt out of here."

Their feet crunched on gravel as they left the cars behind, disappearing into the shadows. Under the canopy of trees, the air felt cooler and their footsteps went quiet as they reached a carpet of grass. Through gaps in the fence, Tanya could make out the wide fairway of the golf course.

"That's the fourteenth hole," Ernie said, pointing. "The pool is on the other side. You can't miss it. We'll leave our clothes here—"

Tanya's eyes got big. "Whu—?"

"Why?" Vinnie butted in. "Seems like we should bring them with us."

Tanya raised a trembling index finger. "What did you say?"

"If the cops come," Ernie said, "they'll blow in the front. Would you rather get redressed here in the dark or while a spotlight is on your ass?"

"Good point" Vinnie said. Grinning, he tore off his bow tie.

"Nobody said anything about going skinny-dipping!" Tanya said loudly. "There's no way I'm taking off my clothes in front of all you people."

"What kind of a prissy prude are you?" Eileen said. "Goody two shoes ain't the right word for you. You're more like a nun and that Granny dress is your habit." She popped the cap off a beer and slugged a long swallow.

Stan eyed the beer. "Just going swimming, huh?" he said to Del.

Del shrugged.

"Forget them," Eileen said. "They're chicken-shits. Let's go."

Tanya huffed, then spun on her heel and stomped toward the car.

Stan chased after her. "Tanya, wait."

She opened the door, then stopped. "Why do they always have to ruin it?"

"It's not ruined," he said. "Not yet anyway."

"Yeah? What'll it be like? Me and the skinny minnies."

"They're not skinny."

She returned a withering look. "Eileen has a body like a Barbie doll. She makes me look like a cow."

"She does not. You've got a great figure, Teedy."

"No way I'm getting naked in front of that crowd!" Tanya cried.

"Well, when you said yes to going swimming, did you think you would wear your prom dress into the pool?"

Tanya's arms dropped to her side. "No, er, not exactly. I mean, um, shit."

"Why don't we strip down to our underwear?" Stan suggested.

A frown creased Tanya's face.

Stan tilted his head. "Same thing as wearing a bathing suit."

A glimmer of hope brightened behind her eyes. "I could do that. But do you think they'll make fun of me?"

"I won't let them," Stan said and grabbed her hand. "Come on." They rejoined the other kids who were already disrobing.

Eileen chuckled. "Can't stand to miss out, can you?"

"We're sweaty from dancing," Stan said. "Gonna cool off in the pool."

Ernie leaned close to Del. "Did you spoon feed her when she was going out with you?"

"What's that supposed to mean?" Stan said.

"It means how come the girl can't speak for herself, huh, Palmer?"

"Me and Stan are only going down to our underwear," Tanya said.

An amused look broke out on Ernie's face. "Suit yourself."

A drunken Eileen flipped the latch of the gate. She paraded to the middle of the fairway, stark naked, hands on hips. "Come on. Let's get this party started. Oooh, Vinnie, nice pecs."

Vinnie playfully smacked her rear. She squealed in delight. Together, they sprinted away followed by the rest of the group in a mad romp across the grass. A few muted shouts of "Wahoo" could be heard.

They circumvented the tennis courts, gained the concrete deck surrounding the pool and leapt through the air, hitting the water in random rapid dives and cannonballs. Water fights ensued, people got dunked, laughter filled the air. Ernie and Margie made out on the steps in the shallow end. On the diving board, Eileen fought Vinnie for position.

Stan and Tanya watched while clinging to the side of the pool, bodies hidden below the surface, elbows plastered to the deck. "Talk about flaunting it," Stan said. "Sorry Teedy, maybe we goofed."

"I think you're right," Tanya said.

"We wanna see Tanya jiggle on the diving board," Ernie yelled.

"No way!" Tanya snapped.

Shouts of "Come on" and "Chicken" filled the air. Tanya's cheeks flushed.

"I'm not doing it," she hissed. "I can't believe you talked me into this."

"Nobody talked you into anything," Eileen snapped. "You came 'cause you wanna see how the cool crowd lives."

"Leave her alone, Eileen," Stan said. "She doesn't have to."

"Then you do it, Stan," Ernie said. "The girls will get a kick out of seeing you flouncing around." Girlish giggling followed his challenge.

"Go pound sand, McFadden," Stan said.

"Don't need to," Ernie said, leering at Margie. "I got Wheels."

Margie snorted an inebriated guffaw. "They don't call me 'Wheels' for nothing." She climbed out of the pool and dashed away into the shadows of the golf course. Ernie quickly followed. There were hoots and hollering from everyone except Stan and Tanya.

The Foiled Knight

"Ugh," Tanya said.

"Wassamatter, Tanya?" Eileen said. "Never been kissed before?"

"None of your business," Tanya said.

"Beat it, Eileen," Stan said, splashing her. "Go annoy somebody else."

"Gladly." She grabbed Vinnie's hand and led him after Ernie and Margie.

Ronnie was already out of the pool, Del in tow, and headed in the same direction. "You two love birds can have the pool," Ronnie said. Their laughter faded away as the darkness enveloped them.

A quietness surrounded Stan and Tanya, the only sounds being the soft lapping of the pool water against the sides.

"Drunken assholes," Tanya said. "I hope they all get pregnant."

"Tanya!" Stan exclaimed. "That was wicked. You don't mean that."

She blew out a gust of air. "I know, they just make me so mad." She swam to the ladder. "But I am glad they're gone." She yanked herself out of the pool and leapt onto the diving board. "Think I remember how to do the back-flip?"

"No brainer," Stan said. "Try something a little harder."

She stepped forward in that measured way a diver calculates their take-off and soared high, her body cutting across the moon. She reached for the water and disappeared. A few strong breast strokes propelled her to Stan. She crested the surface just before him, eyes closed.

"Beautiful," Stan applauded.

Her green eyes opened wide and with them her smile. "Thanks," she said, pushing her hair behind her ears. The light from below glistened in the drops of water that speckled their faces. She wrapped her arms around his neck and pressed her body into his, kissing him gently on the lips. "I really liked slow dancing with you."

"Me too," he said and kissed her back. The moon emerged from behind a cloud, its light dancing on the glassy surface. The water, warm and perfect, surrounded them in a state of weightlessness. The air, cool yet calm, tickled their skin, raising goosebumps along their limbs.

The blare of a car horn rattled the moment. "Hey, Palmer!" a voice called from the darkness. "Hope you know your way home."

Stan and Tanya broke away from each other, heads jerking about.

"That was Ernie," Stan said, a ripple of fear climbing his spine.

He and Tanya hurried out of the pool and ran in the direction of the voice. Car headlights blazed where they had snuck into the country club. Raucous laughter echoed as the headlights retreated and disappeared into darkness.

"Oh shit, oh shit, shit, shit!" Tanya wailed. "Stan, they're ditching us!"

"Come on!" Stan yelled. Across the fourteenth fairway they galloped, skidding to a halt at the fence line. The gate swung lazily back and forth. Scuttled footprints were visible everywhere.

"They took our clothes!" Stan exclaimed.

"And all the cars," Tanya added.

"Those bastards!" He smacked a fist into his palm. "No wonder Ernie was so adamant about leaving our keys in the ignition. Ah, man, I shoulda known."

"What do we do?"

Just then, a flashing red light appeared from behind the clubhouse.

"Shit!" Stan said. "The cops!"

Stan and Tanya dashed through the gate and cut through the woods, going several hundred yards before emerging onto a gravel road.

"I'll betcha fifty million dollars Del is the one, ouch, who called the cops on us," Stan said. He stopped to extract a pebble from the bottom of his foot. "Let's cut through that neighborhood," he pointed to houses nestled in the trees. "Maybe we'll get lucky and find something left on a clothesline."

Over bushes and through backyards they crept, across decks, and under swing-sets, their only source of light being the pearly-blue glow of the moon. They found an asphalt bike path and hunch-ran for another hundred yards, popping their heads up every so often to check the contents of back yards.

"There," Tanya said, pointing. Through the mangled branches of some hedges, they spotted several strands of clothesline with drying laundry.

Stan plowed through the shrubs, holding open a hole for her. "Hurry!"

In seconds, they were rifling through the garments.

Stan held huge boxer shorts to his waist. "My size?"

"Not unless you're Andre The Giant." She pulled some clothespins off a woman's bra and wrapped it around his head. "Gives a whole new meaning to lift and support." She bent over laughing as Stan mock-wrestled with the garment. "Try these," Tanya said and tossed him some gym shorts.

"Cool, thanks. Here, how about this?" He held up a striped sundress.

She pulled it over her head. "This will work. Come on, let's explore."

With a squeal, she hopped a split-rail fence and crossed the yard, stooping to pick up a volleyball and hurl it at Stan before climbing onto a trampoline. In three bounces, her head was at the second story level.

"Teedy, not so high!" Stan howled in delight.

She soared once again. "Come on, join me."

Timing his jump, Stan quickly caught up to Tanya's height. They had to hold hands to keep from sending each other flying off in different directions.

"Hey, check out the next yard over," Stan said. On the other side of a row of pine trees, they spotted a tether ball game.

"When is the last time we played?" Tanya asked.

"Doug Fitzgerald's party, eighth grade."

"You game, Flouncy?"

He laughed. "Bring it, Jiggles."

They collapsed their knees to kill their bounce, jumped to the ground and slipped between the pines.

Tanya served, the ball soared over Stan's head for two revolutions until he slammed it back at her.

"Could you ever imagine our prom turning into a scavenger hunt in our underwear?" Stan said

"Not in a million years," she said, blocking his hit, then snorted a loud laugh as Stan toppled backwards over a child's Big Wheel left askew in the grass. His momentum knocked over a trash can. The contents spilled across the ground. She rushed over and helped him up. "You all right?"

"Yeah. Holy crap, look at that slop pile."

Tanya kicked at twisted aluminum foil scattered in the debris. "Somebody

The Foiled Knight

had grilled corn on the cob for dinner. Here help me."

Together they scooped up the mess.

The backyard suddenly turned yellow as the back porch light came to life. Stan grabbed Tanya's arm and whispered hoarsely, "Run!"

They dashed behind a pile of firewood. The screech of a rusty screen door sounded as a man holding a baseball bat exited the house.

"Who's there?" the man said loudly into the night.

Crickets chirped a reply as Stan and Tanya ducked down. After several moments, the screen door screeched again as the man went inside.

Stand and Tanya fell over, gasping for air.

"Oh man, that was close," Stan said.

They both stood and walked along the asphalt path a ways more.

"Teedy, look." Stan pointed to a large built-in pool with a long and twisting fiberglass tube that descended from a tall ladder.

"A serpentine slide," she said. "Just like on the boardwalk in Wildwood."

"You thinking what I'm thinking?"

"But I just found this new dress. Be a shame to get it wet."

They grinned at each other. The dress hit the ground before Stan could kick off the shorts. In seconds, they were at the top of the ladder.

"Last one in the water is a rotten egg," Tanya said. Slipping and sliding, they toppled from the top step and down the tube's throat, smashing into each other and the fiberglass sides. In a thrash of arms and legs, they hit the water, the freshness cooling their skin. They dove to the bottom for a touch of the drain and an exchange of underwater smiles as their hair floated about them. She motioned for a high five. He attempted to return it, but missed when she moved her hand to play-smack him in the forehead. Bubbles exploded from their mouths. A strong thrust with their legs brought them to the surface. Sputtering and choking with laughter, they swam to the side and climbed out.

Stan nabbed two beach towels that hung over the back of a chair. They wrapped themselves up and lay side by side on the wooden deck, staring up at the stars, heads touching.

"Having fun yet?" she asked.

"Tons," he replied. "Don't get to do this every day."

"Couldn't ever see me doing this with Del."

"He's not right for you, Teedy."

"Don't start in on me again."

"He doesn't care about you—"

"—He needs help!" Tanya blurted. "His parents are div—"

"—if he cared," Stan interrupted, "he wouldn't have ditched you. But he can't stand it if anyone else has you either. That's why he's so willing to get me in trouble tonight. He thinks we're being arrested right now and that it'll make me look like such a shit, your parents won't ever let me go near you."

She stayed silent for a few moments then shook her head. "No, he's not that smart. This is Ernie all the way. When Del's parents split up, neither of them wanted anything to do with him. Unfortunately, he started following Ernie. Must make Del feel like he belongs. Doesn't make it okay, but I sorta understand it." She rubbed her thigh against his. "Instead, I'm lying with you under the moonlight having the time of my life." Then she sat up.

"What's wrong?" Stan asked.

"Nothing," Tanya said, her voice gushing. "Just had a brainstorm." Holding her towel tight, she disappeared into the night toward the houses.

Stan heard a slight rustling noise like a raccoon scavenging a camping site.

After a minute, Tanya reappeared holding up a handful of mangled aluminum foil.

"What were you doing?" he asked.

"You'll see," she replied as she bent and molded the foil into shape. After a minute, she finished and held up a miniature figure of a person in a muscleman's pose. She handed it to him. "To Stan the man Palmer, my hero."

"Hey!" Stan beamed. "It's The Foiled Knight."

She touched his hand. "It's for saving me tonight."

"I accept with honor." He intertwined his fingers with hers. "Gotta admit, this will make the Stan and Tanya highlight reel."

"How can I repay you?"

"Wait till you see my bill," he said. "You might need to mortgage all your Monopoly properties."

"Always the comedian," she said, stroking his forearm. "What do you want to do now?"

"Wanna get dressed? Not sure this house will keep that sundress on layaway forever. And you've got a curfew."

"I know." She kissed his hand and then choked out a half-laugh, half-cry.

He rose up and leaned on an elbow, stroking her cheek with the back of his hand. Her eyes glistened in the moonlight. "Hey, Teedy, you okay?"

"Yeah. It's just... I don't want this night to end."

"It doesn't have to end yet, does it?" There was a crookedness to his grin.

"Not *just* yet." She ran her fingers through his hair and pulled him close.

Chapter 17

Ciquero stared at a photograph of Holly Mathews. With a frustrated sigh, he tossed it into the case file and shoved the folder across his desk. It slid over the edge onto the floor.

Ray O'Hara, Glenside's grizzled police chief, stepped into the doorway. "That good, huh?" He stooped to pick up the file and groaned. "Making the boss bend his bad back. You trying to send me to retirement?" He closed the door to the noise of the stationhouse, limped to the lonely visitor's chair and eased himself in. "What's the latest?"

"I got nothing, Cap," Ciquero said, massaging his forehead. "No clues, no leads, no theories."

"You talk to everyone in the surrounding area?"

"Yep. Nobody saw nothing."

"Any suspects?" O'Hara said, scratching his gnarled nose.

"Nope. We checked all the registered sex offenders and came up empty."

"Similarities to the others?"

"Young girl, caught alone," Ciquero said. "Not enough for a pattern."

"At least the ones we know about. Feds any help?"

"Gave me access to their database, but doubt we'll get a body to help us."

O'Hara put on thick glasses and leafed through the case file. "What about that 911 call?"

"Timing looked good, but it was made by a guy in a car accident."

"Did you interview him?"

"Can't. He's laid up in Abington Hospital in a coma."

"So you don't know if he knows anything. What did you mean about the timing looking good?"

"The 911 call came in not too long after the girl disappeared."

O'Hara peered over the top of the case file, his white scalp visible through the thinning hairs of his marine crew cut. "That sounds promising. Anything in the call give you a clue?"

"No. It all checks out. I interviewed the bartender at Fitzy's. The guy stopped in for a beer before heading up to his folks for dinner."

"He was at Fitzy's at the same time the girl disappeared?"

"Yup. Coincidence."

"What do you know about him?"

Ciquero shrugged. "Good kid growing up, Eagle Scout, decent grades, stable family. Clean record. By all accounts, an okay guy."

"Pays his taxes and helps little old ladies across the street," O'Hara added.

"Don't forget that he's a church goer and volunteers time with the Rotary Club," Ciquero said with a frown. "What are you getting all crotchety about?"

"That there might be another possibility," O'Hara said. With a grunt, he stood and handed the case file to Ciquero. "Let's go outside."

Ciquero followed O'Hara through a back door to the alleyway.

O'Hara removed a pipe from his shirt pocket, stuffed it and lit a match, hovering the tiny fireball over the tobacco chamber, all the while studying Ciquero. "Mike, how do you know *he's* not the kidnapper?"

"There's nothing in his upbringing to suggest that," Ciquero said.

"That's his youth," O'Hara said. "What about his recent history? Anything happen that might have caused him to snap?"

"I interviewed his family, neighbors, co-workers. It's all good. He's a bookkeeper at the mill. Hard worker. Dependable. Gets along with folks. Everybody that knows him says the same thing. He's a good guy."

O'Hara motioned to the file. "He went to Furman. Why is a guy with a college degree working as a lowly bookkeeper all these years?"

"I don't know," Ciquero said. "It's not a crime. And who said he's lowly?"

"You have to look deeper, Mike. Does he have a girlfriend?"

"No. He's a single guy, lives alone."

O'Hara stared into the alley, smoke encircling his head. "Single white male, late thirties, loner, lives in the same town as the victim, underachiever, difficulty with women, lurking in a smoky bar across the street scoping out victims."

"Woah," Ciquero interrupted. "You're twisting things."

"You can't ignore it fits some of the profile and you haven't ruled him out as a suspect." O'Hara pulled on the pipe. "Does he go to strip joints?"

"Whu—" Ciquero started to say, then paused. He shoved his hands into his pockets. "I don't know. Didn't seem necessary."

"Mike, if he lives alone and has no girlfriend..."

"That's a reach," Ciquero said.

O'Hara bit down on the pipe. "Mike, wake the fuck up! You've placed him in the bar right across the street from the theater - at the same time the girl's movie lets out - and all of a sudden he just leaves?"

"He was going to dinner at his parents. I confirmed it at both ends."

"Great alibi. Maybe he's got everyone snowed."

Ciquero shook his head. "I just can't see it."

"Is that your gut talking?" O'Hara said, his scratchy voice rising in intensity. "Or the facts you got right there in the file? Don't you think it smells that we haven't heard anything from the kidnapper for the same period of time that your coma guy has been out of commission?"

"Maybe, but come on Captain, you know it's doubtful there will be a ransom request. None of the others had one and the Mathews family hasn't got any money. We're lucky if the girl is still alive."

O'Hara tapped the pipe against the brick wall, its smoldering contents fell to the ground. He ground them with the heel of a polished boot. "Get a warrant, Mike. Toss his place. And his computer." Opening the door, he turned to Ciquero. "Sometimes you've got to put yourself in the dark to see darkness."

Chapter 18

The pick-up truck found the break in the guardrail along Terwood Road, shock rattling the frame as it lurched down and hard into the ditch. Mud and slush splattered in a bronco-buck across Sawtrigger's Creek and up the opposite embankment. The brute force of four-wheel drive powered the truck over the crest, the diesel engine roaring as the front end vaulted into the air, muck flying from spinning tires. The pick-up blasted through a row of bushes and jounced to a halt on level ground.

Shifting gears, the driver followed a path that hugged the base of the snow-covered mountain. Many years earlier, the path had been a convenient shortcut to the town of Horsham until the construction of the Pennsylvania turnpike dissected the path, rendering it useless.

Deep into the forest, the road curved sharply around a large outcropping of rock that jutted from the mountainside. Evergreen trees lined the ridge atop the protrusion forming a picketed berm of earth and wood. The driver pulled off the road and parked, grabbed his package and whiskey bottle, jumped out and circled around the formation.

On the other side, the forest opened up into a circular clearing with dense trees on the left that when combined with the rock outcropping on the right and mountain in the background, created a natural enclosure with the sky for its ceiling.

Nestled into the side of the mountain, built just beneath a rock ledge, squatted a small cabin. Rough-sawn cedar siding hung haphazardly from a crooked frame. Two triangle-shaped windows pointed inwards at each other. An exterior walkway surrounded the place, its crooked railing and balusters leering an evil grin. Spindly pressure-treated stilts stretched out at awkward angles. Painted cammo-green, it blended into the foliage and was virtually invisible during the summer from as little as fifty yards away. In the starkness of winter and the fireplace flickering however, the compact wooden box peered out of its nook like an angry Jack O'Lantern.

The driver trudged around back and climbed the steps up to the rickety front porch, paused at the door to take a slug of the rot-gut, then knocked. "Hey, lemme in."

There was a rustling from inside. "Who is it?"

"It's me, Del."

A clicking noise sounded as a bolt unlocked. The door swung open revealing an unshaven Ernie McFadden, dressed in hunting boots, cargo pants, checkered flannel shirt and a green army coat. Stamping his feet, he pulled at the worn woolen gloves with missing fingertips. "Bring me something to eat?"

"Soup and a roast beef sandwich," Del answered. "Just like you asked."

"Better be good," Ernie grunted. "Get in here." He didn't hold the door.

The main room of the cabin was cramped with crooked wooden planks for a floor and cheap paneling. A small flame gnawed at paltry logs in a crumbling stone fireplace. Kerosene lanterns hung from nails on three walls. The kitchen consisted of a battered table, a propane-powered camping stove on one side, cases of beer on the other. Newspaper and adult magazines lay strewn about an old couch with ripped cushions.

Ernie shoved a pillow and blanket aside and flopped on the couch. He tore open the bag of food while Del warmed his backside by the fire.

"Damn it's cold in here," Del said, squirming from foot to foot.

"Don't be such a pussy," Ernie said and ripped a hunk of sandwich.

"Why don't you build up a bigger fire?"

"Big fire, big smoke… numb-nuts."

Del's face scrunched into a scramble of puzzlement. "Oh, right." He helped himself to a beer. "But how can you stand it?"

"You're worse than the girl."

"Up yours," Del said. "How is she?"

"Still tied up like a little lamb." Ernie scratched his throat as he chewed. "Don't even bother to fight anymore." In four bites, he devoured the sandwich, then popped the lid off the soup and drank it straight down.

"Jesus, how do you do that?" Del said.

Ernie laughed. "Man, in the army, you got used to wolfing down your food." He took a long guzzle of beer and forced out a wet belch.

Del smiled. "Good one."

Ernie waved him over. "Okay, so when I checked up on our old pal Stanley, he was still making like a vegetable."

"Did they say if he might come out of it?"

"Doctors don't know nothing." With a tremendous sniff, Ernie hocked a massive lugey into the fireplace. "Damn, new record." He grinned at Del with food-speckled teeth. "But as long as he stays in a coma, we're free and clear."

Del's face puzzled. "What do you mean, *we*? I haven't done anything."

Ernie looked amused. "You're here ain't you? In a cabin in the woods, where a scrawny teenage girl is tied up in the slaughter house."

"But that ain't—"

"—bringing me food," Ernie added. "Stocking my beer, lugging my firewood…"

"I haven't touched her."

"No, but you been making sure she don't get away."

Del held up a silent index finger.

"I'd say that's about as close to aiding and abetting as it gets," Ernie continued. "Probably get you ten to twenty in Holmesburg."

Del scratched his head at the spot where his brain hurt. "Hmm, didn't think about it that way."

"Of course you didn't. That's why I do the thinking around her."

"But why did you have to do her up here where someone like Palmer could see you through the window?"

"Not enough room in the shed," Ernie said. "And quit bitching at me. You're the one who started shooting at him."

"He saw everything!" Del squealed. "What did you want me to do?"

"Use your brains, dickhead. While dip-shit Palmer was enjoying the show, one of us could have gone out the back door and snuck up on him. Then we could of taken them out in the woods, aced 'em and buried them." Ernie cleared his nose by plugging one nostril and blowing snot out the other. "But no. You had to start blasting and chase him off. If you at least could have winged him and slowed his ass up so we coulda stopped him before he reached his car, we wouldn't be in this mess."

"And if you didn't have to snatch a teenage girl," Del barked, "Palmer wouldn't have been snooping and there wouldn't be a mess to be in."

"Clam it! Lucky for us he drove out of here like a lunatic and hit that deer. Racked himself up but good."

"What if he wakes up?" Del asked.

"We'll be in deep shit, that's what."

"Maybe we'll catch a break and he'll stay that way the rest of his life."

"Maybe," Ernie mused. He stroked the prickly stubble on his throat, up and down, slow and methodical. "Can't really deal with *maybe*."

Chapter 19

Dr. DeAngelis gingerly peeled away the wrappings from Stan's face. "Looks like his swelling has gone down significantly."

Sandra and Fenton Palmer looked on from the other side of the bed.

"Oh, I can see him!" Sandra said and clasped her hands to her face.

"Ah, and his coloring is returning to normal," DeAngelis said pointing to Stan's forehead. "Lacerations are healing nicely. Scarring will be minimal."

"You are an incredibly gifted doctor," she said.

"You can thank the plastic surgeon, not me. I did the internal work."

"We need to thank everyone," Fenton said, "because you all deserve it. Any good news is reason to be thankful."

DeAngelis peeked under the bandage on Stan's chest and smiled. "Good! His puncture wound is healing much faster than I expected."

"Does that mean he will be able to breathe on his own?" Sandra asked.

"Afraid not," DeAngelis said. "But, his kidneys are producing good output and his reparative osteoblasts have already begun mending his ribs." There was a slight crinkle at the edge of the surgeon's eyes. "Amazing thing the human body. And when supplemented by modern technology, it can do miraculous things." He winked. "Of course, good family genes help."

"What about his mind?" Sandra asked. "Any feel as to when... if... he might wake up?"

"No way to tell with a coma," DeAngelis said. "The subdural hematoma he suffered was a nasty one. *But*, his EEG shows synchronous activity, which is a good sign. That means his brain is still functioning." He paused.

Sandra stiffened. "What?"

"The problem is time. It's our best indicator of whether he'll come out of it or not. Comas rarely last more than two to five weeks. The longer this goes on, the greater the chances are that Stan will fall into a vegetative state."

"But it does happen, right?" Sandra said. "People do recover."

"There have been reported cases of patients coming back after months or even years in a coma, but they are pretty rare. If this goes past four months, the chances of recovery are only 15%."

"Can you do anything?"

"Not much," DeAngelis said, hesitated, then added with a slight wince. "There have been experiments where doctors implanted electrodes deep into a patient's brain as a way to jump start activity, but not with a lot of success."

"But stimulation could possibly help him."

"Yes, in theory, but we're not at that point yet. We've got him stable and that's the most important thing right now. We can talk about what to do next in a day or so."

"Thank you, Doctor," Sandra said with a sigh.

The Foiled Knight

"You're welcome." He stuffed his stethoscope into the pocket of his lab coat. "Now, if you'll excuse me."

As DeAngelis left, Tanya blew in with red cheeks and scarf flying. "What did the doctor say?"

"Mostly good news," Fenton answered. "Stan is recovering very well, faster in some areas than they originally thought."

"That's great," Tanya said and removed her coat.

"They're still not sure about his mind. Doctor DeAngelis said something about a stimulation procedure. Sounded iffy to me, wish it didn't, but he wants to wait a day before deciding what to do next. I guess time will tell on that."

Tanya shrugged. "Then I guess we wait."

"Yes," Fenton said and put his arm around Sandra. "Gotta go. Call me if there's any news. I want to be here when they tell us."

"Of course," Sandra said. "Have a good day, dear."

"I will. You do the same." Fenton took a moment to gaze at Stan. "Take care, son. I'll see you later." He then glanced at Tanya. "Are you staying?"

Tanya made figure eights in the hair of Stan's arm. "For a few hours anyway. Gotta work later. Why don't you stop in and have dinner?"

Fenton's face stayed expressionless. "I don't think so."

Tanya noticed Sandra subtly step on Fenton's toe. A silent look passed between the married couple. He cleared his throat and faced Tanya.

"Well, okay, maybe," Fenton said. "Haven't been there in a while. What's the special?"

"Meatloaf, whipped garlic potatoes and green beans with bacon."

"Mmmm. Stick to your ribs kinda food."

"Betsy made her famous apple pie. You wouldn't want to miss that."

"Double mmm. Okay, you convinced me." He buttoned his coat. "I'm outta here." He kissed Sandra and left.

"I can't stay long myself," Sandra said to Tanya. "But before I go, I have something to give you." She pulled a worn manila folder out of her purse.

"What's that?" Tanya asked.

"It's a story Stan wrote."

"Really?" Tanya said. "What's it about?"

A twinkle flashed in Sandra's eyes. "Don't know, but I imagine you'll enjoy being the first one to read it."

"What? He never got it published?"

"Really now, Tanya, don't you think you would have heard if Stan had been published?"

A knowing look took over Tanya's face. "Guess you're right. But where's it been all this time?"

"I found it today," Sandra said. "In the attic. I was cleaning out some things. Get this: I found Stan's old baseball glove in there. There were other stories too. Figured you'd like something to read while keeping your vigil."

"I would love that," Tanya said. A memory flashed before her of the conversation at the train yard where she and Stan had confessed to each other their future dreams. And then in college, he had asked her to proofread an early draft of a short story for an English Lit assignment.

Sandra handed the folder to Tanya. "Why don't you read it to him?"

The two women made eye contact. Stan's life support equipment chirped repeatedly, filling the temporary silence. They both turned to gaze upon him.

"Think he can hear me?" Tanya asked.

Sandra shrugged. "What can it hurt?"

Tanya shrugged back. "You're right."

"You'll call me if he wakes up?"

"Won't need a phone," Tanya said. "You'll hear the scream across town."

Sandra tried to laugh. "Precious. Be back in a few hours." She scooped up her coat, kissed Stan on the forehead, hugged Tanya, and left.

Tanya took a moment to watch Sandra walk away. Such a nice woman. Generous, tender, and ever caring. Always thinking of others. A calmness settled over Tanya that made her feel appreciative of her own parents whom she knew would do anything for her or any of her friends. Or at least try.

She plopped herself into a chair and emptied faded yellow parchment papers into her hands. Looking at Stan, she held the crispy pages to her nose, relishing the scent of old pulp. "Well, Mr. Palmer, let's see what twisted ideas you've been hiding up in that mischievous brain of yours." She raised her chin and read, her voice an exaggerated nasal imitation of Charles Emerson Winchester III. "When Ink Bleeds — a short story by Stan 'The Man' Palmer."

Tanya Davis snuggled in the deep recesses of a chair in the back of the public library and slid her fingers behind the page of a book. Her alert, green eyes peered over the top of the cover, spying patrons as they wandered about. She pushed a sheet to the left, her fingers gliding over the crispness of the parchment, her nose breathing in the musty smell of pulp. Never once did she look down at the printed text. Would the mysterious man brave the cold and take up his usual spot in the chair across from her? She pulled her winter parka up around her cheeks and turned another page.

* * *

Stan Palmer tilted his face away from the fierce January wind and scurried across the parking lot and into the library. A gentle warmth greeted him. He peeled off his scarf and worked his way through the aisles of fiction to his favorite spot. The woman with auburn hair was already burrowed into her chair in the corner. He dropped a hard-back novel into the seat and studied her fuzzy boots as she crossed her legs. He held his breath as her hand adjusted the bottom of her sweater, an emerald-green, cashmere v-neck. Mmmm.

Looking up, he was startled to see her staring at him. Her eyes flicked back to the book, a slight crinkle forming at her temples. Stan smiled, hung his coat and leaped his lanky frame into the chair. "Yowch!" He contorted his body, reaching awkwardly underneath him to extract the book. Flustered eyes glanced in the woman's direction. The book in her hands jiggled and he thought he detected muted laughter.

The Foiled Knight

Later that night, after they had conquered their mutual shyness and talked for hours over coffee and cheesecake at a nearby diner, Tanya carefully penned a bold prediction in her diary that Stan Palmer could be the one.

* * *

Tanya blinked at the words on the page and did a double-take to make sure she read them right. Convinced she wasn't dreaming, she shook her head and returned to the story, a strange sensation fluttering her insides.

* * *

Nats Remlap stared at his word processor, hands hovering above the keyboard, fingers quivering, waiting for his mind to release its creative genius. All of the ingredients were in place: deer skin moccasins, a lambs wool sweater, his pipe, and a gentle fire crackling in the fireplace. A glass of port glowed under the kelly-green lamp. When Vivaldi burst from the stereo, his fingers attacked. The words came fast. Ideas flowed through him, each one fostering more brainstorms. The clacking from the keys bounced from one bookcase to the next. He was in the zone.

Two hours later, the fire lay smoldering, the glass of port half full, and the computer screen jammed with genius. Smiling, he interlocked fingers and cracked his knuckles.

A voice called from upstairs. "Nats, it's after midnight. Give it up. Come to bed. And don't forget to finish your drink."

"In a minute, Eileen," he yelled. "Chapter one is complete."

"It won't matter."

"This one is different," he said. "It's from the heart."

"What part of 'Nats, we don't like your stuff anymore' don't you get?"

He got up from the wooden desk and punched the off button on the stereo and whispered, "Thanks for all your steadfast support. *Dear.*"

Returning to the computer, Remlap sent the newborn manuscript to the printer. He slugged the remaining port in one gulp, the burn shuddering his body. Scraped the pages out of the print tray, laid them on the desk, then lurched to the window, staring mindlessly at the moon.

Remlap lifted the window a crack and pressed a wrinkled forehead against the glass. He rolled his head from side to side. So cool and smooth. Unfortunately, Eileen was right. There had been countless tries at a comeback, but he couldn't convince the publisher. Too long, too boring, too fantastic. He wondered if this story would suffer the same fate.

His breathing had fogged up the window. With a delicate index finger, he traced the letters SP and TD in the condensation. Sighing, Remlap kicked off his moccasins and climbed the stairs for bed. He never heard the puff of wind that blew the beginning pages of the manuscript behind the desk.

* * *

The next night, Stan and Tanya strolled along the sidewalk until they reached the diner. She smiled as he held the door for her. They found a table near the window and ordered finger sandwiches and coffee.

"That is so great that you are a writer," Tanya said.

"Haven't been published yet. It's a lot harder than everyone thinks. But it's only a matter of making it happen."

Tanya scrunched up her face. "You mean get lucky, don't you?"

"No. A man makes his own life. Got you here didn't I?"

Her eyebrows arched. "Excuse me, I came here out of my own free will."

"This isn't free will," he said. "This is fate."

Blushing, she fed him the last corner of a sandwich.

* * *

"Nats, your writing doesn't sell anymore," the publisher said over the phone. "I'm sorry, there's no zing. Why not try some of the other houses?"

"I have," Remlap said. "Gimme another shot, I can do *zing*."

"Sorry guy." *Click*.

Remlap tried to slam the phone into the cradle, but it skittered away and fell behind the desk. "Damn." He knelt and slithered an arm into the narrow crevice, felt the edge of paper and extracted some pages. *So that's where chapter one went*, he thought. He stood and wandered aimlessly around the den, re-reading his work. His chest cramped. A bead of sweat trickled down his temple. This was his best stuff; reduced to "drivel." The room began to swirl around him and he dropped the pages in the trashcan. Massaging his forehead, he leaned on the desk, his breath short. Tears, large ones, dangled from the end of his nose. He adjusted his head so that he was directly over the trash can. The teardrop released. It hit the parchment without a sound.

* * *

Stan and Tanya left the diner, holding hands. They were halfway to the library parking lot when a single raindrop hit Stan on the cheek. He looked up at the sky and gawked.

"What's wrong?" Tanya asked, noticing the wind had picked up.

"For a moment, I could have sworn I saw the stars forming two giant eyes." He tasted the raindrop. "Huh. Salty."

She glared at him sideways. "Stan, how much coffee did you have?"

* * *

A week later, Tanya sat in her corner of the library waiting for Stan to arrive. Two cups of steaming coffee sat on the table. He was late. But then, so was everyone else. In fact, the place lay empty. And then she noticed no lights were on. Not even in the parking lot. She figured that was because all the windows were foggy and she just couldn't see out. But when she tried to wipe away the condensation, nothing happened. *That's weird*.

She picked her way through the aisles of fiction. All of the chairs were empty. She booted over a trash can. As the container rolled away, the hair on her forearms stood on end. Not because nothing spilled, but a metal trash can sliding across a tiled floor should make a noise. "Hey," she shouted and immediately froze when she realized not only was her hearing gone, but she hadn't felt the impact of her toe against the trash can. *What's happening?* she thought. *My mind is still working. I'm able to think and breathe and see, but my senses seem to be…dying.*

Tanya cracked open a book, hoping for the musty smell of pulp. Nothing. She ran, back to the table with the coffee, took a drink, then immediately spit it out. Dark liquid splashed on her ankles as the cup hit the floor. No burning sensation hit her. Tears welled in her eyes. She screamed.

"Tanya!"

She whirled and spotted Stan kneeling on top of a bookcase, beaming a smile. Her heart leapt and she ran to him. "Stan! Can you hear me?"

"I can hear you just fine, sweetheart," he said, his voice deep and velvety.

"Why can I hear you, but I can't hear myself?" she asked.

"We hear what we can live with," he said and smiled again, the whiteness blinding her. "I don't think any of this is real."

"I don't understand."

He jumped down. "Look what I found," he said, holding up a hard-back book. "It's a novel by Nats Remlap."

"Who cares?" she blurted. "Where is everyone? Why can't I feel or smell or taste anything? And why is your skin glowing like that?"

"Calm down," he said, patting her hand. "I'll explain. But I need to ask you some questions. Let's start with what kind of car do you drive?"

Her forehead wrinkled as she wracked her brain. "I…I…I don't know."

"And where do you live?" he asked, his eyes twinkling.

She looked at him with confused eyes. "I don't know that either!"

"What's your mom's name?"

Tanya's jaw dropped. "How is it I don't know my mother's name?"

"Maybe you never had one," Stan said.

"What?"

"If you asked me those same questions, I wouldn't be able to answer them either. It all started the night the raindrop hit me. After I left you, I went to the parking lot to look for my car. Guess what? I don't have one! So I went back into the library and everything felt normal again. It's like, when I'm here, I belong here. The librarian saw me acting weird and asked me what was wrong."

"What did you tell her?"

"That I didn't have a life outside of the library. She told me I sounded like

I was stuck in a Nats Remlap story." He held up the novel. "Remlap was once a famous writer. Had a few good sellers, but then hit a dry spell, began to drink and stopped writing. This is the last thing he ever published. It's about a man and a woman who fall in love, but are torn apart when one of them goes crazy thinking the library is his home."

She held up her hands. "Wait. We're getting away from the important stuff. What about my senses, and all the people, and your skin?"

"This will sound crazy," Stan said, "but I think I'm a real person."

"Excuse me?"

"When I got hit by that salty rain, something changed. I feel alive. I can touch things, smell them, hear, see and feel emotions like never before."

"But we've always been able to do those things."

"Believe me, Tanya. You've never experienced anything like this."

She lay on her back. "You're right. It's too surreal."

He stood. "Let's find out," he said, extending his hand. "Follow me."

A surge of comfort filled her chest when she felt the warmth of his grip. They sprinted to the front of the library and he pushed open the door. "There, tell me what you see."

Tanya stared at a blanket of white. "When did it snow?"

"That's what it looks like to you?" He took several steps outside, turned, knelt and ran his hand along the ground. "Touch it."

Tanya reached out with tentative fingers, expecting to scoop up a handful of frigid snowflakes, but nothing gathered in her hand. "I can tell it's smooth."

He thought for a moment. "Like an empty sheet of paper?"

"Yes...I guess. It's just that I can't...feel it."

"Can you come out here?"

Tanya tried to take a step forward. Her body halted, as if an invisible barrier blocked her. "Whu—?" With jittery eyes, she looked at her feet and then at him. "I can't go past the threshold."

Stan re-entered the building, took her hand and led her to a chair. "Tanya, I think we used to be characters in a novel and I somehow came to life, but you stayed the same. That's why you can't leave the library. You only exist in stories. The snow you saw was a blank page of a book. The next chapter in your life. Unwritten."

Her mouth gaped.

"I know, it's too fantastic," he said. "But I found out that Remlap was in the middle of writing a book when he just disappeared."

Her hands trembled. "Do you know the name of the book?"

"*When Ink Bleeds*. He never wrote the ending."

"But what difference does it make? Why does it matter?"

"Tanya, *we* are the characters from that unfinished story. That's why you're losing your senses. You're fading away, I'll prove it to you." He ran over to a bulletin board and pulled out a thumbtack. "Give me your hand."

She shrank away.

"Trust me," he said, calmly taking her palm. With a deft touch, he pricked her index finger. A smear of black liquid oozed from the puncture. Her hand recoiled.

"What the hell!" she exclaimed.

He handed her a tissue. "I was right. It's ink."

She sank to her knees and began to sob. "What is this nightmare?"

Stan held her by the shoulders. "Tanya, we've got to find Nats Remlap."

Her arms went to her sides and she looked up at him with puffy, but hopeful eyes. "So he can finish writing the story?"

"Exactly."

* * *

Jenny knocked quietly on the door. "Hi, it's me again. Can I come in?"

"Of course," Tanya said, putting down the story.

"I need to roll Stan so he doesn't develop bed sores. Fortunately, skinny guys are easy. It's the bigger ones that are, well, you know… "

Tanya stretched her arms. "I don't know how people in the medical profession do it, face sickness every day."

"You get used to it."

"Yes, but still. Doesn't it get depressing?"

"I try to look at it from the perspective that I'm helping people."

"Well, you're good at it," Tanya said, a warm feeling spreading through her chest. "Thank you for everything you've done for the Palmers."

Jenny smiled. "No sweat. How about you?"

Tanya nodded toward Stan. "Been better."

"Oh, right. Sorry, that was stupid of me."

"Don't worry about it."

"Were you two," Jenny's index finger wagged from Tanya to Stan, "seeing each other?"

"No, we're just friends."

"But good ones," Jenny said and tilted her head, admiring the way Tanya looked at Stan. Her eyes crinkled and a contemplative tone seeped into her voice. "I believe good things happen to good people."

Tanya looked up. "Mmm?"

"I mean look at Stan," Jenny continued. "There he was, crushed in that car, bleeding. If that motorist hadn't come along when he did and called the paramedics, Stan probably would have died."

"I should write a letter thanking him for helping," Tanya said. "Stan was always helping others. Maybe you're right. Maybe it was God's way of rewarding him for being a good guy."

"Seems like he has a lot of friends. One of them stopped by the other day."

"Yeah?"

Jenny nodded. "Old football buddy."

"No, you mean baseball," Tanya said. "Stan never played football."

Jenny studied the ceiling. "Pretty sure it was football and this guy was big like a gorilla. He said Stan was quite a hitter. Oh! Maybe he meant a *baseball* hitter and I just heard him wrong."

"Stan was a really good pitcher too," Tanya added.

A pang of sadness hit Jenny as she noticed the forlornness that had draped itself across Tanya's face. "So how do you think Stan will do it?"

Tanya shook back to attention. "Huh? Not sure what you mean. He can't do much of anything."

"Not this Stan," Jenny said. "That Stan." She pointed to the pages in Tanya's hands. "How do you think he'll get the two of you out of it?"

Tanya's mouth opened. "Have you been listening in?"

Jenny's eyes bugged. "We all have. You two are the talk of the floor."

"Whu—?"

"It's okay," Jenny gushed. "We love it and we're all rooting for you. Anything you need, you just let us know. All right?"

Tanya returned a dazed expression. "All right, I guess."

As Jenny left, Tanya returned to the story, a grin on her face.

* * *

Stan climbed on top of the bookcase, removed a panel of the library's drop-ceiling and pulled himself through the opening. A dark and narrow corridor stretched before him. Near the end, a flicker of light licked at the ceiling and walls. He plunged into the gloom, trickling his fingertips along the wall, feeling the spines of books forming a tunnel of literature. Arriving at a window, he peeked into the room.

A modestly furnished office sat in silence: upholstered chairs crouched peacefully in the corners, a portrait of Edgar Allen Poe hung above an antique desk, embers in the fireplace still glowed, and a giant stuffed moose head jutted out from the wall above the hearth. He lifted the pane and crawled over the ledge. There was a sucking noise and the window disappeared, his back now against a floor-to-ceiling bookcase. Then the sound like a swishing garment snapped his head.

"Hello Stan," a woman's voice floated out to him from the darkness. "I always knew you would come."

Stan slithered along the wall and into the shadows. "Who are you?"

A rustling of leather, then heels on the hardwood floor. The barrel of a gun broke the plane of moonlight pouring in through a skylight. The outline of a woman came into focus. She stepped into the light.

He gasped. "Tanya!"

The woman leveled the gun at him. Her throaty laugh filled the room. "Not quite, but you're close. My name is Eileen."

Stan squinted. Facially, Eileen looked remarkably like Tanya. High cheekbones, full lips and petite nose, the seductive eyes, but more wrinkles and graying hair, and not as curvy. Forty years ago however...

"Nats Remlap was my husband." She waved the gun at the chair. "Sit."

"What do you mean *was*?" Stan asked.

She laughed again and strutted to the moose head above the fireplace. Reaching up, she stroked the stuffed animal. "Nats, would you agree that we are no longer married?" She leaned close as if listening to the response. "Yes dear, Stan is very astute, just like I wrote him to be. Like you never were."

"Like you wrote—?" Stan's face puzzled. "What?"

A wry smile formed on Eileen's face. "Nats was not an attractive man. But in his writing, he could be anything." She pointed the gun at Stan. "And look what he created: Stan Palmer. Intelligent, athletic, handsome. Nearly perfect. But his leading lady. What a tramp. So after I slowly poisoned him to death, I rewrote both characters more to my liking. I never liked the name Eileen. I always wanted to be someone exotic, like a Tanya."

A trickle of fear leapt across Stan's scalp. "My God. You're insane."

She whirled on him, eyes ablaze. "You don't know my anguish. Lonely dinners. Forgotten anniversaries. Crying myself to sleep while he wrote. The bastard cared more for his characters than he did his own wife."

Eileen leaned on the desk and cried big tears that splattered on the pages of Remlap's manuscript. "What does that say about me?" She snatched up the papers, crumpled them and hurled the ball of pulp into the fireplace.

Stan moved to get up, but Eileen jammed the barrel into his nostril. "He cared more about you than he did me," she snarled, eyes wild, spittle flying from her mouth. "But I'm in control of his character now." Her finger curled around the trigger. "Goodbye, Stan Palmer."

Fwump.

Eileen's eyes bulged and she staggered forward. The gun fell. She gurgled something unintelligible and collapsed onto Stan's knees.

He shoved Eileen's limp body away and looked incredulously at the dagger embedded into her spine, then toward the bookcase. The wall of books rippled, like a theatre curtain. Now swirling, a whirlpool of brown and gold. A profile materialized. At first pure white, then turning to peach. The shape solidified. Clothes and auburn hair appeared. Stan gawked as Tanya appeared, slightly bent over, the pose of someone having thrown something. She stepped forward, eyebrows singed, her clothes in smoking tatters.

"Goodbye Eileen Remlap," Tanya said and faced Stan. "Good thing you made her cry, isn't it?"

"Couldn't have written a better ending," Stan said and took Tanya in his arms. "The bad girls always get the guy in the end." They kissed.

THE END

* * *

Tanya leaned back in the chair, holding the pages of Stan's story close to her chest. She dabbed at the corners of her eyes with a tissue and stared at him. He lay on his back, head tilted slightly toward her, tubes dripping, monitors beeping and wheezing away.

Her pocket vibrated as her cell phone rang. "Hello?"

"Hi Tanya, it's Fitzy."

"Hey stranger," Tanya said to her former schoolmate. They had become friends in fourth grade when his family moved out of the inner city to the safety of the suburbs.

"Did I catch you at a bad time?" he asked.

"No, this is good. I'm sitting with Stan."

"Oh, how's he doing?"

"Good on the outside," she said, "no idea on the inside."

"Shit."

"Yeah."

Fitzy cleared his throat. "So how are you doing?"

"Hanging in there. You? How's the bar?" Tanya sometimes went to Fitzy's on her day off from the diner. Most times for a drink and to catch up on gossip. But sometimes she just needed someone to talk to. Fitzy was a great listener.

"Same ole. Hey, listen, I'm in the waiting room at the doctor so only have a minute. Something weird happened the other night. A police detective came by the bar asking questions about Stan, thought I should check it out."

"What kind of questions?"

"When was the last time I saw him, did his bookkeeper job require him to work Saturdays. Random stuff."

"What would he want to know that for?" Tanya asked.

"That's what made it weird. I musta asked him that three times and he just kept saying he was just checking on something, real vague like."

"Was that it?"

"No," Fitzy replied. "He asked about what we talked about, when did Stan leave, that kind of stuff."

"What did you tell him?"

"I couldn't tell him anything. Stan came in for a beer, we talked a bit and he left."

"What did the detective say?"

"Nothing."

"What do you mean, nothing?" Tanya said. "He comes in, grilles you and then just clams up?"

"Uh-huh. Said he was sorry, finished his beer and walked out."

"That is weird," Tanya said.

"So you don't know of any reason why Stan might be in trouble?" Fitzy asked. "Maybe something to do with his job?"

"Stan? No way."

"Money?"

"You'd probably know about that better than me," Tanya said.

"No, not really, he's been keeping to himself lately. Doesn't play basketball with us anymore. Rarely see him on poker night. Anything going on with him that I wouldn't know about?"

"Can't think of anything."

"Huh. Okay, well I guess I just needed to talk to somebody about it. Figured maybe you might know. And they're calling me in so I gotta go. Hey, why don't you stop in sometime so we can talk longer?"

"I'd like that, Fitzy. Maybe this week."

"Okay, catch you later." He hung up.

"Bye," Tanya murmured at the phone. She then turned her gaze toward Stan. A surge of emotion ripped through her limbs ejecting her out of the chair and to his side. She pressed her forehead gently to his. The sounds that escaped her mouth were more whisper than words. "What's going on Stan? Did you get yourself into something?"

Chapter 20

Ernie parked the pick-up in the car port under the cabin, tramped up the steps and barged in the door.

Del turned from gazing out the window. "Where've you been?"

"Taking care of something."

"Like what?"

"My garden," Ernie said laughing. "Had some planting to do."

"Plan—" Del's face curled into a wrinkled mess. "What?"

"Never mind," Ernie said and tossed a small log into the fireplace. "Hey, something's been bothering me. How the hell did Palmer know we was here? That has been bugging me ever since we took the girl." He gave Del a long, accusing stare.

Del held his palms up. "Don't look at me."

"He's never been back here before," Ernie said, tugging on his whiskers. "Not that I know of anyway. Nobody knows about this place. Only reason I do is 'cause my dad was friends with old man Sawtrigger and they used it for hunting and fishing. But that was years ago. Ever since they put in the turnpike and cut off the old dirt lane, nobody comes out here anymore."

"Didn't Palmer's father use to work at the saw mill?" Del said.

"Palmer's old man is foreman at Peterson's lumberyard."

"I'm talking before that. If he worked with Sawtrigger, he might have known about the cabin. Hell, Palmer's dad probably even came here with your dad."

"Palmer's old man would never hang out with mine," Ernie said.

"Why not?"

"Because nobody hangs with scuzz, that's why."

"Huh?"

Ernie took off his coat and rolled up the sleeve of his shirt. Dime-sized red circles littered his skin. "Wanna know how I got these burn marks?" He rolled up the other sleeve to reveal several crescent shaped scars. "And these?"

"Shit," Del said. "What happened?"

Ernie sat down. "Compliments of my father." He picked up one of the adult magazines and opened it to the centerfold. "I used to break into his stash of porn." Ernie rubbed his eyes and took a deep breath. "He didn't like that so he used to light up his cigar and brand me."

"Jesus Christ," Del whispered.

"No, not Jesus Christ," Ernie said. "More like Charles Manson. But instead of stopping, I used to do things to get back at him." He licked the centerfold. "I used to whack off into the mags so the pages would stick together so he couldn't read them."

"I'll bet that ticked him off," Del said, snickering. "What would he do?"

The Foiled Knight

"This." Ernie motioned to his other arm. "He used to take his fishing hook and shove it through my skin..."

Del winced. "Holy fu—"

"...then rip it out."

The skin on Del's face went slack.

"Like I was a fish he'd caught that wasn't worth keeping." Ernie hurled the magazine into the fireplace. It ignited into a fireball. "Told me I was worthless and that he wished I'd never been born."

"Nice guy," Del said. "Is that how you got that gash under your eye?"

"Nope, got that one first day of first grade," Ernie said. "Compliments of your ex-wife." He half chuckled at Del's confused look and held up a hand. "True story. Tanya nailed me with her lunchbox."

"Damn. She's as bad as your Dad."

"Nah, no comparison. I started that one. When a man picks a fight, if he gets his ass kicked, he deserves it. But I didn't have to do anything for that asshole of a father to shit on me. He was one nasty mean-ass rotten mother-fucker. One time, I came home and walked in on him banging my girlfriend."

"What! You're full of it."

Ernie held up his hand again. "God's honest truth."

"Was he raping her?"

"Nuh-uh," Ernie said. "That's what's messed up about the whole thing. She'd been doing it with him for weeks. Willingly."

"What a skank," Del said.

"Totally," Ernie said. He got up and wandered to the fireplace. "Turns out she loved it. Said he gave it to her like I never could." Pausing, he reached into the tool cradle for the poker and placed the tip into the coals of the fire. "I couldn't handle it. I freaked out and threw a lamp at him."

"What he do?"

Ernie shrugged. "He went wild. Started whipping me with an extension cord and calling me a faggot. I crawled in a corner to get away, but he just kept coming so I kicked him in the stomach. Man, that sent him into orbit and he got his gun. Practically rammed the barrel up my nose." Ernie went silent for several moments. The muscles in his jaw clenched and his face went to granite. "He shoved me to the floor, tied me up and forced me to watch him do her from behind."

Del said nothing, a gasp of disbelief draped over his face.

"So the next day," Ernie continued, "I sprang in on them while they were doing it in my bed. I bashed him over the head with a shovel. Then I socked her a good one and knocked her unconscious. Gagged and tied both of them up, threw 'em in our pickup and came here."

Del's eyes were wide like fried eggs. "How old were you?"

"Sixteen."

"What did you do to them?" Del asked.

"Check it out. I laid the fishhook treatment on the old man so he could know what that felt like. As for her, I wanted her to remember me as having given her the best sex of her life." By now, Ernie's voice was a haunting drone of empty emotion. He removed the poker from the fire. Its tip glowed a smoldering orange. "And I gave it to her all right."

"Holy mother of God," Del croaked.

"So…yeah," Ernie said. "My father was a twisted piece of shit. And that's why Palmer's father would never want to hang out with him."

Ernie's eyes glassed over and he drifted away. To the insults if he asked for help with homework. To being told to go away when he wanted to have a catch. Being thrown out of the house, stark naked, if he broke a plate. The whiskey breath. Undergarments of other women hanging from the banister. Then the ugly sound of his father's ring hand connecting with his mother's cheek. And the buckle end of the strap if he ever talked back or refused to fetch another beer.

"Living with a maniac does things to you," Ernie said. He remembered digging the hole in the woods. Deeper than normal. And then throwing in a bucket of fish bait before dumping in the bodies.

And smiling.

Chapter 21

The late afternoon sun sank rapidly behind the main office of Peterson's Lumberyard, dropping the temperature another five degrees. A whipping wind turned the aisles of stacked lumber into blustery tunnels.

Fenton steered the forklift around the corner of the warehouse and under the canopy. With a deft hand, he navigated the turns, eased close to the wall and lowered the dual tongues, setting his load onto timber runners. He turned the engine off, reached for the clipboard and recorded the delivery.

Coming on quitting time, the parking lot emptied quickly as customers and employees departed. Fenton liked the yard at the end of the day. Quiet and peaceful, like the day after Christmas. Gone was the buzz of the saw blade, its raging replaced by the muffled applause of string pennant flags and the soft whistle of wind through the rafters. And messy, like after a good party. Remnants of string and paper receipts tumbled across a carpet of sawdust. And the smells. Mother nature's reminder of the beauty only she can produce. Mahogany's musk and the sweetness of hickory. Syrupy pine, oak's pepper and the richness of cedar. The aromas filled his nostrils and he breathed them in deeply while flexing aching muscles. Another solid day of work at the yard.

He jumped off the forklift and yanked down the retractable aluminum door before trudging across the asphalt parking lot. Up the wooden steps and through the doors of the office. Kicked off his metal-toed boots and opened his locker. Tossed the worn leather gloves inside, hung his hard-hat and goggles and sat down on the bench. A black and white photo, taped to the inside of the locker door, stared out at him. A much younger Fenton stood shaking hands with Jim Peterson, the owner of the lumberyard. On Fenton's shoulders sat a young Stan, his arms raised in the air, a beaming smile on his face in celebration of his father's promotion to foreman.

For thirty years, Fenton had worked at the yard. Good years too. Honest and worthy. Never high paying, but enough to cover a mortgage, take Sandra to a nice restaurant once in a while, and get Stan through college. Jim was a good boss. Firm and fair. One knew where they stood with Jim and Fenton liked that. No mind games, just work. Sure they had fun, like who could do the best imitation of a cow mooing over the PA system or playing broomstick ball behind the warehouse. On Saturdays, Sandra would drop off Stan during lunch hour to pitch to the guys. Jim didn't mind as long as the work got done and customers were satisfied. Fenton knew pizza lunches on the boss' nickel were never a coincidence. A happy workforce produced.

He pulled the laces tight on his Timberline hiking boots, then made a sweep around the office, turning off the lights and locking all doors. Glanced at his watch: 6PM. He made for the car. He'd told Sandra not to expect him; that he would eat at the diner where Tanya worked.

As a way to say thank you for being so helpful during the tragedy, he stopped and picked up a box of chocolates. The discussion at the restaurant had ended awkwardly. He and Sandra had discussed the situation and agreed it wasn't Tanya's fault Stan had selected her to make medical decisions on his behalf. Hopefully, she would accept the gift.

Once out of the parking lot, he shifted his 4-wheel drive Blazer into gear and sped down Easton Road to the diner. The Palm Grille Diner, an Abington attraction during its early years, had degraded over time into a bad greasy spoon. The parking lot was littered with potholes and the building's once silver exterior now pocked with rust marks where kids had thrown rocks. The neon sign blinked sporadically as did the interior fluorescent lights that could not be seen through the smudged windows.

Fenton pulled into a parking spot between two salt-splattered pick-up trucks and went inside. The smell of meatloaf filled his nostrils as he passed through the door. Fifties-style booths with red leather seats and miniature juke boxes lined the windows. Patsy Kline's *Crazy* wafted in the air. The ting of spatulas on grilles of stainless steel mixed with clinking plates, glasses and silverware as dishwashers struggled to keep up. Turning right, he glanced at the faces of patrons as he looked for his party. The recently mopped floor was slippery and he skidded rounding the corner to the back section when he spotted arms waving in the air.

"Yo, Fenton." Kurt Davis, wearing a green Eagles sweatshirt, got out of a booth and walked toward him, hand extended. "How've you been?"

"Hey bud, good to see you." They shook. "Thanks for meeting me."

"You bet," Kurt said. "Take a load off. How's things at the yard?"

"Fine." Fenton hung up his coat and sat opposite Kurt. "Busy. How about you?" He placed the box of chocolates on the seat and shoved them to the side.

"Same old, same old," Kurt said. "When are you going to retire? You've been working for Peterson for what, a hundred years?"

The lines at the corners of Fenton's eyes crinkled. "You've been teaching high school biology longer than that. Tell me again what kind of student Abe Lincoln was?"

Both men smiled wryly. Fenton held out a clenched fist.

Kurt bumped Fenton's fist with one of his own. "Heh. I hear you brother."

A waitress came by with coffee and took their order.

After she'd left, Kurt spoke. "How are you and Sandra holding up?"

"We're slugging our way through it; she's handling it better than me."

"Sandra is one tough cookie," Kurt said. "I think she and Laura were cut from the same cloth." He added three packs of sugar to his coffee and stirred. "They're the best things to ever happen to us. Without them, we'd be nothing but two piles of dog crap. I can't imagine what you must be feeling, but you gotta stay strong."

"I'm trying, man," Fenton said, frisking his hands together. "I really am trying. But it's tough."

"What's the latest on Stan?"

"We had good news the other day. Externally, he's healing just fine, looks much better. And the docs did a good job patching him up inside too. The

The Foiled Knight

question now is his brain. No one can predict whether he'll wake up or not."

"Huh, that's tough."

The two men went quiet, trying to think of something to say. They each reached for spoons at the same time, paused, stirred, another pause before dual clinks on the top of their mugs detached any residual coffee, another pause, now a nervous glance at each other. Both spoons met their respective napkin.

"So was there something on your mind that you wanted to meet for dinner?" Kurt asked.

"Yes, something's been bugging me."

Kurt eyed Fenton and the way his forehead twitched. "Those chocolates aren't for me, are they?"

Fenton's lips formed into a thin line. "No." He rapped the table with weather-worn knuckles. "Sandra and I had dinner with Tanya the other night. We talked about Stan's will."

"I knew it," Kurt said, leaning back. "Tanya told Laura and me about it. Must've been an awkward conversation."

"You can say that again. I figured I'd bring her something."

"Okay, I'll buy that," Kurt said. "But you should hold onto them for a bit."

Fenton's face showed puzzlement.

Kurt spread his palms. "The tough part is yet to come, isn't it?"

"That's true," Fenton said, bowing his head.

"Is that why we're here? You want me to influence Tanya about Stan?"

Fenton stayed quiet for several moments. His forehead rippled some more as he played with the salt and pepper shakers. "Yes."

"You know I can't do that, Fenton. You know how close they were."

"*Are*," Fenton snapped. His eyes were hard.

"Sorry, how close they are. But Stan entrusted her with this responsibility."

"But—"

"I can't interfere."

"You could—"

"No. There's a reason why he did that, Fenton. And you should respect that. I just can't."

Fenton sat back, his cheeks bulging with a buildup of air. He let it out in a gust. "You're right. I don't know why I even asked."

"Hey, I don't blame you. I'd feel the same way. Gotta be frustrating."

"You have no idea," Fenton said. "He just lays there."

Reaching across the table, Kurt braced Fenton by the shoulder. "Let me ask you something. Have you actually sat down and talked to Tanya about where her head is at on all of this?"

"No, Sandra and I figured we'd wait for the doctors to do all they can. Maybe we're in denial. We're still hoping they can bring him out of it."

Kurt let go his grasp. "And? What's your gut telling you?"

Fenton took a long time to answer, then shook his head.

"Well! To what do I owe this wonderful surprise?"

Both men turned to see Tanya, dressed in her waitress-blues, carrying their food. Her white sneakers squeaked on the damp floor. She set their plates down, leaned across the table and kissed Kurt. "Hi, Dad."

"Hi sweetheart," Kurt replied, grasping her hand.

"Hello Mr. Palmer, long time no see." Her eyes dipped as she adjusted her apron.

"Hello, Tanya," Fenton said and picked up a fork and scooped some mashed potatoes. "How are you?"

"Fine. Didn't expect to see you two here together, what's up?"

Fenton didn't answer. Drove his fork into the meatloaf and shoved a bite into his mouth.

"Just two friends having dinner," Kurt said.

Tanya glanced from one man to the other. "Uh-huh." She toyed with her ponytail.

Several long seconds ticked by.

Finally, Fenton stirred and reached for the candies. "Here Tanya, these are for you."

She took them, her eyes quizzical.

Fenton shrugged. "Sandra and I wanted to say no hard feelings about the other night." He hoisted another fork-full and tipped it into his mouth.

"Oh. Okay. I mean, um, you didn't—"

Kurt cleared his throat and gave her a look.

"Thank you," Tanya said quickly.

"You're welcome," Fenton said.

Kurt slid over in the booth. "Here Tanya, take a break."

She sat down. "So, do you think we'll get more snow anytime—" She stopped as Kurt elbowed her. She glared at him.

He glared back, motioning with his head ever so slightly toward Fenton.

She widened her eyelids in response. "Mr. Palmer," she said, "I've been meaning to talk to you about something."

The fork in Fenton's hand snapped decisively against the plate as he chopped off a huge chunk of meatloaf.

Tanya looked at her father who nodded. "I'd like to come over some time and discuss what to do about Stan. Would that be all right with you and Mrs. Palmer?"

Fenton crammed the meatloaf into his mouth and chewed. And chewed. After several moments, he reached for a napkin and wiped his hands, eyebrows arching, forehead twitching, never once looking at Tanya.

"We need to," Tanya said more firmly.

Still Fenton said nothing.

Kurt flicked a pack of sugar at him.

Fenton's eyes fired up at Kurt, then softened as he leaned back. "Yes, you're right. We need to discuss it."

"Great, I'll come by one night this week."

A nod of the head from Fenton. He squirmed in his seat, then reached for the pepper.

"Excellent," Kurt said. "I'm glad we got that out of the way."

Fenton cleared his throat. "Me too."

"Good news about Stan, huh?" Tanya said. "I thought he looked good."

"Yes, I was glad that we are seeing some improvement," Fenton said.

The Foiled Knight

"Especially for Sandra."

"A friend of Stan's stopped by," Tanya said, then she laughed.

"What's so funny?" Kurt asked.

"Jenny, the attending nurse on duty, she got it wrong. Thought the guy said he was a football buddy of Stan's. Said Stan was a good hitter."

"Stan was a lousy hitter," Fenton said.

"What do you mean?" Tanya said. "I watched him play. I thought he was a good player."

"He was good," Kurt interrupted, "at pitching. But hitting? Well, let's just say it…"

"It wasn't his best thing," Fenton finished. "I would've liked to have talked to one of his teammates. What was his name?"

Tanya shrugged. "Don't know, didn't leave a name."

"Huh, odd. What did he look like?"

"I don't know, I wasn't there. Jenny said he was a big guy. Like a gorilla." She looked at her father, then at Fenton. "Do you know any of Stan's friends?"

"Sure, I know some of them," Fenton said. "But that doesn't ring a bell."

"Oh well, what difference does it make?" Tanya said.

Fenton leaned back. "It doesn't."

"Better get back to work," Kurt said to Tanya. "Before you get in trouble."

"I don't really want to."

"Go on."

"Dad, I'm allowed to talk to customers. It's actually good for business."

"Tanya," Kurt started, an edge to his voice.

Fenton cut across him. "Police came by our house the other day."

Both Tanya and Kurt swiveled toward him.

"A detective," Fenton continued. "Asked me some questions about that missing girl, Holly Mathews."

"What's that got to do with you?" Tanya asked.

"Nothing really," Fenton said. "Their investigation had dried up. They were checking out a random possibility."

Kurt arched an eyebrow. "Random?"

"Yes, something unusual happened the night she disappeared which also happens to be the same night as Stan's accident."

"So?"

"So the 911 call Stan made came in around the same time as when the Mathews girl was last seen."

"I don't get it," Tanya said.

"I do," Kurt said. "The police were hoping maybe Stan saw something related to the kidnapping."

"Right," Fenton said. "But they didn't know about his—"

"Wait, what?" Tanya said. "Stan made a call the night of his wreck?"

"Yes," Fenton said. "From the accident."

"How?" Tanya asked. "He was hurt."

Fenton shrugged. "The detective listened to the tape. He said there was only part of a phrase that was understandable."

Both Kurt and Tanya leaned close.

"All they could make out," Fenton continued, "were the words 'in the woods.'"

Tanya's mind whirled to her conversation with Jenny at the hospital. "But that's impossible."

"Why?" Kurt said. "The accident was on Terwood Road. It cuts right through the woods."

"Because it wasn't Stan who called the paramedics," she said. "Jenny told me another motorist who came upon the scene, some man, made the call."

Everyone paused for a moment to process the statement.

"That's right," Kurt said, nodding. "They both called. Stan probably tried right after the accident, but was too injured to finish it. This other guy Jenny told you about made another. Two calls."

"Oh," Tanya said. Her shoulders fell. "Didn't think about that."

"Makes sense to me," Fenton said, "but what doesn't make sense to the police is what was Stan even doing way over on the east side of town? He was coming to our house for dinner so—"

"—so why didn't he take Easton Road?" Kurt said.

"Exactly," Fenton said.

"Oh, God," Tanya shuddered. "The police think Stan did it!"

"That's crazy," Kurt said.

"Just the other night," Tanya said, "a policeman asked Fitzy a whole bunch of questions about Stan."

"I told them to do that," Fenton said. "Because of the 911 call, they wanted to know where Stan was right before the accident. I didn't know, but Fitzy had mentioned he talked to Stan earlier that night."

"What did Fitzy tell them?" Kurt asked Tanya.

"Nothing. That Stan stopped in for a quick beer and left."

"It's still crazy," Kurt said.

"Yeah, maybe to us," Fenton said. "And they might get desperate and look for someone to blame, but I didn't get that sense."

"How'd you leave it with the detective?" Kurt asked Fenton.

Fenton lifted the pepper shaker, then set it down gently. "That was their last lead. It's over, case closed."

"You mean they're not going to look anymore?" Tanya asked.

Fenton shook his head. "They might put something in the paper, ask for the public's help, but it's been weeks. The chances that she's still alive are—"

Spatulas tinged and glasses clinked as he let the words hang there.

Chapter 22

"I wonder how often they change his sheets," Sandra said sinking down into the chair by Stan's bed, crossing her legs at her ankles.
Tanya glanced toward Stan. "Every couple days."
"Better not be. If this were *my* hospital, they'd be changed every day."
"Well, Jenny checks his IVs and all that stuff every day."
"I like that Jenny," Sandra said. "She's nice."
"But firm. Have you noticed how she gets on that medical assistant?"
"They squabble like Fenton and me," Sandra said and gathered up the cards strewn on the table. "Another hand?"
"No, I can't keep my eyes open."
"Want to get some coffee?"
"No thanks," Tanya said. "I've had two cups already. If I drink any more, they'll hook me up to a catheter."
"Heh, welcome to the world of weak bladders. And it only gets worse as you get older."
"Want me to get you a cup so you can be alone with Stan?"
"You're a sweetheart for offering," Sandra said, "No, it'll be good for me to stretch my legs, but why did I have to mention weak bladders because now I have to go again." She set the cards down. "Be back in a few. I'll pick up the newspaper on the way."
She had only been gone a minute when there was a knock at the door.
Dr. DeAngelis breezed in. "Just want to take a quick look at Stan's chart. I want to look into some stimulation tests." He paused to examine the clipboard. "And everything looks good."
"I've been reading to him," Tanya said.
"I've heard. It's good for him."
"Good for me, too."
"Keep it up," DeAngelis said smiling, then paused noticing a vase of flowers on the window ledge.
"Oh," Tanya started.
"It's okay," DeAngelis said. "Sandra called me. Stan's healed up nicely so I said it would be all right."
"Good."
"Gotta go," DeAngelis said. "Take care." He swooshed out of the room.
Sandra returned a short while later, newspaper and coffee in hand.
"You just missed Doctor DeAngelis," Tanya said.
"Did he say anything?"
"No, he just laid there, beeping and wheezing. Kinda like that old station wagon he used to drive."
A blank look cast upon Sandra's face. She swiveled to stare at Tanya. "Not

Stan, silly. The doctor. Did the doctor say anything?"

Tanya jerked. "Huh? Oh!" Her faced flushed.

Sandra smiled warmly and squeezed Tanya's shoulder.

"I can't believe I said that," Tanya said. "Maybe I do need coffee."

"You're a dear," Sandra said, waving a hand. "I remember that old station wagon. Used to drive Fenton bonkers. Dripped oil all over the place. Every time you hit a bump, you swore your butt would fall through the floor and scrape the roadway." She held Tanya's hand. "Oh, and the looks on your faces when the two of you came home without it after the prom—"

"—at dawn, four hours late," Tanya injected.

"—sopping wet and with filthy feet," Sandra added.

"—in stolen clothes that didn't fit us."

"I'll never forget what Fenton said when he noticed neither of you in your prom attire." Sandra buried her forehead into her palm and started to giggle.

Tanya made her voice deep as she went into her best Fenton Palmer impression: "'Holy Mack-a-noly, I see proms just aren't as fun as they used to be. Hello Tanya, Irma la Douce called, said she wants her dress back.' And then to Stan: 'dude, where's the car?'"

Sandra broke into a nervous mixture of crying and laughter. "To hear Fenton say 'Dude' was priceless."

"I know," Tanya said. "And I was like, who the heck is Irma la Douce? I thought we were in so much trouble."

"Never," Sandra said, shaking her head. "If I told you the story of Fenton's and my prom, you kids would never respect us ever again."

Tanya's eyes widened. "Mrs. Palmer!"

"Oh, shush, it wouldn't be appropriate to tell you while my son lays there in a coma. But enough foolishness. What did the doctor have to say?"

"Said something about a stimulation test for Stan. I said okay."

Sandra nodded. "He mentioned that might be the next thing they try. Did he want to speak to me?"

"Mmm, no, didn't sound that way."

"All right, then I'm going to go. Fenton will be home soon. We might stop back after dinner."

"Okay," Tanya said. "You don't happen to have another story for me to read to him, do you? Doctor DeAngelis said it's good therapy."

"How'd you like the first one?" Sandra asked.

Tanya kicked off her boots. "I loved it. And so did everyone else." She relayed how the hospital staff had listened in.

"Glad we could be of service," Sandra said, handing over the newspaper. "Here, best I can do."

Tanya snapped the crisp pages open and quickly scanned the headlines. "Flyers won last night."

"That's nice. Anything about the weather?"

"Hmm, looks like more snow on the way. Better get to the grocery store and stock up on milk."

"And toilet paper," Sandra chuckled. "People can be such idiots."

A frown creased Tanya's face. "Ugh. Listen to this. There's a follow-up

The Foiled Knight

story on the young girl that was reported missing."

"The police stopped by and talked to Fenton about it."

"I know, he told my dad and I about it."

"What's it say?"

"'...last seen the night of the storm,'" Tanya read. "'Walking home from the Keswick movie theater. Police are asking anyone who might know anything to call the hotline.'"

"Oh dear. Did they give a description of the girl?"

"There's a picture." Tanya held the newspaper so Sandra could view the photo of a pretty young girl with freckles.

"Do the Police have any leads?" Sandra asked.

"It says she may have been tricked into getting into a stranger's car."

"Good God. What a treacherous world we live in. That's why Laura and I always taught you kids to—"

"—Never go anywhere with anyone we didn't know," Tanya interrupted.

"Exactly," Sandra said. "Parents always give the wrong advice of 'don't talk to strangers.' Well, that's just silly. You have to talk to people every day. Just don't *go* anywhere with them, that's the right advice. I hope they find the poor child, but I can't think about that right now. I've got my own problems."

Tanya came up behind Sandra and caressed her shoulders. "I'll be here when you get back."

"You hear that Stan?" Sandra said. She caressed her son's cheek. "You won't be alone."

Tanya leaned forward, resting her head between Sandra's shoulder blades and wrapped her arms around the elder woman.

"He's lucky to have you for a friend, Tanya."

"I'm lucky to have him."

They stood in silence, each lost in thought.

"Mmm," Sandra said. "I probably shouldn't ask, but this whole ordeal has me wanting to flush all the bullshit in the world and just speak my mind."

"What is it?" Tanya said, a slight queasiness gurgling her stomach.

Sandra turned with a troubled, but earnest gaze. "Tanya honey, why didn't you and Stan ever get together?"

"Oh, God."

"You know each other so well. So much in common."

"Mrs. Palmer—"

"You've helped each other through the worst of times."

"That's not true," Tanya said, her eyelashes beginning to flutter.

"What? I've watched you both grow up. I've seen how you two come to life when you're around each other."

Tanya massaged her forehead then hooded her eyes. "Please don't."

"You complement each other's strong and weak points. You're like... reflections in the mirror."

"That was another life."

"Now there's bullshit. If ever there were two people meant to be together, it's you two."

"Not really, I don't know. At one time. Maybe. But things change."

"How?"

Tanya breathed heavily and brushed fallen hair away from her face. "There's so much you don't know. We were so young." She sighed as her face fell. "Living fire begets cold, impotent ash."

"What's that from?"

"It's a quote from a book we read in high school. *Things Fall Apart* by Chinua Achebe." Tanya sniffed and set her jaw.

"What could possibly have happened to—"

Tanya shook her head violently. "Things were said. And done. Things that can't be taken back."

Sandra stared, puzzled. "Does this have to do with your dancing—"

"Please don't ask, it'll only rip open old wounds."

"But—"

"Please, Mrs. Palmer."

"I just—"

"Please!"

Sandra slumped. "All right, I'll let it go." She grabbed her coat, stood a flustered moment, turned to go, then stopped, kissed Stan on the forehead and left.

But Tanya couldn't let it go. A pang of want crawled into her stomach. Up until a certain point, it could have happened, she and Stan could have gotten together. But after college, nothing was the same.

It had been the Tuesday before Thanksgiving of her senior year. Stan had driven up from Furman University to give her a ride home for the holidays. Furman was not far from Elon. She remembered looking out the window, seeing him arrive at Good Shepherd House, the all-girl sorority house.

There had been a party. Girls wearing grass skirts used the couch for a trampoline. Beer sloshed over the sides of their mugs as they sang at the top of their lungs. A Frisbee soared through the air, interrupting a couple kissing by a poster of tanned male body builders. A boy lay passed out in a sudsy puddle, his head covered by women's underwear, his fingernails painted optic pink.

Tanya's room was on the third floor, measurably smaller than the lower floors and less riotous. She remembered his knock and unlocking the door.

"It's open," she said and crawled back to bed.

Stan pushed into a chamber of chaos. Clothes hung from open drawers. A lamp lie flickering in the corner. Beer cans littered the floor. Text books were piled carelessly before the computer monitor. Against the bureau leaned an empty wine bottle covered by a lampshade. A poster peeled from the far wall next to a bunk bed that was a shambles of blankets, pillows, magazines, candy wrappers, tissues and a spilled carton of Buffalo wings. Stan took a step closer to the bed and spotted Tanya in the shadows, bundled in flannel pajamas, rainbow socks drooping, the hood of her Elon sweatshirt pulled over her face.

Stan dragged over the desk chair, tossing away a pair of ballet shoes draped over the back. "Teedy, what's the matter?"

A moan, followed by a nose blowing. "You don't want to know."

"Hey, I'm here to take you home. Aren't you glad to see me?"

She tried to sit up, but her elbows slipped. Her skull banged on the

The Foiled Knight

headboard. "Ouch. Shit." She removed the hood. Stan drew in a sharp breath.

Tanya's eyes were red and puffy. Snot dribbled from her nose. Chapped lips bled. Her hair was in greasy tangles and she smelled like dank laundry.

"You're totaled," Stan said.

"No doubt about that." She drained the remainder of a beer. Her arm fell from the bed and hit the floor. The can rolled away, a dead soldier in a tiny aluminum barrel.

"Great. We got eight hours in the car and you go and get plastered."

"Lay off," she said. "What are you my mother?"

"No, your chauffer, but you just demoted me to nanny."

"Well, Happy Thanksgiving to you too."

"Whatever," Stan said. "Just sleep it off in the backseat. I'll drive."

She shook her head. "I'll puke."

"We'll bring a trash can."

"Didn't pack," she said, waving at the room. "Can't you tell?"

Stan scanned the room, intently studying things more closely. A thermometer stuck out of a plastic cup on the shelf behind her. "Are you sick?"

"You could say that," she cackled, then snorted while reaching for a tissue. Missed. He snared one for her. "Thanks," she mumbled.

"What have you got? Flu?"

"Wouldn't that be great," she said and blew her nose loudly.

Stan's face scrunched. "What? Teedy, what the hell is going on with you? I can't tell if you're drunk off your ass, on the rag, or got Bubonic Plague."

She threw the covers off and tumbled from the bed. "Don't feel so good." She stood, took a few wayward steps toward the bathroom, then careened sideways into the closet. Hangers clanged together in a cacophony of tangled drunkenness. After a few seconds of silence, she spoke in a meek voice. "Stanny, help me."

Stan strode to the edge of the closet. Amidst the dirty laundry, shoes, and hanging clothes lay Tanya, hair strewn across her face, chin smashed into her chest, one leg curled uncomfortably beneath her.

"Ah, Teedy, why did you do this to yourself?"

From the depths of the shadows, Tanya's hand reached out to him. It wavered in mid-air, a lonely vine searching for its trellis. "Please Stanny, I think I'm going to be—" She turned her head and threw-up into a shoebox.

The sound of it splattering brought a cringe to Stan's face. Yet he made no move. Standing silently, he watched as her body wretched. After a few moments, the convulsions stopped, replaced by moans and spitting.

"You okay?" Stan said.

A groan in response. Then the sound of lungs sucking air and quiet sobbing. A vomit covered hand crawled across the rug to Stan's shoe.

Stan leaned into the closet. A raunchy smell like that from a trash dumpster hit him full in the face. He ignored it along with the crimson colored oatmeal mush that clung to her hair. "Augh, what were you drinking tonight?"

"Wine mostly."

"Let's get you outta here." He pulled her up and led her into the bathroom.

"Where we going?"

"Get you cleaned up. We're not going anywhere tonight."

He propped her against the wall, holding her with one hand while reaching in to the shower to turn knobs with the other. While the water heated up, he stripped her to her undergarments.

"Get in," he commanded.

She turned her head toward the sound of the water and lunged for the curtain rod, but snared the shower curtain instead. The sound of vinyl ripping was followed by a *konk* as she keeled face first into the tub. Metal rings clattered across the floor.

"Ah, for Pete's sake," he muttered and climbed in with her.

She flopped against him. "Please don't hate me."

He rubbed her hair furiously to dislodge the muck. "I don't hate you."

"Yes you do." She grabbed the bar of soap and began washing his back.

"You're not helping," Stan said, forcibly removing the soap from her hand.

"You think I'm a slob." She turned an open mouth toward the showerhead, gathered a mouthful, then spit a stream of water into Stan's face. "Ut-oh, shouldn't have done that."

"You're not a slob," he said, "but you *are* being a royal pain in the ass."

"Told you you hate me."

"If I hated you, I wouldn't be here." He shut off the water and manhandled Tanya out of the tub, wrapping her in a towel. "Come on, you need to sleep this off." He guided her back to the bed. While Tanya leaned against him, he rummaged through her bureau and found pajamas. "Here. Get out of that wet stuff. I'll go in the bathroom while you change."

"What about you? You're soaking wet."

"I'll be fine," Stan replied and fished out a pair of maroon sweatpants from the bureau. "These will do." He held up a gold T-shirt. "And, unfortunately for me, we're the same size." He darted to the bathroom.

"Gonna crash over at the boy's dorm?" Tanya said as she changed.

"No," he called out. "I'm going to make sure you don't flip onto your back. If you throw up again, you might clog your airway and fry your brain."

Tanya shuddered. "Ugh."

"Exactly. Machines keeping you alive, tubes coming out of every orifice, all you do is lay there like a piece of broccoli."

"If that happens," Tanya said, "just shoot me."

Stan emerged from the bathroom and sat on the floor. "I hear you. Would you do the same for me?"

"Never."

"There's no way I'd want to be kept alive like that. Artificially I mean."

"I know, but I—" she paused for a moment and looked as if she might vomit again, "—couldn't do it."

A lengthy silence engulfed them.

"Hey Stan?" Tanya said. "Any chance I can talk you into sleeping next to me? I would really like to fall asleep with your arm around me."

"Promise to keep your hands off me?" Stan asked.

"I promise, if you promise to keep me off my back."

Stan moved to climb onto the bed. A crunching sound caused him to jump.

"Damn all these beer cans," he said and kicked aside dancer's leggings to reveal a glossy white cardboard box with a Johnson & Johnson logo. He snatched it up. "What's this?"

Tanya's trembling hand hid her eyes.

"Is this what I think it is?" He turned the box over and studied the diagrams indicating positive or negative.

She said nothing.

He grabbed her arm. "Answer me."

She turned away from him.

"Oh my God, you're pregnant."

Still more silence, but after a moment she nodded.

He let her go. "Is it Del's?"

Her head snapped at him. "Who the hell else's would it be?"

Stan recoiled at the ferocity of her voice. "Whoa, I didn't—"

"Yeah, you did. You think that I screw anybody and everybody. Well I'm not a slut, and I don't need you making accusations."

"Hey!" Stan barked. "I didn't mean it like that. And go to hell for taking it that way. How long have you known me? When have I—"

"You never liked Del." She sniffed. "Ever."

"Why'd you get back with him? He's an idiot."

She wiped her nose with her sleeve. "He is not."

"Yeah he is, Teedy. Is he the one who talked you into going all the way?"

"He said he loves me."

Stan's eyebrows rose. "You always said you'd wait till you were married."

"Stupid notion," Tanya said. "Everybody's doing it."

"Since when do you give a shit about what everybody else is doing? When everyone else was doing pot and cocaine, you didn't. You always thought for yourself. What did he do to change your mind? Did he lay some guilt trip on you that he," Stan made quotation marks with his fingers, "has needs?"

"Listen to you," Tanya spat. "Mister holy man. You sayin' you don't have 'em? Needs?"

"Don't compare him to me. I would never put you at risk just to satisfy something I could take care of with my hand."

She threw the covers off and stormed across the room. "Who the hell do you think you are?"

"Your friend."

"I need more than that. Del loves me."

"Right. Did he wear a condom?"

"No, he said—"

"—that he didn't need it anymore, that it made it better for him."

She went quiet. "Yes."

"See?" Stan said. "*His* pleasure. Forget about what it means for *you*."

Tanya kicked at a beer can.

"Does he know?" Stan asked.

"I called him this morning."

"So where is he? Where is he when you need him most?"

She looked around confusedly. "He's, he's—"

"Not here," Stan finished.

They were silent for several moments, the only sound the alternating gusts of their breathing.

"I'm keeping it," Tanya said.

"What about your dancing?"

She hesitated. "I can do both."

"How can you possibly tour with a dance company with a baby?"

"I'll take him with me."

Stan punched the wall. "You haven't thought this through. You haven't got any money; where will you live? Is Del going to marry you? I doubt it. Even if he did, what kind of job will he ever have? He can't keep the one he has now and all he's doing is pushing a broom. So you can forget dance because you're going to have to find a job. Who's gonna look after little Del while you're at work? Your mom? That wouldn't be fair to her. See how it all falls apart? Ask yourself: what kind of life would you have?"

"Better than anything else I've got going on," she said. "He's the only guy that's ever showed interest in me."

"Here we go again," Stan said, massaging his forehead. "You think your life is defined by the man in your life. That the only way to happiness is to be married, even if it's to a loser." He reached for Tanya's hands, but she pulled away. "What do you think life for you and the baby will be like if he abandons you during tough times?"

Tanya's green eyes flared. "He won't." She threw open the door and disappeared into the hall. "He'll change."

"Just like he looked out for you the night of the prom," Stan said, chasing after her. "I know you're obsessed with him. Some kind of misguided mercy, martyr, physical…delusion. You're blind. He doesn't have what it takes to commit to you. Remember how he blew up at those little kids at your parent's house last Thanksgiving? He hates kids. Any idea what it's like to grow up in a house where your father is an abusive louse? It sucks. Ask Ernie McFadden. Is that the life you want for your baby?"

"It won't be like that."

"What's happened to you?" Stan asked. "You're… different. College has changed you. Why did you let this happen?" He stood back. "Were you so fed up with guys acting like you didn't exist?"

Tanya's eyes widened.

"You did, didn't you?" Stan said. "You figured if you started putting out, you could get a guy to like you."

"Go to hell!" Tanya screamed and ran toward the stairs.

He caught her by the arm and pinned her against the wall. "How come you never put out for me?"

Tanya struggled against his grasp. "Ouch, Stan, you're hurting me!"

"Was I so putrid looking? Is that it? I'm not good looking, like Del?"

"No!" The tension in her arms slackened. "Wait. What?"

Stan's voice cracked. "Is that why you never showed interest in me?"

"Don't blame me," she said. "I've *always* been your friend. *You're* the one who never made a move."

The Foiled Knight

"You can't do this, Tanya. You'll regret it the rest of your life. I love you."

"Ha! Where's that been the last four years?" she said. "How come you never told me before?"

"I was scared...you always went for other...didn't think I—"

"Yeah, and now I'm pregnant. Face it, you're too late. Del has plans that will make us rich. You're satisfied with being a measly accountant. You and I can never be more than just—"

His fingers dug in deep. "Don't say it."

"—friends."

"You don't mean that."

"Yes I do. I've found a good looking guy who wants me. I'm going to marry Del and have this baby and make a life for myself."

Rage built up within Stan. A cramping fury scalded his neck compounded by bone crushing pain in his chest. He clawed his shirt, but air would not come to his lungs. Shapes and colors blurred before his eyes. A molten sun exploded in his brain and suddenly everything went white as the muscles in his hands tightened. "Then get out of my life," he said and turned to leave.

"Wait, Stan, don't—" She remembered reaching for him.

Her foot had slipped off the edge of the top step and she stumbled sideways, arms flailing wildly for the railing. She fell into space, tumbling awkwardly down the wooden steps. Halfway down, Tanya's lower leg had slipped under the balusters. There was the sound of a tree branch cracking as Tanya's tibia bone snapped in two, the jagged tip ripping through her skin. The party went quiet as her screeches of pain shook the walls.

Tanya stared at Stan in his hospital bed, rubbing her leg where the scar suddenly itched furiously, and wondered if the incredible pain she remembered rivaled an antler through the chest.

Chapter 23

Ciquero parked in the snow-covered driveway that stretched to what looked like large pine trees.

"My first time here," Ciquero said, "the place looked totally innocent."

Falbo shouldered his tech bag and opened the door. "And now?"

"The place looks creepier than hell," Ciquero said.

"Funny how a different perspective changes everything."

"Cap did a good job of spooking me." Ciquero checked to make sure his gun was loaded, then did a quick assessment of their surroundings. "The place is small to begin with, but because it's set so far away from the street and hidden by trees, you'd almost think it was just a field."

"Remote area," Falbo said, "far away from town, hardly any traffic, plenty of space from the neighbors."

"Like a recluse," Ciquero said and retrieved a nylon bag from the trunk.

They trudged through the snow toward the house, making their own pathway between the trees. Falbo stamped his boots on the front porch where a single Adirondack chair sat next to the peeling screen door. Ciquero walked around the corner of the house.

"Where are you going?" Falbo asked.

"Front door is locked," Ciquero said. "And nobody's home, so I'm gonna try to get in through a window."

Falbo checked the door knob. It wouldn't budge. "You're right."

"That's why I'm the detective."

"Touche," Falbo said with a smirk.

Ciquero checked all of the first story windows. When none would open, he moved to the rear of the house where he found double French doors with small glass panes. He tried the knob. Locked.

Ciquero rummaged through the nylon bag and removed some duct tape. Cutting several strips, he affixed them to the glass pane closest to the doorknob.

"Why didn't you just get a key from the family?" Falbo said.

"If he's our guy, we don't want them to do anything to cover for him," Ciquero answered. "And the law says that if I have a warrant and nobody's home—" he punched the glass; it splintered with a dull crack, "—I can force my way in." He gingerly folded the taped shards and extracted the panel from the frame, reached in and opened the door.

One by one they entered the kitchen, a sparsely stocked room consisting of a skinny stove, a refrigerator, and a tiny sink. A two-person table fit into the corner. The smell of dead air filled their nostrils.

"What do you want me to check first?" Falbo said.

"Find his computer. See if you can access his files."

"Roger that," Falbo said and disappeared toward the front of the house.

The Foiled Knight

Ciquero surveyed the kitchen, making a mental note of the absence of "things". No magnets or pictures on the fridge. No shopping list or phone numbers on a pad. No car keys on a hook. He shifted to the adjoining room, his alert eyes scanning. Hardly any furniture. A table with no chairs, bare walls and nothing on the windows except cheap blinds. He ran into Falbo.

"Pretty small digs," Falbo said. "Nothing much in the front room other than a TV, couch and coffee table. Not even a bookshelf."

"And?"

"And nothing. There's no computer unless you found one."

"Did you check the upstairs?"

"Same thing. This guy's life is pretty drab. Creepy. What about the basement?"

"I think the entrance is where we came in," Ciquero said. He went back to the kitchen and tried the knob of a door to the right of the refrigerator. It opened with a squeal. Their eyes met. "Nobody would ever sneak up on someone down there," Ciquero said. He tried the light switch. Nothing.

"Okay, I'm officially beginning to freak out," Falbo said.

"Come on," Ciquero said, rolling his eyes. He fished a flashlight out of his bag. The bright beam lit up a narrow wooden plank stairwell. Ciquero tested the top step and turned to Falbo. "I think it'll hold us, but if I suddenly cave through into a pit of black oil and the house starts whispering 'Get out', save yourself."

"Very funny," Falbo said as he followed Ciquero down.

They stopped at the bottom landing.

"Here's the fuse box," Ciquero said and opened the metal door. He quickly found the tripped circuit and flipped it back to the "On" position. Light burst about them. Immediately they were transported to another world.

Paintings and a stuffed moose-head adorned the wall to their left. A stone fireplace with a timber mantle spanned the right. Floor to ceiling bookshelves lined the center wall, every inch crammed with tomes. Beneath the stairs, they found an entertainment system complete with wide screen TV and stereo system. A massive antique writing desk dominated the center of the room along with an upholstered chair. On the desk surface sat a pipe rack, a brass lamp with a Kelly-green lampshade, and a computer.

"Talk about night and day," Falbo said. "What a plush writer's den."

Ciquero studied the painting of a man that appeared to be from the 1800s. "Edgar Allen Poe."

From his crime kit, Falbo produced two pairs of latex gloves, pulled on one and tossed the other to Ciquero, then sat at the writing desk and turned on the computer. The large flat screen flickered to life.

"Think you can get in?" Ciquero said, snapping on his gloves.

"As long as he didn't password protect his hard drive, we should be able to access almost everything…and looks like he's not that smart because we are in." A standard desktop with numerous icons and shortcuts blinked on.

"Huh," Ciquero grunted. "Didn't think it would be that easy."

"Most people only password protect their work computer. Where do you want to start?"

"Check his browsing history. Let's see where he went."

"Okay, gimme a sec." Falbo tickled a few keys and clicked through menu options. In moments the screen filled with pornographic images. Falbo leaned back. "Jackpot."

"Holy mother of Christ," Ciquero whispered. He opened a desk drawer and pulled out several adult magazines featuring young girls.

"Woah, this guy is really into child smut," Falbo said.

Ciquero flipped through the pages. "Mmmm."

"Check this out," Falbo said and opened a word processing document. "When It's Right, a short story by Stan 'The Man' Palmer." His eyes widened as he read. "Holy shit, Mike. This guy writes stories about fourteen year-old girls. I think we caught your creep."

"Certainly looks that way," Ciquero mused.

"What's the matter?"

"Don't know." He dropped the magazines into an evidence bag. "Spidey sense is tingling."

"Mike, this is good evidence."

"It's all circumstantial."

"Pretty damning circumstances if you asked me."

"Uh-huh."

"And it's the most we've got so far."

"Exactly."

"What's with you?"

"Nothing," Ciquero said. "Take the mags back to the station. Have them fingerprinted and see if you can trace a subscription. We need to be sure."

"You want me to leave you here?"

"I only needed you in case I couldn't get into the computer. Send a forensics team back to process the scene. We need something that directly ties him to a victim."

"What are you going to do?"

Ciquero eyed a pair of moccasins under the chair, nudged a box of videos and photo albums, and poked at a CD of Vivaldi. "Visit with darkness."

Chapter 24

Tanya parked her 1968 Camaro on the shoulder of Terwood Road, behind shrubs and away from oncoming traffic. She had been chomping at the bit to explore an idea, but her shift at the diner never wanted to end.

Killing the motor, she stared out the window at the winter day. A dreamy stream of pink and orange clouds whispered across the horizon. Yet the road lay barren, a deserted, frozen tundra of snow-covered gravel that twisted along in a dark tunnel through the forest. Terwood was never a busy road, even at rush hour. There were no other cars around leaving her alone with her thoughts. A strong wind whistled, rocking the car gently.

It had been a long time since she had visited the general area that held so many memories for her. The bus accident in fourth grade. Doing backflips into Sawtrigger's Creek. Holding hands with Stan as they walked to the train yard - the day of the dog attack. Hiking with her dad. The post-prom fiasco turned magical. And now this, the scene of Stan's accident. Another blast of wind nudged the car. A calm silence followed and a shiver ran through her frame.

Memories were a funny thing. Some good, some bad. Some easy to forget, while others burned. They were like snapshots in a photo album, only better because the sounds, smells and emotions lived in memories. She leaned her forehead against the side window. And then she realized they kept bringing her back to key moments of her life, and one key person: Stan.

Sandra's probing questions had hit deeper than Tanya wanted to admit. Questions of "why?" that were really challenges of "why not?" Challenges that may have been true if she were honest with herself. Challenges she had no answer for. But more importantly: what was she going to do about it?

Why hadn't she and Stan gotten together? Could pride be that powerful? Or did she refuse to admit her cowardice? He had said he loved her. Even if a last ditch effort, he had said it, meant it. But he hadn't said it since. And though they'd remained cordial toward each other, they had drifted apart. Not totally fallen out. But enough. To the point she didn't really know his state of mind in recent days. Is it possible he'd been swallowed by loneliness, grown distraught? Despondent enough to disconnect himself from society? Devolved into something less than her memory of him? Could there be any microbe of validity to the police's investigation into Stan as a suspect?

"No!" She pounded the steering wheel. "That's not you! I'll prove it."

Taking a deep breath, she forced her mind to change gears. To the diner conversation with her father and Mr. Palmer. Something about it gnawed at her. The detective had been so positive of Stan's words in the garbled 911 call. He couldn't have gotten it wrong, could he? Yes, two people made calls that night, but something didn't seem right. With a head trauma, Stan would have been bleeding, an antler piercing his lung, delirious. She squeezed her eyes shut, trying to chase away the thought of the pain he must have felt. Her hand slithered to her heart and gripped her sweatshirt. She couldn't imagine how he could even punch buttons on a cell phone. Her eyes snapped open.

"Punch buttons?!" she exclaimed. "Forget that!" *He wouldn't have been able to breathe or hardly talk,* she thought. But Stan *had* made a call, there was no disputing that. And the time was right, around seven-thirty, the police had proof. But it still didn't make sense.

Tanya scraped her scalp with tense fingers, then gingerly took hold of the steering wheel. *Focus. It'll come to you.* She closed her eyes again. At first, there were only jumbled images and flashes of a driver education horror film. *Relax. Think about what it must have been like.* She exhaled a long, shallow hiss of air and emptied her mind. Slowly, a curious mix of images began to take shape. Crumpled metal and plastic around a massive tree. White snow swirling like dandruff against black smoke. Lights sporadically blinking. Electrical circuits buzzing and flashing. Motor fluids dripping. The rank smell of battery acid and burning rubber. Pieces of glass falling to the ground. The wind howled again, carrying away the smoke from her vision. And there Stan lay, slumped in the car, bleeding, hurt, unconscious. All went quiet and the car stopped rocking. Calmness settled over her and a thought emerged from the shadows. No way he could have made the call *after* the crash. Her eyes opened. "You made the call *before* the accident, didn't you?" Tanya whispered. "Why would you do that? What was the matter?"

A leaf tumbled across the hood of the car. It drew her eye to the trees lining the road. "And what was happening that you didn't see the deer? The blizzard? Yeah. Okay. Maybe." Out of the car now. She walked along the road for a while before stopping at a gap in the guardrail. "The road to Sawtrigger's cabin," she mused. Looking down, she could make out tire tracks. Huh. She followed them as they dipped down the embankment, temporarily disappearing into the creek and then reappearing back up the other side. Pursed her lips. "And why would you be making a 911 call and say 'In the woods?' Hmm, Stan? What was the emergency? What did you need?"

Donning woolen gloves, Tanya leapt across the gurgling stream and scrambled up the embankment. As she was about to plow through the hedges, she noticed two gaps in them about five feet apart, roughly the width of a set of tires. She knelt and fingered deep tread impressions where the bushes had been squashed to the ground, trampled by thick tires. A truck?

Gashes in a tree to her left drew her attention. Two holes. She examined them closely. The bark had been blasted away from the trunk, the wood beneath still white. Pure. "What the—?"

Tanya zipped up her coat and set off along the path. Twenty steps later she stopped and glanced back at the damaged tree, sure now of what she had seen: bullet holes.

Chapter 25

"Yo!"

Del, asleep on the couch in the cabin, started at the realization of Ernie's fingers snapping in his face.

"Wake up," Ernie said. "We need to talk about how Palmer knew we brought the girl here."

"Huh? Yeah, I mean no," Del said and sat up, rubbing his eyes. "I have no idea how he knew. Maybe he saw you nab the girl and followed you?"

Ernie shook his head. "No way, I was careful to wait till she was on a quiet street." He moved to the fireplace and held his palms out to warm them. "Nope, something must have tipped him off. Or somebody."

"Wasn't me," Del said. "I know how to keep my trap shut. Contrary to what Tanya used to say about me."

"You still pissed at her?" Ernie said. "After all these years? What's the deal, you still hoping she'll take you back?"

"Why the hell are you bringing that up for?" Del asked. He didn't face Ernie when he asked the question. Didn't want to. He already knew the why.

* * *

Del had been a wallflower before he met Tanya. Shy with an undiagnosed learning disability, he struggled in school. His parents cared little for him. Their relationship, one of constant criticism and emotional abuse, inflicted his psyche with low self-esteem.

Even he thought himself a loser. It was Tanya who boosted his confidence when his parents split up which helped him excel in athletics. She taught him how to get over his social awkwardness so the "cool" crowd would idolize him, even if they didn't accept her. He wouldn't have made it out of high school without her tutoring. But she always took it too far, nagging him about never having deep philosophical discussions. It wasn't his fault, they were beyond him. When she asked what he thought about the use of metaphors in a book, his brain buzzed from inner circuitry overload. Go to the museum? What, and look at paint swirls? Show his sensitive side? What was he, some kind of a girly-man?

Their relationship had always been one dimensional—physical. She wasn't the most attractive teen. None of the other guys would go near her freshman year, but he often caught her looking at him, always checking him out. When she started to blossom senior year of high school, they started dating. She had all the right equipment and a willingness to experiment. In the back seat of his car, she scored a perfect ten. At least he thought so. But now that he searched his memories, there was never anything else. No foreplay or intimacy afterwards. There was just...it.

After they were married, they never went out. Not even pizza and a movie. To Del, the perfect Saturday night consisted of a six-pack and the game. Any game. If no game, then the sports channel. At parties, she danced by herself because he was all stumps, content to hang at the keg. She wanted her own bank account and to have a ladies night out once a month. What kind of nonsense was that? But the final straw came when she insisted he take her to see a theater production in New York.

"I'm not going to any ridiculous dance recital," he said.

Her face crumpled in a crestfallen sag of surrender. It was at that moment he knew she had given up on them.

* * *

Del tilted his beer can and took a long deep swallow, finished it, then crushed the can in his hand. "She ain't never taking me back."

"Huh," Ernie grunted, pensively scratching his throat. "Funny the timing of things, you know? Somehow, dip-shit Palmer finds us here, gets in a wreck and lies near dead and all of a sudden," he smiled, "your ex-wife is by his bedside." He stretched out and picked his teeth with a toothpick. "Things that make you go hmmm."

Several seconds elapsed before a flash of understanding registered on Del's face. "What? You think she's got a thing for him?"

"Those two been having a big-time thing ever since grade school, bro."

"That's bullshit." Del stuck out his chest. "She married me."

"Then divorced your ass. And the only reason she married you is she liked the way you smiled." Ernie chuckled to himself. "That and Palmer being a chicken-shit coward." A wistful faraway look entered his eyes and he whispered to the ceiling. "He never even made a play." He thought of all the chances Palmer would have had, but other than the prom, he couldn't think of one instance where Stan had attempted to get with Tanya. And Abington was a small town. Everybody knew everything about everyone else's business. Secrets never remained so for long.

"Think Palmer would have got her if he had made a move?" Del asked.

"Delward, wake up, if Tanya had gone with her heart, instead of her—" Ernie pulled at his crotch, "—you'd have been out in the cold."

"Go to hell, Ernie!"

"Hey, don't be pissed at me. It's the truth…and you know it."

* * *

Del did know it. The signs weren't hard to spot. He just chose to ignore them, at first anyway. The greeting cards that seemed to come at random. On the outer envelope would be cryptic sentence fragments like: "Don't count out the knight in shining foil." or "Never the dogs will bite" or "Choose your lunchbox and prepare to duel!" At first, the cutsie little notes made his head hurt. Who the hell would bother to send such stupid cards? There was never a return address. So Del started taking a steam iron to open and read them before she returned home from work. He never found a name in the cards, but they always made Tanya smile, like she had been whisked away to some secret world where he wasn't invited. And then he found the painting someone had given Tanya years earlier. A painting of a young boy and girl holding hands as they walked barefoot along a dirt path into the sun. She wore pigtails and held a daisy in her other hand. In the corner were the initials "SP".

The Foiled Knight

* * *

Del hurled his beer can into the fireplace. "I hate that asshole Palmer."

"I don't blame you," Ernie said. "I would have kicked his ass a long time ago."

"I know he's the reason why Tanya lost the baby."

Ernie blinked. *"What?"*

"In college. Tanya got pregnant."

"Get the hell outta here."

"No it's true. She messed up with her pills or something."

"Stupid broad," Ernie said.

"You're telling me. You shoulda seen me when she hit me with the news. Man, did I wig out. Got plastered at a bar. Palmer went to see her—"

"Palmer?" Ernie asked. "Went to see her? Like, right after she told you?"

"Uh-huh. Why?"

One of Ernie's eyebrows went up. "Huh. Nothing. Just weird is all. So what happened?"

"They got into an argument. She fell down some stairs and lost the baby."

"Holy shit," Ernie said.

"What? I never told you? She broke her leg something awful. That's why she can't dance no more."

Ernie strode to the table by the window and clipped off another beer, glaring intently onto the clearing below. "How come I don't remember any of that?"

"You weren't here," Del said. "You were in the army."

"Of course it was almost twenty years ago," Ernie said, then his head tilted and a confused look covered his face. "Hey, where the hell did you park?"

Del belched. "By the rock formation, why?"

"You moron, I told you to park this side of it. If somebody comes down the old path, they'll be able to see the truck."

"Oh, shit."

"Yeah, oh shit is right. Get your ass out there and move it." He grabbed Del by the front of his jacket, opened the door, and shoved him into the howling wind.

After the truck had been moved to the carport, Del returned to find Ernie leaning with elbows on the fireplace mantle, eyes alertly following the flickering flames. Del grabbed another beer and flopped on the couch.

"What are you thinking about?" Del asked.

"Tanya. I'm trying to put it together. Can't understand how come I don't remember anything. I mean, yeah, I kinda remember the leg thing now that you mention it, but I never knew nothing about no baby before."

"She never told nobody, not even her parents," Del said.

"Of course she didn't," Ernie whispered. "Hush, hush, avoid the embarrassment." He was silent for several moments, eyebrows dancing. The glow of the fire turned his face orange. It came out as the thought hit him. Whirling, he pointed a finger at Del. "Palmer killed your kid."

"What?"

"You said they argued."

Del's forehead wrinkled. "So?"

"So she was probably trying to get away from his pontificating righteous bullshit. You know what an insufferable altar boy he was." Ernie scratched the stubble along his throat as he paced. "He chases her. They argue some more. She tells him to piss off. He can't take it. Blows his cork and shoves her down the steps."

"Shoves her…what? You don't know that."

"Anyone else see it happen?" Ernie asked.

"No, the party was downstairs. Only time anybody knew there was a problem was when she started screaming like a stupid banshee."

"Why didn't you just punch her in the stomach if you wanted to get rid of the baby?" Ernie said, speaking wistfully to the ceiling again.

"What are you talking about?"

"But making it look like an accident?" Ernie said, his eyes shining bright. "Oh, that was brilliant. You brilliant son-of-a-bitch."

"Who's brilliant?" Del asked.

Ernie turned to Del. "Don't you get it? Palmer was in love with Tanya. Been so his whole life. But if she marries you and has the baby, well, that just blows his whole dream of a storybook romance out of the freaking water."

"You're saying he did it on purpose?"

"That's exactly what I'm saying."

Del went quiet.

Ernie placed an arm around Del's shoulders. "That asshole is the reason why you and Tanya split up, buddy boy. She's probably at the hospital right now, holding his hand, crying: 'Oh Stanley, why didn't you marry me? I miss you so much.'" Ernie paused to watch Del's nostrils flare. A snake-like smile wriggled across Ernie's mouth. He continued in a pathetic voice: "'You were always the one for me, Stanley. Please wake up and take me away from all of this.'"

The veins in Del's neck began to bulge.

"We gotta take him out, brutha," Ernie said. "If that puke Palmer wakes up, not only is he gonna tell the cops about us, but she's gonna run off with him and any chance you had to get back together will be shot to shit. We'll both be screwed sideways."

Del stood before the fireplace, hands flexing into fists. The reflection of the fire roared in his eyes. "We gotta take him out."

Chapter 26

Tanya trudged along the snow-covered road. To her left, nothing but woods and dense foliage. To her right, the mountain, also covered with trees and shrubbery. Behind her, the sun began its dip below the horizon, its rays casting her skinny shadow onto the road before her. The wind screamed, blowing her backwards a step. She made fists and leaned into it, the cold vapors raking her skin like a curtain of broken glass.

She threw the hood of her parka over her head, bent slightly to shield her face from the sting and plowed ahead, one foot in front of the other. Not quite sure where she was going, or even why. What could possibly be out here in this barren wasteland? More trees? The lake? Definitely some deer. Sawtrigger's cabin was used for hunting and fishing. She stopped. What about bears? She glanced about in a nano-second of panic until her father's voice in her head calmed her.

* * *

"The men who come out here hunt quail," Kurt said.

They had been out hiking in the woods on one of her Girl Scout merit badge missions.

"Are there wild animals?" she asked.

"Rabbits and deer, nothing dangerous."

She pointed at the mountain. "Dad, what's that?"

"Sawtrigger's cabin. That's where the men who come here stay."

"Looks neat," she said.

She would never forget the tone of her father's voice as he replied: "Tanya, that place is a coward's castle."

"Huh?"

"They don't come here to hunt and fish, honey. They come here to run away from their lives. Away from their responsibilities."

As a child, she couldn't understand what he meant. But as a woman having experienced a failed marriage, it now made perfect sense. Del was never around. Even when he was, he wasn't. Lost in his sports, basking in memories. Anything to relive the glory days from high school.

When she tried to get him to engage in the relationship, he retreated to his man-cave. Deeper into the reclining chair or off to some boondoggle with the buddies, only to return drunk and wanting one thing. Then treating her so roughly, he often made her bleed. They never talked about her ruined dream of joining a dance company, sharing intimate thoughts was simply beyond his capacity. It hurt worse that he didn't care. What happened to the shy, awkward boy that was so in need of her help?

She signed them up for a pottery class to give them something to do together. He refused to go. It came to a boil when she bought tickets to see *A*

Chorus Line on Broadway for their anniversary. The tickets, having been paid for and non-refundable, would give him no excuse to back out. She was so wrong. He exploded at her for having purchased something "so expensive and ridiculous." The back of his hand across her face was the final straw.

* * *

Tanya rubbed her cheek at the memory and sniffed back a tear. She may not have known why she was tramping in the woods, but at least the 'what' made sense. At least she was *doing* something. Thinking. Searching. Being proactive. Taking some control – something that she desperately lacked in her life. Somewhere out here lay a clue that would help Stan or at least uncover another question that would lead to an answer. At least she was *trying*.

The deeper she plunged into the woods, the more the darkness swallowed her. Other than the wind, the woods lay silent. No airplanes, no honking traffic, no sirens. Just the sound of her plodding feet and tree branches swaying and groaning. A full moon emerged from behind the mountain, replacing the sun that had now fully disappeared. It cast a spooky light on the barren trail of snow. The barely visible remains of tire tracks swerved to the left as they followed the contour of a twenty-foot-high rock outcropping. Tanya stopped abruptly and sniffed. Firewood burning? She quickened her pace.

As the road continued on, she rounded a large cluster of boulders on the right where an opening appeared in the rock wall. She froze in place. There to her right, embedded into the side of the mountain, hid Sawtrigger's cabin, still as rickety as she remembered. On the second floor, a dim light flickered in the side-by-side windows and through a crack in the bottom of the door. She shivered, not from the cold, but from the cabin's evil grin. A vehicle sat parked in the dark shadows of the carport underneath the cabin. She squinted, but in the gloom, the wheeled block of black offered no answers.

Tanya crept forward, careful not to step on anything or trip over a rock. She reached the ramshackle building and grabbed a porch pillar. An owl hooted. The wind blasted through her and she rammed her hands into her pockets. She thought about running back to her car, then reconsidered. Turning left then right, she pondered what to do, then made for the side of the cabin. Around the corner, she found a narrow fissure of a walkway against the mountainside.

Protruding stones forced her to turn sideways to navigate in the constricted space. She stepped over firewood, around trashcans and between hunting traps. Light filtering through gaps in the building guided her way. At the back, a stairwell stretched up to the house. Next to it squatted a beaten shed with a dim bulb dangling from a power cord. A thick, wooden board had been wedged into metal brackets and across the doorway, a crude, but effective lock.

The sound like a twig snapping jerked her head back down the narrow alley. Then a slight moan from her feet. She glanced down and spotted what looked like the end of a ponytail protruding from beneath the door. Tanya dropped to her knees. Her eyes widened. Within a foot of her reach lay a young girl, bound and gagged. The hair on Tanya's neck prickled.

"Pssst," Tanya whispered. "Hello, can you hear me?"

The girl did not move. The wind howled.

"Hey," Tanya said slightly louder.

The Foiled Knight

This time the girl stirred and turned her head toward the sound of Tanya's voice. She tried to speak. Only a muffled mumble made its way through the gag, but the girl's wide eyes screamed a terrified plea for help.

Tanya jumped to her feet and attempted to lift the wooden board from the brackets. Heavier than she thought, it slipped from her grasp and landed on the ground with a thud. Then a shadow rose up on the door before her.

She started to turn. Stars exploded as the battering ram that was Ernie's fist smashed her cheek.

Chapter 27

Kurt stood at the woodpile at the rear of the Davis backyard, tossing firewood into a leather sling, his breath billowing bright white in the moonlight. He inhaled deeply, enjoying the aroma of fires burning in neighboring houses, and the yellowish glow emanating from their windows. And the silence, the peaceful sound of nothing but nature. A rabbit skittered under his neighbors fence. The jangling of the phone hurried him back to the house. Kicking open the back door, he dropped the logs on the mudroom floor and snatched the receiver off the wall.

"Davis residence."

"Hey Kurt, it's Fenton."

"Hey, long time no talk to."

"You busy?"

"Just bringing in firewood," Kurt said, closing the door. "What's up?"

"It's probably nothing, but something about the visit from the police is bothering me. I was wondering if you would go with me to the hospital."

"Why?"

"I can't explain it," Fenton said. "Something about Stan being on Terwood Road during the storm, the emergency call, the missing girl, the coincidence of the timing. I know it sounds wacky, but I just can't shake the feeling that something's wrong."

Kurt halted, then took a seat at the kitchen table. "You think maybe Stan did know something about the missing girl."

"Yeah, I think Tanya was right," Fenton said. "There's no way Stan makes that call *after* the wreck. He must have made it before."

Kurt softly thumped his fist on the table, like an accountant stamping an invoice paid. "Yeah…why would he make a 911 call immediately before his accident unless there was a real emergency?"

"Exactly."

"But why do we need to go to the hosp—wait, you don't think Stan's in some sort of danger do you?"

"Kurt, listen, I don't know, but what if I'm right? What if Stan did see something related to that girl's kidnapping?"

"If he wakes up—" Kurt began.

"—he can identify the creep," Fenton finished.

"And Stan's lying there, defenseless in his hospital bed."

"And remember the other thing Tanya told us the nurse said. About the high school buddy checking up on Stan at the hospital."

Kurt recalled the diner conversation. "That he played football with Stan."

"Yeah, things like that. I mean, come on, would any of your buddies forget what sport they played with you?"

"No way," Kurt said with another thump of his fist, this one a four-knuckled knock that drew a call from Laura Davis in the adjoining room.

"Kurt? What's that banging?"

"Nothing, sweets," Kurt said loudly. "I'm talking to Fenton Palmer."

"Is everything all right?"

"Tell you in a minute."

"The nurse said the guy was big, like a gorilla" Fenton continued. "I think I know who it was."

"Who?"

"Remember Ernie McFadden, Bart's kid?"

The image of a goon in a prom tuxedo flashed before Kurt's eyes. *Thump-thump.* "Yeah, Bart that you used to work with."

"Bart that was an asshole," Fenton said.

"Passed it on to Ernie, from what I remember," Kurt said. "Didn't he get busted for indecent exposure in a girl's restroom or some shit like that?"

"I think he beat it in court."

"Still, not much of a leap to go from peeping to snatching."

"You think I'm crazy?" Fenton asked.

Kurt frisked his buzz haircut. "No, but why not just call the police?"

"Already tried that," Fenton said. "They told me I'm just being paranoid."

"Tanya is with Stan now," Kurt said. "I'll call her and have her give us a read on the scene at the hospital."

"Good idea."

"Hold on," Kurt said and ripped his cell phone out of his pocket and speed dialed Tanya's cell phone. Her away message picked up after several rings. *Thump-thump-thump.*

"Kurt?" Fenton said. "You there? What did she say?"

Kurt kicked the chair away. "Get your coat."

At the sound of the chair skidding across the linoleum floor, Laura ventured into the kitchen to investigate. "Kurt? What is go—?"

She gawked at napkins and curtains flying about in a blustery vortex powered by an icy wind that sailed through a wide open door.

* * *

Ernie watched Tanya collapse, then stalked to the truck. Rummaged through the tool boxes, found duct tape, a rag and some rope and quickly bound and gagged Tanya's limp body. He opened the shed door and threw her next to Holly. A muffled ringing sound startled him. Frantically, he searched Tanya's pockets and found her cell phone. Checked the caller ID: Dad.

Shutting off the device, Ernie removed the battery and stuffed the pieces into his pocket. "Sorry mister-has-been-free-safety, but she's mine now."

Chapter 28

Morty and Jenny sat across the nurses' desk from each other, going over charts. The night had been quiet, only a few new cases. The clock ticked its monotonous tock and Morty's eyelids began to droop.

Jenny slapped the counter. "Morty, stay with me, we're almost done."

Morty's head snapped. "I can't help it. The floor is so quiet and that damn clock won't let me stay awake."

"Then go get another cup of coffee."

"I've already had three. Any more and I'm going to have to pee like a race horse."

"Thank you for that visual," Jenny said. "Seriously, go splash water on your face, then stick your head out the window. I don't care, just wake up."

"Okay, okay." He pushed his chair back and reached for her coffee mug. "You want me to get you a refill?"

Jenny didn't look up. "No, or I'll be joining you at the starting gate."

Morty paused, his eyebrows arching intermittently trying to catch up.

"But I've got a craving for an apple," Jenny said and vibrated her lips before breaking into laughter.

"Ha ha, Secretariat," he said grinning. "I'll see what's on the menu at the stables." He ambled off to the break room.

* * *

Ernie stood silent in the equipment room, invisible behind shelves of medical supplies. His dark eyes shifted slowly from the window to the hallway. All quiet. He put a finger to his lips and motioned with his other hand for Del to stay put. They both froze as alternating squeaks of sneakers on linoleum approached.

"I'll see what's on the menu at the stables," a voice said. Then a chubby orderly waddled by and turned into the next doorway.

Ernie tip-toed to the door joining both rooms and curled an eye around the corner of the small window.

* * *

With an experienced eye, Jenny studied Stan's chart. And frowned. On the outside, he looked to be healing quite nicely. Whatever might be going on inside his skull, however, was another story. The results of the brain scan were disappointing. She tapped the eraser end of a pencil against her chin. *The longer he goes*, she thought.

* * *

Morty hummed a tune while pouring himself a coffee. Found the artificial sweetener, ripped open a pack and dumped in the white powder. He tapped his toe to the music in his head as he stirred. Behind him, the door from the equipment room opened silently.

The Foiled Knight

* * *

Jenny made calculations on Stan's chart. Most of his vitals were fine. Strong heartbeat. Blood pressure solid. Temperature normal. *That's good,* she thought. *No infection.* Blood work came back with no problems. Urine output was productive meaning his kidneys had not shut down - yet. She set the chart down. "So why," she murmured, "are your EEG readings flipping out, huh Stan? Brain waves shouldn't fluctuate like short-circuiting Christmas lights." Her head jerked at a shattering noise. "Morty, you all right?"

Tick-tock from the clock.

Tossing her stethoscope on the counter, Jenny strode in the direction of the break room.

"What did you do, fall asleep in the middle of fixing—" She rounded the corner of the doorway and went quiet. Her face puzzled at the million pieces of a broken coffee mug still scattered across the floor. She looked about the room. Empty. "What the—? Hey, Morty, you okay? Where are you? Why'd you leave these pieces all over the place?"

Poked her head out into the hallway. Nothing. Turning, she began picking up some of the larger chunks when a clanging of metal on metal from the equipment room drew her attention. "Hey, hurry up with the broom," she said. "We'll never be able to pick all this up by hand." Several moments went by and Morty still did not reappear. "What the hell is he doing?" she muttered under her breath.

She crossed the floor and ducked her head into the equipment room. "What's the matter, can't you find—?"

A rustling to her right, then crushing pain and flashing stars.

Everything went black.

Chapter 29

"Still no answer?" Fenton asked as he and Kurt shoved through the front doors of the hospital. The lobby area appeared the same as every night: sparsely attended, calm and organized.

"No," Kurt said, punching the 'Up' button on the elevator. "Can't figure it. Tanya's always been good about returning calls."

"Maybe she's at a movie where she can't get reception."

Kurt hit the button again. "She said she was going to sit with Stan tonight."

"Not supposed to have cell phones on in the hospital," Fenton replied. "Probably just shut it off."

"Right," Kurt said. "Forgot about that." He began thumbing the button in rapid fire. "Come on. Christ, I'm freaking out."

The elevator arrived. They climbed in. Kurt hit nine. They rode in silence, the only sound their fingertips tapping the change in their trousers. With nervous eyes, they fixated on the flashing of floor lights as they waited for their stop.

* * *

Ernie ripped off two pieces of duct tape and affixed them over the mouths of an unconscious Morty and Jenny. He then double-checked the tightness of their bonds and the handkerchiefs stretched across their eyes. "That should hold them."

Del appeared with some bed linens and covered their bodies. "Do you think they saw our faces?"

"Nope," Ernie said. "Help me get them out of sight."

Together, they dragged the bodies behind some laundry bins.

"What next?" Del asked.

"Now, you go and take care of Palmer."

Del hesitated. "Okay, but tell me again why this will work."

"Simple. He's on the edge of being brain dead anyway, so if you just unhook a couple of things for a few minutes and hurry it along, no one will be the wiser."

"Yeah, but what about—"

"Quit whining and go," Ernie commanded with a whack on Del's back. "Sooner you go, sooner we're out of here."

"All right, all right, quit your nagging," Del said and stole down the hallway to Stan's room.

* * *

With a ding, the elevator-doors slid open. Fenton and Kurt burst into the hallway. And slid to an immediate halt.

The floor lay quiet as a country meadow. Soft tones of medical equipment beeped from side rooms. The aura purred calm and organized. No one seemed to be around. The utter stillness and tranquility slowed their juices. They passed by an empty reception desk, all papers stacked, all pencils aligned, clipboards neatly organized in a wire basket. The two men made eye contact.

"I guess we got all amped for nothing," Kurt said.

"Mmm," Fenton mused. His brow furrowed. A half-full coffee mug near the edge of the desk drew his attention. "But isn't there supposed to be someone on duty 24-7?"

"Yes there is."

"I'm going to check on Stan," Fenton said and strode briskly away.

Kurt reached over the counter and snatched the phone. "Good. I'll call security, just in case."

* * *

Ernie reached for the handle of the equipment room door and immediately flinched. A shadow passed by the window. Ducking, Ernie studied the new arrival through the tiny window. A man, well-built, graying at the temples, but not elderly. Walking with powerful strides. A man with a purpose. Leather coat, jeans and work boots. Not a cop. Not security. And not a doctor. Or is it? Maybe answering a late call? Ernie opened the door a crack. *Who the hell is this guy? And where's he going?* Ernie's eyes widened as the man approached Stan's room. *Shit!*

Chapter 30

At first, nothing. Blackness. Empty.

Then a distant sound. Or a sensation of one. More like a drone.

Closer now. Maybe a mumble. Someone talking? Yes, but from under a blanket. A thick one.

Tanya opened her eyes slowly, slits only, then wider. Temples throbbing. Head pounding. Muscles aching.

And pain. Like a hot knife in the eye.

Now repeated scraping. In-synch with a persistent nudging.

Brain activity increasing. Cold. Trembling lips. Shaking limbs. And numbness. It ran the entire length of her side and in her face.

Where am I?

She took in the dank surroundings. Wooden boards, all standing upright. Rusty tools on hooks. Spider webs in a rotting ceiling. More focus now. A shed. Wind whistling. It brought the smell of blood and entrails to her nostrils. The stench of death. No, worse, slaughter. A searing stab of agony from her cheek brought back the events from earlier.

Another nudge. And more muffled words. Tanya twisted her head to spot a terrified face partially shielded by a bandana. Eyes, puffy and wild. Forehead grimy and rippled. A young girl with brown hair. Tanya tried to speak. Another stab from the hot knife. Her eyes watered then slammed shut. *Oh my God, that hurts!* She forced herself to lie still. There. A calm place, no more heat. She focused on breathing.

Tanya opened her eyes again. The girl was trying to say something. More garbled nonsense. Tanya tried to move. Couldn't. Something holding her hands together behind her back. Her ankles immobile as well. And then she realized her hands were tied to her ankles. Hog tied.

A thump, then another. And again. Tanya twisted her neck, searching for the sound. It was the girl, banging her head on the splintery floor. *What? Is she trying to tell me something?*

Tanya tucked her chin into her chest and rubbed the side of her face against the rough floor. The duct tape loosened some. A second try. More slack. Again. Now even with her mouth. Blood seeped from the gouges in her cheek. One last scrape, a violent and desperate skin-peeling attempt to rid herself of the gag. She forced her teeth above the edge. Free.

Mimicking Tanya, the girl dropped her chin and tried scraping off the bandana. Two and three times, but it wouldn't loosen.

"Come close," Tanya croaked.

The girl contorted her body until her cheek touched Tanya's mouth. With a vicious snap of her teeth, Tanya ripped the gag left then right until it sagged beneath the girl's lips.

The Foiled Knight

"Help me!" the girl gasped. "Please help me."

"I'll try," Tanya said. "Are you Holly?"

"Yes. Holly Mathews. Who are you?"

"My name is Tanya. Are you hurt?"

"No, well yes, I mean no, nothing's broken. You gotta get me out of here, before that man comes back."

Tanya squeezed her eyes shut to fight off the pain in her cheek. "Can you get your hands loose?"

"No, the ropes are too tight."

"Try rotating your wrists in opposite directions."

Squirming, Holly struggled against her bonds. "Doesn't work."

"Look around," Tanya said. "Is there anything we can rub the ropes against to maybe cut through them?"

"No. Every day I try to find a sharp edge, but nothing's worked."

"How long have you been here?"

"I don't know. Weeks maybe." Holly paused as if suddenly remembering something. "Where's your partner?"

"Partner? What? I'm alone."

Holly's eyes squinted. "You're not police?"

Catching her insinuation, Tanya went still. "No."

With an exhale of frustration, Holly lay back, her whole body sagging into the unforgiving floor. All of the physical aches evaporated. The chafing, the bruises, the hunger, the cold. All of it faded as her senses numbed to a dark realization. Tears slid from the corners of her eyes and down her bleeding cheeks. Dirt and scum of captivity collected in the streak of hopelessness.

"We're both gonna die."

Chapter 31

Fenton entered Stan's room, immediately struck odd by why the privacy curtain had been pulled around the bed. At the same time, his subconscious registered a distinct lack of sound. Gone was the usual beeping and wheezing of the life-support equipment. He stepped in and another pang of oddness hit him. Beneath the curtain: a pair of leather boots. It took a moment to decipher why boots and not white sneakers typically worn by medical staff. He threw open the curtain. Every hair on his body leapt to attention. Next to Stan, mangled wires and tubes in his hand, stood Del Guidry.

"Hey!" Fenton shouted and hurled his body at the man.

Wires and tubes flew as Del pitched sideways. He crashed into the far wall and toppled over the pot of daisies. It broke into pieces, casting water across the floor. Fenton attacked, but a kick to the stomach threw him backwards into Stan's bed, his spine smashing hard against the chrome railing. Grimacing, he went down on one knee. Del tried to kick him again, Fenton blocked the strike with an iron forearm. Thrown off balance, Del fell to the floor. Both men leaped up. Del swung. Fenton sidestepped it and landed a counter-punch to the gut, followed it with a hard right to the jaw. He then grabbed the dazed man by the shirt and drove a vicious fist into his face. Del collapsed in a puddle of water that quickly turned red as blood dripped from his broken nose.

Fenton hurriedly attempted to reattach the wires and tubes to Stan. Anxiety pounced. *Christ, I'm not a doctor! I don't know what goes where.* "Hey! Help! I need a doctor!" He had just connected the breathing apparatus when he heard a loud metallic click. Against the silence, it sounded like a cannon in a gymnasium. He turned. Just outside the doorway stood the hunching mass of Ernie McFadden. In his meat hook of a hand, he held a gun, the barrel pointed at Fenton's heart.

"Should have taken the night off Mr. Palmer."

* * *

"I don't know where everybody is," Kurt spat into the phone at the hospital security operator. "Get somebody up here!" He jumped at shouts for help from somewhere on the floor. Jamming the receiver back into the cradle, Kurt set off in the direction of the sound. He turned the corner. Ten yards ahead, a man stood in the hallway, his back to Kurt, pointing a gun into a patient's room.

Chapter 32

Ciquero replaced the last of the videos on the shelf of Stan's basement entertainment center. There had only been a few with none containing any further incriminating evidence. And that was beginning to wear on him.

After finding the magazines and the computer data, he expected there to be more, that it would have permeated a suspect's entire existence. A second walk through of the upper floors with the DNA team had revealed nothing.

A photo album attracted his attention and he scanned pages of typical pictures from diapers to adulthood. He paused at one taken at the beach of a teenage Stan with a redheaded girl on his shoulders. Flipping back through, Ciquero noticed the same girl in a lot of the childhood photos, but not so much the recent ones. There were no names or captions.

"Everything seems normal," he said to no one and glanced around the room. The computer's asteroid shower screen saver gave him an idea. He grabbed the mouse and quickly navigated to the browser's history file.

The list of recently visited sites, while vile, was not long, another fact that nibbled at his brain. *It should be longer. Unless he's good at wiping his trail. But why would someone who lives alone need to do that?*

Ciquero organized the list into "Detail" view. Nothing immediately jumped out at him. The files were all relatively small. *Huh, no videos*, he thought, *a deviant mind would want that*. A click on the tool bar offered more sorting options. Just as he selected "Last Accessed", his cell phone rang.

"Ciquero."

"Mike, it's O'Hara, there's been a disturbance at Abington Hospital."

Ciquero barely heard. The dates that the sites were last visited populated the computer screen. "What's happened?"

"Don't know," O'Hara said, "but isn't your coma guy there?"

Ciquero tried to focus on the conversation, but something about the list didn't make sense. All were within minutes of each other—and the same day.

"Mike? You there?"

"Yeah," Ciquero said, staring hard at the display. Minutes apart. All the same day. The date burned his corneas. Yesterday. "Cap! Get some guys over to the hospital. Now!"

"Why?" O'Hara said.

Ciquero took the stairs three at a time. "Palmer is being set up!"

Chapter 33

Fenton held up his hands. "Ernie, don't!"

"You shouldn't have come tonight," Ernie said. "You almost messed everything up. But you're too late."

Fenton blinked as it happened.

Ernie in the doorway, leering a toothy smile.

Then a green missile exploded into his ribs, bending him in half.

The gun's muzzle flashed. An ear-splitting explosion and a puff of air by Fenton's ear.

Doorway now empty. Reverberations.

Tinkering shards of glass. A burst of cold.

And then... quiet.

A moment later, Kurt reappeared in the doorway, his face flushed with worry. "Fenton! Are you all right?"

Fenton held up a shaking hand. He looked down at his body, then at the large hole in the window behind him. It took a few moments for him to find a voice. "He missed me."

"Thank Christ," Kurt said.

"Did you get him?" Fenton asked.

"Yeah, and the gun too." Kurt pulled the weapon from his back pocket, showed it to Fenton, then shoved it back. "I need to tie him up, but I hit him plenty solid. He's out. And security should be on their way." Kurt paused, noticing the concerned look on Fenton's face. "What did they do?"

Fenton swiveled toward Stan. "Del ripped out his breathing tube and some wires before I got here." Their eyes locked in a grim, knowing stare.

"How long?" Kurt asked.

"I don't know. Maybe a few seconds, maybe a few minutes."

"His heart monitor is still going along all regular like," Kurt said. "Maybe you put it back in time." The words were hardly out of his mouth when Fenton cried out in pain, gripping the back of his leg.

From behind, Del crouched with a broken piece of flower pot in his hand. Blood laced its razor sharp edge. He stood, desperation wracking his face. "Move, or I cut his throat."

"Fuck you asshole," Kurt hissed. "You touch him and I'll rip you apart."

Del buckled as Fenton kicked the jagged piece of porcelain out of his hand. With a warrior's cry, Kurt sprinted and launched himself through the air and into Del. The crunch of Kurt's forearms broke rib and jaw. Del catapulted through space. There was another splintering sound as he crashed through the broken window and disappeared from sight.

Kurt and Fenton waited for it. The sound neither had heard before, yet one they'd know to be exactly what they thought. Dull. Gruesome. Final. And it

The Foiled Knight

came. A pumpkin splattering on pavement.

There were several seconds of silence as Kurt and Fenton gawked at the hole in the window. Cold air flooded the room.

"Oh my God," Kurt gasped. "I killed him."

Fenton staggered to his feet and peered through the broken glass at Del's broken body on the sidewalk below. He turned back to Kurt and braced the shaking man by the shoulders. "Kurt! Listen to me! They tried to kill us."

Kurt's face glazed in disbelief.

"He got what he deserved," Fenton continued. He shook Kurt again. Nothing. "*Come on!* My leg is cut. You have to get Ernie before he escapes."

Kurt's forehead rippled. His eyes rounded and squinted in spasms of confusion. Of all the football hits he had delivered in his playing career, none compared to this. His mouth trembled and his muscles clenched, but in no way could he move.

"Augh, I'll do it myself," Fenton grunted. Holding his hamstring, he limped to the hallway.

Rushing footsteps approached. Several security guards appeared. Fenton raised a bloody hand.

All weapons turned on him. "Freeze!"

Fenton collapsed against the wall and slid to a sitting position. Blood pooled under him. He looked left then right, but Ernie McFadden had disappeared.

The guards surrounded him. "Don't move."

Fenton's world swam. Lights blurred. Shouts faded to mumbles. With a wobbly finger, he pointed toward the stairwell. "I'm not the one you want." A dark curtain snapped. He blacked out.

At that same moment, Stan's eyes opened.

Chapter 34

"We're not going to die," Tanya said and squinted to peer through cracks in the wall of the shed. A circle of amber light played on the ground just outside the door, a ghostly specter shifting to the will of the wind.

"If you're not police," Holly replied, "how did you know my name?"

"I read about you in the paper." Tanya glanced at Holly's bare feet. "Where are your shoes?"

"He took them."

"We've got to get you out of here," Tanya said. "Keep trying to loosen your hands. All we need are a few fingers free. I have a cell phone in my pocket."

"No you don't," Holly said. "He took it. He takes everything."

"What? How?"

"It rang after he threw you in here. I pretended to be asleep. I do that sometimes, hoping he'll leave me alone." Holly paused and her face pinched. "But it never works."

"How many of them are there?" Tanya asked.

"Only one that I know of." She started to sob.

"Holly," Tanya said. "Listen to me. We're going to figure it out. I promise. But you've got to try and stay calm."

"Stay calm!" Holly barked, her face an eruption of tears and anger. "Are you out of your mind? That pervert kidnapped me, beat me, peed on me, and, and…" She whimpered. "He… raped… me."

Tanya's heart stuck in her throat. For the first time she noticed the dried blood clotted in Holly's hair. "I know honey," Tanya said, her voice as small as she could make it. "And we're gonna get him for that. But look at me. Please!"

Taking huge sucks of air, Holly stared into Tanya's eyes.

"We're going to make it," Tanya said. "I promise."

"Yeah right. You're stuck like me."

Tanya paused a moment. *This isn't working,* she thought and studied their surroundings. *I need to change the energy.* She came back to Holly. "When is the last time you ate?"

Holly's eyes went incredulous. "How can you think of food?"

"First order of survival. I need to know what kind of condition you're in."

"I don't get it."

"Just tell me."

"I get fed once a day," Holly huffed.

"Have you been fed yet today?"

Holly gawked trying to comprehend the question.

"If he's already fed you today," Tanya continued, "that means we've probably got another twenty-four hours till he returns."

"Oh." Holly's eyes fell. "Sorry."

"Come on, don't get like that."

"Easy for you. You've been here, what, a couple hours? I've been here, like, forever."

"If we're going to get out of here, we have to be a team and you need to believe we can do it."

Another stare.

"What in God's name have you got to lose?" Tanya said.

"Nothing. Except my life."

"We're never going to get anywhere with an attitude like that."

"Don't tell me about attitude," Holly said. "You can't possibly understand what I've been through."

"You're right. I have no idea what it's been like. But maybe you can cut me a break. I'm just trying to help."

"How? You came out here all alone, at night, you're tied up as tight as me and you haven't got a knife. Even if we did get loose, you haven't got a cell phone or a weapon. So how are you going to help?"

"That's not fair," Tanya said.

"Neither is being kidnapped and thrown into a slaughter shack from hell."

They rolled away from each other and did not move for several minutes. The wind howled around them, its wail like the scream through a hollow tree.

They had been lying like that for almost ten minutes when a bug slithered through the floor boards and into Tanya's hair. She screamed. "Augh! Something's on me."

"It's just a bug," Holly said. "Relax."

"Get it off me."

"Just Ignore It."

"I can't, ewe, get it off."

"Oh for Pete's sake," Holly said and rolled over toward Tanya. "Don't be such a wuss." She dove into Tanya's hair with bared teeth and snatched the crawly insect, ripped it free and spat it across the room. The bug scurried under the door. "There, all gone."

It took several seconds for Tanya to calm down. "Thank you."

"You're welcome."

With one huge gust of air, Tanya forced her breathing to return to normal. "Has that happened to you a lot?"

Holly remained still.

"I hate bugs," Tanya said and flicked her eyes at the girl.

Silence.

"One time, my friend Stan and I were exploring this creek, he caught a crayfish and stuck it in my face. I screamed like a hyena."

More silence.

"But the worst was when he slipped a worm in my swimsuit."

Nothing.

"Down my crack. You should have seen me wiggle to get it out."

A slight upturning at the edge of Holly's mouth.

Tanya turned to face her. "Hey, Holly, I'm sorry about before. I can't even imagine the hell you've been through." She bit her lip, forcing herself to say nothing for several moments. *She's got to meet me*, Tanya thought.

The silence that followed lasted several minutes, at first peaceful, almost therapeutic, but no less awkward. The hushed space around them graduated to a state of defiant ignorance, the quiet ironically increasing in volume. The wind screeched as if urging them to break their stubborn vows.

Finally, Holly's somber voice broke the darkness. "Sometimes the bugs go up my pant leg, other times in my ear. Eventually they go away."

"Good God," Tanya replied softly. "How do you stand it?"

"Don't have much choice, do I?"

"Didn't mean it that way."

"I know, I just squeeze my eyes shut and think of something else."

"Like?"

"Like something good, something positive."

"Something to live for?" Tanya said.

"Yeah, I guess."

"And what's that for you?"

"Doesn't matter," Holly said. "That's what's frustrating. It'll never happen."

"Don't say that."

"Why? It's true. Everyone is against me."

"Who's everyone?"

"I told you, it doesn't matter."

"Why do you say that?" Tanya asked.

"Why do you want to know so bad?"

"Because I care."

Holly rolled her eyes. "Yeah, right."

"No one should have to experience something like this," Tanya said. "What's happened to you is horrible. You deserve to have something good in your life."

Holly said nothing.

"You need to be given encouragement," Tanya continued. "Confidence, your self-esteem boosted."

"You sound like an evangelist."

Tanya half-laughed. "Not really.

Holly studied Tanya. "Who are you?"

"I told you, my name is—"

"Yeah, yeah, you told me that. What I meant was, who are you that you say you care to give me advice?"

"I'm nobody."

"Nobody," Holly repeated.

"Well, maybe not nobody," Tanya said. "Maybe more like someone who wishes they had a daughter they could teach things to."

Holly studied Tanya some more. This time longer and deeper, the kind of examining stare of a person trying to peer into another person's soul. "It's my mom. She doesn't…we don't…um…it's complicated."

"Things at your age usually are," Tanya said. "I know they were for me, especially with my dad. But try okay? I really want to know."

Holly started slowly, her tone a low mumble, as if she had travelled in her mind back to a very early age. "My whole life I've loved to draw and paint. In school, at home, didn't matter, I found a way to doodle. Anytime we took long family trips in the car, I colored. At carnivals, I could spend hours at the booth where you dribbled paint from a squirt bottle onto a spinning card to make psychedelic designs, do you know what I mean?"

"I do," Tanya said, remembering when she and Stan used to spend entire days at Willow Grove Park, tossing rings, riding roller coasters and eating cotton candy. There had been an art center to make pottery and paint with oil-based paints. "I'll bet you were good."

"I was," Holly said. "My stuff was always selected for display in the glass cases at school. I won a blue ribbon once at a contest with the Girl Scouts."

"And do you still paint today?"

"A little. My cousin, Joanna, she's older than me, she's this awesome artist and is studying art in Italy. I mean, how cool is that? That's what I want to do, go to art school in Europe."

"That's a great dream."

"Yeah, well, my mom doesn't think so. She's always harping about how I should learn to cook and all this idiotic stuff."

"Moms are like that," Tanya said.

"She's always on my case. Holly! Watch your weight. Holly! Why don't you want to learn how to sew? How are boys ever going to find you attractive when you dress like that? It's like she doesn't think I can take care of myself."

"Maybe that's how she was raised."

"Nuh-uh. She doesn't think I have what it takes to be a good artist. And my friends aren't very supportive either. They all want to do ridiculous things like become models or go on reality TV shows. I can't stand any of that. They all make fun of me, tell me I won't ever do it, like I'm some kind of loser."

Ignoring the pain in her shoulders, Tanya rolled onto her back and blew out a gust of air. "Don't ever let anyone tell you that you can't do something, Holly."

"Sounds like something your parents say to you. Like becoming President of the United States."

"No, more important than that."

"What could be more important than being president?"

"Learning how to do a back flip, that's what."

Holly snorted. "Your parents used a back flip as their example for accomplishing anything?"

"No, a friend of mine."

"The same guy who got you with the worm?" Holly asked.

"Yep."

"Some friend."

"He is," Tanya said, her smile surprising her. "My best."

Chapter 35

Coffee made its way around the break room of the hospital where the police had set up a temporary command post. Officers bustled about. A janitor swept up the remains of the broken coffee mug. Jenny and Morty, groggy and haggard, huddled in the corner, pressing ice packs to the backs of their heads. A policewoman stood by them, methodically jotting notes in a notebook. The area around Room 9 had been taped off and a tarp crudely stapled to cover the gaping hole in the window. Stan was relocated to another room.

Detective Joe Westerman sat in the center of a circle of cheap plastic chairs, his steely grey eyes flitting to everything happening around him. Lean with thinning white hair, the thirty-year veteran had never conducted a crime scene investigation in a hospital before. Across from him sat Fenton, one trouser cut at mid-thigh; a thick bandage of gauze and tape wrapped his wound. Kurt rocked back and forth, staring at the floor. One of the legs of his chair came off the floor every time he surged backwards, followed by the *click* of metal on linoleum as he leaned forward. Click. Rock. Click. Kurt's trembling hand raked across his scalp every few seconds. Ciquero leaned against the wall, arms folded, studying Kurt.

Westerman flipped open a notepad. "Even though Abington isn't in his jurisdiction, I've known Detective Ciquero for years and asked him to join us since some of this might be related to his missing person's case in Glenside."

Ciquero nodded. "Thanks, Joe."

Westerman addressed Fenton. "Mr. Palmer, when did you know something was wrong?"

"We saw the nurse's station empty," Fenton said, "I knew it had been a while since somebody had been there because of the stale coffee. I left to check on Stan while Kurt called security." Fenton winced as he shifted to take pressure off the injury.

"Tell us what happened."

Fenton pursed his lips. "I walked into Stan's room and immediately knew something was up because the curtain had been drawn and none of the machines were working."

"How'd you know that?" Ciquero asked.

"No sound. They make this chirping and beeping noise that you never get used to. And then I looked down and saw a pair of boots, not medical booties, but leather hiking ones, so I threw open the curtain. Del was standing there with all of Stan's tubes in his hands."

"Did he say anything?"

"No. He was just… there, so I jumped him. We went at it."

"You knocked him out?"

"Yes, well, obviously not all the way."

The Foiled Knight

"Then what?"

"I tried to reattach Stan's tubes. I didn't know what I was doing. Everything was so jumbled. There were wires and tubes all over the place." Fenton's face contorted into a silent cramp and he pressed a fist into his palm. "I did the best I could."

Westerman snared a passing medic and whispered something in his ear. The medic glanced toward Fenton, nodded subtly, and went to his medical kit spread on the counter.

"So is that when McFadden tried to shoot you?" Ciquero asked.

"Yes. He just… appeared… said something… pointed…it happened so fast. One second he was there and then—"

A hand in Fenton's face holding two white pills stopped his recounting of events. He looked up at the medic. "What's this?"

Westerman grasped Fenton's forearm. "Mr. Palmer, I asked the medic for a sedative. I need to ask you these questions, so we can begin looking for the man that got away." He looked at the medic. "Mild, right?"

"It'll take the edge off," the man replied.

Fenton took the pills and downed them without water.

"You're going to be fine," Westerman said as the medic left. "Keep going. One second McFadden was there, and then…"

"It's all a blur. I saw the gun and heard the shot. He flew sideways. And then Kurt was yelling at me, showing me the gun, so figured we were safe. Del must have woken up and grabbed a chunk of the broken vase to slice my leg."

"Jagg-off."

All three men stared at Kurt who had spoken for the first time in nearly thirty minutes. And just as quickly, he went back to rocking his chair. Click. Rock. Click.

"He had no other weapon?" Westerman asked, focusing back on Fenton.

"No."

"Did you hit him again?"

"I wasn't even thinking at that point. He threatened to slash my throat. Kurt yelled something to distract him. I kicked the thing out of his hand. Lucky actually. That's when…"

Click. Rock. Click.

Fenton looked at Kurt. "That's when Kurt hit him and—"

Click. Click. Silence.

Fenton paused, then turned back to Westerman and made a tumbling motion with his index finger.

Westerman mouthed an "Ah."

Click. Click. Click.

Westerman faced Kurt. "Mr. Davis?"

Click. Rock. Silence.

"Can you tell me what you remember about tonight?"

More silence. Kurt's gaze never left the floor.

"Mr. Davis?"

Finally Kurt shook and rubbed his face with both hands. "Yeah?"

"What do you remember about tonight?"

"What?"

"What do you remem—"

"You know," Kurt said, cutting across the detective, "in all the years I played ball, I never injured anyone seriously?" Click. Rock.

Westerman leaned back in his chair, stroking his chin. A quizzical look overtook him. Lips pouted in that pensive way a man judges something. Finally, eyebrows rose over thoughtful eyes. "You only missed one game your whole career."

Kurt stopped rocking. "That's right." He tilted his head at the detective as if trying to figure the man.

"Concussion," Westerman continued. "Compliments of Nick Yanosek."

"You saw the game?"

Westerman nodded. "One of the most violent collisions I've ever seen on a football field."

"Why do you think I got out of the game and became a teacher?"

"You never shied away from anybody, no matter how big they were. You were the last line of defense. Playing free safety took a lot of balls."

"So does running towards a man with a gun," Ciquero added.

Kurt shrugged then scratched his head. "What did you want to know again?"

"Tell me what happened tonight," Westerman said.

Kurt filled his cheeks with air, paused a moment looking like Louis Armstrong on a steroid trumpet, then let it escape in a hiss. "Pretty much exactly the way Fenton told it. When we came on the floor, there was nobody here. Fenton went to check on Stan while I called security. I was on my way down the hall when I saw this guy—"

"McFadden?" Ciquero asked.

"Yeah. Him. Big bastard. I saw him creep across the hall with a gun raised."

"Did he see you or say anything?"

"Not to me. He said something to Fenton, but I wasn't listening anymore."

"What did you do?"

"I just reacted. I didn't think these old wheels would get me there in time, but I hit him with everything I had. Got him right in the midsection." He paused. "And I heard a crack."

Westerman scribbled in his notebook. "You think maybe you broke something?"

"Oh, I know it. He was totally exposed, wasn't ready for it and I nailed him full blast. I can't believe he just walked away."

Fenton leaned in. "You nearly cut him in half. Detective, if you check some of the other hospitals, you might find he went to an emergency room."

"I was thinking the same thing," Westerman said and motioned to a policeman.

A blond man approached. "Sir?"

"Call around to the surrounding hospitals, emergency care units, clinics, anyplace that somebody might go to get treated for broken bones. Get it out to our guys on the street."

"Roger that."

Westerman turned to Fenton. "This McFadden," he checked his notes,

"Ernie. What can you tell me about him?"

Fenton considered the question as his mind retrieved data bits from days long since gone. "He's a local guy, grew up right here in Abington. Kind of a loser, wrong side of the tracks. Went to school with Stan, same year, but they weren't friends. I knew his father, we both used to work at the mill years ago. Did some fishing together, but I stopped going."

Westerman's eyebrows perked. "Yeah, why?"

"Bart McFadden was a strange guy. Wrapped a little too tight. Cynical, you know what I mean? Extreme. He would flip out over something as stupid as losing his lure. Violent too. I think he might have given Ernie the back of his hand a lot."

Ciquero interrupted. "Is the father still alive?"

"Don't know. Word is he just up and left when Ernie was still a teenager. Never heard from him since."

"Too bad," Ciquero said. "He might have been able to tell us where Ernie might go to hole up."

"What about the mother?" Westerman said.

"I think she died a while back. Lung cancer or something like that."

Westerman made notations. "Let's get back to Ernie. What else can you tell me? Does he have a family?"

"I don't know," Fenton said. "Stan told me he was shacked up in a trailer park with somebody named Margie Wheeler. Think they went to school together. But that was years ago, probably split by now."

"We can check that," Westerman said. "Any idea where we can find her?"

"Talk to the younger guys at the lumber yard. Seems I heard one of them talking about her being an exotic dancer over at the Landing Strip."

More scribbles. "What about a job? Places he would hang out? Friends?"

"I doubt he has a job. Ernie was bad news."

"That's the truth," Kurt chipped in. "When our kids were young, Ernie was behind everything bad that happened in school or the surrounding area. He would unscrew people's Christmas lights and piss into the empty socket and blow all the fuses in the house. Throw mud balls at cars, break open the vending machines behind the shopping center and steal all the quarters. He was banned from the shopping mall for a year by Pinkerton Security."

"Sounds like a real punk," Ciquero said.

"He was," Kurt said. "And naturally, he escalated to even worse stuff. Pretty soon, he was dealing drugs and stealing cars. Crafty son of a bitch though, could never catch him in the act. Remember the fire that took out Daisy's Five and Dime?"

Westerman returned a blank look. "Must have been before I transferred in to Abington."

"Never proven, but he did it. He got tossed out of the Army, I never did hear what for. Probably got caught having sex with an officer's daughter."

Westerman held up his hands. "Okay I get the idea. Not exactly a model citizen." He looked at Fenton. "What's he got against your son?"

"Ernie and Stan have been enemies all their lives," Fenton said.

"Why try to kill him?"

"Here's the thing," Fenton said. "That's sorta what led Kurt and me to come here tonight."

"What do you mean?" Ciquero asked.

"Kurt and I were having dinner the other night and got to talking about the 911 call you came to see me about. The one Stan made the night of his accident."

"I remember," Ciquero said. "But we figured the timing was wrong."

Fenton shook his head. "Actually, the timing is perfect. You said it yourself: what was Stan doing all the way over on that side of town during a snow storm? There's no way he made the call *after* he hit the deer. It had to have been before."

"Before? But why would he do that…unless…" Ciquero let the words hang there. "Wait, you think—"

"Yes I do," Fenton said. "You were right. I think Stan saw something that had to do with the kidnapping of that girl, what was her name?"

"Holly Mathews."

"Right, and was trying to report it when the accident happened."

Ciquero pulled up a chair. "You think the kidnappers snuck in here to pull his plug."

Both Fenton and Kurt nodded.

"What led you to believe that? Stan's been laid up for a while, why tonight?"

"I've had a bad feeling about this ever since you came to see me," Fenton said. "The timing of Stan's call, why didn't he come up Easton Road, the report of the Mathews girl in the paper." He shrugged. "We started putting pieces together. And then I learned a guy fitting McFadden's description came to visit Stan here in the hospital."

Ciquero's jaw dropped. "What! When did that happen? Why wasn't I informed?"

"I only just found out," Fenton said. He pointed toward Jenny still answering questions. "Jenny told Tanya. The guy said he played football with Stan."

Westerman scratched his head. "So?"

"So Stan never played a down in his life," Fenton replied. "He was a baseball pitcher. The visitor was obviously lying to worm information out of Jenny to find out what kind of shape Stan was in."

"If Stan wakes up," Ciquero said pensively, "he can I.D. the kidnapper."

"Bingo. Ernie probably got antsy and came cruising. We got lucky tonight, detective."

"I'll say," Ciquero said, then his face scrunched into a puzzle. "So let me ask you again. Why did you expect trouble tonight and not sooner?"

Fenton and Kurt shared a look.

"Because Tanya's not here," Kurt said. "And we can't get a hold of her."

Westerman's brain began to hurt. "Who's Tanya?"

"My daughter," Kurt replied. "She been coming here almost every night."

"Stan's wife?"

"No, it's a long story," Kurt said. "Stan and Tanya have had a thing for each other since they were born." He looked at his feet and ran a hand through his hair. "It didn't work out the way it should have." His voice trailed off.

The picture of the redhead on Stan's shoulders flashed in Ciquero's brain.

Westerman rattled his head. "I'm lost."

"Detective," Fenton said. "If Stan wakes up, everything will be clear for them to get together."

The look on Westerman's face was one of bewilderment. "What in the hell does that have to do with what happened here tonight?"

Fenton placed a hand on Westerman's forearm. "Tanya was married to Del. Long time ago. Been divorced for years, but he never got over it."

"Del," Ciquero said, his voice as flat as black paint. "The guy who's lying on the sidewalk below."

"That's right," Fenton said. "He and Ernie were tight, like blood brothers. Ernie was always pulling Del's strings."

It all came clear in Ciquero's mind. "Ernie can't risk Stan waking up and fingering him as the kidnapper. So Ernie needs Stan dead. And instead of doing the dirty work himself, Ernie winds up his little puppet Del with a story that if Stan wakes up, he'll run off with Tanya, so Del needs him dead too."

"Right," Fenton said.

And with Stan dead, Ciquero thought to himself, *we probably would have pinned him as the kidnapper.*

"Where is Tanya?" Westerman said. "We need to talk to her."

Kurt pulled out his cell phone and dialed again. Tanya's answering message kicked in. He held the phone up for the detective to listen. "No one knows where she is."

"Is it like her not to answer?" Ciquero asked.

"No."

"Is it possible she's just—"

"I've already asked myself all these questions," Kurt said, punching a thigh. "I don't know anything."

"Calm down," Ciquero said. "When is the last time you saw her?"

"Night before last, at the diner. She waited on Fenton and me." He blew out a gust of air. "Shit, for all we know, she's at the movies, but she's been coming here most nights."

Ciquero stroked his mustache. "I don't want to take any chances. I'm going to put it out on the wire for everyone to be on the lookout for her. Joe, can you help me there?"

"You got it," Westerman replied.

"We'll need a photograph," Ciquero added.

"I'll go home and get one," Kurt said.

"Good, when you get to the station, ask for dispatch." Ciquero tugged on his mustache as his eyes bored through Kurt. "Give me her cell phone number too. We might be able to trace it through GPS software." Another tug. "And we'll check with her friends and people she works with to see if anyone has been in touch with her."

"What about other places she goes to, like the gym?" Kurt asked.

"Good idea," Ciquero said. "Give us as much as you can." He stroked for several seconds then threw his hands up. "That's all I got, Joe. Thanks for letting me inside on this."

"No sweat," Westerman said, then turned to Fenton and Kurt. "I think we're done for now. If you want to, you can go home. But let me know if Tanya gets in touch with you. Hopefully you're right and she's just somewhere safe with her phone off."

"Okay, I'm on it," Kurt said. "Fenton, you want to come with me?"

Fenton grimaced as he stood. "I need to check with the doctor first to see what's going on with Stan. I don't understand why his eyes are open, but he's supposedly still in a coma." Gritting his teeth, he limped out the door.

Chapter 36

Sunlight speared its way through cracks in the shed wall as Tanya woke from a restless sleep. Her eyelids fluttered open and she immediately felt the gnawing ache of having slept on a hard surface. Lips trembling, head splitting, stomach growling, she moved and froze as a bolt of pain shot into her neck.

"Good God," Tanya groaned.

Holly stirred beside her. "Hurts, don't it?"

"Yeah," a pause, "but it can't be as bad as what you're feeling."

"Everything's numb," Holly said. "I know the pain is there, but I'm so banged up that I can't feel it anymore."

"At least the wind isn't blowing like it was."

"Yeah, but if that were truly a good thing, we'd be able to smell breakfast cooking. I can't smell anything."

Tanya focused on the air. If Holly hadn't said anything, she never would have noticed that the only thing she could detect, other than the stench within the shed, was the smell of pine trees somewhere nearby. "Did he usually bring you something in the morning?"

"Not every day," Holly said, "but I could smell food every day. Bacon, eggs, coffee. Drove me crazy."

"But now—"

"—there's nothing," Holly finished

"Huh," Tanya mused. "I wonder what that means?"

"Doesn't mean anything. He could just as easily have gone somewhere."

"Then it's a good time for us to try to get out of here."

"How?" Holly asked. "I've tried everything."

"But you didn't have someone to work with," Tanya said. "Turn over."

"On my back?"

"No, so that we are back to back."

"Why?"

"Just do it," Tanya said.

"Yes ma'am."

They struggled to flip themselves into opposing positions.

"Now what?" Holly asked.

"Adjust your body until your hands are near mine. I'll try to untie your ropes with my hands."

"Okay, hold on," Holly replied and squirmed until she felt Tanya's searching fingers. "There, can you feel them?"

"Yes, a little more… there, that's perfect. Don't move."

Fumbling blindly, Tanya tried to undo the ropes around Holly's wrist, but her frozen fingers could not loosen the knots. After several minutes, she gave up. "Shit."

"Let me try," Holly said and began attacking Tanya's bonds. It took only a minute before both realized she would have no better success. With a shout of frustration, Holly stopped.

They lay still for a few seconds. "Now what?" Holly asked.

"Can you stand up?" Tanya asked.

"No, I already tried. The way my hands are tied to my ankles, I can't keep my balance."

"Maybe I can bite through your ropes," Tanya said. "Don't move." She quickly rolled over and gnawed at the knots. They tasted of oil and something foul. A raunchy smell burned her nostrils. The smell of something dead. She slammed her eyes shut to it and tugged savagely. Again and again she bit and pulled, switching to her molars for added strength. Never once did they budge. A vision of a hunter lashing a carcass to the hood of his truck flashed in her brain. With a groan, she gave up.

"Dammit, there must be something we can do," Tanya said and scanned the inside walls at the rusty tools hanging from hooks. "Hey, I know it hurts like hell, but slide over here next to me and lay on your back."

"Why?"

"See those tools hanging on the wall? If we pound the walls with our feet, maybe we can get one of them to fall."

"Okay, here I come," Holly said with determination. "Make room."

Writhing like snakes, they wiggled around until they were side by side, on their backs.

"This is going to take some coordination," Tanya said. "Both of us, on three, kick the wall as hard as you can. Got it?"

"Got it."

Tanya took a deep breath. "One...two...three, go!"

Together they pulled their knees into their chests and lashed out. Tanya, the stronger of the two, hit first with Holly a split second later. A quick *thump-thump* vibrated the wall, but did nothing to shake the tools from their hanging position.

"Again," Tanya said.

Once more they struck, this time at the exact same moment, but the rope that connected their hands to their feet restricted them so greatly that the impact was only enough to cause the slightest of vibrations.

"Come on!" Tanya shouted. "Everything you have, try to break through the boards. One, two, three, now!" They thrust their legs with as much power as they could muster.

The walls rippled slightly, but the tools remained unshaken. They collapsed in frustration.

Tanya rolled onto her side, the floor hard against her cheek. "Dammit."

Holly rolled toward Tanya, a look of despair on her face. "We're not getting anywhere. And I can't stay in that position, it hurts too much."

"We'll try again later."

They took a few moments to catch their breath and regroup.

"So what do we do in the meantime?" Holly asked.

"Good question. I suppose we could try to think of details the police might need, if we ever get out of here. What do you know about the kidnapper?"

"What do you mean? Like his face?"

"Yes, anything that could identify him."

Holly thought for a few moments. "I don't know hardly anything."

"Physical description, tattoos?"

"No."

Tanya's mind scrambled for questions. "Scars, weird haircut?"

"I never saw him."

"Did he ever speak around you?"

"No."

"You sure he's alone?"

Holly thought for a moment. "No," she said with a disgusted thump of her head on the floor. "I never heard anyone talking; I just assumed it. About the only thing I know is he's got a truck."

"What kind?"

"A pick-up."

Tanya paused, vaguely remembering the vehicle she had seen parked in the carport of the cabin. A vehicle in shadows. She forced her mind to try to picture it, but it had been night and her focus on the cabin. "What color?"

Holly thought a moment. "Dark green, I think."

"Do you remember what kind of tires?"

"What? I don't know."

"Try to remember, picture them in your mind."

"I'm trying." Holly stared at the ceiling as if it held the answer. "They were big."

"How big?"

"I don't know!"

"Come on, think. Details matter here. Were they monster truck big?"

"No, not that big. But they were fat."

"Like off-road?"

"Yeah. And they had no hubcaps."

"Good," Tanya said. "What else?"

"The front door panel was smashed in."

"Like it had been in an accident?"

"No, like someone had kicked it in."

Tanya started. "Kicked in?"

"I don't know. Why?"

"No reason. Keep going."

"It had a rack... thingy... on top, for like, carrying stuff."

An uneasy feeling gurgled in Tanya's stomach. "Like long pieces of wood or siding?"

"I think so. It had tool boxes on the side... and a decal. Some kind of construction company."

"Did you see the name of the company?" Tanya asked, the uneasiness in her gut solidifying into a knot.

"Yeah, but it isn't coming to my mind real quick, but I remember it began with an 'M'."

The apprehension caught in Tanya's throat like hot paste. "Long? Short?

Common?" She hesitated. "Maybe an ethnic name?"

"Not very common. And, oh! Yeah, I remember now it was an Italian name. Mancini's or Marucci's. Something like that."

Tanya's spirit sank into the floor as she conjured the logo of Macino's Construction Company in her mind. Several weeks before, Del had visited Tanya, uninvited, begging for her to give him a second chance. The visit ended in another shouting match. Del had stormed outside and kicked in the door of his company vehicle. She rammed her eyes shut. "The decal on the door, did it have an Italian flag?"

"Yes, do you know it?"

Tanya hissed air like the slow leak of a balloon as she debated telling Holly the name of the company for which Del worked. "I think I've seen it around town. Macino's."

"That's it!" Holly said. "That's good, right? Can't be many companies with that name. The police should be able to find it easy. That's terrific."

Tanya sniffed. "Yeah, terrific."

Chapter 37

John DeAngelis sat before Sandra and Fenton in the quiet confines of the surgeon's office. Sweat outlined the neck of his operating scrubs. Hardly a word had been spoken the entire meeting. DeAngelis looked up with tired eyes from his folder containing Stan's most recent EEG.

Sandra gripped Fenton's arm.

"Mr. and Mrs. Palmer, I have bad news for you. The attack on your son caused his life support equipment to become disconnected for several minutes, depriving his brain of oxygen." His eyes glanced from both parents, then down to the charts in the folder then back to them.

"Please tell us," Sandra said. She leaned closer into her husband who wrapped a comforting arm around her.

But the surgeon could not bring himself to speak. He stood, paced to the window, then placed two palms on the glass. "Stan's condition is worse. We ran him through a battery of neurological tests. He's unresponsive to anything we do."

The words hit like a punch to the stomach. Neither Sandra nor Fenton said anything. A blankness saturated their faces. Jaws slackened, mouths opened. Yet no sounds escaped their throats. Both heads drooped.

Holding Sandra tight, Fenton whispered at the floor. "Does that mean he's brain dead?"

"No. Stan's CAT scan shows he still has some brain activity, but it's not what he had. Topography tests indicate there is some brain damage."

"But his eyes open once in a while," Sandra said. "How can that be?"

"Some patients progress out of a coma and open their eyes," DeAngelis said. "Some even go through sleep wake cycles."

"I'm confused," Fenton said. "That sounds better than before. When he was in a coma, he wasn't…looked…he didn't do…anything."

DeAngelis spread his arms wide as if asking for forgiveness. "I admit, it seems contradictory. Usually, we don't know why patients move from one state to another. In Stan's case, the traumatic shock of being disconnected from his life support caused the change. What worries me is his unresponsiveness. His brain impulses are weak, pupils are fixed and dilated, there's no reaction to stimuli—"

"That sounds like brain dead to me," Sandra said, more of a murmur than a statement.

"No, brain death is the absence of brain activity. Total necrosis of cerebral neurons. Usually the result of severe blood loss or oxygen deprivation. It's irrevocable." He paused noticing Fenton and Sandra's eyes grow wide. "I'm not saying he's there yet, but in my professional opinion, the oxygen deprivation has thrown him into something called persistent vegetative state."

"Oh," Sandra moaned and buried her head into Fenton's side.

Fenton rubbed the back of his leg. "What does that mean…exactly?"

"In laymen's terms, it means he only looks to be awake," DeAngelis said. "But he's not aware of anything going on around him."

"And that's…"

"Not good."

Sandra's head rose. "Define 'not good'."

DeAngelis stared out the window for several moments before returning to stand behind the desk. Heavy hands went to his waist. Shoulders slouched under the weight of a profession that rarely fought fairly. "It means that there is virtually no chance that he will ever achieve higher level functioning. And the longer he stays that way, the more he'll spiral downward."

"And then?" Fenton said.

"Eventually," DeAngelis began, then stopped and shuffled his feet. Slowly he reached for the cap covering his head and dragged it away. He didn't bother to smooth his now mussed hair. "Eventually, his brain will just…"

Fenton leaned forward. "Quit?"

Bloodshot eyes nodded a confirmation.

Chapter 38

How could this be true? Tanya thought. How could she be so clueless? Though she had divorced Del, to have even attempted a life with such a piece of scum. Especially after all she had done to help him. To have once had his child in her womb. The bile in her gut scorched her throat as the awful realization stabbed at her heart. She swallowed hard, forcing it back down.

"Holly, do you mind if I ask you some questions?"

"Why?"

"I'm not good with silence, that's all. Who knows, maybe it'll help us."

"What do you want to know?"

"How did it happen, the kidnapping, how did he get you?"

Holly remained silent for several moments. She closed her eyes, then reopened them, a sense of resolve in her voice. "I was coming home from the movies. It was snowing like crazy. Normally I would walk along the sidewalk, but the cars kept splattering me with slush so I cut through some alleys." She paused to acknowledge Tanya's silent look.

"I know, that was stupid," Holly continued, "but I've walked to the theater by myself before, I knew the neighborhood and I've always felt safe there. I never thought I would be in danger. Anyway, somebody jumped out at me from behind a trash dumpster and grabbed me. He clamped his hand over my mouth so I couldn't scream for help. I got a glimpse of the pick-up before he threw a bag over my head and tossed me into the back. I tried to yell for help, but the bag muffled everything. Ended up here. That's it."

"And you never saw his face or heard him talking to another person?"

"No, I told you, he wore something over his head and kept a bag over mine most of the time." Holly shivered. "And it smelled too, like B.O."

Tanya winced. "How awful."

Holly sighed. "I just want to go home."

"I'll second that."

"Are you married?" Holly asked. "Your husband is probably as worried about you as my parents are of me."

Tanya fought hard to repel the explosion of disgust that wanted to erupt from her mouth. "Not anymore," she said, turning her head.

Holly bit her lip. "Sorry."

"Not your fault."

"Still."

"Do you have a boyfriend, Holly?"

"Not at the moment." A pause. "But I'm hoping."

"What kind of guys do you like?"

Holly thought for a moment. "Cute ones."

"Hmm. Do they like you?"

"Well, of course."

Tanya rolled to look at Holly. "I mean do they like you for *you*?"

"I don't know. The boys all tell me I'm pretty."

"I'm sure."

"What's that supposed to mean?" Holly asked.

"Nothing. I just hope you're not the kind of girl that is superficial and ignores substance."

"Er, not sure what that means."

"It means would you choose a hot guy over a good guy?"

Holly considered. "I'd take the good guy."

"Even if he was ugly?"

"I'm not like that."

"Mmmm." Tanya hesitated knowing the next question would likely light fireworks. "Yet when I asked you what kind of guy you liked, the first thing out of your mouth centered on looks."

"So? What's wrong with that?"

"Everything." A faraway look entered Tanya's eyes. "But you can't help it. At first, you probably told yourself looks didn't matter. But then everyone started dating and other girls were getting asked out and you weren't. Maybe guys wouldn't sit with you at lunchtime. They'd never flirt with you at your locker like they did other girls. You sit by the phone enough on Saturday nights and you begin to wonder. Is it me? And you know what? You find out you'll do anything to belong. Anything."

Tanya drew in air. "And just like that, you decide to change your life. You begin looking around at what others are doing, how they're dressing, who they're hanging out with. Before you know it, you decide who your friends are *because* of what they look like and not whether they're nice or not. And those friends will reinforce that whole lifestyle. How you dress, how you walk, how you talk, where you go, what you do. Everything.

"And then, if you're lucky, a guy will show interest in you. Maybe even a good-looking one. And despite everything in your head saying stop, you go for it. And you do it because you can't believe a guy is attracted to you. What's better is he's not what everyone thinks; he's got issues, weaknesses, things you can help him overcome. He actually needs *you* and that makes you feel like you're doing a good thing. So you'll do anything to keep him. Tell him anything. Do anything for him. Even things you know you shouldn't be doing. All because you are so convinced, beyond any rational thought, that if he stops liking you, you'll never find another guy in the whole universe that will be attracted to you. So scared that you'll never find another guy that will ever talk to you.

"And then you marry him. This hot guy. The guy you think everyone else is jealous of. Of course, you refuse to listen to the whispers that say the relationship isn't based on the right things. At first, everything is great. No responsibilities, and you think: how can life get any better? But then there are bills to pay and somebody loses a job or a family member dies. Life gets hard. And all of a sudden, that guy you did so much for doesn't even like talking to you anymore or can't be bothered to fix a leaky pipe or keep a job to pay the mortgage. Then he's going out more with his buddies than he is you. When you confront him with the things you don't like about your relationship, he smacks you around, like you're some kind of pestilence…"

Tanya's voice trailed off. There were several moments of silence filled only with a slight sob as tears welled in her eyes.

Holly's voice was meek. "You're not talking about me anymore, are you?"

"No," Tanya said, sniffing.

She fell into a silence as deep as a ditch on the side of a country road. The rut that was her life's regret. From its depths, she watched as endless rows of memories and emotions paraded on that same road, a rampaging trumpet section of mistakes and poor decisions. Of peer pressure and the path of youth lined by rose bushes. A path where flowers bloomed within arms-length, but still behind the thorns that grew early like acne. The scars of immaturity. Where chasing wealth and appearances ended in irony. Numbers on paper, but not wealth. Cosmetics, but not beauty. Where stubbornness trumped common sense and the brutal honest advice of friends and family.

Tanya's whisper crawled along the rotten floorboards. "I really thought I could help him."

Chapter 39

Vinnie Macino stood in the doorway of his six-bedroom house that backed up to the Huntington Valley Country Club. Snugged his Jerry Garcia tie and smoothed his hair before glancing down at his Italian shoes. Perfect. Clicked un-lock on the remote to his Porsche parked in the driveway. The oil-black vehicle responded with a quick two-tone chirp.

He tossed his leather satchel containing blueprints for a new mega-mall in the passenger seat, hopped in and gunned the engine to life. It was only a ten-minute drive to his penthouse office. Checked his knockoff-Rolex watch. Time enough to swing by Starbucks for an early morning soy latte. Looked up at his wife who waved goodbye from the upstairs window. He waved back and mouthed 'Love you' before she closed the drapes. He smirked. Maybe even enough time to drop in on Eileen for a quickie. The rap at the passenger side window startled him. Ernie McFadden, unshaven and looking like a bad Saturday night, peered through the glass. Vinnie hit the down window button.

"What the hell?" Vinnie said. "You scared the crap out of me."

"Heh, is that all it takes?" Ernie said. Coffee grounds, a wrapper from a stick of butter and maggots littered his army coat. His breath reeked of whiskey.

Vinnie frowned. "You look like you just crawled out of a dumpster."

Ernie found a piece of eggshell on his sleeve, picked it with grimy fingernails and flicked it into the backseat.

"Hey!" Vinnie exclaimed.

"Shut up," Ernie rasped and opened the door. "I'm in trouble." He struggled into the cramped interior, gasping with pain as he held his side.

"What's the matter with you?"

"I think I got busted ribs." Ernie glanced around. "Read the paper yet?"

"No, I usually pick it up on my way into the office."

"Huh, then you'll find out when everyone else does."

"What happened?"

Ernie scraped at his stubble. "Let's just say I got into a fight, all right?"

"Why don't I believe you?"

"I don't give a shit what you believe," Ernie grunted and swatted at Vinnie's gelled hair, getting only part of the way there before grimacing again.

"We can't talk here," Vinnie said. He backed out of the drive and pulled down the street half a block. "Ernie, you should go to the hospital."

"No can do, bro. Can't go home to the trailer either. I swiped some medical tape from the drug store and wrapped myself up tight. Broke into your neighbor's house looking for painkillers. Your neighbor's got a sweet-looking daughter by the way. You tappin' that?"

"She's fifteen."

A greasy grin slid across Ernie's face. "And your point?"

The Foiled Knight

Vinnie's eyes narrowed. "You haven't changed a bit."

"Up yours. Look, I need your help."

"I can't help you," Vinnie said, eying Ernie warily. "For whatever you've done. I probably shouldn't even be seen with you."

"I guess putting me up for a few days is out of the question, huh?"

"The dumpster suits you," Vinnie said. "And if I hear of anyone getting mugged for their groceries in the ACME parking lot, I'll know who did it."

"Some friend you are, douche bag."

"You burned that bridge when you tried to finger me for helping Del swindle that retirement money, remember?"

"Told you a thousand times," Ernie said. "That was Palmer, not me."

"Yeah, right. Like your word carries any weight."

"Whatever, dude. You got off, so no harm, no foul."

"Get the hell out," Vinnie snapped. "I'm late for work."

"Don't bullshit me," Ernie snarled. "I know where you go most weekday mornings." He slapped Vinnie in the shoulder. "Eileen Harding, huh? You're one to talk about who hasn't changed."

"Beat it, Ernie or I'll get my lawyer to file a restraining order against you."

"Big talk, mister big shot Huntington Valley developer, think you're shit don't stink. Well, I know all your shit, *remember?*"

"I'm clean now."

"Maybe, but the crap I know goes back eons. Juicy too. Bribing the Zoning Commission, tsk, tsk. Kind of stuff the newspapers devour."

Vinnie's eyes went wide. "You're a snake."

"The slimiest," Ernie said. "But you're pretty slimy too. So, for insurance, if you don't help me out, word just might get back to your little wifey up in the window about your affair with Eileen."

Vinnie massaged his forehead. "What do you want?"

"I need some dough, and your hunting rifle."

"No way. You're not wasting anyone with my rifle."

"Who said anything about wasting anyone? I need to get out of town and lay low for a while, maybe go camp out in the mountains for a bit."

"How do I know that's really what you're going to do?"

"You don't," Ernie said, grinning. "But it don't matter. The cash isn't traceable and you can always claim the rifle was stolen." The grin disappeared behind a scowl of stone. "Gimme what I want Vinnie, or you'll have some 'splaining to do to your wife."

Vinnie shifted into gear, set his jaw and stepped on the gas. "You suck, Ernie. Always have."

Chapter 40

The sunlight that had temporarily chased the darkness away from the shed retreated behind the horizon, pursued by another, more powerful demon: time. The wind, dormant during the day, returned. Bleak and random, it burped and howled in intermittent bursts, like an old man honking into a snot rag. Bugs came and went, their visits lasting only the few seconds necessary to sniff for food before disappearing through cracks. Through it all, the cold stayed, enveloping everything with no appetite for escape, a penetrating invasion of privacy. Raw, biting and consistent, it chewed its way to the core of Tanya and Holly's bones.

They had been lying still, drained and weary from hours of trying to loosen their bonds. Their wrists were chafed and bleeding, their voices reduced to ragged rasps from fruitless yelling. Spirits ebbing, they curled on the hard-knotted floor, sometimes touching, most times not. Soft growls from their stomachs mixed with the surges of wind.

"You awake?" Tanya asked.

There was a rustling noise. "Yeah, too hard to sleep," Holly said. "My side is numb again."

"Roll over, helps keep your blood circulating."

"I have been, but I can't go more than a few minutes before I get sore again."

Tanya noticed that Holly's voice seemed smaller than even just yesterday. It had been more than twenty-four hours since either of them had last eaten. If she herself was hungry, the kid had to be starving. Tanya's stomach growled again. A cramp of emptiness gnawed at her insides. "Have they ever gone this long without bringing you something to eat?"

"No," Holly said. "Think that means something?"

"I don't know. Maybe it's good, maybe it's bad. If they're just out doing things like getting more provisions, that's one thing, but—"

"—Getting provisions wouldn't take this long," Holly interrupted.

"No, it wouldn't."

"Maybe they've moved to a different hideaway."

"Maybe they've been caught by the police," Tanya said. "Either way…"

Neither said aloud what both were thinking. If the kidnappers had fled, there was no way they would be getting food or water anytime soon. And if the kidnappers had been arrested, but refused to talk, the police wouldn't know where to search. The wind screeched.

"What'll we do?" Holly asked. "My stomach hurts really bad. I'm really tired and can't hardly move my tongue… so thirsty."

"Me too. I don't know what to do, but we can't give up. If the creep has been caught, people will be out searching for us. My dad is probably out looking right now."

"Yeah, but how's he gonna know where to look?"

"The same way I found you," Tanya said, trying to sound confident.

"Which was?"

"I returned to the scene of the accident."

"What accident?" Holly asked.

"My friend's."

"The guy with the worm?"

"Yeah, him," Tanya said.

"What happened?"

"Hit a deer with his car."

"Ohhh," Holly gasped.

"Yeah, he's hurt really bad."

"Is he going to be all right?"

"Dunno," Tanya said, her voice catching a bit. "Tubes and wires…"

"Oh, sorry to hear that."

"Thanks. I've been visiting him every day. Had been anyway."

"What's his name?" Holly asked. "You talk a lot about him and the things you did together, but you've never once said his name."

Tanya rolled onto her side so she could face Holly. In the diminishing light, the girl looked ghastly. Eyes sunken into her head, skin stretched tight over her face, she looked like a bloodied scarecrow. "His name is Stan."

"Stanley?" Holly mimicked with a whine in her voice.

"Heh, don't let him hear you say that. He'll get really mad."

"Okay then, how'd you meet him?"

"We've known each other our whole lives, grew up in the same neighborhood, went to the same school."

"He your boyfriend?"

"No. We did things together all the time. Used to explore. He saved me from this rabid dog once." Tanya felt a pang of hurt cramp her chest.

"That must have been pretty scary."

"Mmmm. But funny thing, that same day, we were each other's first kiss."

"He liked you?"

"Yeah, I guess he did. And wasn't afraid to show it."

"How do you mean?"

"On my thirteenth birthday, he gave me a painting, that he did himself, of him and me holding hands."

"Awe! How sweet."

"I know, it was the most endearing present anyone has ever given me." Tanya closed her eyes remembering the thrill when she had unwrapped it in front of everyone at the party.

"No guy I know would be caught dead doing something like that," Holly said.

"He took a lot of crap from his buddies for it, but it didn't seem to bug him too much. And then he wrote an adventure story where he and I were the main characters."

"You guys sound tight."

"We were close all right. Pretty much shared everything, knew every little detail about each other. Even the dirt. But we never declared or anything like that. Although we did sort of end up together after our prom. I guess that's the closest thing we've ever done that could constitute a date."

"What do you mean, didn't you go together?"

"No. It's a long story. Stan's date bagged him and my date was in on a practical joke. Stan saved the day." She smiled. *Just like The Foiled Knight.*

"What's so funny?" Holly said.

"Nothing. It's just ironic that a lot of people I know hated their prom and it turned out to be one of the best nights of my life."

Holly thumped her head against the floor. "I just hope I get to go to my prom at this point." A sob. "But the way things are going…"

"Hey!" Tanya said. "We're not thinking negative thoughts. We're gonna get out of this. We've just got to work together and figure a way. Okay?"

No response.

"I said okay?"

Holly sniffed back her tears. "Okay."

"You're gonna go to your prom, Holly, I promise you that. And you're going to have a great time. Maybe not as great a time as I did, but hey…"

"I thought you said your date played a trick on you?"

"He did, but he wasn't the mastermind behind the trick, he wasn't smart enough…" And as the words trailed away, a sudden dawning of illumination came upon Tanya. *Del isn't smart enough to pull off something like a kidnapping. And who else would he be in cahoots with but Ernie McFadden?*

"Hello?" Holly said.

Tanya started. "Huh?

"He wasn't the mastermind…"

"Oh, right. But he went along with it. And then Stan came through. A bunch of us went skinny dipping, and the kids we were with took mine and Stan's clothes and ditched us."

"Left you naked?" Holly asked wide-eyed.

"No, we had our underwear on, but still, as a shy eighteen-year-old, it was traumatic. And then they called the cops on us so we ran like maniacs and barged through people's backyards looking for clothes. Didn't get home until dawn. Stan told my parents it was all his fault that I got home so late."

"He sounds like a good guy," Holly said. "How come you never got married?"

"Augh," Tanya sighed. "That's an even longer story."

"Like we got anywhere to go."

"Nor is it a happy one."

"I find that hard to believe," Holly said.

"Trust me, it's full of warts. I never told anyone the whole story before."

"Well, look at it this way; I might be the only one, you know?"

Tanya looked at Holly with concerned eyes. They shared a moment.

Holly's eyes pleaded. "It would be a shame if you never got to tell this secret. Who am I gonna tell anyway?"

"I guess you're right," Tanya said and sucked in a chest full of air. "All right, don't say I didn't warn you."

"I've been warned," Holly said, her cheeks stretching a tiny bit in an attempt to smile.

Tanya paused and suddenly felt elated at seeing Holly's happiness. There hadn't been much of that in either of their lives recently. It felt good to have some semblance of feeling good. And then she blinked. *And in a weird way it's all because of Stan.*

"Why do you keep doing that?" Holly asked.

"Do what?" Tanya asked.

"You like... go somewhere... in your mind. I can tell. You just drift off and get this look in your eyes. And then you always smile. Wherever you go, must be someplace nice."

"Yeah, I guess. I never thought of it that way."

"So, how come you two never got married?"

"Not gonna let me skate, are you?"

"Nope."

"All right. So it was when we were in college, right before Thanksgiving break. He came to pick me up and give me a ride home, but I wasn't ready."

"Hadn't packed yet?"

"Not exactly. Truth is, I had gotten really drunk."

"Oh. Great timing."

"Yeaaaah... so, anyway, we talked and he found out why."

"Why?"

Tanya paused. "Even if we make it out of here, I don't ever want you to repeat this, okay?"

"I swear," Holly said.

"I was pregnant."

"Oh my God."

"Yeah," Tanya said, grimacing. "By the hot guy."

"Figured," Holly said. Her eyes widened at Tanya's scowl. "Sorry. So what happened?"

"Stan flipped out. We argued like never before. Nasty crude. I mean we were vicious at each other."

"Things that neither of you is willing to take back," Holly added.

"Worse," Tanya said. "Stan tried to talk me out of having the baby, but I was bullheaded and told him I was going to have it. I was young, I didn't know anything. And then I said the thing that hurt him the most."

"What?"

"I told him the most we would ever be is friends."

"Ouch. I'll bet that hurt. What happened then?"

"By that time we were yelling at each other, furious and all, and he told me to get out of his life." Tanya paused to suck in some air. "We were arguing at the top of the steps in my sorority house." She closed her eyes to gather her strength, then reopened them a moment later. "I lost my balance and fell down a flight of steps."

"Oh no!"

"I broke my leg real bad." Tanya felt her voice crack. "I wanted to be a dancer and join a professional touring company, but the injury was too severe. I know it was an accident, but still…"

"What about the baby?"

Tanya sucked in more air. "I lost it."

"My God!"

"It was horrible. Poor Gracie."

Holly's brow furrowed. "Who's Gracie?"

"That's what I would have named her if it had been a girl. No one else knows that by the way, besides you. I was devastated. Got all depressed. I never finished school. And you know the real tragedy? To this day, Stan thinks it was all his fault. He carries the guilt of not only having ruined my dream of dancing, but he also feels responsible for what happened to the baby."

"Oh my goodness," Holly cried. "That is so sad."

"I told you it was not a happy story."

"I can't believe it. You two sound like you were so right for each other."

"Were."

"You never tried to reconcile?"

"Sort of. We talked and made up, but it was never quite the same. He couldn't bear to look me in the eye." Tanya sniffed. "We've stayed in touch. My marriage, was, well, I told you, Stan helped me through the tough times."

"How?"

"When things got bad between me and my husband, I would phone Stan. And he always took my call, no matter where he was or what he was doing or what time I would call. Such a good listener. I could tell he was still pissed, but in spite of everything that happened, he never judged me. And he never tried to solve my problems either. He just let me talk. I think he knew that most times I just needed someone to vent to." She paused. "He knows me so well. And the really sad part is I never really appreciated that. At least not until now." Tanya's voice caught. "I never appreciated how deep our bond is."

A few moments of silence passed. The wind continued its sporadic wails. In between gusts sounded the soothing whispers of breathing.

"I read a book once," Holly began, "that said the greatest display of commitment to another person that you have feelings for is unconditional acceptance. Warts and all, you accept them for who they are and never tear them down."

"Pretty powerful stuff if you can ever find that," Tanya said.

"I hope I find a guy someday that I can be that close to."

"You will, Holly. Don't ever give up on your dreams. I remember Stan used to tell me: 'If you give up your dream, you die'. Even though we weren't together, he never gave up on me. That's why he wrote that story about him and me. It was always his dream to be a writer. It was his way of keeping our relationship alive. So I can't give up on him. This may sound strange, but I had to try to pick up for him. That's why I came back to the scene of the accident."

"Yeah, about that," Holly said. "How did visiting the scene of his accident lead you to find me?"

Tanya relayed her theory about Stan possibly knowing something about Holly's kidnapping and getting chased by the criminals.

The Foiled Knight

"I heard gunshots that night. You think they were shooting at Stan and that's what caused him to crash?"

"Yes," Tanya said. "Well, I can't be sure, but I found two bullet holes in a tree." Suddenly she blurted: "My car!"

"What?"

"My car! It's parked by the side of Terwood Road. Somebody will find it."

"Terwood Road?" Holly said. "That's where we are?"

"Yes, this is good. Maybe it'll be reported to the police. Abandoned car or something. They'll trace my license plate."

"How far away from the road are we?"

"I don't know. I'm not good with distance. Pretty far."

Holly looked doubtful. "What's going to cause them to search in the woods? You said hardly anyone knows about this cabin."

Tanya shook her head. "Stan's father knows about it. And so does mine. They'll figure it out, just like I did."

Chapter 41

Kurt kicked the back door closed on the windy evening and lugged a load of firewood into the Davis family room. He tossed another log onto the fire. "Laura? Fenton? Can I get you anything while I'm up?"

Perched on a folding chair, Laura curled her feet underneath her and shuffled a deck of cards. "I'm fine dear." She scooted closer to the green-felted card table, took a quick sip of tea and set the cup down in her saucer with an intentional *tink*. She arched amused eyebrows. "Another round of Hearts, Fenton, or have you had enough?"

"I surrender," Fenton replied. "If Kurt shoots the moon one more time, I'm conking him over the head with a log."

Kurt slid back into his seat at the table opposite Fenton and raised a mug of hot chocolate. "I won't do it again."

"Don't fall for that idle promise," Laura said. "I'll get a new kitchen before he keeps that one."

"Very funny," Kurt said. "How's the leg, Fenton?"

"Little stiff, no biggie."

"You're one tough nut."

"Makes two of us," Fenton said and held out a fist that Kurt thumped. "No word yet from Tanya?"

"No."

Fenton studied the tautness in Kurt's face and the death grip he held on the mug. Having a daughter had been tough on Kurt. Mostly conservative, he never mastered Tanya's delicate transition from childhood to adolescence. The early years had been easy. Physical comedy and hugs went a long way. But when puberty arrived, all of the rules changed. Tanya started to think for herself and assert her own personality, a character value that, while encouraged by both parents, worked more for Laura than Kurt. Laura and Tanya's relationship thrived as they dealt with peer pressure, drinking, sexuality and other social issues. In contrast, Kurt's connection with Tanya suffered as she no longer responded to the old jokes.

"We'll find her, bud," Fenton said. "Don't worry."

"I'm not worried," Kurt said. He took the cards from Laura and began shuffling them in spastic jabs.

"I know you're not," Fenton said, making eye contact with Laura.

The hardest part, by far, had been the dating. Kurt never completely trusted any boy to be responsible for his little girl. Once, when Tanya went to a "girls only" sleepover where the parents were supposedly chaperoning, Kurt parked in the shadows down the street. Around midnight, he busted up a no-parents-at-home party where boys tried to sneak in alcohol through a basement window.

"Too bad Sandra isn't here," Laura said. "We could play guys against the

The Foiled Knight

girls. What time was she staying with Stan till?"

"Till they kick her out," Fenton said. "But don't think we don't see through the sham going on here. Last minute card game…this smells of a Sandra and Laura caper to give Kurt and me something to do so we don't drive everybody crazy."

"Everyone's stressed," Laura said. "We're just trying to help."

Fenton placed a reassuring hand on Laura's. "I know and I appreciate it, but what we really need is a chore."

"Like what?" Laura asked, eyes shifting from one man to the other.

"A task," Kurt added.

Laura held up a hand. "Wait a minute you two, I'm not—"

Fenton stood. "A quest."

Kurt kicked his chair away. "For the missing daughter." He set his mug down, disappeared into the mud room and returned with two coats, tossing one to Fenton.

"Where are you going?" Laura asked.

"Been working on a hunch," Fenton said. "We're going to check it out."

* * *

They jumped into Kurt's SUV and headed east out of Abington along Old Welsh Road. A busy thoroughfare during the day, Old Welsh had been heavily salted by plows and thus clear and coated white. Traffic was light in the post rush hour period; the night calm, but still bitter. Kurt fired up the heated leather seats and flicked on the radio. Gordon Lightfoot's *The Wreck of the Edmund Fitzgerald* played on the oldies channel.

"Thanks for going with me, Kurt," Fenton said, pointing to the left. "Here's the turn."

Kurt down-shifted the SUV, kicked in the four-wheel drive and made the left turn onto Terwood Road. Immediately, he needed his full concentration on the less-travelled road as the thawing and refreezing winter cycles had created a myriad of jagged tire ruts that jolted the vehicle about. He fought the wheel a few seconds before regaining control. "What do you think we'll find?"

Fenton shrugged. "No idea. The cops have been searching everywhere, but sitting around on my duff was driving me bonkers." He snapped off the radio.

"You know," Kurt said, "if you're right about the timing of the 911 call in relation to the accident, maybe we'll get lucky." He squinted out at the thirty yards of frozen white chop illuminated by his headlights. Trees and shrubbery flashed by. The road snaked and twisted deeper into the woods.

"How much farther?" Fenton asked.

"Not far, we're along the back of the country club." He pointed to his left. "You can just barely make out the glow from the clubhouse through breaks in the trees. In the summer time, you can't see shit because of all the leaves."

"We'll be at the cave pretty soon," Fenton said.

"No, that's still a ways," Kurt replied and turned the wheel sharply around a bend. "Stan's accident should be—" He went silent as his headlights lit up the rear of a car tucked behind dense foliage on the shoulder of the road. "Hey, that looks like Tanya's Camaro. What's it doing hidden like that?"

"Pull up behind it," Fenton said.

They parked, grabbed flashlights and jumped out. The cold night ripped at their skin with razor teeth. Turning up the collars of their coats, they approached the vehicle from the rear.

"It's definitely hers," Kurt said, kicking at the thick tires. "I remember when she had it painted." He pointed. "And made the guy order vintage '68 midnight blue metallic paint."

"What's inside?" Fenton asked.

Kurt played his flashlight around the interior. Specks of dust floated about the bright beam of light. "Nothing."

"Keys? White distress rag?"

"Nope. Empty, like someone abandoned it." He flashed the beam up and down the road. "Desolate."

"Yeah," Fenton said shining his flashlight into the woods. Evergreen trees swayed side to side, their branches floating about in a spastic octopus-like thrash. "And creepy."

Kurt aimed the light at the ground. "I got footprints from her door," he pointed, "heading that way. Come on."

They walked side by side along the shoulder of the road, each sweeping the wilderness with criss-crossing beams of light. Their boots crunched. The wind howled and whistled through the trees. Fallen leaves rustled. Away from the ambient light of town, stars were easily discernible in the night sky. The half-moon, low in the distance, cast a glow over the valley, not quite enough to see by, but just enough for them to make out shapes.

Fenton stopped. "Look." He pointed his light. "There, down into the creek and up again and then through those trees."

"Tire tracks," Kurt mused. He looked up and lit up the side of the mountain with a beam of white. "Hey isn't this…?"

"Yes it is," Fenton said, his pulse quickening. "It's the old dirt road that goes back to Sawtrigger's cabin."

"You don't think…?" Kurt said letting the sentence hang there for the wind to whip at it.

Their eyes locked.

* * *

"Do you really think someone will find your car?" Holly said.

"Yes, I do," Tanya answered. "And when they do, we've got to find a way to get their attention."

"How?"

"I don't know, exactly. Think MacGyver. Maybe we can signal them. Smoke, or sound, something."

"We can't do anything the way we are tied up," Holly said.

"We've got to find a way to free our hands," Tanya replied. "Hell, even if we could get our hands in the front of our bodies, that would be an improvement. If I could slide my hands under my butt, I might be able to get my legs through."

"I can't do that," Holly said. "Already tried. I'm not flexible enough."

"Maybe not, but I am. Even though I stopped dancing, I never stopped stretching and doing my exercises. I can still put my leg behind my head."

* * *

The Foiled Knight

Ernie switched the rifle from one shoulder to the other as he trudged through the forest toward the cabin. His face, beet-red from the long walk from town, hurt from the biting wind. Vinnie had refused to provide any more taxi services and dropped Ernie at a roadside diner with forty dollars before peeling away. The ragged army coat provided little protection. Toes frozen, ribs throbbing, stomach growling, Ernie marched. Over boulders, through bushes, around trees, he pressed into the darkness, guided only by an internal compass that worked on autopilot.

He had to get back before the police figured everything out. They could already charge him with assault on the hospital staff. That didn't bother him. The attempted murder charge, however... Unless a lawyer could find a technicality or swing a jury to believe that Del acted alone, he was toast. A stretch, he knew, but there would be no stretching the truth about kidnapping or rape if Tanya or the girl survived.

A close grouping of trees appeared over the last rise. *Perfect*, he thought. *I'll do a little recon of the area, just to be sure it's safe.* He settled gingerly into the crotch of the trees, minimizing the twist on his ribs. Lifted Vinnie's rifle to his shoulder and peered through the magnifying scope at Sawtrigger's cabin, three hundred yards away. Nestled into the mountain, the house lay cold and quiet. Because of the ridge, he could only make out the top half of the house, but there were no lights on and no smoke from the chimney. Not that he expected the police to be dumb enough to light a fire. The house was dead.

He panned the scope around the surrounding terrain all coated white with snow. Nothing moved. Down the access road, through a grove of trees and toward Terwood Road. He froze. There, two shadowy figures were examining the trees by the side of the road. The beams from their flashlights flicked back and forth from the ground to holes in the tree trunks. "God dammit!" *Who the hell are these assholes?* As if in response, the one figure illuminated the face of the other. Fenton Palmer. *Shit.* Ernie eased his grip on the rifle and pressed the scope to his forehead. What to do? *If I ignore them, they might come to the cabin.* The pressing quickly escalated to a repeated ramming of the scope against his skull. *But if I take them out, they can't tell anyone anything.* The cold steel jolted his brain.

Repositioning the scope to his eye, Ernie blew out a slow stream of air, focused the sights on the back of the man's head and pulled the trigger.

* * *

Tanya tucked her knees into her chest and stretched her arms as far as the rope would allow until her hands were at her lower back. She rolled onto her back. For the first time in hours, she was able to lie flat backed on the floor.

"So far so, good," Tanya whispered. "But here comes the hard part." Grimacing, she fought off the pain from shoulder muscles not designed for such movement. Her hands reached her tailbone and she worked to slide them across her jeans. The fit was tight. "Ooof, I'm stuck." Tanya grunted and tried again. Her hands slid a bit more.

"Keep going," Holly said. "You're almost—"

Crack! The muffled explosion echoed all around them.

First silence, then eye contact. Holly's eyes bulged. "What was that?"

"Sounded like a gunshot," Tanya said. "Maybe it's a hunter. Yell."
"Help! Somebody! Help us! We're in here!"
"Quiet," Tanya said, "Let's see if they answer."
The wind howled a depressing wail.
"Nothing," Holly said.
"They'll never hear us while we're in this shed."
"We gotta get your hands free."
"I need more slack," Tanya said.
"Stretch."
"I can't get any traction."
"Then we'll make some," Holly said, her voice full of purpose. "Here, turn your back to me. Press your feet against the wall. I'll brace myself against this wall and push your hands past your butt with my feet."

They squirmed and wriggled so that Holly could brace her shoulders against the wall and use it as an anchor. On the other side, Tanya turned her back to Holly and placed her feet against the wall. By doing so, leverage was applied to the middle.

"Okay, ready?" Tanya said.
"Ready," Holly replied. "One, two, three, go."
They both pushed. Tanya's hands moved an inch. And with it came pain. The stretching of her shoulder ligaments shot daggers throughout her body. "Augh!"

Holly slackened for a split second before Tanya barked at her: "Don't you dare stop. Come on! Shove!"

Holly thrust her feet forward, hard and frantic. She sensed movement. Another inch. Now two. She heard Tanya scream.

Tanya slammed her eyes shut, tucked her chin and gritted her teeth. "Harder! I'm almost—"

Holly sucked in air and pushed, a desperate, unthinking heave fueled by two weeks of anger. Straining, her own rope bonds tearing at skin, Holly heard another scream. Her own. And then the release as Tanya's hands cleared.

* * *

The impact of the bullet into the tree trunk sprayed bark into Fenton's face. Shards of wood splinters ripped his skin. He threw himself to the icy ground. "Get down!"

An experienced hunter himself, Kurt recognized the rifle shot and dove to his belly behind a massive pine. "You hit?"

"No." Fenton touched his hand to his face and came away with a smear of blood. "Got strafed by some wood chips, but I'm okay. Kill your flashlight."

"Okay. Where'd it come from?"
"The mountain."
"Hunter?" Kurt asked.
"No way, not at this time of night."
"Who then?"
"It's a wild guess," Fenton said, "but whoever caused Stan's accident may also be responsible for Tanya's disappearance."

"What'll we do?"

"Stay outta sight, that's what."

Kurt glanced left, then right. "We can't just lay here, we're sitting ducks."

"He can't see us if we keep our flashlights off."

"We gotta get him."

"Not we," Fenton said and pulled out his cell phone. "The police." He flipped it open and began dialing. "We're outgunned and he's got the high ground. If we try to—"

Blood spurted as the phone exploded in his hand.

* * *

Ernie howled in delight as his second shot found its mark. The elder Palmer hadn't thought that even the dim display of the cell phone would glow like a beacon in the powerful magnification of the rifle scope. After missing his first shot, Ernie had chided himself for not having accounted for the wind. A quick adjustment to his scope put him back on target.

He scanned the dense copse of trees. Except for branches swaying in the wind, there was nothing. His prey had learned quickly.

* * *

"There's another one," Holly shouted as the second rifle shot echoed across the valley. "We gotta get out of here."

Tanya struggled to stand and hopped to where she remembered seeing a saw hanging high on the wall, too high to reach with her hands. With her face, she probed around until she felt the hard metal frame. Stooping, she used the top of her head to push the saw towards the rafters until it cleared the hook. It clattered to the floor. Tanya pounced and searched blindly with her hands, found the tool and positioned it between her thighs, sharp teeth facing up. Back and forth she scraped the ropes across the jagged edges. The stubborn knots frayed and in seconds she was free. "I did it!"

"Hurry," Holly urged. "Untie me."

After sawing through the rope around her own ankles, Tanya feverishly cut Holly free. Together they stood. Almost immediately, Holly's legs buckled.

"Why can't I stand?" she cried.

"You've been tied up for so long," Tanya said, "your muscles are weak. We need to get some blood flowing through them." She rubbed Holly's thighs and calves briskly. "Come on, let's try again."

Tanya helped Holly to her feet.

The young girl wobbled for a few moments, but stayed erect. "I'll be okay," she said and felt her way in the dark. She tried rotating the wooden latch on the door, but it wouldn't budge. "It's locked. Shit!"

"We need more light," Tanya said.

"There's a camping lantern on the wall."

They scoured the walls with fumbling hands until Holly latched onto the lamp's wire handle. "Found it," she said and began playing with knobs. A click sounded and the interior filled with light. "There." She hung the lamp on a nail.

Tanya whirled around looking at the blood-stained walls for anything they could use to hack their way out. "Here!" She pulled a rusty pick-axe from its hook and almost fell over from the weight. Regaining her balance, she set her feet and swung clumsily at the door. A dull thud sounded, but the wood remained intact. She tried again with the same result. "I'm not strong enough."

"Both of us," Holly said and grasped the handle with both hands.

Together they raised the heavy tool into the air.

"Aim for the handle," Tanya said. "Now."

Down came the thick iron blade square on target. *Crack!* The head of the ancient pick snapped off and fell to the floor, leaving them standing with only a wooden handle in their hands.

"Dammit!" Tanya growled and flung the handle. Her eyes became slits of fury. She grabbed Holly by the arm. "Come here."

"What are we doing?"

"Getting out of here. I'm sick and tired of this bullshit." Tanya pointed at the side wall. "The door looks new, but the walls are rotting. If we run at it, I'll bet we can blast right through it."

Backing away, they leaned against the far wall. "Ready?" Tanya said. "One. Two. Three. Go!"

In two strides, they hit the opposite wall with their combined weight. A splintering noise sounded as rotting posts gave way and the entire shed tipped over and then fell apart. Tanya and Holly floundered into a frigid night and a howling wind.

"Help! Help! If you are hunters, don't leave! And don't shoot us! We're by the cabin!"

* * *

"Sonofabitch!" Fenton cried. He clamped down on his left hand. "What was I thinking!"

"Where'd he get you?" Kurt said.

"My hand. Goddam it hurts." He drove both hands into the snow to numb the pain. "We gotta get out of here, that maniac is out of control!"

"He knows exactly where we are," Kurt said. "If we move, he'll nail us when we run."

"He could be changing position right now to get the angle on us," Fenton said. "We've gotta move."

"You bleeding bad?"

Fenton extracted his hands and removed his glove. A dark expanding stain oozed from the center of his palm. "Yeah."

"Get some pressure on it," Kurt said. "Here." He yanked a handkerchief from his pocket and tossed it to Fenton.

Fenton wrapped his hand tightly, tying the knot with his teeth.

"What do you think about splitting up?" Kurt said.

"Good idea; maybe it'll confuse him long enough for one of us to get to the car. We can call the police from the Mobil station on Welsh."

The sound of wailing shouts reached their ears. They exchanged worried glances.

"Did you hear that?" Fenton asked.

"Yeah. Sounded like a woman shouting."

The wails sounded again. "Help! We're by the cabin!"

"That was Tanya!" Kurt shouted and scrambled into the open. He burst into a flat-out sprint toward the voices.

The Foiled Knight

"Kurt!" Fenton hollered. "Get outta sight." He stared in frantic horror as Kurt hurtled into darkness. "Shit!" He spun around trying to decide what to do. He couldn't leave them, his phone was destroyed and he had no weapon. And neither did Kurt. "Fuck it!" Leaving his hiding spot, Fenton scaled the mountain in the direction of the gunshots.

* * *

Ernie panned the scope around the entire perimeter of the cabin. Still dark. Still no movement. He could hear the bitches shouting, but he couldn't see them. *Must be hiding under the stairwell*, he thought. *How the hell did they get out of the shed? It doesn't matter...*

A dashing shadow appeared from behind the trees. Ernie couldn't tell the man's face, but the athletic frame and speed told him it was Kurt Davis. Ernie tried to catch him in the crosshairs, but the man disappeared behind the large rock outcropping. Ernie's attention jerked in the opposite direction at the sound of a snapping twig. Then another. The adrenaline boost tightened his grip on the rifle. *Someone's close.* More thrashing. He smiled. *Someone's dead.* Slinging the rifle over his shoulder, he belly-crept away from the copse of trees.

* * *

Kurt raced around the rock outcropping toward the cabin. "Tanya! Honey, it's me."

"Dad! I'm here." The hysterical reply came from the darkness beneath the cabin. "Is it safe to come out? We heard gunshots."

"No, don't come out," Kurt said. "I'll come to you." Taking care to shield his flashlight, Kurt approached the cabin until he spotted Tanya hiding in a gap between the mountain and the house. He rushed in and wrapped his arms around her. "It's all right baby, I've got you. Are you hurt?"

"No, just really dehydrated and hungry." Tanya turned toward Holly still in the shadows. "It's okay; you can come out. This is my dad."

Holly crept forward on scrawny legs.

Kurt gasped at the girl's appearance. "Are you the Mathews girl?"

"Yes," she said, her voice weak. "Can you get us out of here?"

"Gonna try," Kurt said. "But we've got a problem. There's a lunatic on top of the mountain with a rifle. We've got to stay out of his sight."

* * *

Ernie slid silently from tree to tree. It had been several minutes since he'd heard the last of the snapping twigs. Either his prey had found softer ground or had stopped moving. He brought the scope to his eye and scanned the area. Stars exploded when the rock hit him in the side of the head. Reverberations rattled through his skull; the rifle fell from his hands. Then searing pain. Vision blurring. World spinning. He fell to the ground, blood trickling from the gash in his temple.

* * *

Like fog at dawn, Fenton crept through the woods. *Get to a new spot*, he thought. The rock he'd thrown had hit the assailant solid, Fenton was sure of it. Not sure enough however to rush the nest. Idiot should have knelt to make himself less conspicuous. But he's hurt now. The thud and way the man went down meant he would be disoriented. And mad as hell when his head cleared.

That was okay though. As long as Kurt and Tanya could get away.

* * *

Ernie half-staggered, half crawled through the forest. *Keep moving!* His military training had taught him if the enemy knew your location, don't stay put. A freight train roared through his skull, fire scorched his ribs. He scrambled behind some boulders and cursed at himself for being spotted. Grimacing in pain, he crouched to a sniper's tucked-kneel and tried searching the forest through the scope. Salty sweat poured into his eye; he pawed at it with a bloody hand. The sting made him want to cry out; he swallowed it. *Don't give away your position.* But the wind and darkness weren't cooperating. It was difficult to distinguish tree branches from human limbs. Ernie kept at it, looking for sudden bursts of a shadow instead of gentle swaying.

* * *

Crab-walking low, Fenton scurried beneath branches and slithered over felled tree trunks. The moon cast eerie shadows through the trees and helped light his way. He took care not to step into a clearing. Jumping a small ravine, he came upon a triangle of thick Leyland Cyprus and crawled into the center. From here, nature had formed an enclosure. He squatted with his back against the largest one, mindlessly rubbing sap from his palms. Couldn't get Kurt and Tanya out of his mind. Probably weak, she would move slowly. *Need more time. Think man – improvise!* Fenton studied his environment. The elements were in his favor with one huge exception: *the man has a rifle and all I have are rocks.* He glanced at his boots.

* * *

Movement was everywhere. Branches were breaking in the wind. Ernie forced himself to stay slow and methodical in his scouring of the area. Blood gunked up the scope; he did his best to wipe it clean. At it again: up, down, adjust, past some dense pines. *There!* Behind a cluster of trees, a man in the shadows. From Ernie's original position atop the mountain, the hiding spot would have been totally obscured. But from this new angle, he had a clear line of sight to the target. *I have you now.* Bringing the rifle level, he placed the man in his crosshairs.

* * *

"Who is he?" Holly asked.
"Dunno, but he almost nailed us twice," Kurt said.
"How did you find us?" Tanya asked.
"We found your car by the road. Come on!" He moved to leave.
"Wait," Holly said, motioning to her bare feet. "I need shoes."
Kurt glanced around, then at the house. "I'll check the cabin, stay here out of sight." He stole up the steps. A minute later, he returned with Holly's snow boots and two blankets. "Hurry, we've got to—"
The explosion of three rapid-fire rifle shots cut him off.
Tanya and Holly screamed.
"Be quiet!" Kurt hissed. "They weren't at us."
"Who else is with you?" Tanya asked.
"Mr. Palmer."
Tanya's hand flew to her mouth. "What if he's been shot?"

The Foiled Knight

"You don't know that," Kurt said meeting Tanya's eyes. He couldn't hold her gaze. "Let's get out of here."

* * *

Ernie silently approached the man's hideout in the grove of trees. As he reached the largest trunk, he swung into view, rifle poised for action. And froze. There, speared onto the top of a six-foot tall cross made of tree branches, was a chunk of snow the size of a man's head. A winter coat hung from the horizontal piece of wood. The crude prop teetered as the wind changed. Ernie studied how the branches had been lashed together with shoelaces. He shoved his fingers through three holes in the upper back of the coat.

* * *

"Stay close to the rock outcropping," Kurt said. "We'll use it as a shield." With the girls weak from their imprisonment, he braced each with a strong arm and practically carried them into the woods. His powerful legs drove them forward through the heavy snow and around the trees. Eventually, they burst through the forest and into a clearing by the road.

"Dad," Tanya cried, "we can't just leave Mr. Palmer back there! He might be hurt, or—"

"We don't have a choice," Kurt cut across her. "The bastard has a rifle and we don't have anything."

"But—"

"Look, I'm worried too," Kurt said, "but Fenton has training, he knows how to take care of himself. Right now, the best thing we can do is get to a phone and call the police."

Rustling sounded from the trees. A sweaty-faced Fenton pushed his way through the foliage, panting with exhaustion. "You made it," he said and hugged Tanya before shaking hands with Kurt.

"Thank God," Kurt said.

"We thought you'd been shot," Tanya said.

Fenton held up his bandaged hand. "He got me once."

"Oh my God," Tanya said. "Are you all right?"

"I'll be fine."

"Where's your coat?" Tanya asked. "And you've only one boot."

"Never mind," Fenton said, then paused noticing Holly. "Who are you?"

"I'm Holly. Holly Mathews. I'm the reason why your son is in the hospital."

Fenton's only reaction was to blink.

Tanya turned to Kurt. "Dad, I think it's Ernie McFadden. And I'm pretty sure Del is in on it with him."

Kurt and Fenton exchanged glances. "She doesn't know," Fenton said.

"Know what?"

"We, ah," Kurt stumbled. "There was…"

Tanya leaned forward, the sinking feeling returning. "What is it?"

"I'm afraid I have some bad news."

"Later," Fenton said. "We're exposed standing in this open area. Let's get you girls to safety." He guided them toward the car. "We'll come back for the Camaro, after we call the police."

They all jumped in the SUV. Dual rooster tails of snow and ice shot from the thick tires as they sped away.

* * *

Anger built up inside Ernie and he roared a guttural scream. He went wild, thrashing the coat about, ripping it to pieces, stomping it, a baboon in a frenzied tantrum. He stabbed the shredded fabric with his rifle, eventually flinging it into the upper branches. But the rage would not subside and he beat the ground with a fist. After several minutes, he collapsed. Cursing, he spat blood and tottered to his feet, rifle dangling loosely from an index finger. With his other hand gripping sore ribs, he lumbered toward the lake, a mass of frustrated fury. The darkness had long since swallowed him up when the sirens sounded.

Chapter 42

The day after the rifle attack in the woods, Stan's new hospital room attracted the most attention of any patient on the floor. Sandra Palmer and Laura Davis hunched in chairs while Fenton, Kurt and Fitzy leaned against the window sipping coffee. Tanya nestled next to Stan. Detectives Ciquero and Westerman, bundled in parkas, caps and hiking boots and looking fatigued, stood at the foot of the bed.

"We searched the woods and the surrounding area," Ciquero said. "Found the spots where McFadden was shooting from. We had plenty of men looking, but he didn't leave anything behind to tell us where he might have gone." He lifted his cap and ran a gloved hand across disheveled hair. "We did find footprints that led to the road where he likely hitched a ride, but…"

"But he could be anywhere by now," Kurt finished.

The detective's perspiring face fell. "We did our best, but there was too much acreage to cover and with the head start…well…" He paused and shifted weight from one leg to the other as his forehead wrinkled and melting snow dripped from his boots to the floor. "How's the gunshot wound, Mr. Palmer?"

"I'm fine," Fenton said, waving him off with a heavily bandaged hand. "What about the cabin?"

Westerman removed his hat and smoothed his white hair, sending pine needles falling to the floor. "Searched that too. We collected plenty of physical evidence against McFadden. Combined with the girl's testimony, we've got everything we need to arrest him."

"Do you think you can catch him?" Fitzy asked.

"McFadden's face is posted all over town and with every news station," Westerman replied. "We've notified the airport, bus and train stations. Port Authority too."

Fenton leaned close to Kurt and whispered. "He's had over twelve hours head start." The two men exchanged knowing looks.

As if sensing their doubt, Ciquero added: "We've also sent an artist's sketch of McFadden to all the surrounding precincts. His face will be on every newscast today. If he surfaces, we'll nail him."

"I don't like the idea of a maniac with a rifle and a vendetta running loose in our neighborhood," Laura said. "What can be done to protect our families?"

"We'll have a squad car parked in front of everyone's house for the next few days," Westerman said.

Kurt stared out at the overcast day. The muscles in his forearm twitched. "Are we supposed to stay indoors all day?"

"Might not be a bad idea for awhile," Ciquero said. "Give us a chance to search for him."

"What about the press?" Fenton asked. "I don't want a bunch of reporters on my lawn."

"Don't blame you," Ciquero said, massaging his forehead. "Talk to them, don't talk to them, it's your choice." He hesitated. "*But*, it might work in our favor if both Mrs. Palmer and Mrs. Davis were seen on local TV broadcasts saying McFadden must be caught."

"Holly's parents will be doing the same thing," Westerman said. "The public will be much more in tune with looking for McFadden if they see sympathetic moms they can connect with."

Sandra reached for Fenton's arm. "I'm doing it."

"Me too," Laura added.

Kurt and Fenton made eye contact, followed by several moments of reading each other's minds, then a subtle nod from each. No one noticed the exchange except Westerman and Ciquero, who in turn traded knowing glances.

"Good idea," Fenton said.

"I hope it helps us nail the slimeball," Kurt said. "Who could do such perverted things to a little girl? Scumbag."

"Kurt!" Laura exclaimed.

"What? Every father in the community should be allowed to harpoon the bunghole up his ass for what he did to Holly."

"Amen," Fitzy said.

Laura's jaw dropped at the same time Westerman elbowed Ciquero.

Ciquero placed a steady hand on Kurt's arm. "Mr. Davis, please calm—"

"How is she?" Tanya asked, sensing the building tension. "How is Holly?"

"She's doing fine," Sandra interjected quickly. "I checked on her. Severely malnourished and dehydrated, but she's hooked up to IVs. The doctor said she should be fine in a few days." She glanced at Fenton. "Physically anyway."

"The hospital has good people that Holly can talk to about this," Westerman said.

"Maybe even go back to school this semester?" Laura asked.

Westerman frowned. "No. At best she'll go back in the fall."

"Her parents will likely be up to see all of you sometime today," Ciquero said. "They want to thank you for rescuing their daughter."

"Well I'm going to thank them," Tanya said, raising everyone's eyebrows. She glanced around. "Holly's a tough little nugget. There's no way we could have gotten out of that shed without her."

Jenny snuck in, carrying a clip chart. "Hi everyone, no reason to leave. I just need to take a few readings."

"How are you feeling, Jenny?" Fenton asked.

"I'm okay, just a bad bump on the head. Nothing serious like getting shot at like you all."

Tanya squeezed Jenny's hand. "That's good to hear."

"Never mind me," Jenny said, speaking directly to Tanya. "How are you holding up?"

"Don't know how to answer that." The veins in Tanya's neck went taut like guitar strings. "I'm still numb. I just can't believe that Del would get mixed up in something like that." She paused. "Both of his parents are dead so I'm going to take care of the funeral."

The Foiled Knight

Everyone went silent as Tanya absentmindedly took Stan's hand.

"I don't think I'm ready for that," Tanya finished.

"I'll help you," Fitzy said.

Sandra rose from her chair and stood next to Tanya. "It'll be all right, dear. We'll all help you through it. Just like you've been helping us through this."

Tanya looked at Sandra with moist eyes. "He's not going to wake up, is he?"

Sandra's lips trembled as she stared at her feet. Tanya's eyes shifted to Jenny.

A flush of heat flared across Jenny's collar. She glanced from one set of worried eyes to another. The scrutiny choked her throat. Adjusting her stethoscope, she hurried from the room mumbling that no one should give up hope. Heads turned at the sound of a clipboard clattering to the floor and Jenny's muffled sobs.

Chapter 43

To the citizens of Glenside, it was the end of a winter day like any other. A day of work or school. A day for shoveling, shopping, skiing, or chopping firewood. A day to drink hot chocolate, watch old movies, or catch a cold.

Traffic had died down by the time Tanya pulled her Camaro into the parking lot of Fitzy's bar. She locked the door and dodged patches of black ice as she trudged to the front door.

With a yank on the wooden handle, she was in. A cloud of aromas hit her in the face as the door thumped her in the rear. Buffalo wings, blue cheese dressing, fries with brown gravy, beer, winter coats, leather gloves and melted salty snow. She looked around at the happy hour crowd. Unlucky souls who had something go wrong with their day made up for it by feasting on a hot and gooey Philly cheese steak, washed down with a cold draft.

Tanya removed her coat and saddled up to the bar. *"Searching So Long"* by Chicago played on the juke box. The flat screen on the far wall featured a college basketball game. LaSalle was crushing Villanova and the commentator in danger of abusing his quota of 'Yeah, baby!' expletives.

The door from the back room yawned. Bright light filled the door frame for a fleeting moment before a large and dark silhouette stepped into view. The shadow materialized into Fitzy carrying a tray-load of freshly washed mugs. He made eye contact with Tanya, hesitated, then with a grunt, set the tray on the bar and set about polishing them one by one before hanging them on hooks in the rafters. "You here for advice on life?"

Tanya half smirked. "You don't waste any time."

"You're not exactly a newbie that I have to get to know first," he said with a sideways glance.

She arched her eyebrows. "Heh."

Fitzy positioned a mug under a tap.

She cleared her throat.

Fitzy paused.

Her stare fixed him.

A tilt of his head. "Tequila?"

"Mmmm."

He laid a beefy hand on the bar, open palm up. "Keys."

She furrowed her brow.

"Solves that," he said and pulled the tap. "Just one, agreed? And something to eat or else I'm driving you home."

"Agreed," Tanya sighed.

"Be right back." He leaned into the kitchen to convey instructions to some unseen person. He returned to find Tanya rolling the mug between her palms.

"You know Fitzy," she said, "for a good guy, you sure can be a royal pain in the ass."

"Thank you," he beamed and clanged the bell normally reserved for when a customer leaves a healthy tip.

"Did they teach you that in bartender school?" she asked.

Fitzy laughed. "Never went to bartender school. Or bar owner school. Or people manager school."

Tanya set the mug down, leaned forward with elbows on the bar and interlocked her fingers. "So how'd you get so good at all three?"

"The shingle in my office," he made a thumbing motion over his shoulder, "says I've got a college degree from LaSalle, but I've learned more about how to be an entrepreneur by listening to businessmen spill their guts here at the bar than anything I learned in college."

"Entrepreneur?"

"Go ahead, make fun, but I deal with the same issues any Fortune 500 company faces." He accepted a used mug from a customer and dunked it in a basin filled with soapy water. "Customer service." He rinsed the mug and held it aloft. "Product presentation." Unfolding a lunch menu, he pointed to the list of choices. "Pricing, merchandising, spoilage." He tapped a button on the register and pointed at the opening cash drawer. "Cash flow, inventory, employee theft." With a thump from his hip, he shut it. "Supply, demand, competitive pressure. You name it, we got it."

"Wow," Tanya said. "No one's ever explained it so clearly for me before."

"I always figured I would take over the bar from Dad. It's not such a bad life. I don't answer to anybody but me and I'm not digging ditches. I sponsor all the local athletic teams which brings me return business and I get to meet new people every day."

"You provide a place where people can belong," Tanya added.

"And, for no charge, I get to offer up my worldly advice."

"So what would the all-powerful, all-knowing Swami's advice be to me?"

"We'll get to that," Fitzy said, patting her hand. "First things first. How are you doing, physically? Can't imagine being tied up in a cabin in the woods in the middle of winter to be the best thing for one's health."

"I'm good. I ate like a horse and drank a thousand gallons of water after we got to safety. The doctor checked me out and I'm fine."

"That's great."

The front door banged as a new patron entered.

Tanya's entire body flinched, then relaxed as she tried to act calm.

His face contorted into a look that silently said, *Fine, huh?*

She shrugged. "You blame me?"

He shrugged back. "Nope. Anything new on Ernie? Do the police have any idea where he is or what he's up to?"

"No, they think he's fled the country."

"Good riddance. Hard to believe someone we went to school with could turn out to be such a slimeball."

"Monster is more the word."

"I wish I could have been there that day in first grade when you and Stan beat the crap out of him."

"We could have used you," Tanya said. "All we had were lunchboxes."

"And now he's on the run, with a rifle. Scary."

"It's terrifying is what it is," she said, shivering. "Ugh. Can we not talk about him?"

"Absolutely. What would you like to talk about?"

Tanya blew out a gust of air. "I don't know. Life."

"The cosmos," Fitzy added.

"Yeah," she said in a whisper. "What's the meaning of it all?"

"Keeping it light, huh?" he said with a grin.

She smiled along with him. It felt good to be with someone who understood her. But the smile soon faded and a faraway look blanketed her face as her mind took her through a summation of her life. A wonderful childhood, the difficult teenage years, the life changing events in college, her short and miserable marriage to Del and finally, the re-emergence, though catastrophic, of Stan. Finally, she took a sip of beer.

"Fitzy…"

"Mmm?"

"Did you ever think growing up around here," she spoke more into the mug than to him, "that our lives would end up like this?"

"When you say 'end up like this' do you mean in a good way or…"

"Both. Neither. I don't know."

"Not sure how to answer that," Fitzy said. He scrubbed his scalp with calm fingers. "But what I think you're trying not to say is, how did you waste your time with Del, am I right?"

"Something like that."

Fitzy sucked in some air. "Well, pretty sure you are not going to like this, but you did come to me, and I am your friend so I owe it to you to speak the truth." He brought his fist down silently on the bar. "So kick me the hell out of my own bar, but there's a reason you haven't got on a stitch of black. You're not exactly mourning him are you?"

Tanya's eyes riveted on Fitzy's. He bored back with equal effort. The stare down went on for several moments until finally she relented.

"I can't hide it, can I?" she said.

"Maybe from most folks…"

"Does that make me a bad person?"

"No."

"Does that make me a sinner?"

"Of course not."

"Well then, what's it make me?"

"It doesn't make you anything," Fitzy said. "It just means you're human."

She took a long swig of beer. "Why did I think I could help him?"

"Dunno."

"What did I owe him?"

"Nothing."

"He was a lousy husband," Tanya spat.

"Here we go," Fitzy said under his breath.

She rapped the bar with hardened knuckles. "He complained about everything I did. Never had a nice thing to say."

"Whiner."

"Never wanted to do anything, or go anywhere."

"Lazy ass."

"Treated me like shit."

"No doubt about that."

"Then he lost his job and was content to live off unemployment benefits… that was the beginning of the end."

"Moocher."

Tanya waived an arm in the air. "And look what it led him to. The fact that he was messed up in the whole Holly kidnapping thing just makes me want to puke for eternity." She pretended to stick her finger down her throat.

"Scum bag," Fitzy said.

"He's worse than a scum bag!" Tanya exclaimed.

Fitzy's eyebrows rose.

"But you know what?" Tanya continued. "You know what hurt more than anything else? More than the beating, more than the low life friends, more than anything, what hurt most of all was he made me feel like a loser."

"He was a shit, Tanya."

"You can say that again."

"You, are not a loser."

"Damn right I'm not. A martyr maybe, but definitely not a loser."

Fitzy slapped the bar. "You know what I think you should do?"

"What's that?"

"I think you should just bury the asshole and move on."

"Bury him."

"Bury him like a cat buries its shit and spray sand in his face."

A lurid smile crept across her face. She stood with a fist in the air. "Bury that shit!"

The bar went quiet as all eyes focused on them.

They looked back in defiance. A lonely crack of the billiard table sounded from the back room.

After a second, Fitzy spread his arms out wide and pointed at the basketball game on the flat screen TV. "What? It was a three-pointer."

The crowd went back to its business.

Plopping down onto the stool, Tanya gave Fitzy a subtle high-five. "Nice save!"

"I'm adding PR and spin doctor to the list of entrepreneurial skills."

She sighed. "Boy, that felt great."

He stood to his full height. "I'm glad to hear you say that. Vee ahr makeeng eggzellent proggrez, my dear."

She gave him a withering look.

A waiter appeared and set down a plate overflowing with a Philly cheese steak and fries.

"Oh. My. God," Tanya said and sank her teeth into the soft and moist Amoroso roll. "Mmm." She motioned to her empty mug.

Fitzy poured another.

"So tell me, Swami," Tanya began. A glob of cheese oozed from the corner of her mouth. A flick of her tongue wicked it away. "What other worldly advice do you have for me?"

Fitzy snatched the dish towel from his shoulder, planted his feet, and started drying a newly cleaned mug. His eyes focused on Tanya, lips in a tight, thin line, hands working slowly and methodically. Inside and out he worked the towel, until the mug gleamed. Never once did his eyes leave her. Finally, he hung the mug on a hook and spread his palms flat on the bar.

"Are you sure you want to go there?" he asked.

She blinked as a flush rushed across her face while heat built up on her neck. She set the sandwich down. "Whu—"

"Don't back away now, Tanya. The Del question was just a dodge. You haven't given a shit about him in fifteen years. But with this one, well, you open the proverbial box."

"I didn't think—"

"Yes you did," Fitzy said. "That's why you're really here, isn't it?"

"No, I, um—"

"Hummina, hummina, hummina," Fitzy said. "Look, let's cut the bullshit. What you really want is for me to tell you what to do about Stan."

Tanya's jaw clenched shut as her eyes and nostrils flared. "Sonofabitch, you did it again."

"You can't go to school with someone since fourth grade and hope to get away with crap like that, sweetheart. I about said the same thing to Stan the night of his accident."

"Yeah?"

"Yep." He squinted and pointed a pistol-finger to a spot three feet from Tanya. "Sat at that stool right there."

"What did you guys talk about?"

Fitzy poured himself a beer. "Eileen Harding."

Tanya's face contorted into a wretched twist. "What? Why?"

"She got all pasted then crash and burned while jamming."

Holding up a palm, Tanya signaled for a stop. "You need to translate that."

Fitzy rolled his eyes. "She got drunk and fell down on the dance floor. Made a total fool of herself."

"Sounds just like her."

"Of course it does. But the reason I'm telling you is because of what happened next."

Tanya came to attention, but said nothing.

"Stan, just like the good guy he is, leapt to the rescue and helped her up."

"And that," Tanya said, "despite it being Eileen Harding, sounds exactly like Stan."

"Yeah, but she looked at him like he was from another planet and just slithered away, didn't even bother to say thank you."

"Skank."

"That's what I said," Fitzy said laughing.

"So what'd Stan say?"

"He said some things never change."

Tanya's forehead rippled. "I don't get it."

"Let me finish. I answered him by saying that was a good thing."

She scanned the ceiling with roving eyes. "Still not following you."

"Then follow this," Fitzy said. "What is good is how you two have always felt about each other. That's never changed."

She clunked her forehead to the bar, moaning, "Here we go again."

Fitzy's big belly laugh reverberated throughout the bar. He lifted her chin. "You have no idea how alike you two are. Last time Stan was here, I laid into him too about how you two should just bury whatever is eating away at you and he did the same forward face plant you just did."

"I'll bet mine was more graceful."

"Nope, you're both pathetic, actually."

"Whatever, look, Fitzy, don't preach to me, okay?"

Fitzy leaned on the bar with his Popeye forearms. His face was so close, Tanya could count the pores in his nose. But it was the intensity in his eyes that shot nervousness to her core.

"I'm not preaching," he said. "But let me ask you something personal."

She recoiled slightly. "Uh, oh."

"No, it's all right" he said. "I promise."

She moved close to him again.

"When you were tied up in that cabin, did you think you were a goner?"

Tanya set her mug down slowly. Her arms unconsciously went across her chest and she tucked her hands under her armpits. "Yes."

"It's okay," Fitzy said. "I would have been scared too." He extended an open palm.

She slid her hand into his and gasped. "Oh." So soft and gentle. He stroked her hand, slowly, back and forth, then across.

"And who did you think of most of the time?"

Tanya's face pinched a bit as she fought back the horribleness of the treatment and the fact that her ex-husband had been a part of it. "All I could—" Her lips trembled.

"It's all right," he said, his voice tender. "I'm right here."

"All I could talk about was Stan."

A silence settled around them in a bubble of privacy that drowned the outside world to a distant hum.

"I can't help it," she continued. "I still have feelings for him."

"Always have."

She nodded. "Since day one."

"That's right. Don't ever forget that. Think about all of the adventures you two have had over the course of your lives. All the secrets you shared."

"We could talk to each other about anything."

"Probably trusted each other with your most intimate thoughts."

"We were best friends," she said, nodding.

"Are."

She smiled. "Are."

He leaned forward and kissed her on the forehead. "That's what I wanted to hear."

A boulder of tension lifted from her shoulders. She pressed her forehead to his. "Thank you, Fitzy."

"No charge, sweetheart." He leaned back and resumed drying mugs. "Any idea what you're going to do?"

"Not yet."

"Hmmm," Fitzy hummed while stroking his chin. "So my work isn't entirely done here."

Tanya looked at him. "What?"

"Here's the thing. The last time I saw Stan, all he was doing was helping people. Before he got here, he helped dig out a family stuck in the snow. Then he tried to help Eileen, even though she's a witch who didn't deserve it. Then he gave money to a complete stranger so the old codger could have a beer to soak his woes."

"So what's your point?"

"My point, my dear, is that guys like Stan are one in a million. The world needs more like him to help the rest of us sorry slouches make it through life. If there was ever a guy that deserved a break, it's him."

Tanya shook her head and nibbled on a french fry, silent, munching for a while processing the statement. "You know, Stan didn't wish to be kept alive artificially."

"Sounds like him. Doesn't want to be a burden."

"It's so hard to see him just lying there, wasting away."

"I know," Fitzy said. "What's his prognosis?"

"Not good. He's in something called persistent vegetative state."

"What the hell does that mean?"

"It means that if he doesn't improve in the next month or so, he probably never will."

Fitzy was silent a long time. He threw his mug into the soapy sink. "Shit."

"And you should also know Stan's parents want to honor his wishes."

"But it's your call isn't it?" Fitzy asked, nodding slowly.

"Yes it is," Tanya said, then suddenly she rattled her head. "How'd you know that?"

"Alan Malone."

Tanya's jaw dropped. "That's confidential information!"

"Can I help it if Alan gets loose lipped when he drinks?" He pretended to watch the ballgame.

Her eyes slanted. "Or maybe you intentionally pumped him full of booze and tricked it out of him?"

Fitzy's head swiveled very slowly toward her until guilty eyes came into view. When his mouth opened, but nothing came out, she continued: "You can't go to school with someone since fourth grade and hope—"

"All right, all right," Fitzy said. "I may have slid him a free beer or two."

"Or six."

"Actually it was closer to eight."

They stared at each other for a few seconds before Tanya lowered her glare. "Ah, what the hell, I would have done the same thing."

"So?" Fitzy asked.

The Foiled Knight

She hesitated, then wiped her mouth with a napkin. "So, right now, I'm just going to take it one day at a time. It'll come to me."

"Okay, but think about what we talked about just now."

"I will, Fitzy, I promise."

"Have you talked to Stan's parents?"

"Not yet."

"You should."

"I will."

"When?"

She held her hands up. "Criminy, Fitzy, what are you, my mother?"

Fitzy's face exuded a bright glow as if he had just swallowed the sun.

Tanya paused. "What the hell is that look for?"

"I must look a lot like each of your mothers because Stan asked me that very same thing." He stole a fry.

"Oh, for Christ's sake," Tanya sighed. "I'm outta here."

She fished some bills out of her purse and tossed them on the bar. Fitzy balled them up and threw them back at her.

She looked at him quizzically.

His stare was like a tombstone. "On the Fitz."

Tanya took her money and left.

Chapter 44

Fenton rose from his reading chair in the corner of the Palmer family room, tossed his book onto the coffee table and limped to the fireplace, picked up a log and poised to drop it into the fire. "Too cold for you, Sandra?"

Sandra lay the magazine she had been reading on her chest and wiggled her fuzzy slippers. "No, it feels just right dear, thank you." She extended her legs across the length of their couch, adjusted her pillow and went back to the article.

He returned the log back to the pile. "Another cup of tea?"

"No."

"Want to watch a movie?"

"No."

"Play a game?"

"Fenton, I just want to read my mag."

"Wanna fool around?"

She rolled her eyes. "In the family room? Go get yourself a beer if you can't relax."

He fumbled with the top button of his flannel shirt. "I can't help it. It's been a month since the attack. Sitting here doing nothing is driving me crazy. I need a project. Give me something to do."

"You're *looking* for a project?" Sandra asked. She exaggerated the lift of her eyebrows while dipping her head to peer over the top of her glasses. An unspoken gesture, one he'd seen a thousand times before. One he'd never been able to fend off. A look that had nothing to do with Fenton's handiness around the house, that they both knew was beyond contestation and everything to do with challenging him to say what was really on his mind.

"You know what I mean," he said and flopped back into his chair. The leather material groaned in protest. He grabbed the TV remote, clicked the flat screen on and began surfing through channels. After about eight seconds, he turned it off. "Augh, a thousand channels and still there's nothing on."

With a sigh, Sandra swung her feet onto the floor. "I'll never get through this article with you in this mood. Let's talk."

"About what?" Fenton asked.

"About the elephant in the room, that's what."

Fenton went still. "Now?"

"You're looking for something to do."

"Yes, but now?"

"You've been avoiding me all day on the subject," Sandra said. "We have to talk about it." Her face grew hard and her jaw trembled slightly as she gritted through the words. "The doctor said once Stan got to the four week mark in that same condition that there wasn't anything more to do."

Fenton tugged on both sides of the collar of his shirt. "But Tanya is coming over later."

"All the more reason for us to be aligned on this."

"Mmmm." More fumbling with buttons.

She placed the magazine into the rack next to the couch and reached for her tea. "I'm sorry, I don't speak mumble."

"Why do you think she asked to come over?"

Sandra shrugged. "I don't know, I talked to her on the phone today, but she mumbles like you. Said something about wanting to see his old room."

"Why?"

"What difference does it make, Fenton? Stop avoiding the question. What do you think we should do?"

Up out of the chair, Fenton stomped back to the fireplace and tossed a log onto the fire. "Stan wouldn't want to live like this. That's not life."

"Agreed," she said. "But what do *you* think?"

"It doesn't matter what I think."

"Of course it matters, Fenton, we're all that's left. How can it not?"

He huffed. "The only thing that matters is what Stan wanted."

"There's no way he could have wanted this."

"There's no way he could have *imagined* this, Sandra."

She set her cup on the coffee table. "Imagined what?"

"This. This…pressure that we're under now." He snatched the poker and stabbed at the fire.

She rose from the couch, padded softly across the room and encircled her arms around his waist while pressing her head against his back. "It'll be all right. We'll figure it out."

"I don't think I can do it," Fenton said. "I don't think I can pull the plug on my own son."

"Don't think of it that way. It won't be you. It'll be us. And we can do it if we truly love him."

"Some love."

Sandra tugged. "You know what I meant."

"When do you want to do it?"

"First things first," she said. "We've got to convince Tanya that it's the humane thing to do."

Fenton shook his head. "You know she's against it."

"And our lawyer is prepared to contest her position of authority in the whole thing."

"That's just going to get ugly."

"Yes it is," Sandra replied, a tear collecting in her eye. "Did you talk to Kurt?"

"Yes."

"And?"

"And nothing. He's sticking by Tanya."

"Does he know that we know about…?"

"I don't think he or Laura knows anything about what we know, period."

Sandra remained silent, but the squeeze of her arms told him the anguish she was preparing for. Without Tanya's concurrence, there was only one way they could wrestle away power of attorney from her. And the ensuing humiliation would probably drive an irreparable wedge between both families.

With his injured hand, he stroked her forearm. "I'm not built for this."

She pressed her body into his. "Yes you are, Fenton Palmer. You're built like no other man I've ever known."

The heat that had been burning the backs of her hands dissipated as his hands covered hers.

Chapter 45

Tanya eased the Camaro to the curb in front of the Palmer house and let the 454 engine thrum its throaty idle. The slightest of vibrations coursed through the frame, a ridiculous contrast compared to the power that lay beneath the hood. She slid the Hurst stick shift into park and killed the motor. The sad, warbling wail of the electric guitar from "*The Air That I Breathe*" by The Hollies filled the interior. Pressing her head against the window, Tanya stared at the home where she had practically grown up.

While quaint and well maintained, the house showed its age, but for things only she could notice. Gone was the monstrosity of a TV antenna that had broken off in a violent windstorm, landing on the Palmer family station wagon. They hadn't had the money to repair the dent it left in the hood, so the ugly crater stayed for over a year. Tanya knew it had added insult to injury for Stan who drove the jalopy to the prom.

The hedges lining the driveway on the left side of the house had grown to twice the height since the days when she and Stan used them as a poor-man's high jump. Paint peeled from the underside of the wrought-iron railing that met at the corner of the property into a Colonial street lamp, the casing of which sported another dent, compliments of a wayward Stan fastball. A forty-watt bulb glowed dull and yellow inside the lamp's cobweb-filled cavity. It cast a soft halo on the now cracked sidewalk where they used to race their skateboards. During the summer, Sandra Palmer, knowing that a verbal command would only embarrass her son, would click the light off and on in secret code for Stan to come in.

She took a deep breath, tugged the key from the ignition and opened the door. The shock of cold wind hardly fazed her as she trudged up the driveway and around to the back door. Only two kinds of people went to the Palmer's front door: people needing directions and solicitors. Even the mailman knew to go to the back.

Tanya removed her glove and felt the rough texture of the house's stucco walls. When Stan first learned how to ride a bike, he had lost control and crashed into the stucco, scraping the skin off his fingers. His scars had never completely faded.

Cinching up her collar, she rapped on the screen door and glanced at the backyard. The wide garage with matching stucco exterior squatted dark and lonely at the back of the property. Ten feet above ground, a single heavy-duty wire ran from the house to the garage bringing electricity to the two-car structure. The basketball hoop that Fenton had secured to the garage had since been removed. How many hours had she and Stan whiled away playing Over The Wire or HORSE? The garden to the right that had overflowed with tomato plants in summers past was now a snow-covered tundra of withered vines. The creak of the screen door startled her.

"Good Lord, Tanya," Sandra said. "Whatever are you doing standing in this cold weather?"

"Huh? Oh, nothing. Just reminiscing, I guess."

Sandra held the door open. "Come in. Let me make you some tea."

"Yes ma'am."

Tanya stepped past Sandra into the kitchen, the buttery aroma of baking filling her lungs. She glanced around at the smartly arranged workspace: a daisy-outlined shopping list on the fridge door, wooden table tucked snuggly into the corner, potpourri smoldering on the window ledge and golden oak cabinets that matched the hardwood floors. A tingling sensation spread through her.

Sandra donned cooking mittens and opened the oven door. "Fenton is in the family room. Go ahead in. I'll be along in a minute."

Tanya kicked off her boots and padded along the hallway, glancing at Palmer family photographs taken over the years. A squeak from the hardwood floor reminded her of Stan and her failed attempt at a clandestine sneak out to witness a lunar eclipse. She laughed and followed the sound of snapping and crackling to the family room where a bright orangey-yellow fire blazed in the hearth. The hardwood ended and she stepped onto the carpet. The softness caressed her feet and a sense of being home swept over her. A memory of a game of Stratego flashed in her mind. Stan had set his flag close to a lake and lost in less than ten moves. The ensuing argument from Stan demanding a "do-over" resulted in their expulsion from the house by Sandra who insisted they take advantage of the sunshiny day. Still chuckling, her eyes were drawn to an oil painting of 18th century hunters on horseback following dogs chasing a fox; a family heirloom painted by Fenton's grandfather. She covered her mouth remembering how she and Stan had accidently knocked it off the wall when jumping on the couch. They never confessed to the crime.

Fenton sat in the corner in a leather chair reading the newspaper. Upon seeing Tanya, he tossed the paper, stood and crossed the room to greet her with a warm handshake. "Hello Tanya, how are you?"

She noticed the gauze bandages that still wrapped his gunshot wound. "I'm fine sir, thanks for asking. How is your hand?"

"Much better," he said and reached into the magazine rack for a rubber ball. "Gotta love those physical therapists. They come up with the most ingenious methods of recovery."

For the first time, Tanya noticed how powerful Fenton's hands were as he went to work squeezing and releasing. "That's good," she said. "I don't know if I can ever thank you enough for coming to Holly's and my rescue."

"Nonsense," he said with a wave. "You were the smart one who found her. Please sit down."

"Yes sir." She crouched awkwardly onto the edge of an armchair next to the fire.

"And it took a lot of bravery for you to go in after her," he said and tossed the ball into the magazine basket, then hesitated to make sure she was looking at him. "Not many people would have done that."

"Thank you, sir."

The Foiled Knight

Fenton cocked his head. "What's with the 'sir'? Since when have you ever felt the need to be so formal with us?"

Tanya fidgeted, played with her hair, then tugged at the pockets of her corduroy slacks. "I don't know." Her eyes went everywhere but toward him.

"Here we are everyone," Sandra said, carrying a tray of cups, a teapot, sugar, cream and some chocolate covered croissants. "Made these little treats myself." She set the tray onto the coffee table.

Fenton served Tanya, waiting until she met his gaze before letting go of her cup.

Sandra caught the exchange. "Are you all right, Tanya?"

"I'm fine. I guess it'll take a while to get over everything that's happened."

"We are absolutely amazed at how you've been able to maintain your composure. Especially during Del's funeral. That must have been tough."

"It was." She lied. She'd hardly felt any remorse at all. Whether it had showed or not, she didn't know. Her only sense of regret: a decision of youth for which she couldn't ever do anything.

Fenton's face softened a bit as he noticed the rippling lines on Tanya's forehead. He handed Sandra a cup before serving himself. "These look good." He plopped into his chair and bit into the warm dessert. "Mmm, Honey, they're so moist. Terrific, as usual. Tanya, try one."

"I've already had dinner."

"One bite won't hurt you."

Tanya looked at her shoes. "I'm not very hungry."

"You're hurting Mrs. Palmer's feelings."

"No she's not," Sandra said. "Fenton, leave the poor girl alone. It's all right if she doesn't want one." She turned to Tanya. "Don't pay any attention to the grizzly bear in the corner. He's miserable when he's penned up in his cave for too long." She cast her husband a reprimanding glare.

He mouthed back: "All right."

"Well, maybe I should at least try one," Tanya said and slid the smallest croissant onto a plate.

"So what's this I hear you're going back to school?" Sandra asked. "Oh, sorry dear, I didn't mean to catch you with your mouth full."

Tanya covered her mouth. "No it's all right." She swallowed quickly. "The rumor is true. I only need one semester to complete the course work for my college degree."

"That's terrific."

"And I've decided to give dance lessons. I have that big old basement, it'll take a bit of work, but I plan to set up a studio like Mrs. Lehman's. I figure I'll start small and go from there."

"Good use of your natural talent," Fenton said.

"Thank you, sir," Tanya said. Her hand drifted to her leg.

"Again with the sir."

"Fenton." Sandra's tone cut quick.

He lifted his palms. "Sorry."

"So I guess we're wondering," Sandra continued quickly, "why you wanted to come over. And I don't mean to sound like you're not welcome here, because you know you are. It's just that, well, it sounded…special."

Tanya shuffled her feet. "I was hoping to visit Stan's room."

"Why?"

"I don't know. I haven't been up there in forever. I'm hoping it will give me some wisdom. For, erm, well, you know."

"Oh, I see."

Tanya flushed. "If it's inappropriate, I totally understand."

"Nonsense," Fenton interrupted. "You go ahead and take all the time you like. Sleep there if you need to."

Sandra's face sagged into a world-weary frown. "Fenton."

"What?"

"Don't be ridiculous."

"It's all right," Tanya said, almost smiling. "That won't be necessary. I just need a few minutes."

"Do you want to take your tea up with you dear?" Sandra asked.

"Yes, that would be nice, thank you, Mrs. Palmer." She picked up her cup and stood for an awkward moment.

"What's wrong?" Sandra asked.

"Not sure. I haven't been to Stan's room in years."

"It's changed quite a bit from what you remember. We use it as a guest room nowadays."

"Oh."

"But it's still first room on the right," Sandra said and pointed toward the stairs.

"Of course. I won't be long." Turning, she glided down the hall and took the stairs one at a time until she reached the landing just outside Stan's room.

The white wooden door still bore the faint outline of the letters spelling out Stan "The Man" Palmer. Stan had attached letters the summer before he left for college. After he moved out for good, Sandra had scraped off the decals and tried painting over them. Tanya reached for the silvery doorknob and pushed her way inside.

The room was a tiny nine by nine with a single bed next to the lone window. A bookshelf and student's wooden desk were against the opposite wall. The same beat-up beige linoleum tile that she remembered covered the floor, but the royal blue walls were bare. All of Stan's posters were gone as were the model cars. A weight bench collected dust in the corner.

She shifted aimlessly to the bookshelf where the only mementos in the room remained. Her mind wandered through the milestones of a life. A baseball signed by Hall-of-Fame pitcher Sandy Koufax crowned a miniature replica of Veterans Stadium. Stan's baseball glove leaned against it. Shot glasses from the boardwalk in Wildwood, New Jersey. A slingshot. His class ring. Baseball cards. A flat magnet in the shape of the Thunderbolt roller coaster from Willow Grove Park. Two tickets to a Bruce Springsteen concert were pinned to the corkboard along with a photo of Stan in a tuxedo at Fitzy's wedding. Across the top shelf were other photos, all framed. First Communion, Stan's Eagle Scout ceremony, high school and college graduations, and a charity golf tournament group shot with baseball great Stan Musial.

The Foiled Knight

Tanya noticed one photograph lay face down. Setting her teacup down, she picked it up and fought to control the mad rush of emotion that surged into her chest. Staring back at her was an image of a teenage Tanya standing on Stan's shoulders, while he, waist deep in ocean waves, held her hands in a wobbly cheerleader-like grip. They beamed youthful smiles and wore skimpy bathing suits that clung to their wet bodies. Tanya's laughter echoed off the walls as she remembered how Stan had dumped her backwards when she had tried to stuff her toe up his nose. She set the photo upright and stroked her index finger along the side of his face. Once again. And a third time, this one bringing a cringe of hurt. Turning toward Stan's desk, her breath caught.

Atop a block of wood stood a small, but gallant piece of sculpture: Crinkled as ever and somewhat tarnished, the silver four-inch figurine curled its arms in the majestic pose of an Olympian. The Foiled Knight. She took the near weightless object into her hand. Tears welled as she remembered the adventurous evening. The night that had started with so much exuberance, contained the emotional highs and lows of adolescence, a tender dance, the stomach-punch of betrayal, and saved by their resiliency. Turning it upside down, she choked out a laugh at the inscription: "Forged from rare metal alloy by Teedy, Senior Prom."

Tanya sat at the desk and set the statue in the center of the work surface. There was a swish of wind from outside and the hot water heater kicked in, sending clinks and clanks along the baseboard. She smoothed her palm across the varnished wood surface, enjoying the solitude. Opened the top drawer of the desk and found a clump of yellowed manuscript pages stapled together. Three corners curled from age. Pressing them back, Tanya smiled at the title: *When It's Right* by Stan "The Man" Palmer. She removed the pages. On her way out, she would ask the Palmers if she could borrow the story.

Along the side of the desk were four drawers. The first three were empty, but in the last one, Tanya found a small box wrapped in red and green Christmas paper. The name tag read: "To Teedy, from Stan." She lifted the present out and shook it gently. Not much noise and not much weight. She scooped up her discoveries and carried them to the bed. After propping up two pillows, she tossed everything to the far side and climbed on, stretching out on the soft comforter.

She took the present into her hands, undid the Scotch Tape and peeled back the decorative wrappings. A tiny shoebox. Removing the lid, she pushed aside the tissue paper and lifted out a pair of red satin ballerina toe shoes. More tears pooled in her eyes. She had always wanted to be a dancer and here Stan had remembered something she had told him in seventh grade. Normally a very intimate thing, but something he knew she needed. Something maybe only one other person in the world would even consider getting her. The gift receipt fell from the box. She checked the date: one week before the fall down the stairs. Draping the shoes to her chest, she lay back on the pillow, closed her eyes, and let the tears go.

* * *

An hour later, Sandra knocked softly on Stan's door and poked her head in. "Tanya honey, when you're done in here, Fenton and I would like to talk to you."

The sound of soft breathing greeted her. She pushed the door all the way open and stepped into the room. And smiled. On the bed, Tanya lay sleeping on her side, three objects snuggled in her curves: the stapled manuscript pages against her heart, the toe shoes by her belly and The Foiled Knight in her hands that were curled under her chin.

Sandra crept across the room and stood next to the bed, admiring Tanya's still girlish looks. A flurry of snapshots of a backyard campout ruined by rain drifted back from her memory. Youthful squeals for rescue. Fenton tossing mock life preservers while barking rescue instructions over the walkie-talkie. The mad dash for the house. Soaked pajamas. Plush towels and redressing on top of the drier. A makeshift emergency survival tent under Stan's bunk bed. Hot chocolate and finally two lumps under the covers as they went to work on coloring books by flashlight.

Gently, Sandra extracted the objects and moved them to the desk before pulling a soft blanket over Tanya. She ran a loving hand through Tanya's hair and kissed her on the forehead. Returning to the doorway, Sandra clicked off the light and pulled the door shut.

Chapter 46

Fenton poured himself a second cup of coffee and stared out the kitchen window at purplish clouds. "Should we wake her?"

Sandra glanced up at the clock on the wall while stirring scrambled eggs in a skillet. "Let's let her sleep." She set down the wooden spoon and wiped her hands on her apron.

"When I said last night," Fenton said, "that she should sleep in Stan's room, I didn't actually expect that she would listen to me."

"I know."

He spooned sugar into his coffee. "She was out before eight o'clock."

"Poor dear must have been exhausted," Sandra said. She poked at strips of bacon hissing on a flat griddle.

"I hope she comes down soon. I want to visit Stan before we go see the lawyer."

"It's still early," Sandra said. "Fenton, be a dear and drop some bread in the toaster while I cut up these green peppers."

"You know peppers upset my stomach. Why not just chop up some onions the way I like them?"

"Shush. I'm putting the onions in with the potatoes."

"Oh. Want me to look after them?"

"No, I want you to look after the toast." She emphasized the point with a distinctive chop of her knife through the pepper.

"I can handle more than just toast you know."

She winked at him. "Without a safety net?"

"Hardy, har, har," Fenton said and plopped four slices of bread into the toaster. "That time it wasn't my fault."

Sandra rolled her head back. "Fenton, you were trying to juggle four eggs. Who could you possibly try to blame for that?"

"Tanya made me do it."

Sandra turned, wooden spoon still, eyebrows raised. "Made you."

Fenton crumpled under the glare. "She said Kurt could do it easy."

"Kurt has lousy eye-hand coordination. Why do you think he gave up trying to be a receiver and switched to defensive back?"

"That's malarkey."

"You just can't accept that a couple of ten-year-olds could dupe you so easily." She laughed. "And then you had the biggest brain fart by trying to clean up the mess with a broom!"

"I got most of it."

"And the whole time," Sandra continued, "Stan and Tanya were chanting: Eggies go down dee hole." The spoon fell into the skillet as her body shook with laughter. "No way were you going to tell me. Oh, that would have been torture for you. Why, oh why, didn't you just get the mop?"

Fenton crossed defiant arms over his chest.

Sandra waved a delirious hand at him. "And there you were, sliding around on the floor in your bare feet, using up a million paper towels, slopping the yolk all over you." She leaned against the counter and howled in delight. "My God, it was the funniest thing ever."

"What's the funniest thing ever?"

Fenton and Sandra turned toward Tanya's tiny voice. Dressed in the same clothes from the night before, she leaned in the doorway, rubbing puffy eyes.

"Oh Tanya, honey," Sandra said, wiping tears with her apron, "did I wake you with my giggle fit?"

"No problem," Tanya said, "but what's this about yolk all over someone?"

Fenton yanked open the back door. "I'm going out to get the paper." With chin thrust forward, he marched into the biting winter air.

Tanya blinked, then faced Sandra.

"Don't mind him," Sandra said as the door closed. "He just doesn't like looking silly."

"Was it something I said?"

"Not at all. I was re-telling the story of eggie go down the hole."

Tanya smiled. "Oh, that. Well, we *were* instigators."

"Nonsense," Sandra huffed and pulled out a chair from under the kitchen table. "Sit down, I made scrambled eggs."

"I really should go."

Sandra removed the loaded skillet from the stove. "And leave me alone with Grumpypants? You'll do no such thing." She fixed Tanya with a glare.

"All right, I'll set the table." Tanya ambled toward the cupboard.

"Better hurry, here he comes."

Tanya scurried about, placing plates, silverware and napkins on the table.

A blast of cold air threw open the door sending the napkins flying. Fenton entered, eyes watering, cheeks wind-burned and teeth chattering. He clutched the newspaper with pink fingers.

"Cold outside, dear?" Sandra said, winking at Tanya.

"Bah. I've worked in short sleeves on days colder than this. Break out the sun-screen."

Sandra worked hard to suppress a grin. "Tanya's joining us for breakfast." She served Tanya a steaming helping of eggs.

"Good." He moved to the coffee maker, flexing his hand to get the circulation going again. "Coffee, Tanya?"

"Yes please."

"How do you take it?"

"With cream and sugar."

He opened the refrigerator and shoved his face inside. "Milk okay?"

"Yes sir, um, I mean yes, Mr. Palmer."

Fenton didn't seem to have heard. "We didn't get to talk last night—"

"—I'm sorry about that," Tanya interrupted. "That was rude of me to impose upon you to visit and then just conk out like that."

Fenton emerged holding a carton of 2-percent milk. "Forget about it. After what you went through? Hell, I'm amazed you're as composed as you are."

Sandra patted Tanya on the shoulder. "Did you sleep well?"

"Like a rock."

"I noticed you discovered a few things in Stan's room. Do you mind me asking what they are?"

"Of course not," Tanya said and tipped a forkful of food into her mouth. "Mmm. I found another short story and a little toy sculpture I made for Stan our senior year."

Fenton looked up. "What, that foil man?"

"Yes, and I also found what looks like a Christmas present he meant to give me."

"Really?" Sandra said. "Didn't know you two still exchanged gifts."

"We don't. I mean, er, we haven't. At least not for a long time."

"Wonder what made him all of a sudden start up again?" When Tanya didn't respond right away, Sandra searched and caught her eye.

"He didn't start up again," Tanya said, dragging her fork across her plate. "The gift receipt indicates he bought it when we were in college."

Sandra shoved the spoon into the remaining eggs. "I see."

"He must have forgotten it in a desk drawer."

"Did you open it?"

"Yes, it's a pair of dance shoes. Ballerina. Red ones."

"How swee—" Sandra's face fell noticing Tanya's face pinch. "Oh."

The sizzle of bacon seemed to reverberate off the walls.

After several moments, Sandra cleared her throat. "You keep them."

Tanya pushed eggs from one side of the plate to the other.

Sandra glared at Fenton who mouthed a silent: "What?" in return.

The flick of her head toward Tanya was no less subtle than the wide eyes that screamed: *"Say something!"*

"So, you, ah," Fenton stammered, "found another story that Stan wrote?"

"Yes."

"Did you read it?"

"Maybe this afternoon. I'd like to read it to Stan."

"We'll be there this morning, but leaving..." he glanced at Sandra, "...for an appointment. So you'll have plenty of time."

"Good timing."

"But I'll expect a report when we return."

"Okay, no pressure," Tanya said laughing.

Fenton covered her hand with his. "That's a good thing to hear."

"You always could make me laugh."

"It's a gift. Guess I'm naturally comedic."

Tanya glanced at Sandra. Both women rolled their eyes.

"Modest too," Sandra said and turned off the burners of the stove. "So modest that you won't mind doing the dishes, will you?"

He frowned. "Not in the mood. Can't it wait until after we talk to Tanya?"

Tanya looked up.

Fenton focused his attention on her. "That is, if you're up for it."

"I'm the one who asked to come over."

"And do you still feel like discussing it?"

She shrugged.

Fenton leaned forward. "We know this is extremely difficult for you."

"Thank you for saying that."

"It is for us as well."

"I know."

"Fenton's right," Sandra said. "I can't imagine what it feels like being given the responsibility for someone else's life."

"It's not a lot of fun, I can tell you that."

"We want you to know we think the world of you for how you're handling the situation."

"Doing the best I can."

"And your best is all anyone can ask," Fenton began, then broke off.

Tanya caught the unspoken words. "But?"

Fenton studied Sandra before facing Tanya. "But we're concerned."

"About what should be done about his care?"

"Yes."

"I've been thinking about that for a long time now," Tanya said.

"So have we."

"I'm sure."

"We'd like to know your thoughts."

Tanya leaned back. "My thoughts, my thoughts," she mused and gazed out at the cold as a howling wind swept along the outside of the house. "What are my thoughts?"

"Surely he believed that you would heed his wishes on something like this," Sandra said. "He must have thought you knew what he wanted."

Tanya sipped her coffee. "You know, as I was lying in Stan's bed last night, it occurred to me that he and I actually discussed this very subject."

Sandra and Fenton exchanged looks. "You did?" Fenton asked.

"Yes. In college. I got pretty drunk one night and got sick. He took care of me. Made sure I didn't choke on my own vomit."

Sandra covered her mouth. "Oh."

"Sorry, didn't mean to be gross. But he made me lie on my side and I asked him why and he told me if I choked, I'd be in danger of causing brain damage or even suffocating myself to death."

Sandra and Fenton stayed silent.

"And that's when he told me he didn't want to be kept alive if it ever happened to him."

"Goodness gracious," Sandra said.

"I'm sorry, Mrs. Palmer, I don't mean to sound so callous. I've been searching for clarity on the issue during this whole thing and for the first time I'm getting a clear signal of what he would have wanted."

"It's all right," Sandra said, reaching for a tissue. She wiped her eyes. "Fenton and I have discussed the very same thing."

"Good."

"We agree that Stan wouldn't want to live like this."

"No he wouldn't."

"And as much as I can't believe these words are coming out of my mouth," Sandra said, "we agree with you that we should cease life support."

"No."

Sandra and Fenton stared.

Fenton found his voice first. "But you just said—"

"I know what I said."

"But—"

"That's not what I'm going to do. I can't."

"What do you mean, you can't?" Sandra said, her mouth trembling.

"I can't do it. I won't."

"Why not?" Fenton said.

"I can't do it if there is still a chance he might come out of it."

"You heard the doctor, he's persistent vegetative state."

"Doesn't mean it's over."

"Yes, Tanya," Fenton said, his voice carrying an edge, "that's exactly what it means."

"I can't just take someone's life like that."

"It's not a life," he said waving his hand in some far away manner. "Not that anyway."

"Doesn't matter. I don't have it in me."

"But it's what Stan wanted, you even said so yourself."

"I know."

"Apparently you don't," he said and forcibly set his mug on the counter.

Tanya set her coffee cup down in the same manner. "I think I do."

"This isn't a joke, Tanya," Fenton said. "Stan's well-being is at stake."

"Don't you think I know that?"

"No, I don't think you are even close to fathoming what's going on here."

"Fenton, take it easy," Sandra said.

"I know exactly what's happening," Tanya said.

"Then how can you just sit there and let him suffer like that?"

Tears began to well in Tanya's eyes. "I'm not—"

Fenton took a step toward her. "Every beep his machine makes is like a splinter in my eyeball."

"Everybody calm down," Sandra said, trying to wedge between them.

"Don't tell me to calm down," Fenton snarled. He pointed a taut index finger at Tanya. "When did you become so heartless?"

"Who are you calling heartless?" Tanya said wild-eyed. "You're the one who wants to kill his own son!"

"Don't give me that. It's the humanitarian thing to do." He paused and his eyes narrowed into thin slits. "This is all payback for what happened to you in college, isn't it?"

The vein in Tanya's forehead bulged like an engorged worm. "What?"

Sandra covered her eyes and began to shake. "Oh dear, let's not do this."

"Don't act so innocent," Fenton said. "We know what happened that night."

Tanya sucked in air. "You don't know anything!"

"Yeah?" Fenton barked. "We know about the pregnancy…"

Tanya stood with a gaping mouth.

"...blaming it all on Stan," he continued. "Coward."

Sandra's fist pounded the table. "Fenton!"

"You're horrid!" Tanya cried.

"And then marrying that scumbag, Del. I'm glad Kurt knocked his sorry ass out that window."

A shriek from a wounded animal echoed off the walls. "How dare you talk that way!"

Fenton snatched up his mug and fired it against the wall. The explosion of ceramic rained down all around them. "I'll talk to you any goddam way I feel. Just like you think you can do whatever you feel like with someone else's life."

"Oh, Fenton!" Sandra wailed and ran from the room.

His face twisted into that of an oily snake. "There's no way we're going to let you get away with this. I'm hiring a lawyer and finding a way to take back control of my son's life."

Tanya's hands curled into clenched fists, the muscles in her forearms, shoulders and neck going taut. "Yeah, get control of his life so you can turn around and take it away, some father you are."

"Get the hell out of my house."

"Gladly!" Tanya yelled. She stormed to the dining room, gathered up the manuscript, toe shoes and figurine and flew out the door without a coat.

The house went silent until the screech of Tanya's tires rattled the windows.

* * *

One block down the street from the Palmers, Vinnie Macino's Porsche sat quietly hidden behind a large moving van. Vinnie had yet to report the vehicle stolen because for the last several hours, he and Eileen Harding lay bound, gagged and naked in the middle of the tennis pro shop of Huntington Valley Country Club.

At the sight of Tanya emerging from the house, the driver of the Porsche calmly rolled down the window and flicked out a cigarette butt. A half-eaten cheeseburger had grown hard on the floor as stale coffee curdled in the bottom of a Styrofoam cup. *Miss You* by the Rolling Stones played on the radio. A meat-hook of a hand scratched at the driver's three-day-old stubble before returning to his crotch. Anticipation boiled between his legs at the delight he was about to enjoy. He squeezed it hard to squelch the ache. As Tanya peeled away from the curb, Ernie McFadden released his grip, gunned the car to life and eased into traffic.

Chapter 47

"Who the hell do you think you are?" Tanya yelled.

She forced the Camaro up the slope of Rockwell Road. Houses flew by as she crested the hill and then plummeted down the other side. She smacked the steering wheel repeatedly as tears streamed down her face. "You had no right to say those things! Just because you're his father doesn't mean you can treat people like shit." The words bounded off the walls of the car's interior and back at her. "I'm his friend. We've been friends as long as we've been alive." She blew through a red light, never flinching at the blaring horns.

At the hospital, she took the turn at high speed, tires squealing in protest. "We talked about everything, but I never, *ever*, asked for anything like this." She mashed gears and let the clutch out early on purpose. The engine roared in response, shooting the car forward like a rocket, dirt and debris swirling in her wake. She careened around corners, oblivious to everything around her. At the sight of a speed bump ahead of her, she punched the roof and screamed: "I hate you!" and rammed the accelerator to the floor. The car hit the bump and left the pavement, sailing through space for a terrifying moment before jouncing back to the asphalt in a fishtail of fury.

"I didn't do anything wrong!" she screamed and banked the car into a hard turn back onto Rockwell. A school bus approached her from the opposite direction, beeping its horn and blinking its high beams in alarm. Tanya yanked the steering wheel and slammed the brakes. The tires locked sending a massive plume of burnt rubber and smoke into the air. Skidding and screeching, she hit the curb and jolted to a stop. "I didn't do anything wrong," she sobbed, wiping tears from bloodshot eyes. Convulsions of crying took over her body.

Several moments passed before they stopped. She leaned back and breathed heavy gusts of air. Her heartbeat slowed. She wiped her nose on her sleeve, looked around and realized she sat only a short distance from old stomping grounds. Shifting the Camaro into low, she rolled another hundred yards until the abandoned train yard came into view.

The lot was as dilapidated as ever with overgrown weeds and rusty rail cars scattered about. She eased the car into one of the few spots not occupied with scrap metal or railroad timbers, turned off the engine, scooped up the manuscript pages, the gift and the Foiled Knight and exited the car.

The winter air nipped at her skin as she picked her way over and through the minefield of junk. The sun did its best to climb higher in the sky as a strong wind howled and whistled through the decaying machinery. She shoved a rickety hand-cart out of her way. Two rail cars, still connected, blocked her path. Grabbing a handle, she pulled herself up the stairs and passed between the cars to the other side where twin stacks of coal silos loomed before her.

Pocked and pitted, the prodigious concrete sentinels showed the effect of thirty years of nature's relentless onslaught. Lesions of decay speckled the exterior, revealing steel reinforcement bars that were orange from corrosion. Stains of green rain scum ran down the sides in random streaks.

Still holding her three treasures, Tanya made her way past where the dog had attacked her in seventh grade to the twisted ladder leading to their old hideaway. The rungs bent under her weight, some snapping, causing her to quickly dart to a different perch. She nearly fell to the ground several times, but pushed on, refusing to give in to an escalating sense of despondency.

At the top of the ladder, she shoved her way through the cast-iron door and wiggled into the silo. Away from the wind, the temperature felt ten degrees warmer. She closed the door and waited for her eyes to adjust to the darkness. While much of the exterior had degraded over time, not much had changed on the inside except for some accumulated spider webs. The smell of mold filled her lungs. She crawled to the wooden table, peered underneath and smiled. There, still tucked safely away was the flimsy remains of Stan's Thor lunchbox. The clasp opened with a metallic *ka-dunk*. She lifted the lid slowly, afraid it would be empty. Instead, just as she and Stan had left them, she found candles and matches. She lit several and dripped melted wax into nickel sized circles about the table, then anchoring the candles in the puddles of paraffin.

The glow warmed the enclosure. It was just as she remembered: still crumbling, but also quiet and cozy. A greater portion of the ladder scaling the interior could be seen in the flickering light. Not enough to see where it reached the top of the silo, but enough to make out the exit to the exterior catwalks.

She set the toe shoes and figurine on the table and sat cross-legged with the light behind her. The soft-sand shifted beneath her as she removed the binder clip from the manuscript.

Closing her eyes, Tanya covered her face with both palms and took several deep breaths, letting the last one out in a slow, exhausted hiss. "Talk to me, Stan. Tell me a story. Take me away from all of this. Take me somewhere where we can be together." After a few moments, her heart rate subsided and she opened her eyes.

The manuscript appeared before her. At first a blur, then dark letters on a yellowish background. The familiar handwriting calmed her even more. A title came into focus and she began to read: "When It's Right, a short story by Stan 'The Man' Palmer."

* * *

In the dingy hallway of his apartment complex, Stan Palmer leaned against the door to his place, trying to figure out why the key would not go into the lock. As he fumbled around, a quiet, but deep voice snuck up on him.

"Hey good lookin,' welcome home."

Over his shoulder, Stan spotted a scraggly looking woman in zipper-happy cargo pants, high top Chuck Taylor's and a droopy gold sweatshirt with a Phoenix emblazoned on the front. She spied over the top of stylish glasses, doing her best to part bangs of auburn hair that refused to stay out of her face.

"Oh, hello," he mumbled. He resumed wrestling with the lock and key, then stopped. Scrunching up his face, he added: "Tanya."

Many years earlier, Stan had helped Tanya obtain a restraining order against her ex-husband. Not that it did any good. When the creep came cruising for trouble, she hid in Stan's apartment. Twenty-three at the time, she was the same age as Stan and worked in the diner. She couldn't afford the court costs. It was no big deal to Stan; he never bothered to send a bill.

Stooping over, he squeezed his eyes shut then opened them, trying to focus on the task. "How's my neighbor these days?"

"I'm good…now that you're here."

Stan turned around, his upper body moving in slow motion as if it were one piece, the key frozen in one hand, his eyes wide and wary.

"My computer is acting up again," she said. "Can you come over?"

"It's just another virus. Run that program I showed you last time."

"I don't trust myself. Can't you fix me up?"

He returned to the battle, to no avail. Placing his palms on the wall, he banged his head on the door. "Gracie, where are you when I need you?"

"She's at my place, Stan," Tanya chirped. "You were late and she got hungry so I cooked her dinner. She's doing her homework."

* * *

Tanya's breathing stuck in her chest remembering that first day of first grade; how she had told Stan the name of her doll and how she would someday name her daughter Gracie. Her fingers gripped the pages tightly as a gush of emotion surged through her.

* * *

Stan faced her. Peering through the stringy bangs were a set of seductive green eyes Cleopatra would have killed for. He heard a subtle intake of breath and realized it was his own. Recovering, he opened his arms and offered a hug. "Tanya, thank you. What would I do without you?"

"Oh, probably starve or fall victim to some unscrupulous man-killer."

Expecting a grungy smell, he was surprised when a lovely aroma of Freesia filled his lungs as they embraced. They had been cross-the-hall neighbors for years, but he couldn't remember ever being this close to her. "Ever since Linda left," he said, "you've been a wonderful friend. Gracie thinks you're the best."

Her arms tightened around his back as she pressed her body into his. He held her closer, enjoying the comfort of her warmth. A muffled sob drifted by his ear sending a slight tingle up his spine. When they parted, her fluttering eyes darted to the floor, but not before he detected a bit of moisture. "Hey, you all right? Something in your eye?"

She turned away quickly and plunged her key in her lock. "No, I'm fine.

It's...allergies." She turned the knob and opened the door. "I'll tell Gracie you're home. Goodnight, Stan." The door closed with a click.

He stood alone in the hallway, tie undone, shirt untucked, key still in hand. He mouthed in a meek voice: "Goodnight, Tanya."

* * *

"Hello, Capezio Dance? Hi, my name is Stan Palmer. I'm looking to take lessons." A pause as the other party spoke. "I'm thirty-eight and a beginner." Another pause. "Oh, I see, well, thank you anyway." Dropping the phone in the cradle, Stan crossed another studio's name off the list.

"What am I going to do, Gracie?" he said to his fourteen-year-old daughter. "It doesn't seem to want to work out for me. Every place I've called is either too far away or booked up."

Lying on her stomach, half her attention on her homework, the other half on *Gilmore Girls*, Gracie was a pasty-skinned, long-legged teen in patched jeans and rainbow socks. Except for the pigtails and braces, she resembled Stan. She closed the textbook and looked up with big brown eyes.

"Why all of a sudden this urge to learn to dance, Dad? Got a hot date?"

"There's this woman at Fitzy's and the only way to get to know her is to hang with her on the dance floor."

"What about having something in common?"

"Dancing is what we'll have in common."

She wrinkled up her freckly face. "Why don'tcha go to Mrs. Lehman?"

"I thought she closed up shop right after you stopped taking lessons."

"Nuh-uh. The girl I baby-sit for, Siobahn, she goes there."

"Is she listed in the Yellow Pages?"

"Nuh-uh. Word of mouth."

"Did she move her studio?"

"Nuh-uh. Still uses her basement."

"But she teaches kids."

"Uh-huh."

"Gracie, you will, as will your future boyfriends, thank me if I refuse to allow you to speak like a Troglodyte. So will you please stop grunting?"

"Sorry...Father."

"Thank you. Now, about Mrs. Lehman. Does she have anything that I—"

"Father," Gracie interrupted, "do you recall what you yourself illuminated for me when I first embarked with Mrs. Lehman? No? Then indulge me dear parental one. In your own immortal words, however superfluous they may have been, dance is simply locomotion of the body, with or without music. And, if your little grey cells are cramping over my meaning, let me translate: dance is just dance. Father."

As Stan gaped, Gracie turned back to the on-screen bickering of *Rori* and

Loreli, smacking her feet together as she twisted the ends of her pigtails.

* * *

The next Friday, Stan burst into the apartment and flung his briefcase to the corner. His coat went over the back of a kitchen chair, knocking it over.

"Dad," Gracie said, "what's wrong?"

"Wrong? Everything's wrong," he fumed. "Traffic around here sucks, taxes are ridiculous and you would think I could get a decent cup of coffee for less than $3.95."

She cocked her head. "What's really wrong?"

He blew out air and ran his hand through his hair. "That dancer woman made me look like a fool again at Fitzy's."

"What is your fascination with her? She sounds like a monster."

"I swear I have the worst luck with women."

"Gracie, do you have a hair brush I can borrow?" A shapely feminine figure, wrapped in a skimpy towel, walked out of the bathroom, her still wet hair frizzied down the back. The towel barely covered her bottom, drawing Stan's attention to long, toned and curvy legs. So innocent looking, so pure, she moved with a silky softness of someone cherishing a memory.

Stan's entire body locked in place, the amount of exposed skin crippling his brain like an inebriating toxin.

"Oh!" the woman blurted One hand went to her chest, the other to the bottom of the towel.

"Tanya!" Stan exclaimed. "What are you doing here?"

Flushing a deep red, Tanya bolted into the bathroom and slammed the door. They heard the sound of whimpering and things being knocked over.

Stan whirled around. "What is going on?"

"Well, you see..." Gracie started, her eyes flicking left, then right. "It's like this. Tanya's hot water went out, so she asked if she could use our shower. I figured you were gonna be late again, chasing what's-her-face, so I said it would be okay. Did I do something wrong? She is our neighbor and she helps me with my homework and she makes me dinner all the time and helps me pick out clothes and seems to understand all about my boy problems and when Patti and I are fighting, Tanya knows just what I should do to make it right and she showed me how to make my internet site private so weirdos can't get me and—"

* * *

Tanya flipped the page over looking for the rest of the story, but it ended abruptly. She thumbed through two blank pieces of parchment before coming upon a page full of Stan's handwriting, only newer looking than the others and not stapled to the rest of the pack.

* * *

Tanya, I don't know where to start this. My mind is so jumbled with thoughts and emotions. Half of me is frustrated and mad at you while the other half is humiliated at my own stupidity and cowardice. For years we were ~~good~~ best friends and I guess I just assumed we would always be in each other's lives. How did things get so messed up between us?

You know how I feel about you and Del, I've told you a thousand times to the point you probably want to punch me. I kinda get why you got back with him after high school. Okay, if I'm being truthful, not really, especially after the prom, but why you ever married him, well that, again being truthful, took me a long time to come to terms with.

And that's why this letter is so hard for me to write because what I'm realizing now is that I was part of the problem. Sorry it's taken me so long to admit it, but you were right that day we argued in college, the day you fell down the steps. I didn't make a move. But more importantly, I didn't tell you how I felt about you. About us.

I could never forgive myself for what happened. Your dreams. The baby. I could try to hide behind the excuse that I was young and immature. While it would be a true statement, it would also be pathetic. What matters is I was a coward. After the two of you divorced, I should have made more of an effort. It's not like we lived on opposite ends of the planet that I couldn't see you more often or try to bring us closer together. But you didn't try either and that got me thinking you didn't want the same thing. So I bottled it up and buried it. After a while, I lost my nerve. Before I knew it, years had gone by and, well, then it was like, what would be the point? We'd missed our chance.

I'm sorry about what I said to you at lunch yesterday. I had no right to criticize you for what you're doing with your life. I'm not exactly doing great things either, so I've no room to talk.

But it doesn't have to be this way, Teedy! Life is short. We're halfway through our lives and unhappy. Why let that continue? Doesn't our being together sound way better than continuing to be miserable? Why not do something about it? Why not at least try?

I know I want you in my life. There's a reason why all my stories are about us and why you are always my heroine. I need you, Teedy. And there's a reason why you made The Foiled Knight and kept my painting. Because you need me too. We need each other.

I'm having dinner at my parents' house next weekend. Can we have a drink together afterwards? Maybe meet at Fitzy's? Nothing heavy, I just want to give us a chance.

--Stan

* * *

The words on the page blurred before Tanya as tears welled in her eyes. She grasped the pages into her fist and pressed them to her heart.

The cast-iron door creaked and flapped open from the surging wind. Tanya tossed the parchment pages on the table and crawled to shut it. Two feet away, her eyes dilated as fear yanked on her spine. She fell back as the leering face of Ernie McFadden filled the opening.

Chapter 48

"Sweet momma," Ernie said. "Lookee what I done found me."

"Help!" Tanya screamed. "Help! Somebody!"

Ernie shook his head. "That's the trouble with running to a secret hideaway. Ain't nobody around to hear you if you get in trouble."

Tanya scrambled to her feet and across the silo floor until her back slammed against the wall. "Stay away Ernie. I didn't do anything to you."

Ernie crawled through the opening, pulled the door shut behind him and stood to his full height. "Didn't do anything? I disagree." He scratched his beard. "You found out what I been doing in the woods. Then your dad killed my best friend, but that was probably worse for you, wasn't it, seeing as he was your high school sweetheart and all?"

"You're wrong."

"You're glad he's dead?"

"No. I never should have married him in the first place."

"Listen to you, getting all philosophical. You are one dumb bitch. Yet it still wasn't all lost because I coulda have had me some fun, but then you had to go and figure a way to escape. No one's done that before so I guess congratulations are in order. But why did you have to tell the police? Especially since we been friends since grade school. Now that hurt."

"We've never been friends," Tanya rasped. "For as long as I've known you, you've been a pustule of society."

"Pustule?" Ernie said. "Huh, fancy word." He took a step toward the table. His shadow flickered menacingly on the concrete wall, a gargoyle of death. "Trying to rub it in that you went to college and I didn't."

"I'm not rubbing anything," Tanya said, eyes sweeping the room looking for a weapon, but except for some wooden pallets, there was nothing.

Ernie fondled his crotch. "Maybe you should."

"You're a pathetic loser Ernie, always have been."

"Look who's talking."

Tanya kicked sand at him. "You're a waste of a life."

"Yeah? What have you done with yours, you stupid tramp?"

"More than you."

"Bullshit," Ernie spat at her. "You're as much a loser as I am."

"I'm going to do something with it now." Tanya lunged forward and snared The Foiled Knight and stuffed it into her back pocket.

"What was that?" Ernie snapped.

"You wouldn't understand. What do you want?"

Ernie's eyebrows rose in amusement. "Really?" He took another step sending his shadow climbing another ten feet. "You have to ask?"

"Why can't you just leave me alone?" Tanya said.

"Because you need to be taught a lesson," he said and removed his coat, casting it carelessly aside. "A lesson my father taught me." He began to circle around the table. "About respect."

"I don't know what you're talking about," Tanya said. She edged along the wall, keeping the table between her and Ernie. "Why are you doing this?"

"Because you ruined everything, Tanya."

"It wasn't my fault."

"It was *all* your fault," Ernie said. "You couldn't just stay away. You had to stick your nose in where it didn't belong."

"I didn't know what I would find."

"Don't matter none now does it? Whether you knew what you was gonna find or not. Life's over for me." He unbuckled his belt. "So if I'm going down, I might as well have a piece of the ass that snitched on me."

Tanya stared frantically at Ernie and his immense flowing shadow. His eyes were ablaze, reflecting the flame from the candles. She continued to slide along the rough wall of the silo until her right shoulder collided into a solid object. Turning, she recognized the interior ladder that led to the catwalks. She glanced back at Ernie, now lifting his shirt over his head. With a leap, she nabbed the bottom rung of the ladder and pulled herself up.

Ernie's face registered surprise and he struggled to put the shirt back on. "Oh, no you don't!" he yelled and sprang forward.

But the delay had been all Tanya needed to create space between them. Frantically she scaled the ladder, two rungs at a time.

The skeleton of the ladder shook as Ernie grabbed the bottom rung and began hauling himself up.

Tanya climbed faster, her smaller frame working to her advantage. She could hear Ernie cursing as rusty struts snapped under his weight.

Thirty feet up, she reached a landing and tried the door to the exterior catwalks. The ancient door would not open, its corroded hinges unwilling to budge.

"Ha!" Ernie scoffed. "Nowhere to go." Having figured out that the circular safety cage that encased the ladder was stronger than the actual rungs, he moved much faster.

Tanya glanced about and considered her options. If she jumped, she'd probably break a leg. No way to fight against a trained killer and she had no weapon. She looked up at the continuing ladder. Her hand reached for the next rung just as Ernie grabbed her foot.

"Got you."

"No you don't," she yelled and struck Ernie in the eyebrow with the heel of her boot. The blow opened a gash that poured blood down his face and sent him skidding down the ladder several feet until he latched onto a rung.

"You stupid bitch!" he snarled and pressed the heel of his hand to the wound. Releasing the pressure, he inspected his hand that looked as if he had dunked it into a bucket of red paint. "God damn you!" he roared and yanked a snot-rag from his pocket and tied it around his head. "That's twice now."

The delay allowed Tanya to put ten feet between them. The light from the candles below were virtually useless at this height. She kept scrambling anyway and reached a section of the ladder that was severely twisted and dented and nearly detached from the wall. Using her dancer's flexibility, she slid through an opening in the bent metal to the outside of the climbing cage and clambered to just above the damaged section.

She grasped the ladder firmly and kicked at the section below. Decaying rubble and rust fell from the silo wall. Two kicks, three, another. The sharp metal sliced her hands and she cried out in pain.

"Won't work," Ernie yelled, still a ways below Tanya. "You're not strong enough."

"Never let anyone tell you that you can't do something," Tanya barked. Sweat dripped from her nose as she feverishly hammered at the loose area. Again and again she lashed out, but it would not give. Her legs began to tire and the blood running down her forearms made it difficult to hold on. She could hear Ernie's labored breathing, feel his presence close as the ladder shuddered from his combined weight. The stench of his body odor roiled her stomach.

With a desperate leap, he grabbed her foot, holding on to the cage with his other hand. She tried to shake him off, but his grip was like a bear trap.

"Come here…sweet thing," Ernie hissed. "Let me show you what you've been missing all these years."

A fierce energy ripped through Tanya. All the rage of a lifetime of cowardice, bad choices and regret surged through her limbs. She latched onto the ladder's outer cage with both hands and smashed down on the rung just above Ernie with her free foot. "Get your slimy hands off of me!" she shrieked.

Crack! A toaster-sized chunk of concrete exploded from the wall. A groan of bending metal filled the void. Ernie's eyes went wild. A desperate suck of air escaped his lips as Tanya wrenched her ankle free. She crashed using both heels this time. With a screech, the entire caged section below her fell.

Tanya dangled in space and watched Ernie fall fifty feet toward the orangey light below, a dark shadow plummeting into the chasm of hell. His scream reverberated off the walls. She slammed her eyes shut, waiting for the wail of a tortured animal. It never came. What she heard wasn't loud, or long, or anguished.

Crunch.

Chapter 49

Tanya pulled herself to the section of ladder that remained intact with the silo wall. Took a moment to catch her breath before scaling her way to the top where the twelve-inch gap between the silo and its sheet metal roof provided sufficient room for her to spy out. The winter wind greeted her, a welcome refreshment on her face despite the chill. At this height, she could see the entire town of Abington and the top of the hospital building.

She slithered over the top of the crumbling concrete wall to the ladder that ran down the entire length of the exterior and began the long descent to the ground. The wind buffeted her several times nearly causing her to lose her grip on the crusting railings and the wobble in her legs didn't help. Concentrating hard, she took the rungs one by one until she could jump the remaining distance. The crunch of gravel and the solidness of the earth under her boots felt reassuring. She cast a quick glance at the door of the silo and considered peeking in to make sure Ernie hadn't somehow survived, took a wobbly step toward the silo, then stopped.

"No way," she whispered. "He's dead." She staggered to the car.

The Camaro swayed across the center line as Tanya struggled to maintain control. Stoplights blurred. Street signs flashed by. Car horns blared. She ignored them all and hit the gas, continuing to weave through traffic. When she hit York Road, she downshifted and took the turn into the hospital parking lot. Out of the car, she sprinted for the entrance.

* * *

"How long do you think it will take?" Sandra asked. She stepped close to Stan's bed and smoothed her son's hair.

"The legal battle could take months or years for all I know," Fenton replied. "That would get expensive."

"This isn't about money," Sandra said.

Fenton nodded. "I didn't mean it that way." His lips formed into a tense line. "No matter what we do, we lose."

"Are we doing the right thing?"

Fenton took a long time to answer. "Sandra, I don't know." His hand went through his hair. "I really just don't know."

* * *

The elevator beeped and the doors opened onto the ninth floor. Tanya burst from the car and ran toward Stan's room. A hallway policeman spread his arms wide.

"Hold it right there," he commanded.

Tanya slid to a halt. "I have to see him!"

He scanned her rumpled clothing, the face covered with soot and grime, the bloody hands. "I don't think so." His hand instinctively reached down to his holster. "Who are you?"

"There's been an accident. I called the police from my car. They should already be there."

"What kind of an accident? Where?"

"At the train yard. A man fell."

"What man?"

"A bad man," Tanya said, her indignation showing. "His name is Ernie McFadden."

"The creep that kidnapped the Mathews girl?"

"Yes, and the same guy that shot Mr. Palmer and tried to kill Stan."

His eyes rounded. "You're Tanya Davis, the woman who—"

"Yes, I'm the same person."

He whistled. "What happened?"

"McFadden attacked me."

The man's eyebrows shot up. "Attacked!"

"That's right. But he won't be any trouble any more. And now I really need to see Stan. Can you please let me through?"

He scratched under his cap, then reached for his walkie-talkie. "Hold on, I need to call this in." He pressed talk. "Bobby, I got Tanya Davis here asking for access to the Palmer room. She claims she was attacked by the guy that kidnapped that girl." Pause. "Uh-huh, yeah? It's already on the wire? Okay, good." He scanned Tanya up and down. "No she seems uninjured. Couple of nicks, but otherwise fine." Pause. "Will do." He clicked off. "Someone will be out in a few minutes." He motioned with a caring arm. "Why don't you use the time to clean yourself up?"

Tanya looked at her blood-stained hands. "All right." She disappeared down the hall to the restroom. The soap and water stung the cuts in her palms, but the filth washed away in swirls of orange, brown and red. When she returned, Sandra was waiting with arms folded across her chest. Tanya's already slow pace ground to a halt.

The two women made eye contact.

"Tanya."

"Sandra."

"What are you doing here?" Sandra asked. Her eyes were puffy and red, and her body bent as if she had slept on marble stairs.

Tanya's feet shuffled. "I'm here to see Stan."

Sandra glanced over her shoulder at no one. "That's not a good idea right about now."

"Is he all right?"

"Yes, he's fine, well, he's still mad."

"Oh," Tanya squinted.

"What?"

"I, er, I meant Stan."

"Oh." Sandra cleared her throat. "Of course." Now it was Sandra shuffling. "Yes, he's fine too."

"I can come back."

"I mean he's the same as before, not that that's fine." Sandra looked up.

"What? No. You shouldn't—"A shaking hand went to her forehead.

Tanya closed the gap between them and gently gripped Sandra's shoulder. "Look, Sandra, I feel terrible about what happened at your house."

Sandra met her eyes. "So do I. I am so sorry. I've never seen Fenton act like that before in my life."

"He's never been under this kind of pressure before." Tanya circled her arms around Sandra. "None of us have."

The two women hugged, not saying anything. After a few moments, they broke away, each wiping tears with their sleeves.

"I really would like to see Stan," Tanya said. "Do you think you could say something to Mr. Palmer for me?"

"I'll try." Sandra took hold of Tanya's hand and led her down the hall, past another policeman, until they reached Stan's room.

At the doorway, Sandra let go of Tanya and stepped cautiously into the room. "Fenton?"

Tanya waited in the shadows, crossing and uncrossing her hands in front, weight shifting from side to side. She had no idea what she would say, but fully expected a full dose of blubbering and begging. Murmuring reached her ears. The metallic taste of blood caused her to stop fidgeting and she realized she had bitten her own lip. The whispering stopped.

"Come in, Tanya," Sandra's voice said.

Tanya took a measured step into the room. She could see Sandra's back as both she and Fenton were hunched together on the edge of chairs, quietly consulting. When Fenton glanced up, Tanya gasped at his ghoulish appearance.

Haggard and unshaven with bloodshot eyes and purple circles beneath, his hands shook as they held an empty cup of coffee. The skin on his face looked as if it would slide onto the floor. His hair was bedraggled, his shirt untucked, and his socks didn't match. He tried to stand, but winced in pain and grabbed for his lower back.

Sandra reached for him. He waved her off, gritted his teeth and stood to his full height. Rolling his broad shoulders, he lasered molten eyes into Tanya.

Tanya didn't move. She couldn't. Her legs were locked in place, her feet stuck to the floor. She met his glare.

For a long minute, they stared each other down. He with his leathered face, she with her locked fists, they squared off like devil dusted gunslingers, waiting for the first flinch. It came when the memory of Tanya and Stan returning from their prom at dawn filled his eyes with moisture.

"Tanya."

In a vanquished nanosecond, all of the events of the past few days were forgotten and she hurtled across the room into his big bear arms.

"I'm so sorry," Tanya wailed.

"Don't," Fenton said, holding tight. "I'm the one who should apologize."

"You were upset."

"I never should have said those ugly things. Can you ever forgive me?"

Tanya gripped him fiercely. "Of course. You've always been like a second father to me."

Sandra moved close and slipped her arms around both of them. "Everything is going to be all right." The three of them hugged for several seconds.

Jenny entered the room. "Oh, I'm terribly sorry."

The trio broke apart. "It's okay, Jenny," Fenton said. "We just had some… issues… to take care of." He tucked in his shirt and combed his hair with fingers that no longer shook. "But we're better now."

Jenny glanced from person to person as if trying to judge the situation. She faced Fenton. "Detective Ciquero is on his way up, wants to speak with you."

Fenton's face crinkled up. "About what?"

Jenny shrugged. "Dunno. But he sounded stressed. Something about another assault."

"It's because of me," Tanya interrupted.

All heads swung her way.

"After I left your house, I just took off. I didn't know where to go. Somehow the car steered itself to the old train yard where Stan and I had a secret fort when we were kids. Left my coat at your place, so I crawled up into the silo to get out of the cold. While I was in there, Ernie McFadden attacked me. He must have been following me."

Sandra's hand covered her mouth. "Oh dear, what happened. Did he hurt you?"

Tanya shook her head. "He blocked the door, but I got away. We fought—"

Everyone leaned forward.

"He's dead."

Silence filled the room for several moments.

"Oh my God, Tanya," Sandra croaked.

"You're lucky to be alive," Fenton added. "Are you all right?"

"Yes, I'm fine. I mean I've got cuts and bruises, but basically I'm okay."

"But he's so big," Sandra said, still in awe. "And he was in the army. What happened?"

"I tricked him. I climbed the old rusty ladder on the inside of the silo. He didn't know that the section above the catwalk was barely attached. All it took was his weight and the whole thing fell."

"How did you know about the ladder?" Fenton asked.

Tanya tried to smile, couldn't, got it out anyway. "Stan."

Fenton furrowed his brow. "Not following you."

"We used to go there all the time in grade school. Stan explored the place a lot more than I did. I was too chicken to climb that high. He told me about the upper section." She turned her face toward Stan's supine body. "His whole life he's been saving me."

She slow-footed it to the bed and leaned over Stan. Even with the breathing tubes up his nostrils, he looked like the Stan of old. His cuts had healed and his color had returned to normal. It was as if he were sleeping with his eyes open. "Hey, you," she said, stroking his hair. "I've known you my whole life. I never realized just how much we had in common." She caressed his chin. "You taught me all the important things I needed in life. I never realized just how close we were. I mean are. You're my best friend." Folding her hand into his, she kissed the tip of his nose. "And despite all my bullheadedness and all my stupidity, you never gave up on me."

The Foiled Knight

A commotion sounded from outside the room as Detective Ciquero arrived just ahead of a herd of police officers. Fenton raised his arms and blocked the doorway. The men collided into the backs of each other as they skidded to a halt.

"Hold on guys, give us a minute," Fenton murmured and motioned toward the bed. "She's fine."

A gaggle of policemen's hats peered around the corner of the door jamb.

From her back pocket, Tanya pulled out the shiny figurine made of foil, now severely bent and mangled. She worked to mold it back into shape and placed it on Stan's pillow. "I never realized I had the most powerful Knight ever watching over me." With tears streaming, she pressed her forehead to his. "I love you Stanley, please come back to me." A teardrop broke from the end of her nose and hit Stan in the eye.

She stiffened at the squeezing of her hand, but it was the ever so subtle shift of Stan's eyes and how they focused on her that ripped a shiver up her spine.

"Teedy, how many times have I told you not to call me Stanley?"

Epilogue

"There it is."

Stan switched the picnic basket to his other hand and swept aside a tree branch. Thirty yards ahead, sunrays illuminated a large flat rock that jutted out from the side of the riverbank.

"Just like I remember it," Tanya said and jumped across a narrow section of Sawtrigger's Creek. "Careful, Gimps, or do you need a piggy-back ride?"

"Ha, ha," Stan mock-laughed. "After all those months of physical therapy, I think I can handle this." He stepped cautiously on partially submerged stones. Half-way across, his bare feet slipped causing a spastic pinwheel of arms and basket before he regained control, eventually landing safely on the mossy shore. He looked up with a crooked grin. "Had it all the way."

Tanya smiled, then turned toward the swimming hole. "Look at that."

Unchanged by time, the circular pool lay shimmering before them, smooth and inviting, colorful rocks at the bottom visible like that in a fish tank. Tadpoles swam about in the crystal-clear water. A slight breeze rustled the trees around them. From somewhere in their branches, a blue jay chirped.

Tanya unfurled a blanket, allowing it to float to the grass-covered earth. She kicked off her sandals and stretched out across the soft fabric.

Stan set the basket down, flopped on his back and crossed his arms under his head. "Ah, now this is the life."

"Hungry?" Tanya flipped open the lid and removed a cluster of grapes.

"Starved, what else you got?"

She held up a tin of chicken spread and a zip-lock baggie of crackers. "Remember?"

He smiled back. "Perfect. All we need now is—"

Tanya presented a plastic bottle filled with a red liquid. "Cool-aid."

"Teedy, you rock."

"Learned from the best," she said and reached into the basket again, lifting up a pack of yellowed parchment paper stapled in a corner. "Look."

"Uh-oh," Stan sighed. "Which one is that?"

"You'll see. Do you mind if I read it?"

"Not if you mind drivel."

"None of your other ones were bad."

"Then read on, McDavis."

She lay on her back and arranged herself until her head was resting on Stan's belly. He stroked her hair as she read aloud. "Passion Takes Center Stage, by Stan 'The Man' Palmer." A slight pause, then a smirk.

"Give me that," he said and made a snatch for the pages.

She snorted with laughter and held them out of his reach. "No way, Stan *the man*. Your punishment is you have to listen to your own story."

He knocked on her skull with his knuckles. "Then read already and put me out of my misery."

Tanya pressed the back of her head against him. "Never."

He lightly squeezed her arm.

"All right," Tanya said, "Here we go."

* * *

"Tanya Davis!"

A shapely young woman in a short black skirt and green danskin half-top stepped into view from the wings of the stage. With legs spread shoulder width apart and hands confidently resting on her hips, she shook her auburn hair like a gun fighter ready to draw. "Here."

* * *

"Oooo, shapely," Tanya said. "I like it already."

"I thought about using voluptuous," Stan said, "but that—"

"Would have made me sound like Ronnie," Tanya interrupted. "No, shapely is just fine."

* * *

"You're next," said Val Lawler, executive producer for The Walnut Street Theatre. "Ballet combinations first, then tap. Throw in some of your own stuff at the end if you want. Wow us." A former dancer herself, Val was a still-sultry platinum blonde in her fifties. She sat with one hand holding both a cigarette and a clipboard while the other brandished a pen poised to critique. She elbowed the man sitting next to her. "Look alive. This one means business."

Stan Palmer opened his eyes and rose up from his slouch. "I'm awake." Rugged, with dark skin and a dimpled chin, Stan's eternal five-o'clock shadow clashed brilliantly with eyes that were as blue as the Aegean Sea on a sunny day.

* * *

Tanya burst into laughter. "'...as blue as the Aegean Sea on a sunny day'? Are you kidding me?"

"Hey," Stan replied, "Cut me a break. I'm a beginner."

"Mrs. Delaney is rolling over in her grave."

He tickled her in the ribs. "Keep going."

She squirmed in giggles. "Okay, okay."

* * *

"Who we got?" Stan asked, yawning and stretching. Immediately, his eyes riveted on Tanya. "Whoa, never mind." He turned to Val. "Maybe the day won't be a total waste after all."

The twirl of Tanya's skirt captivated Stan's attention. From the last row of the theatre, he watched her strut to the center of the stage on long, toned legs that, although he hated to admit it, reminded him of a racehorse.

* * *

"What?" Tanya exclaimed. "You think I look like a horse?"

"No," Stan said. "Stan does."

"But that's you!"

"No it isn't. It's just a made-up story."

"Yeah, right."

"I think you are gorgeous, Teedy. Always have. You know that."

She flushed and held out her hand.

He squeezed it. "And I know you know it. So keep reading."

* * *

Popping a heel, Tanya turned to profile, her hair shielding her face. Even though she didn't stick anything out on purpose, her costume could not conceal her curves. The audition would only last a few minutes, but that single pose edged Stan forward onto folded hands.

As the music floated through the theatre, Tanya eased into motion. She extended an arm, delicate fingers reaching for the heavens. Her plié was smooth and her pirouette effortless, but her body overpowered it. Every step was precise and the flutter kicks technically correct, but she was, at best, only average. He sat back.

Val nudged him. "What do you think? Worth offering a part to?"

Stan, a part-time dancer in Val's productions, followed the lackluster performance. His judge of potential outpaced his own ability. Val often went to him for advice during auditions. "Eh. She needs to pick it up."

* * *

"Hey!" Tanya exclaimed and playfully swatted at Stan. "My flutter kicks were fabulous."

"Relax," Stan said. "I did that for a reason."

"Why?"

"I'm not giving it away. You'll see."

"Okay, but *you* better pick it up. So far you're not exactly sweeping me."

He stroked the profile of her nose. "Trust me."

* * *

The music shifted from classical to a more modern beat and as if transported into a different body, Tanya's hips came to life. A shake, then a turn, followed by a squat and two hands slapping the floor, she instantly transported to some other place. Stan's mouth opened when she ran from one end of the stage to the other, leaping into the air in a full-out split, her legs going past parallel with the floor. The height was extraordinary, the soft landing and immediate roll into a somersault even grander. She sprang up into a series of lively combinations, regaining the rhythm without any hesitation.

"*Jammin',*" he whispered. "Much better."

Val smirked as she observed Stan rocking in his seat, mimicking Tanya's hand movements. "Remind you of anyone?" she asked.

"Man, she exudes confidence," he answered. "There's an animal lust about her. Huh? Remind me of anyone? Not really. Why?" He never took his eyes off the stage.

Val smiled. "Uh-huh." She remembered when a younger Stan had tried out several years earlier. She still had the 3x5 index card recounting his audition: *Stanley Palmer, 18, technically sound. Instinctive and improvisational. There's a primal quality to him. Because his muscular legs are out of proportion with his upper body, he's not really cutout for a lead role, but would be a solid background performer.*

* * *

"Oh. My. God," Tanya said with a roll of her eyes. "I can't believe you let Val call you Stanley."

"She's my boss."

"I thought you said he wasn't you?"

Stan tapped the pages. "Will you stop interrupting? I can't follow the story."

She laughed. "You wrote it."

"Long time ago."

"How long?" she asked.

"Like twenty years."

Tanya paused to stare at the blue sky, her eyes flitting from one cloud to the next. "That would have been right around when we were in college."

Stan closed his eyes. "Mmmm."

Tanya's head sagged into his stomach. "Oh."

He tapped the pages again. "No more stopping."

Tanya obeyed and read the cozy romantic short until finally the protagonists got together.

"I sooooo love this part," Tanya sighed and read aloud.

* * *

When it came time for the new partners to go on, Stan guided them to the rear of the stage where they would draw less attention. She stiffened when he placed his hand on her lower back. She glanced at him nervously.

"It'll be all right," he said softly. "See the first move in your mind. Then let me guide you."

The music started. Tanya's nervousness showed, the combinations coming back to her a split second later than she would have liked. Stan sensed her tentativeness and slowed their tempo, giving her more time to recall the next move. Towards the middle of the number, the routine called for her to lean into him, backwards. When his arms draped around her, she tensed.

"Close your eyes," he soothed. "Let the music release you." Holding her waist, Stan swayed her side to side, then guided her across the back of the stage, his caring hands always in the perfect spot, sending a signal to her body which way to go. She let her body flow in that direction, his feet moving swiftly to catch her on the other side and redirect her. As his fingers cascaded down her rib cage, she heard the velvety sound of the violins. He lifted her into the air and spun her, causing her hair to fall across her face. Deftly, he caught her so that they were facing each other, her breast at his cheek. He lowered her, slowly, the softness of her skin an exhilaration against his rigid frame. A smooth comfort flooded her muscles.

"Beautiful," he said, his tone calm and full of confidence. "Let your instinct take over."

Tanya dropped to the ground, enjoying the friction generated by slithering against his torso. Reaching eye level, she melted her body into his, relishing the heat unleashed through her veil-thin leotard. The crowd cheered.

"They love you," he whispered in her ear. "Almost home."

He slid a palm down her back, found her hand and flung her away, until only their fingertips were touching. Immediately, he yanked her back through the air. At impact, her legs straddled his thigh, like the perfect fit of a puzzle piece. She tossed her head back and her hair fell away, the light illuminating her face. Glowing, she met Stan's clear blue eyes that remained steady despite the deafening applause.

"Wow!" he mouthed.

* * *

"I'll say wow," Tanya said. "Stan this is terrific."

He smiled. "But?"

"No, I'm serious, I'm impressed at how you evoked the raw emotion a dancer feels. That's so hard to do, but I feel like I'm there."

"Then you're gonna love what's coming up."

* * *

"Where are we going?" Tanya asked, climbing into Stan's '68 Camaro.

Stan patted a wicker basket in the back seat. "How about a picnic?"

"Ooooo, I love it. Willow Grove Park?"

"Nope," Stan said. "I was thinking our old hangout, the swimming hole."

"Sounds wonderful."

They parked by Sawtrigger's Creek and soon had spread a blanket on the ground near the water's edge.

"What did you bring to eat?" Tanya asked and lifted the lid of the basket. There was a sharp intake of breath. Tears filled her eyes. "Stan?"

He smiled. "Teedy…"

* * *

Tanya flipped the pages over. "Wait, what? Where's the rest of it? She sat up. "Where's the end?"

Stan rose to a sitting position, his face inches from Tanya's. "I never finished it."

"This isn't 'When Ink Bleeds' all over again is it?"

He chuckled. "I never really expected you to read it, but I'm glad you did."

The Foiled Knight

She ran her hand through the hair of his forearm. "I loved it, but what did he say to her?" Expecting a smile, she was surprised when he stared at her with serious eyes.

"I always knew how dance made you feel," Stan said. "It brought out the best in you." His eyes went to the ground.

She lifted his chin with an index finger. "But?"

"But..." His face pinched.

"You can say it."

"I always felt..." His voice cracked. "It was your... I can't..." He rubbed his eyes. "I don't think I'll ever be able to forgive myself for what happened."

"Aw baby, come here." She pulled him close and nuzzled her nose into his hair, her lips close to his ear. "I don't feel that way," she whispered. "Not at all.

He squeezed her tight, breathing in the sweet smell of her long-flowing hair.

"I know it was as much my fault as it was an accident," she continued.

They stayed in the intimate embrace, enjoying each other's touch, sounds of nature harmonizing all around them. After several moments, the blue jay let out a squawk.

Stan chuckled. "Mr. Blue Jay wants me to get on with it." He took a deep breath. "I'm glad you said that, Teedy. It makes me feel better." He pulled a small felt box from a side pocket of the picnic basket. "And it makes this much easier to say."

Tears filled her eyes. "Stan?"

"Tanya, I've been waiting my whole life to ask you this." He lifted the lid and smiled. "Will you marry me?"

She fingered the diamond ring and pressed her forehead to his. "I've been waiting my whole life to say yes."

They kissed.

John C. Stipa

Author's Notes

During the writing of this novel, my mother, Nancy Stipa, passed away at the age of 90. I will always cherish the memory of her kind and giving soul, the most unselfish person I have ever known. I dedicate this book to her.

I grew up on Rockwell Road in Abington, Pa. The surrounding towns of Glenside and Jenkintown were my stomping grounds. The book is pretty true to the area although there is no proof that Friday paychecks are gone by Monday and there is no resemblance of any character to real persons. But I really was in a bus accident on Terwood Road with my 4th grade classmates from OLHC grade school. The train yard silos did indeed serve as our secret fort, Tanya's dog attack scene was based on a true story, and the fences surrounding Huntington Valley Country Club didn't go all the way to the ground.

I did take some liberties, however. The Keswick Theater no longer shows movies and there is no creek by the name of Sawtrigger (but there was a nice gentleman by that name who lived across the street from us on Rockwell Rd.) Willow Grove Park was torn down in the late 70's/early 80's to make room for a mall that was partially constructed from building materials I sold as a sales rep for Geppert Lumber on Easton Road (the inspiration for Peterson's). The Cave and Sawtrigger's Cabin were total fictional fantasy, but the PA Turnpike to New Jersey was completed in 1956.

There is no Good Shepherd House at Elon University, but there is a reason why I chose Elon and Furman as the colleges for Tanya and Stan. It's due to their mascots. I'll leave it to you to figure out the symbolism.

A very special thank you goes out to Pat Gillespie, a dear friend who served as the inspiration for the completion of this book. Her letter came to me at a time when I was receiving negative remarks on my first novel that were difficult for a rookie author to swallow. I'd be lying if I said I didn't think about quitting. Pat's words of support lifted me from a hole of self-doubt and gave me the confidence to forge ahead. She became the inspiration for the character of Sandra Palmer: strong, but sensitive; firm yet fair; classy, funny, fiercely loyal, and always so very kind.

This story was written for all the Stan and Tanya's of the world who may not appreciate the endearing beauty of loyalty to friends.

Thanks to the people who volunteered to be advance reading copy critics: Gail, Laura, Disa, Mandy, Lisa, Denice, Loni, Vandana, Rebecca, Jeff, Dianne and my wife and daughter.

Kristen King, thank you for the manuscript critique and honest feedback.

The Writers of Chantilly are on the list to recognize as well. They embraced Stan and Tanya from the beginning and never let me be untrue to their story.

Thanks to Lorrie Herman who once again captured the essence of the story on the cover. Check out her artwork at: www.lorrieherman.com

Lastly, I thank my wife and children, my constant reminders that the reward of a fruitful life is earned by following pursuits of substance and being true to the people that have been true to you.

Made in the USA
Charleston, SC
23 June 2013